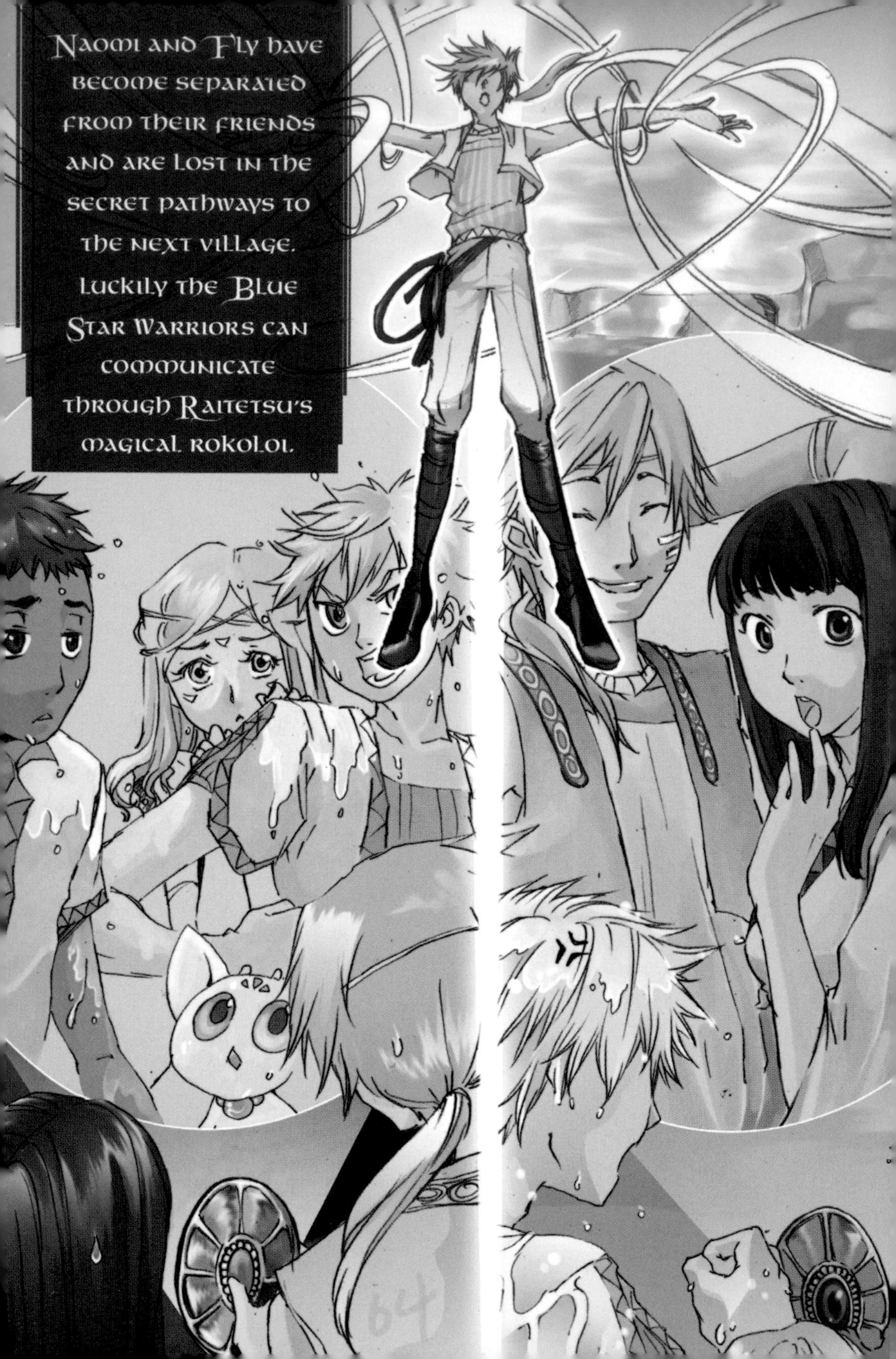
Naomi and Fly have become separated from their friends and are lost in the secret pathways to the next village. Luckily the Blue Star Warriors can communicate through Raitetsu's magical rokoloi.

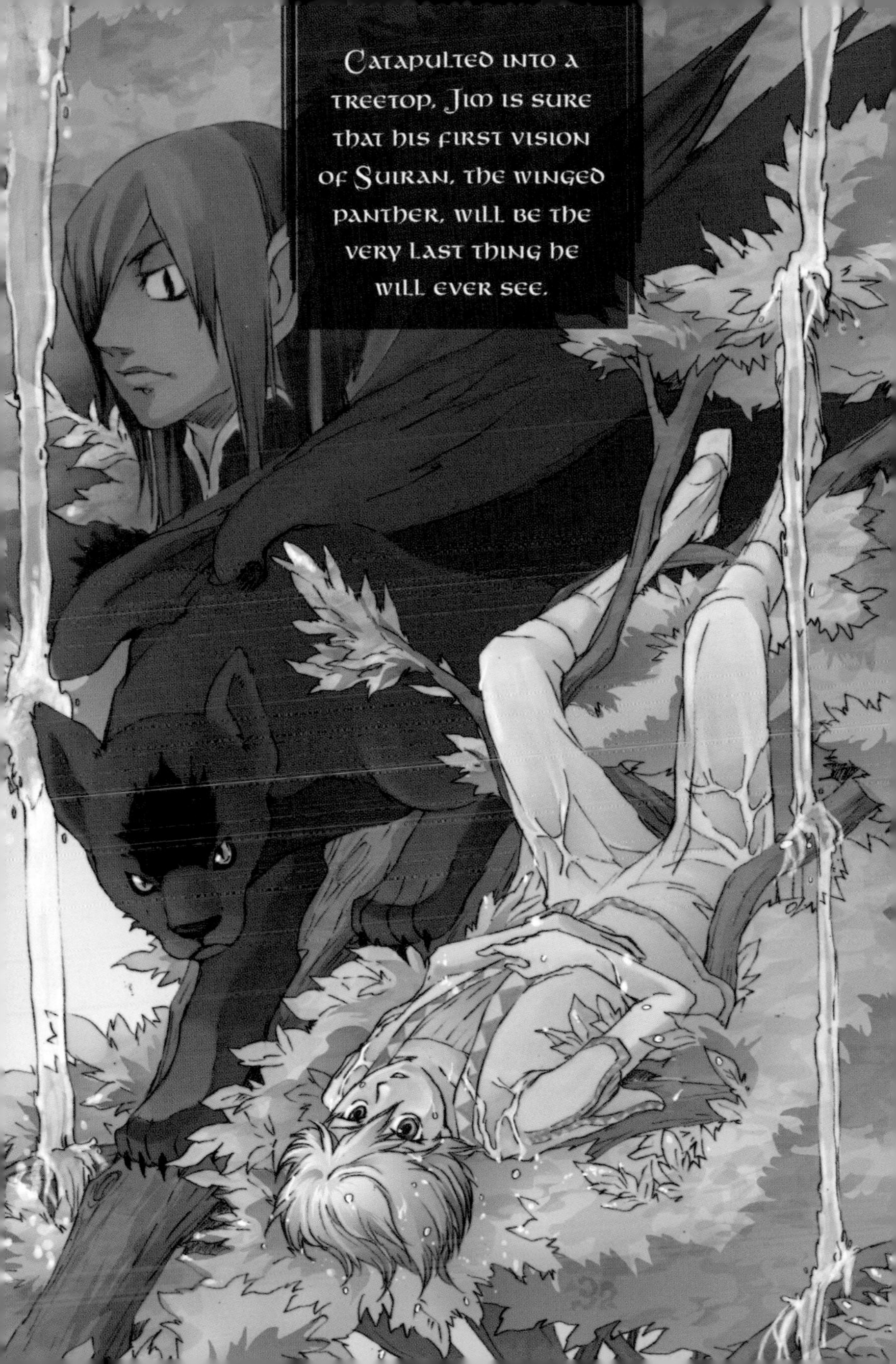
Catapulted into a treetop, Jim is sure that his first vision of Suiran, the winged panther, will be the very last thing he will ever see.

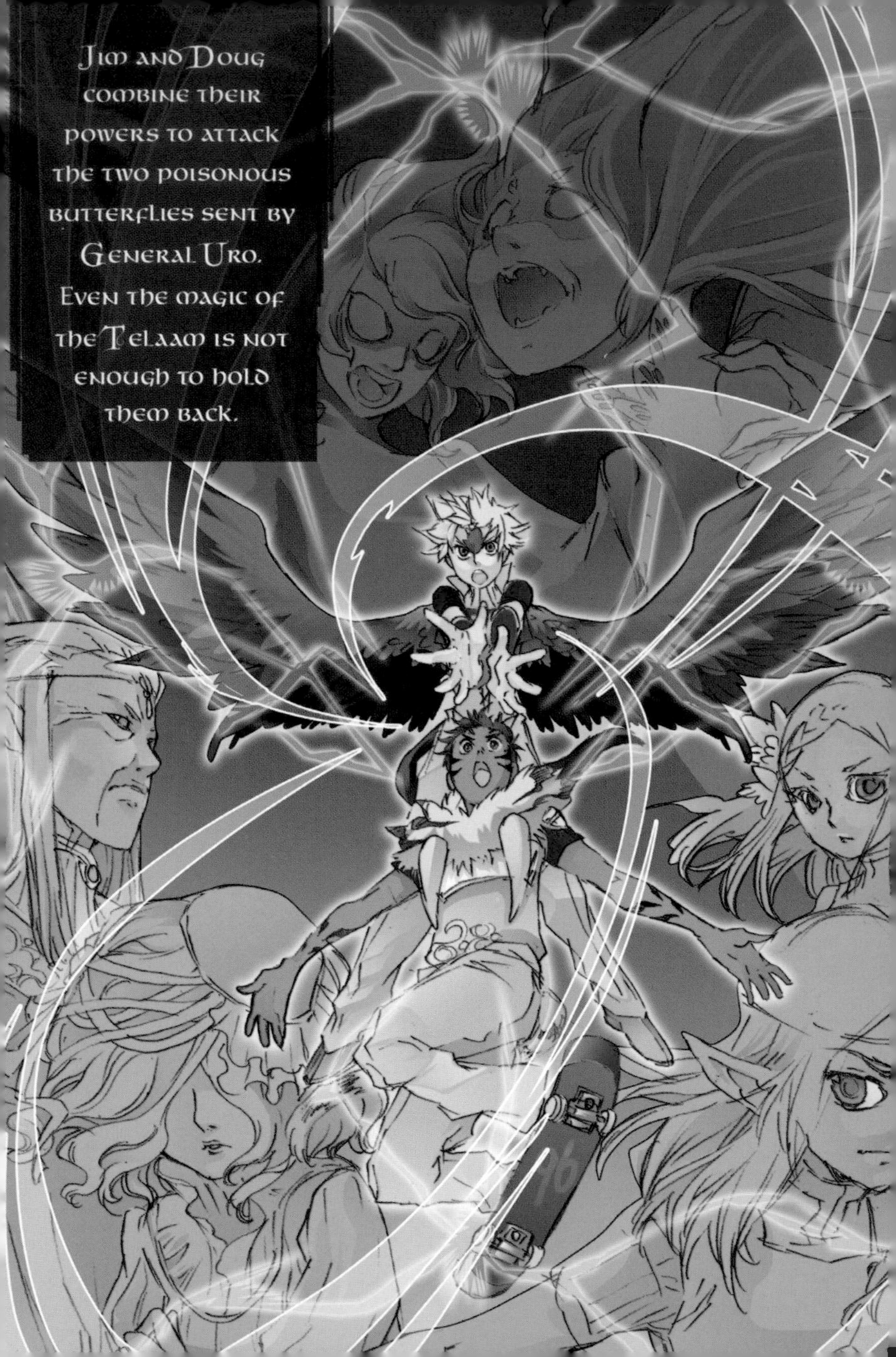
Jim and Doug combine their powers to attack the two poisonous butterflies sent by General Uro. Even the magic of the Telaam is not enough to hold them back.

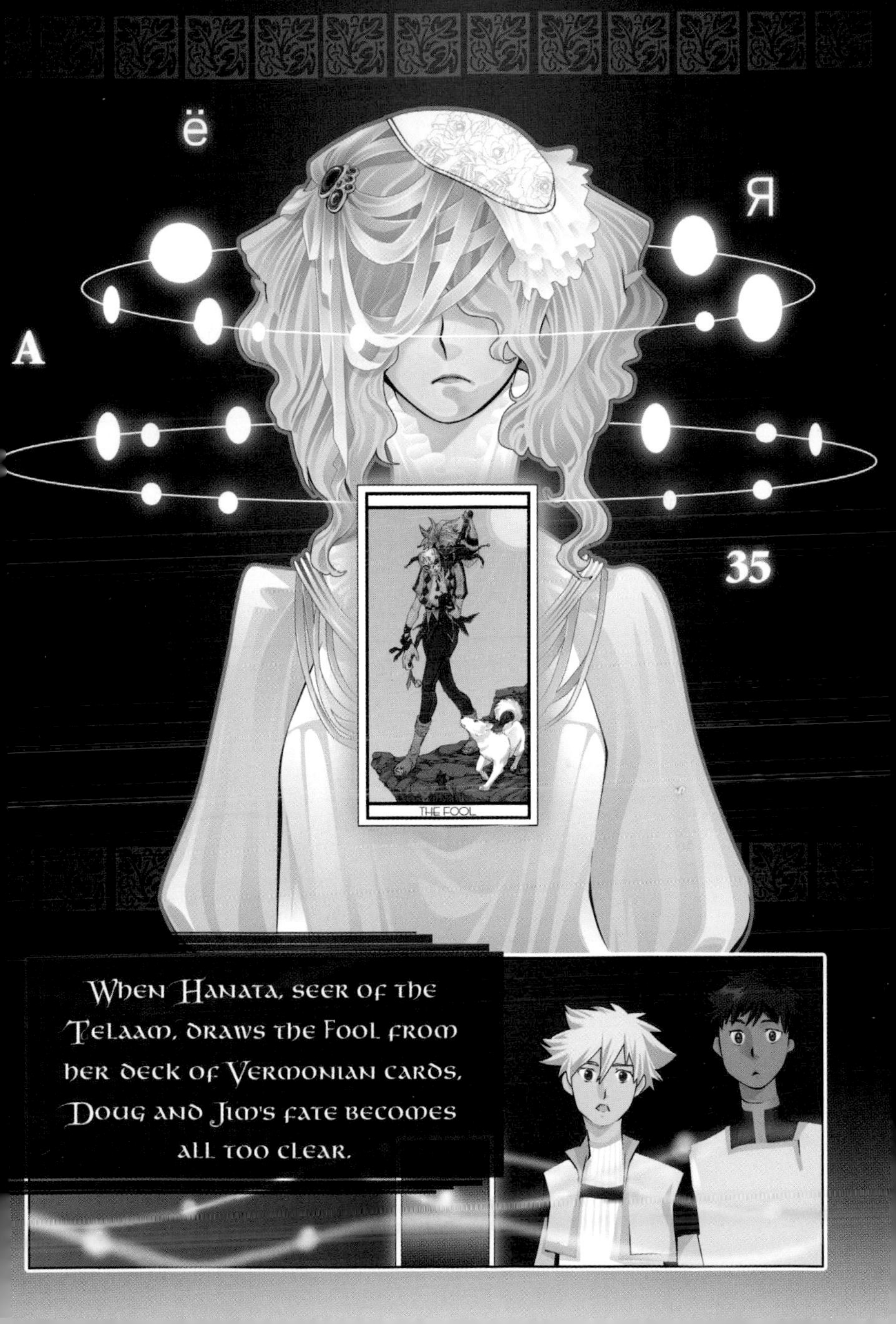
ё
Я
A
35
THE FOOL
When Hanata, seer of the Telaam, draws the Fool from her deck of Vermonian cards, Doug and Jim's fate becomes all too clear.

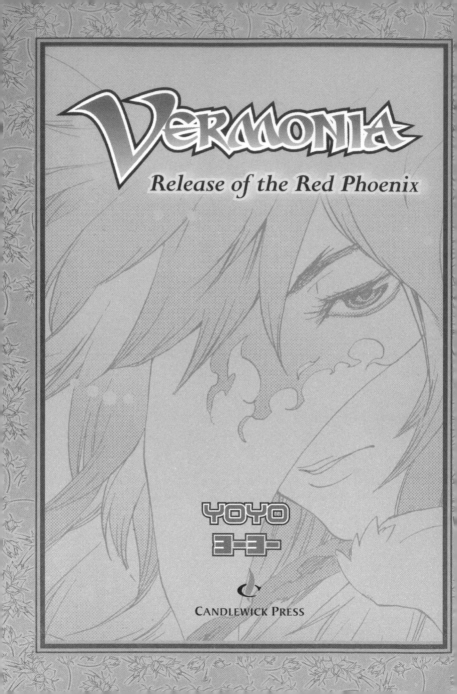

VERMONIA

Release of the Red Phoenix

YOYO
3-3-

CANDLEWICK PRESS

COPYRIGHT © 2010 BY RAITETSU MEDIA LLC AND RAY PRODUCTIONS

FIRST U.S. EDITION 2010

LIBRARY OF CONGRESS CATALOGING-IN-PUBLICATION DATA PENDING

10 11 12 13 14 15 SCP 10 9 8 7 6 5 4 3 2 1

PRINTED IN HUMEN, DONGGUAN, CHINA

THIS BOOK WAS TYPESET IN CCLADRONN ITALIC.

CANDLEWICK PRESS
99 DOVER STREET
SOMERVILLE, MASSACHUSETTS 02144

VISIT US AT WWW.CANDLEWICK.COM

WWW.VERMONIA.COM

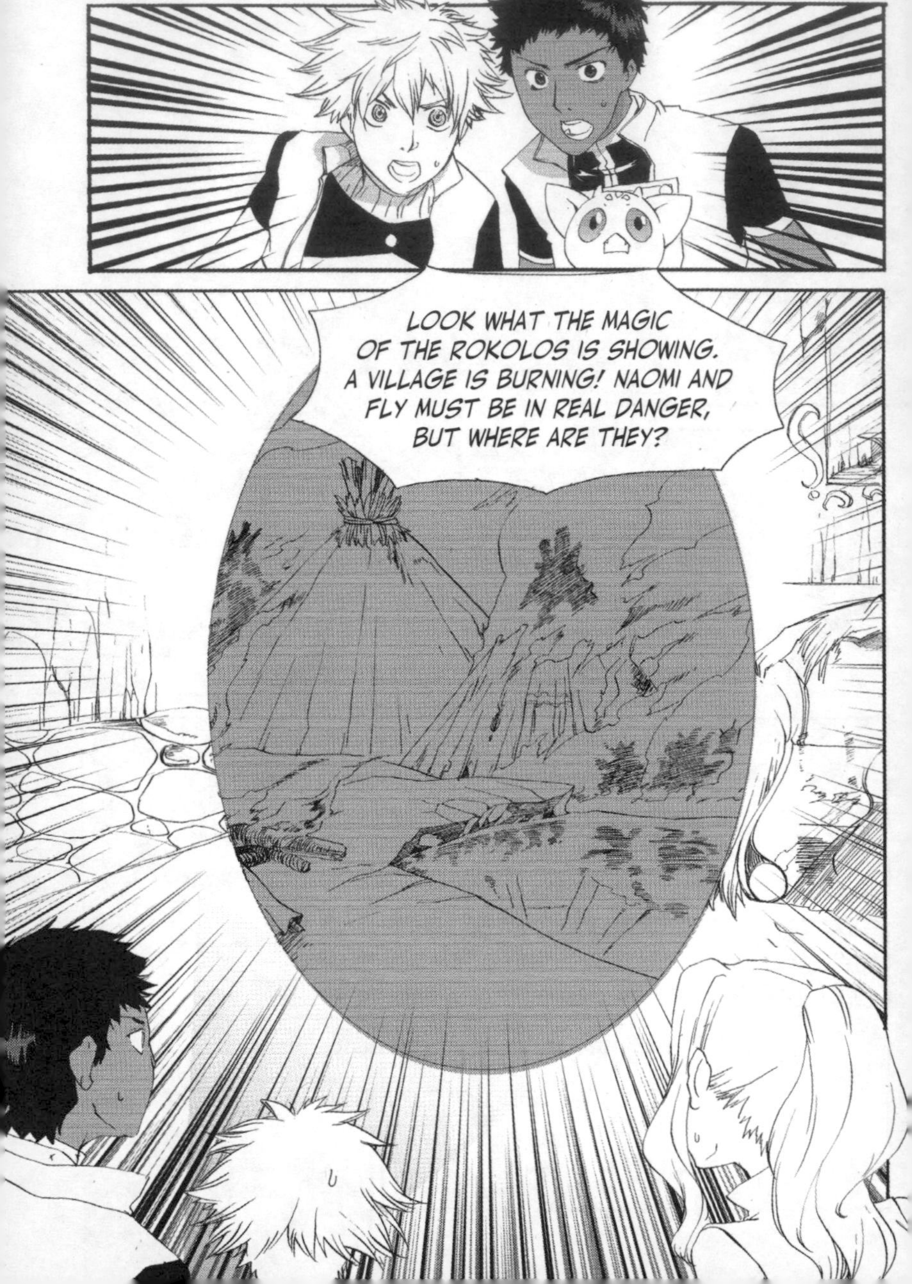
LOOK WHAT THE MAGIC
OF THE ROKOLOS IS SHOWING.
A VILLAGE IS BURNING! NAOMI AND
FLY MUST BE IN REAL DANGER,
BUT WHERE ARE THEY?

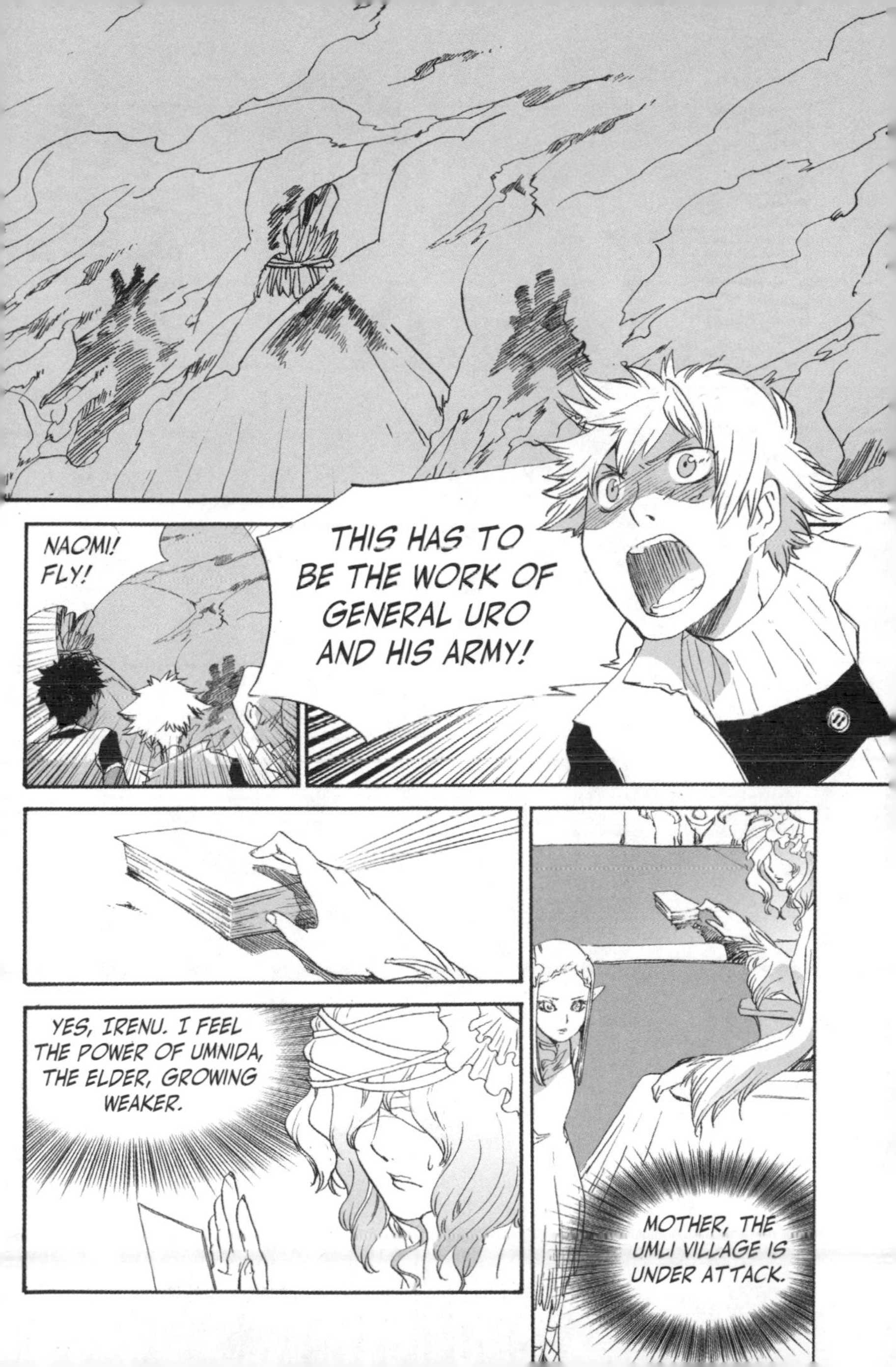
NAOMI! FLY!
THIS HAS TO BE THE WORK OF GENERAL URO AND HIS ARMY!
MOTHER, THE UMLI VILLAGE IS UNDER ATTACK.
YES, IRENU. I FEEL THE POWER OF UMNIDA, THE ELDER, GROWING WEAKER.

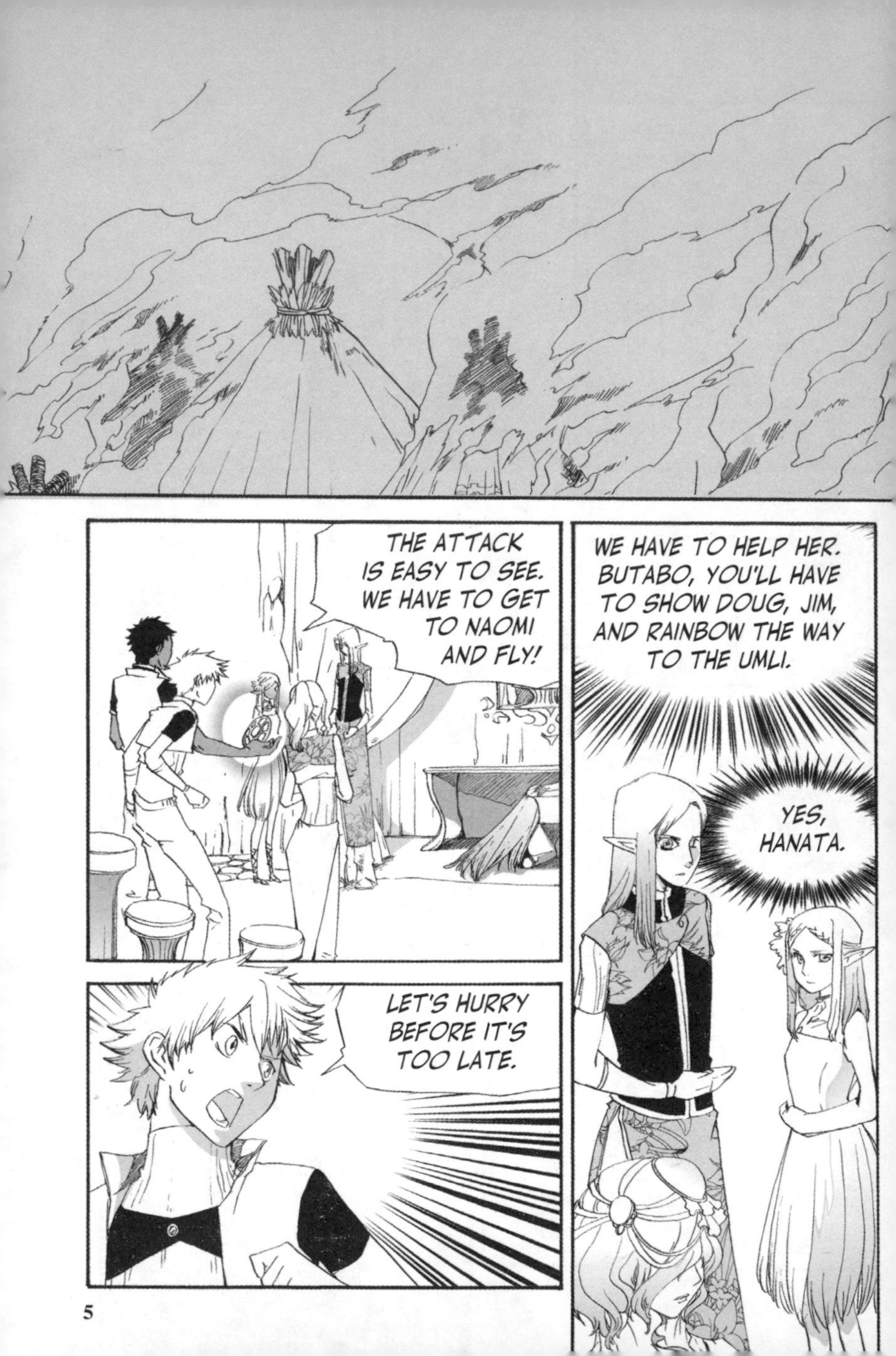
WE HAVE TO HELP HER. BUTABO, YOU'LL HAVE TO SHOW DOUG, JIM, AND RAINBOW THE WAY TO THE UMLI.
YES, HANATA.
THE ATTACK IS EASY TO SEE. WE HAVE TO GET TO NAOMI AND FLY!
LET'S HURRY BEFORE IT'S TOO LATE.

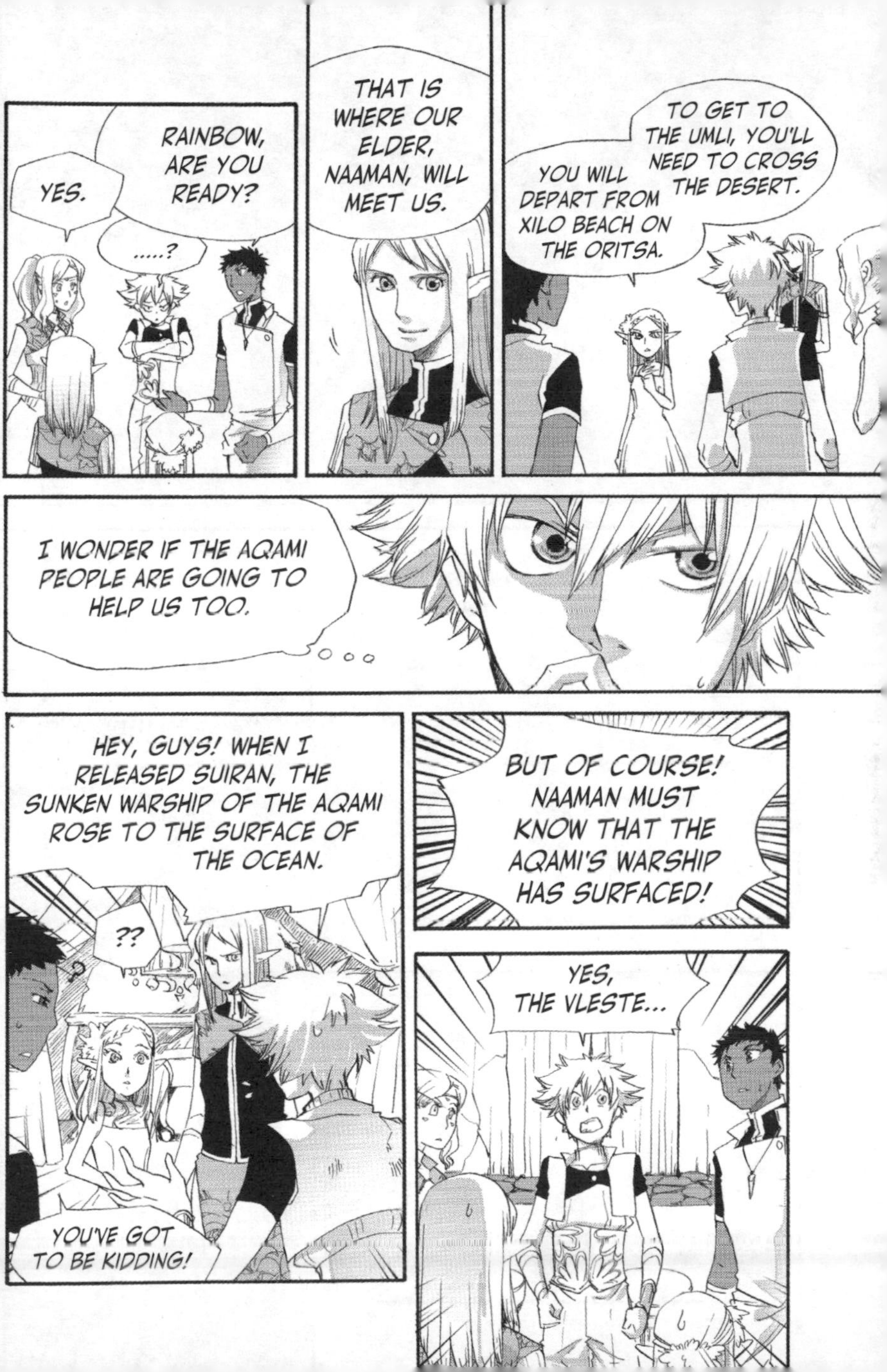
RAINBOW, ARE YOU READY?
YES.
.....?
THAT IS WHERE OUR ELDER, NAAMAN, WILL MEET US.
TO GET TO THE UMLI, YOU'LL NEED TO CROSS THE DESERT.
YOU WILL DEPART FROM XILO BEACH ON THE ORITSA.
I WONDER IF THE AQAMI PEOPLE ARE GOING TO HELP US TOO.
HEY, GUYS! WHEN I RELEASED SUIRAN, THE SUNKEN WARSHIP OF THE AQAMI ROSE TO THE SURFACE OF THE OCEAN.
??
YOU'VE GOT TO BE KIDDING!
BUT OF COURSE! NAAMAN MUST KNOW THAT THE AQAMI'S WARSHIP HAS SURFACED!
YES, THE VLESTE...

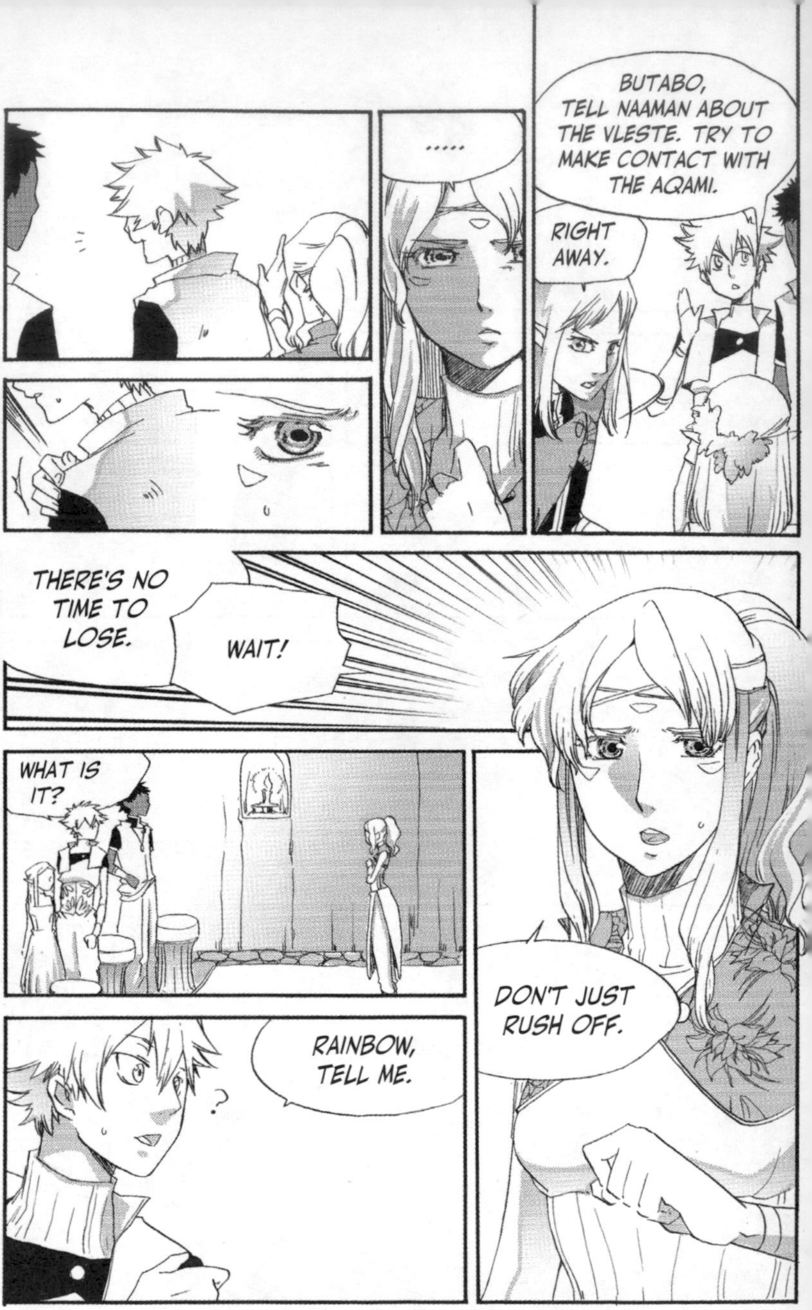
......
BUTABO, TELL NAAMAN ABOUT THE VLESTE. TRY TO MAKE CONTACT WITH THE AQAMI.
RIGHT AWAY.
THERE'S NO TIME TO LOSE.
WAIT!
WHAT IS IT?
DON'T JUST RUSH OFF.
RAINBOW, TELL ME.

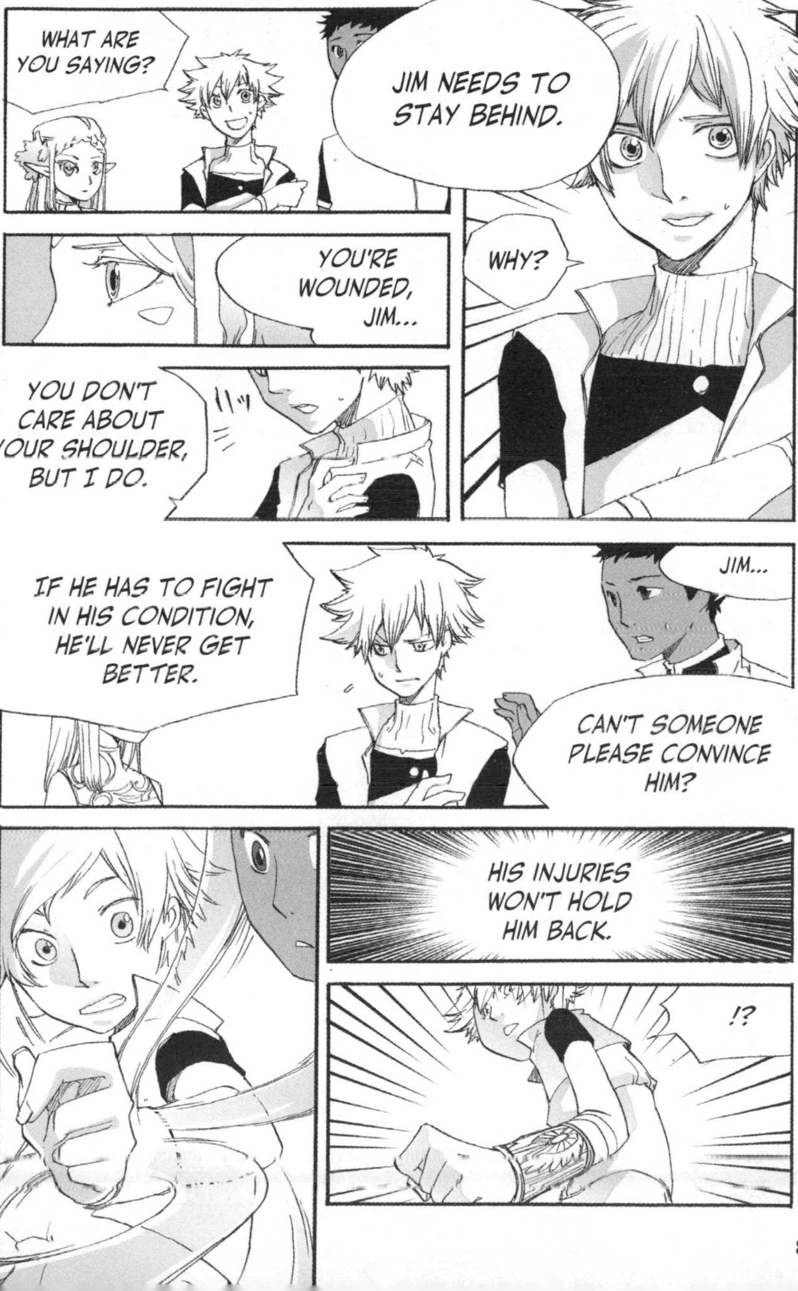
WHAT ARE YOU SAYING?
JIM NEEDS TO STAY BEHIND.
WHY?
YOU'RE WOUNDED, JIM...
YOU DON'T CARE ABOUT YOUR SHOULDER, BUT I DO.
IF HE HAS TO FIGHT IN HIS CONDITION, HE'LL NEVER GET BETTER.
JIM...
CAN'T SOMEONE PLEASE CONVINCE HIM?
HIS INJURIES WON'T HOLD HIM BACK.
!?

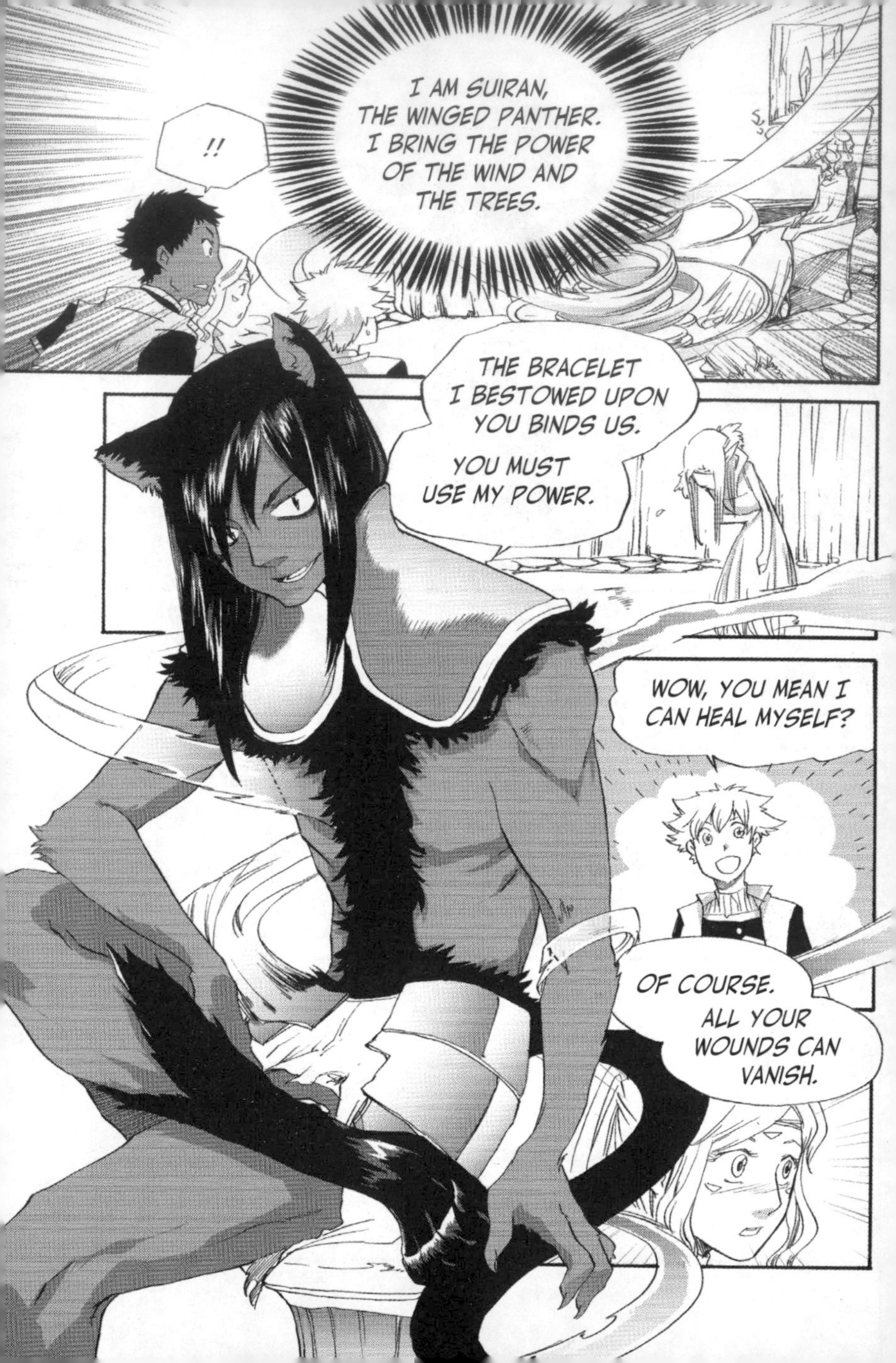
I AM SUIRAN, THE WINGED PANTHER. I BRING THE POWER OF THE WIND AND THE TREES.
!!
THE BRACELET I BESTOWED UPON YOU BINDS US.
YOU MUST USE MY POWER.
WOW, YOU MEAN I CAN HEAL MYSELF?
OF COURSE.
ALL YOUR WOUNDS CAN VANISH.

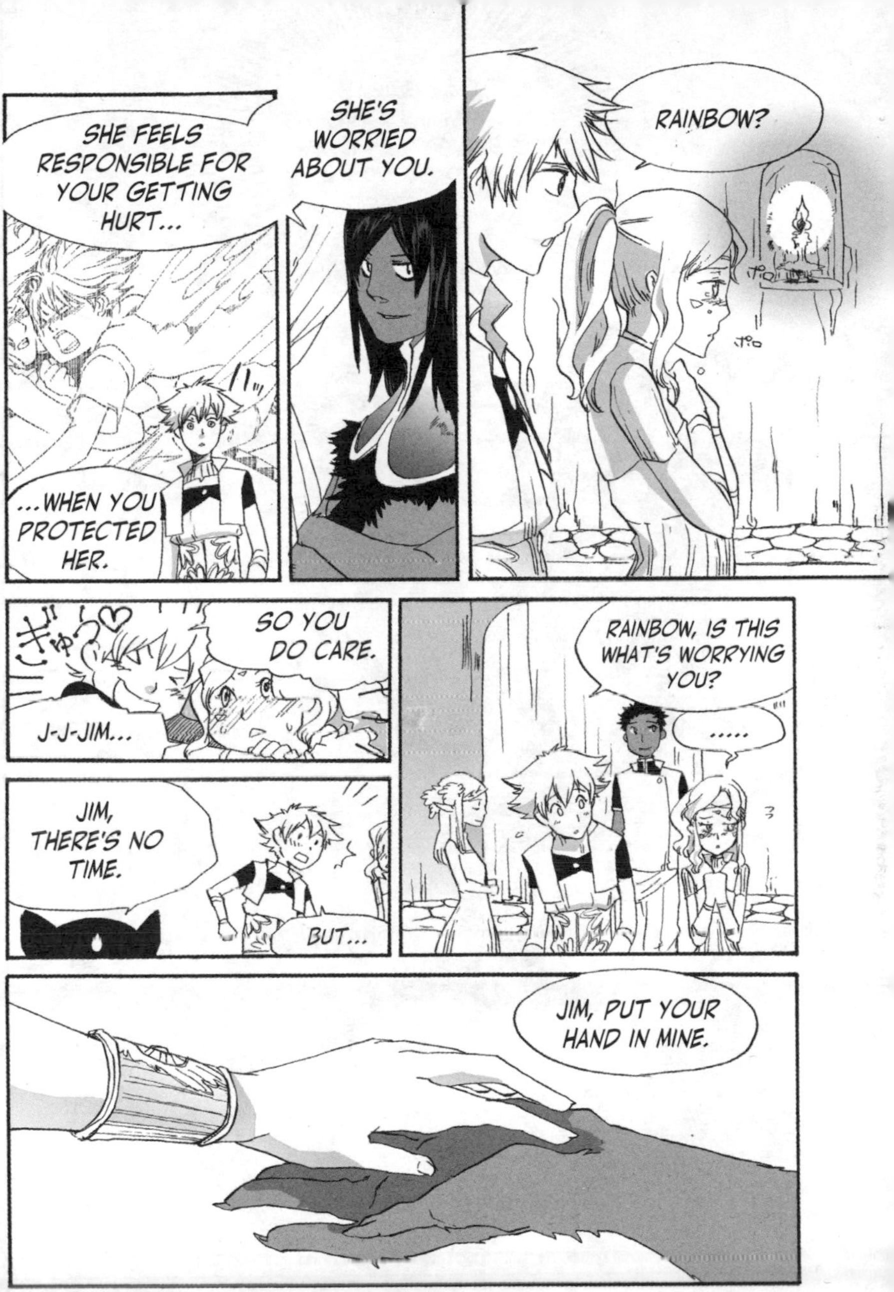

SHE FEELS RESPONSIBLE FOR YOUR GETTING HURT...
...WHEN YOU PROTECTED HER.
SHE'S WORRIED ABOUT YOU.
RAINBOW?
SO YOU DO CARE.
J-J-JIM...
RAINBOW, IS THIS WHAT'S WORRYING YOU?
.....
JIM, THERE'S NO TIME.
BUT...
JIM, PUT YOUR HAND IN MINE.

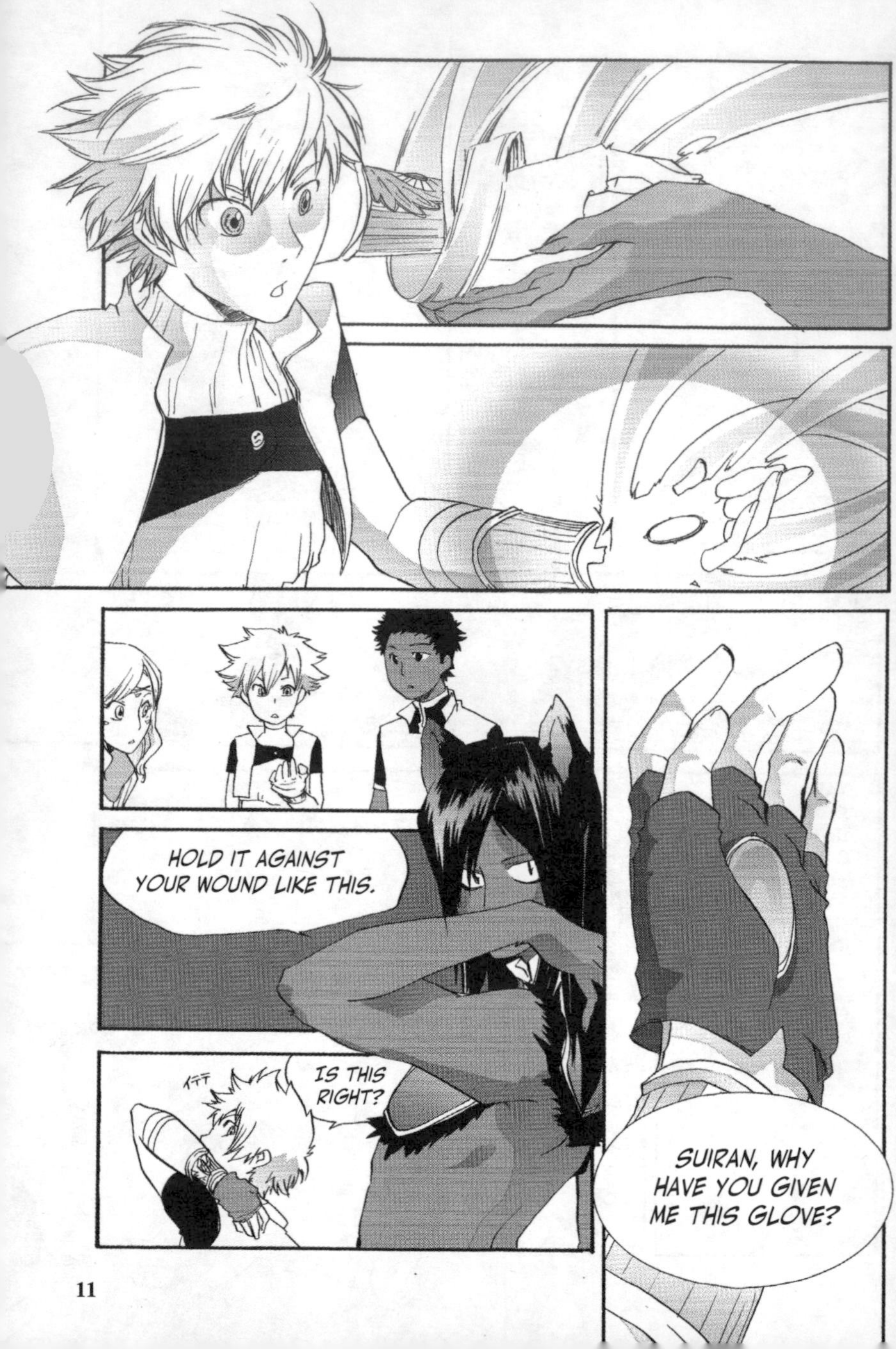
HOLD IT AGAINST YOUR WOUND LIKE THIS.
イテテ
IS THIS RIGHT?
SUIRAN, WHY HAVE YOU GIVEN ME THIS GLOVE?

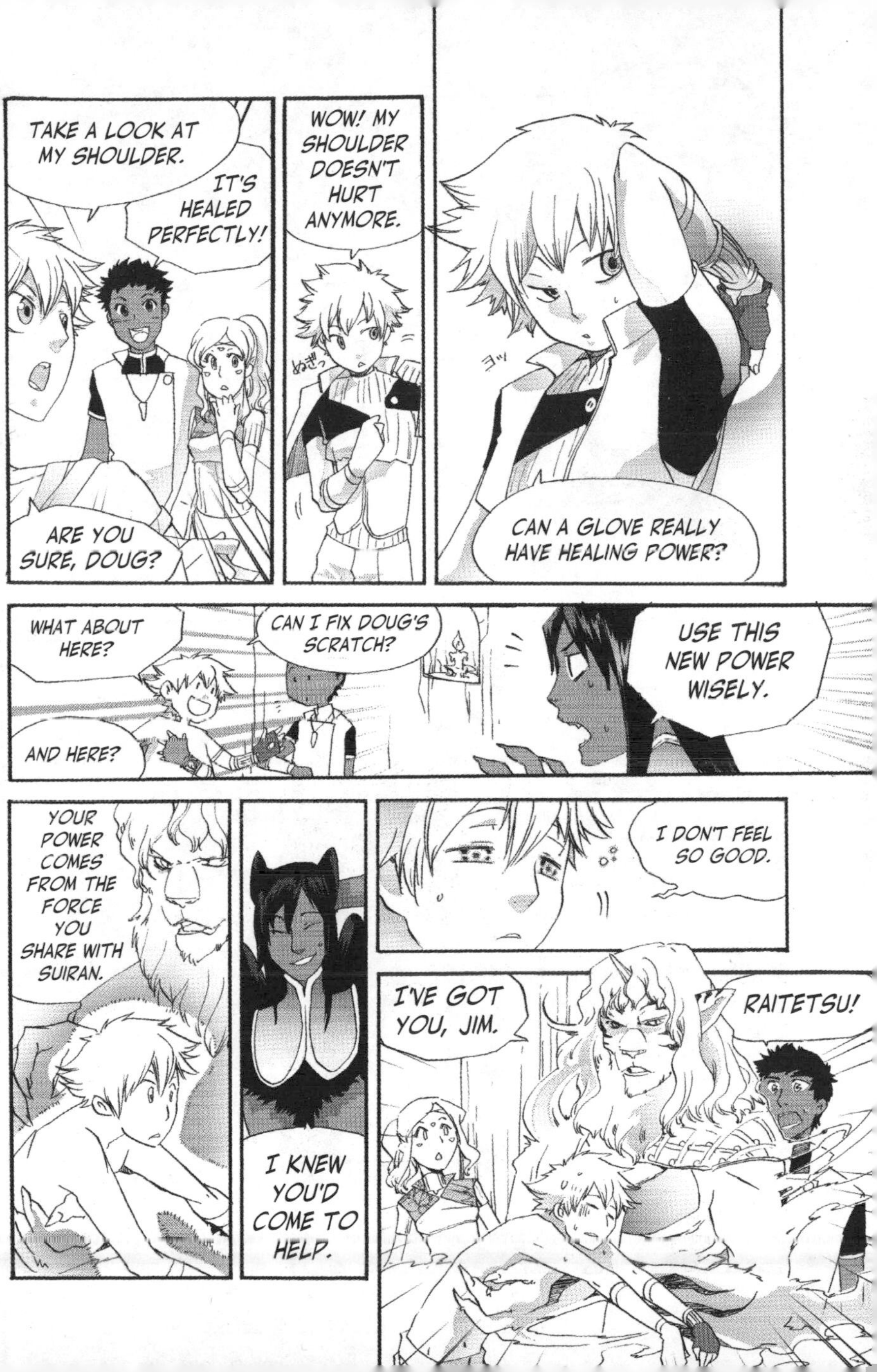

TAKE A LOOK AT MY SHOULDER.
IT'S HEALED PERFECTLY!
ARE YOU SURE, DOUG?
WOW! MY SHOULDER DOESN'T HURT ANYMORE.
CAN A GLOVE REALLY HAVE HEALING POWER?
WHAT ABOUT HERE?
AND HERE?
CAN I FIX DOUG'S SCRATCH?
USE THIS NEW POWER WISELY.
YOUR POWER COMES FROM THE FORCE YOU SHARE WITH SUIRAN.
I KNEW YOU'D COME TO HELP.
I DON'T FEEL SO GOOD.
I'VE GOT YOU, JIM.
RAITETSU!

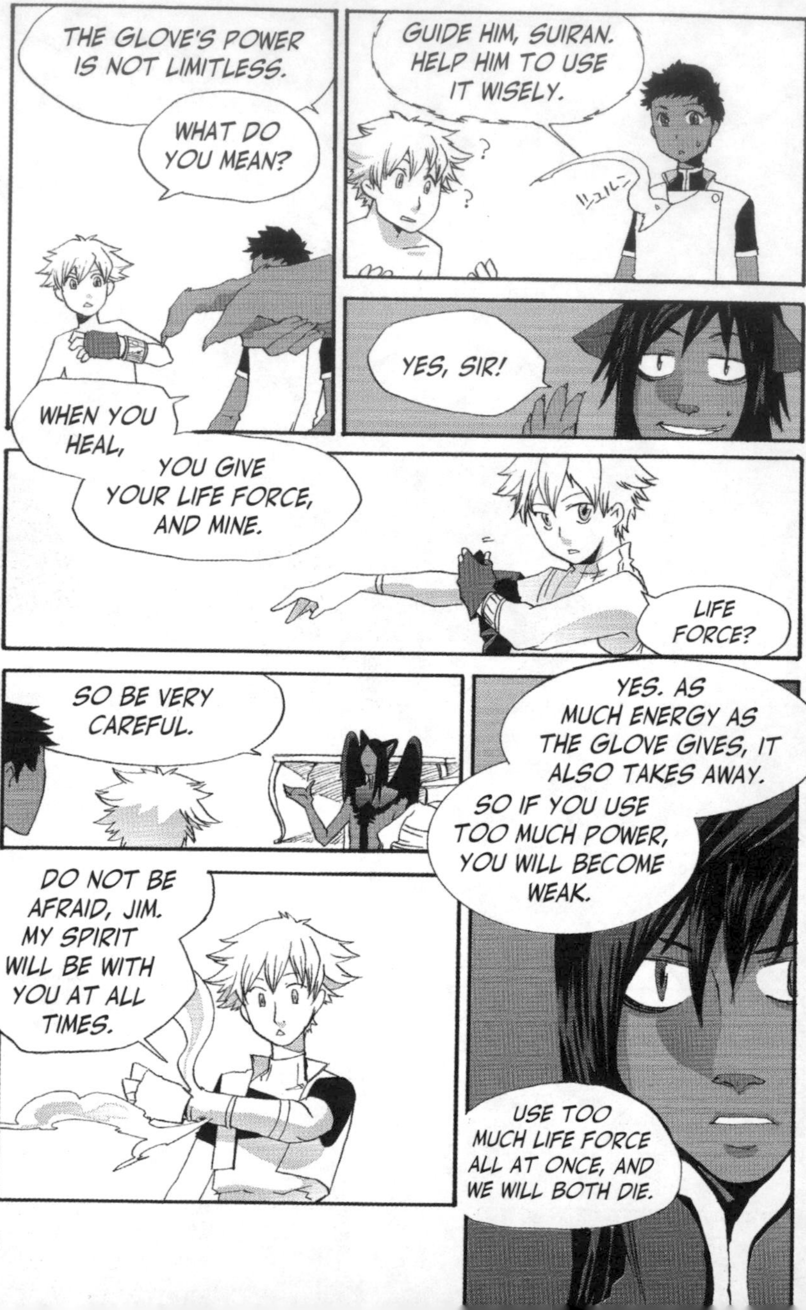
THE GLOVE'S POWER IS NOT LIMITLESS.
WHAT DO YOU MEAN?
GUIDE HIM, SUIRAN. HELP HIM TO USE IT WISELY.
YES, SIR!
WHEN YOU HEAL,
YOU GIVE YOUR LIFE FORCE, AND MINE.
LIFE FORCE?
SO BE VERY CAREFUL.
YES. AS MUCH ENERGY AS THE GLOVE GIVES, IT ALSO TAKES AWAY.
SO IF YOU USE TOO MUCH POWER, YOU WILL BECOME WEAK.
DO NOT BE AFRAID, JIM. MY SPIRIT WILL BE WITH YOU AT ALL TIMES.
USE TOO MUCH LIFE FORCE ALL AT ONCE, AND WE WILL BOTH DIE.

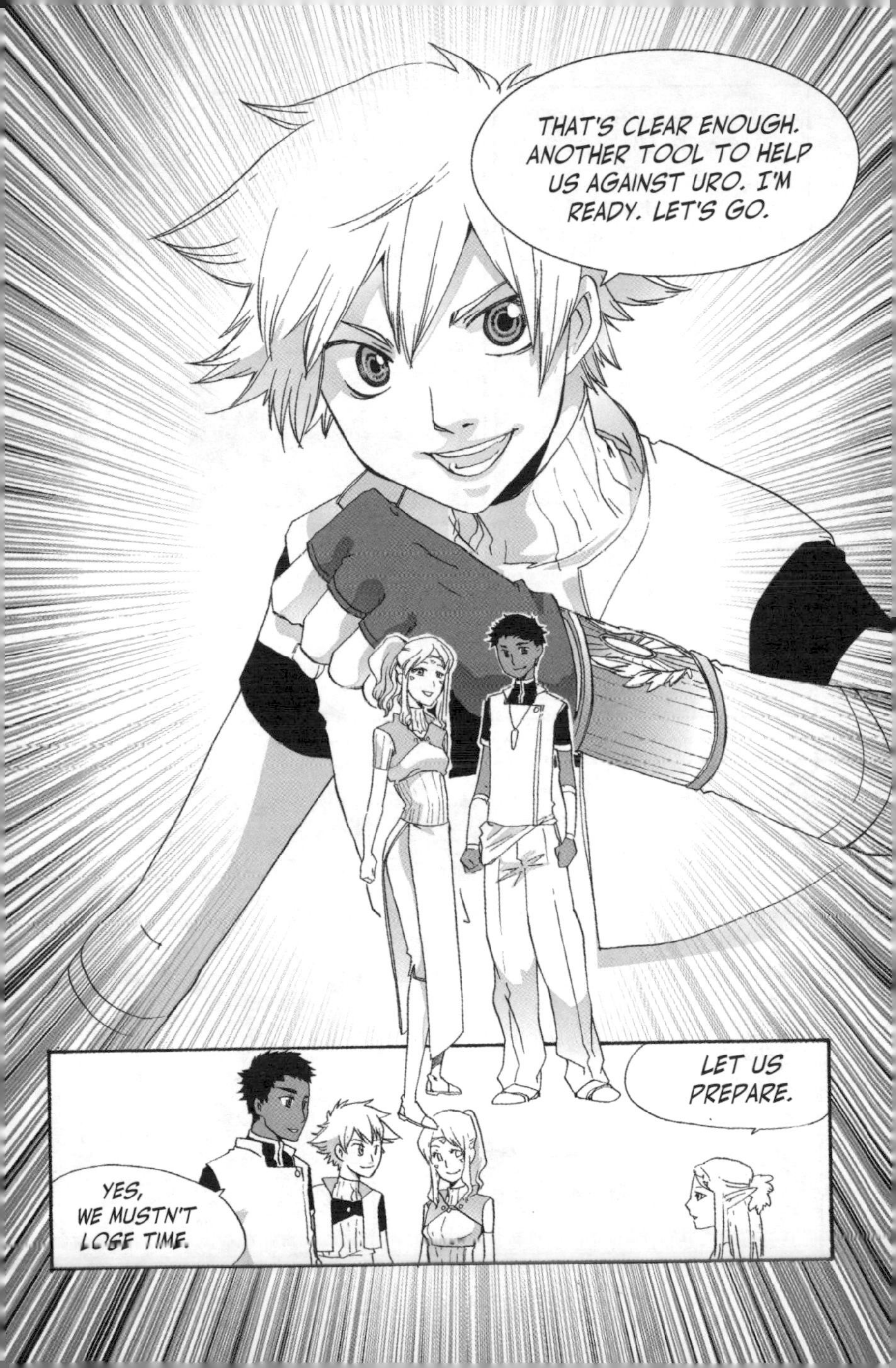
THAT'S CLEAR ENOUGH. ANOTHER TOOL TO HELP US AGAINST URO. I'M READY. LET'S GO.
LET US PREPARE.
YES, WE MUSTN'T LOSE TIME.

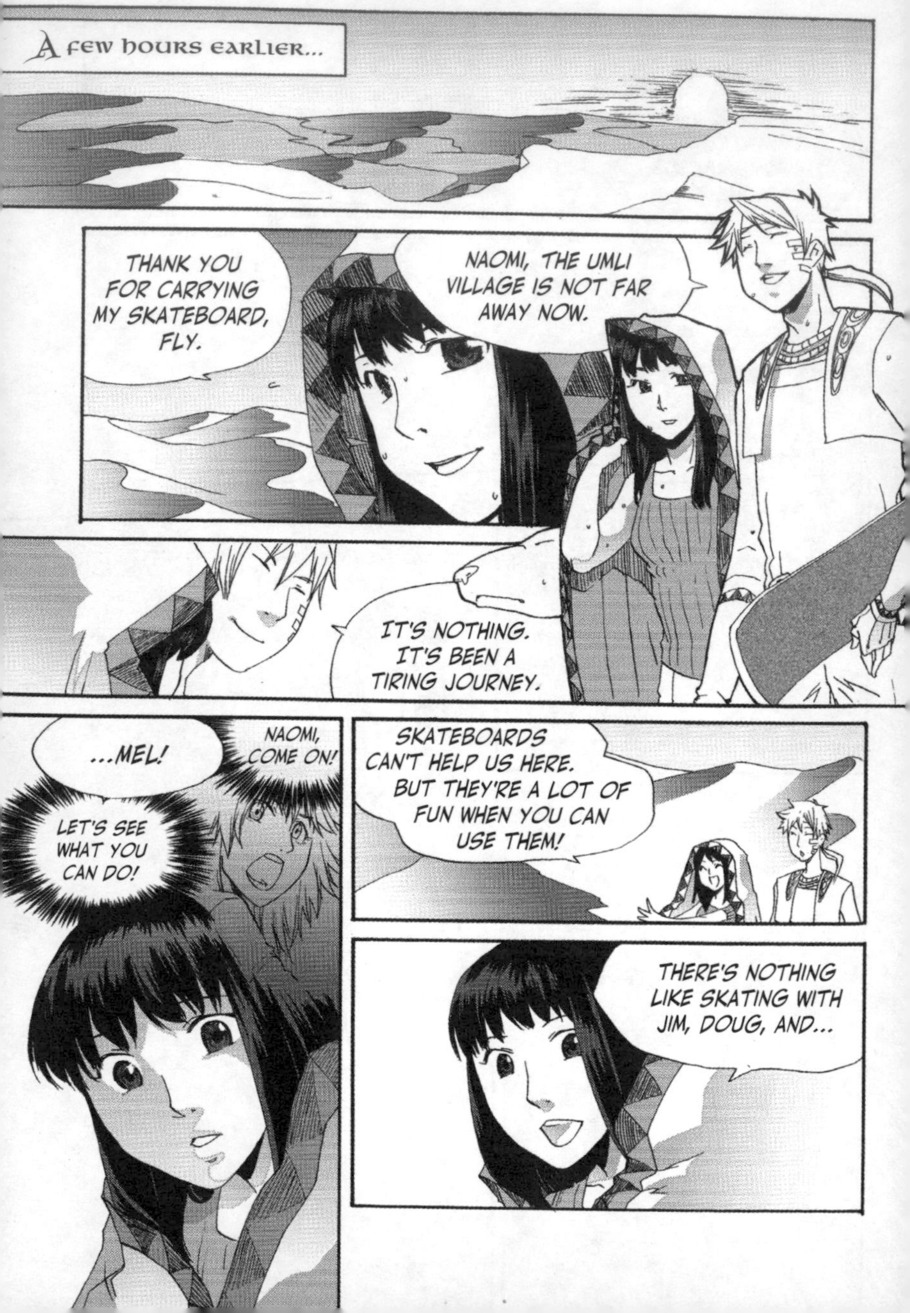
A FEW HOURS EARLIER...
THANK YOU FOR CARRYING MY SKATEBOARD, FLY.
NAOMI, THE UMLI VILLAGE IS NOT FAR AWAY NOW.
IT'S NOTHING. IT'S BEEN A TIRING JOURNEY.
...MEL!
NAOMI, COME ON!
LET'S SEE WHAT YOU CAN DO!
SKATEBOARDS CAN'T HELP US HERE. BUT THEY'RE A LOT OF FUN WHEN YOU CAN USE THEM!
THERE'S NOTHING LIKE SKATING WITH JIM, DOUG, AND...

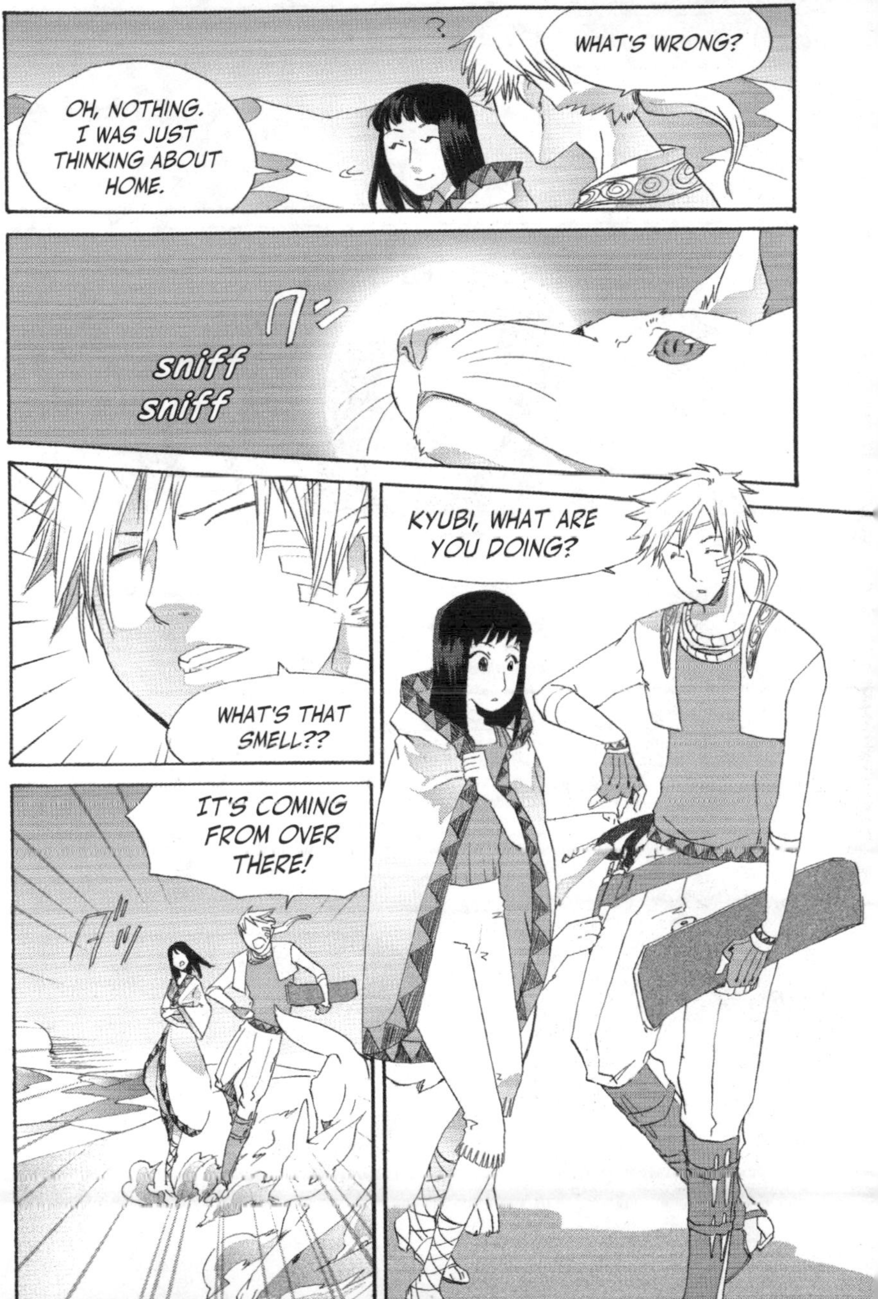
WHAT'S WRONG?
OH, NOTHING. I WAS JUST THINKING ABOUT HOME.
sniff sniff
KYUBI, WHAT ARE YOU DOING?
WHAT'S THAT SMELL??
IT'S COMING FROM OVER THERE!

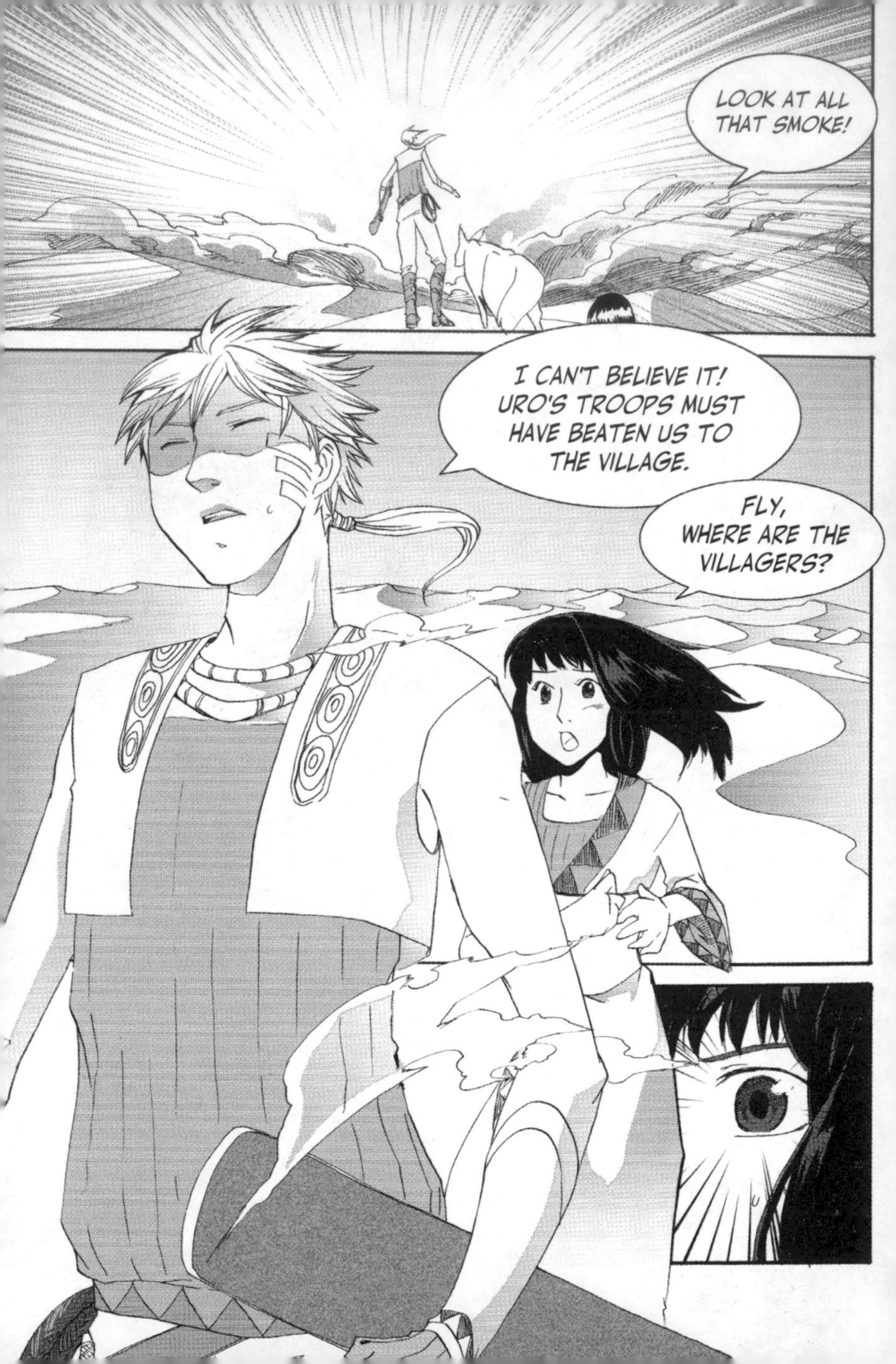
LOOK AT ALL THAT SMOKE!
I CAN'T BELIEVE IT! URO'S TROOPS MUST HAVE BEATEN US TO THE VILLAGE.
FLY, WHERE ARE THE VILLAGERS?

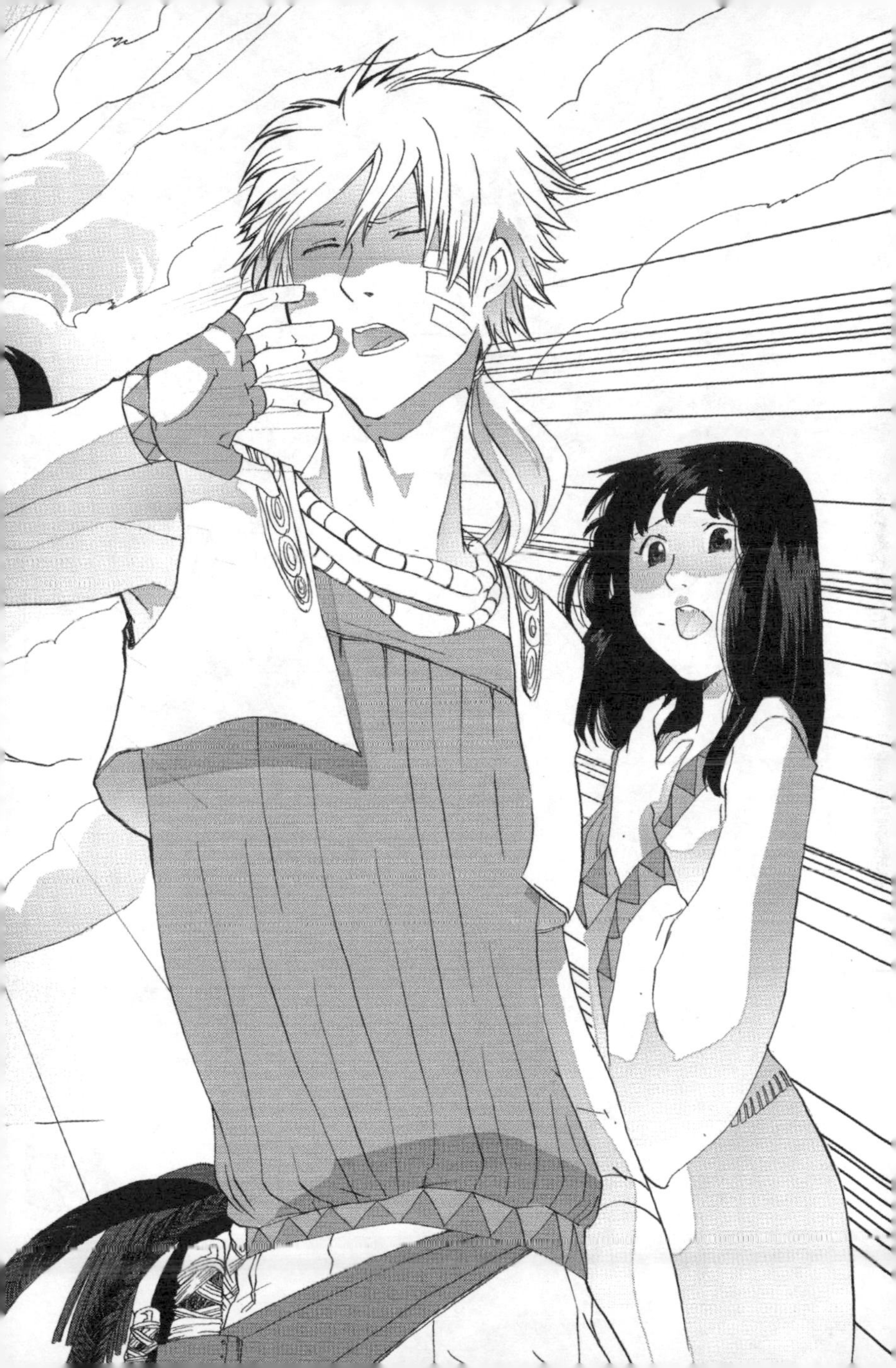

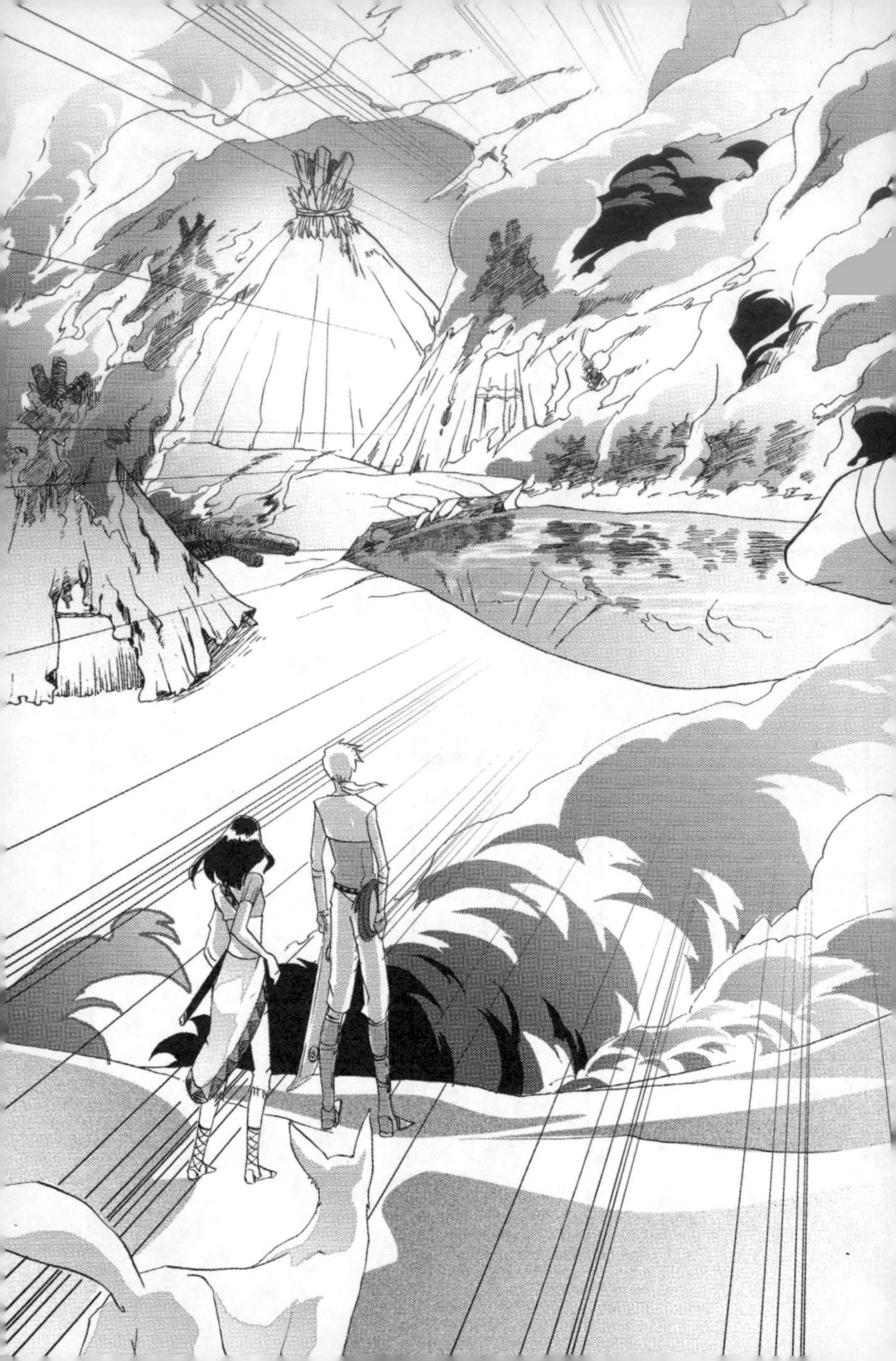

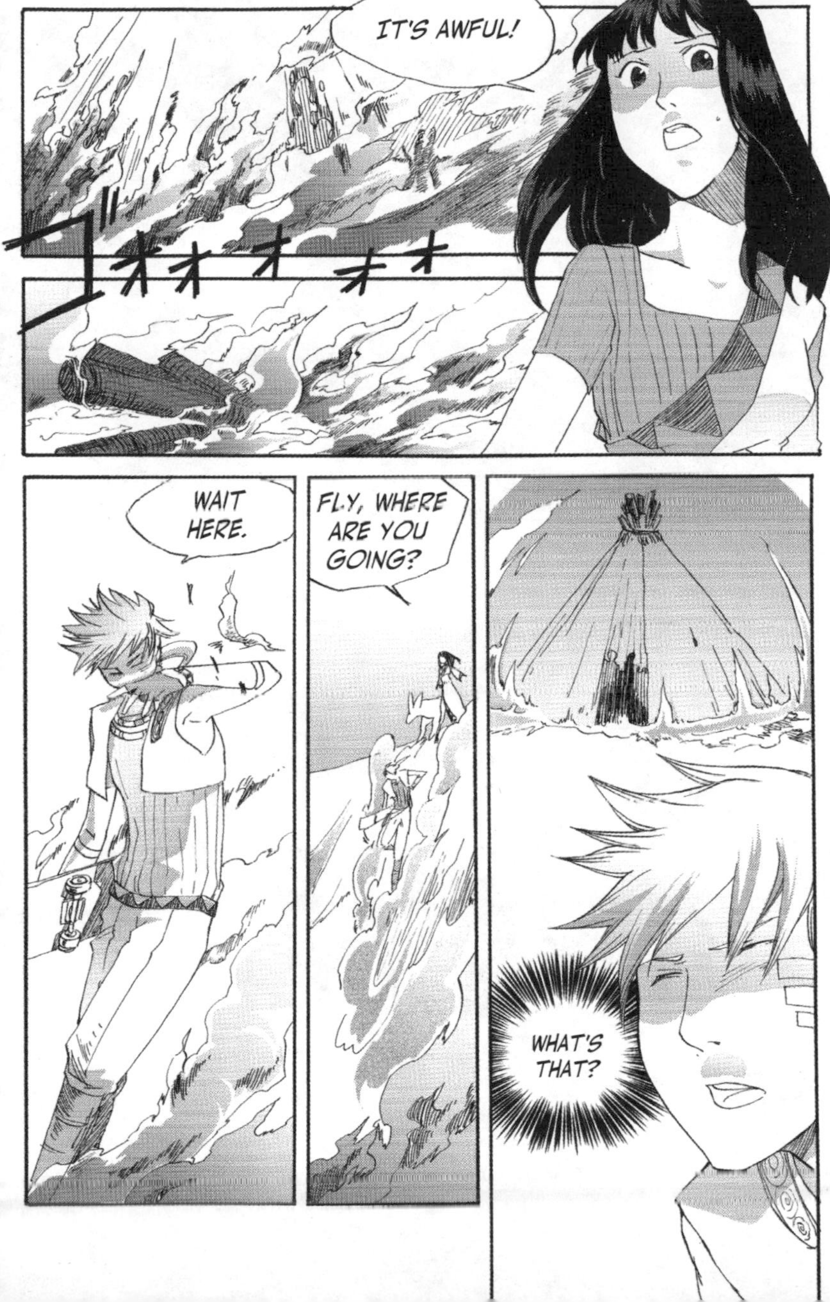
IT'S AWFUL!
ゴオオオオオ
WAIT HERE.
FLY, WHERE ARE YOU GOING?
WHAT'S THAT?

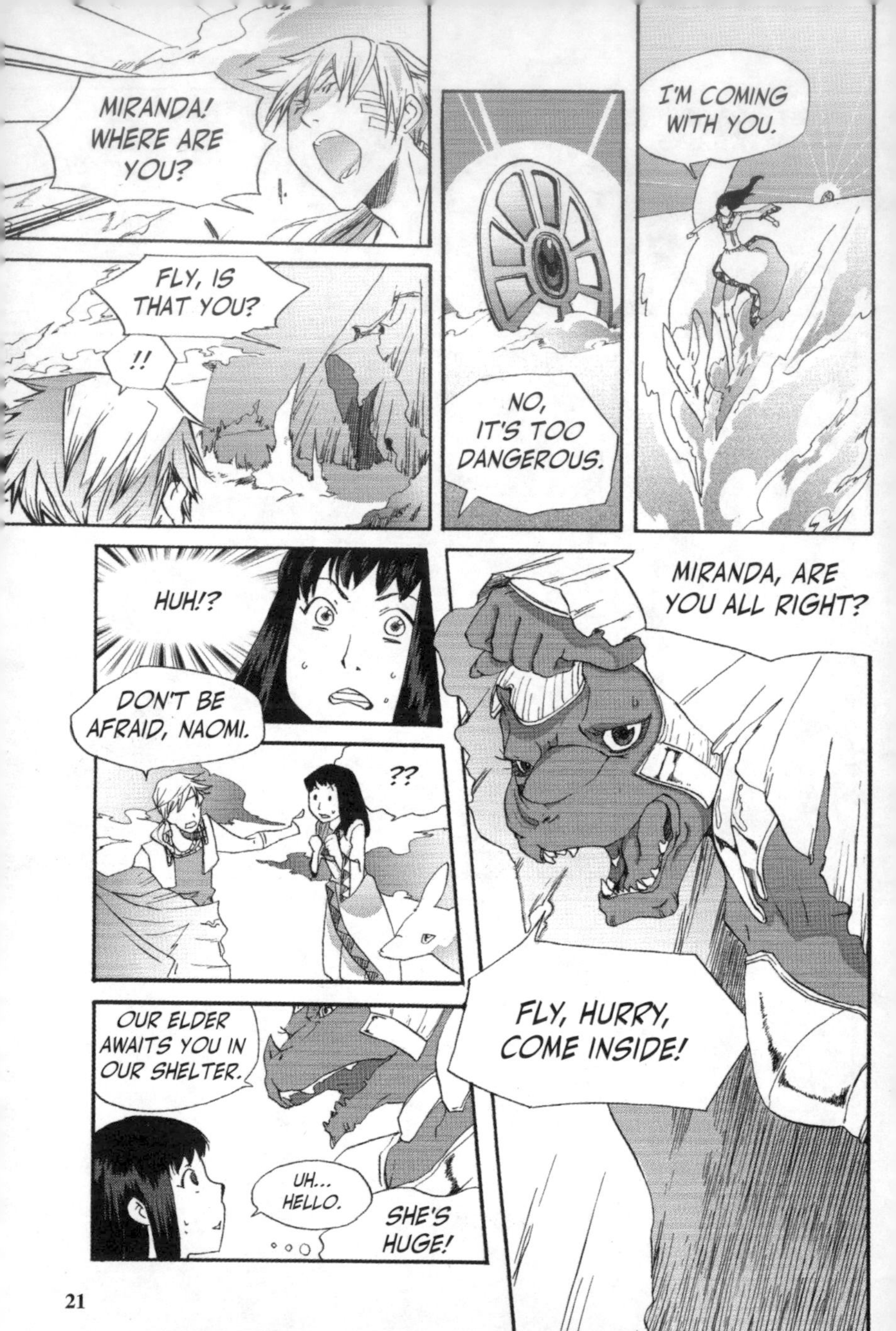
MIRANDA! WHERE ARE YOU?
FLY, IS THAT YOU?
!!
I'M COMING WITH YOU.
NO, IT'S TOO DANGEROUS.
HUH!?
DON'T BE AFRAID, NAOMI.
??
MIRANDA, ARE YOU ALL RIGHT?
OUR ELDER AWAITS YOU IN OUR SHELTER.
UH... HELLO.
SHE'S HUGE!
FLY, HURRY, COME INSIDE!

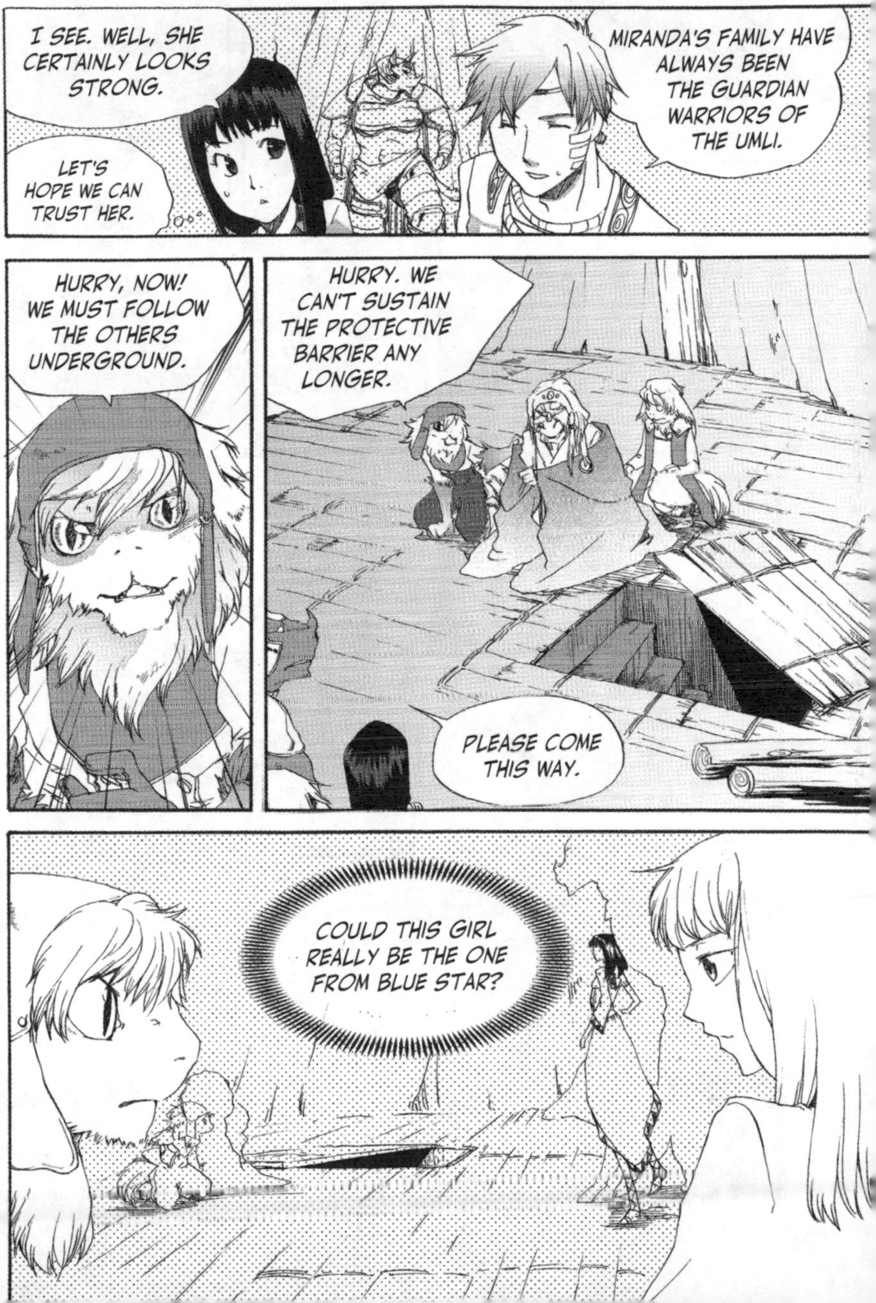
I SEE. WELL, SHE CERTAINLY LOOKS STRONG.
MIRANDA'S FAMILY HAVE ALWAYS BEEN THE GUARDIAN WARRIORS OF THE UMLI.
LET'S HOPE WE CAN TRUST HER.
HURRY, NOW! WE MUST FOLLOW THE OTHERS UNDERGROUND.
HURRY. WE CAN'T SUSTAIN THE PROTECTIVE BARRIER ANY LONGER.
PLEASE COME THIS WAY.
COULD THIS GIRL REALLY BE THE ONE FROM BLUE STAR?

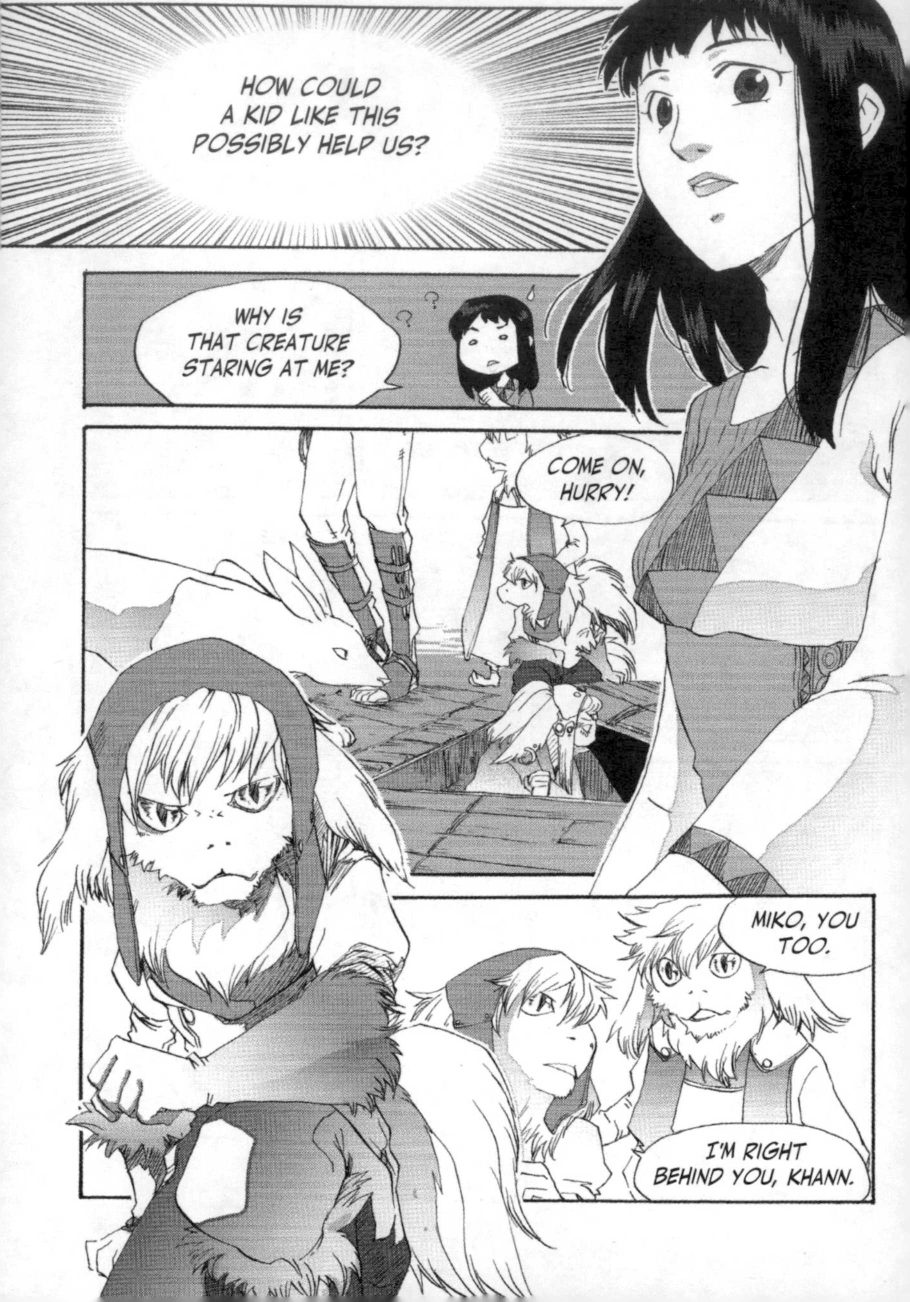
HOW COULD A KID LIKE THIS POSSIBLY HELP US?
WHY IS THAT CREATURE STARING AT ME?
COME ON, HURRY!
MIKO, YOU TOO.
I'M RIGHT BEHIND YOU, KHANN.

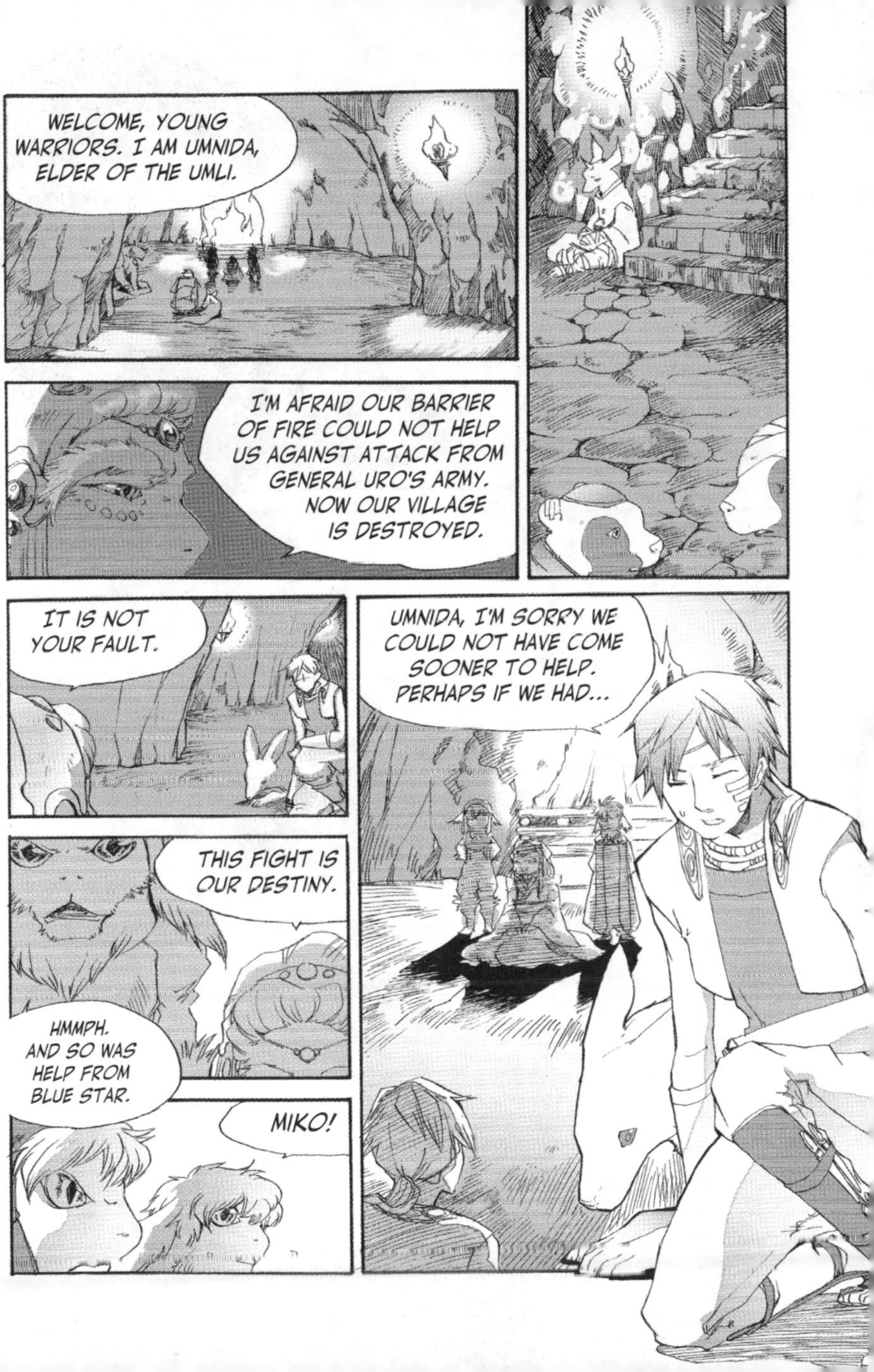
WELCOME, YOUNG WARRIORS. I AM UMNIDA, ELDER OF THE UMLI.
I'M AFRAID OUR BARRIER OF FIRE COULD NOT HELP US AGAINST ATTACK FROM GENERAL URO'S ARMY. NOW OUR VILLAGE IS DESTROYED.
IT IS NOT YOUR FAULT.
THIS FIGHT IS OUR DESTINY.
HMMPH. AND SO WAS HELP FROM BLUE STAR.
MIKO!
UMNIDA, I'M SORRY WE COULD NOT HAVE COME SOONER TO HELP. PERHAPS IF WE HAD...

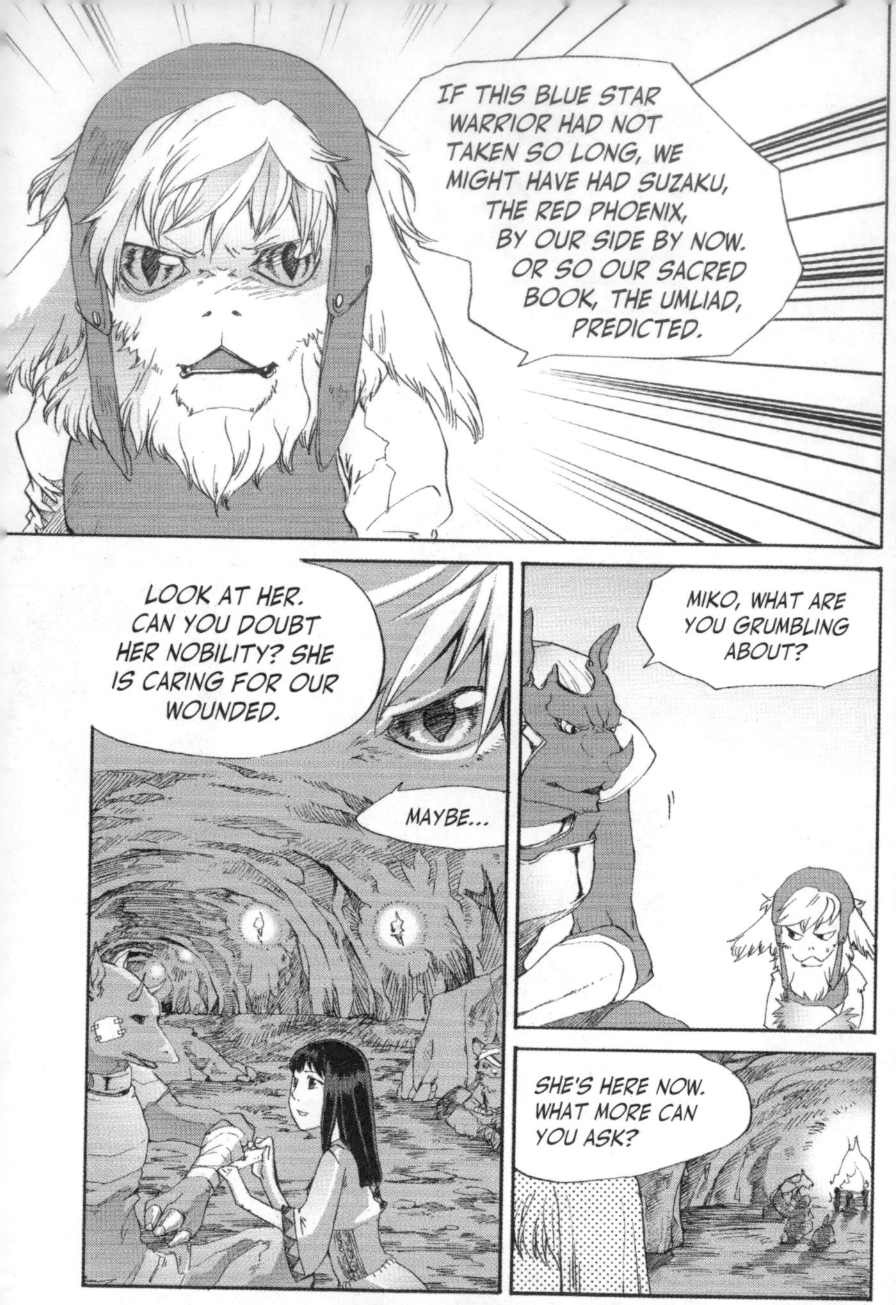
IF THIS BLUE STAR WARRIOR HAD NOT TAKEN SO LONG, WE MIGHT HAVE HAD SUZAKU, THE RED PHOENIX, BY OUR SIDE BY NOW. OR SO OUR SACRED BOOK, THE UMLIAD, PREDICTED.
MIKO, WHAT ARE YOU GRUMBLING ABOUT?
LOOK AT HER. CAN YOU DOUBT HER NOBILITY? SHE IS CARING FOR OUR WOUNDED.
MAYBE...
SHE'S HERE NOW. WHAT MORE CAN YOU ASK?

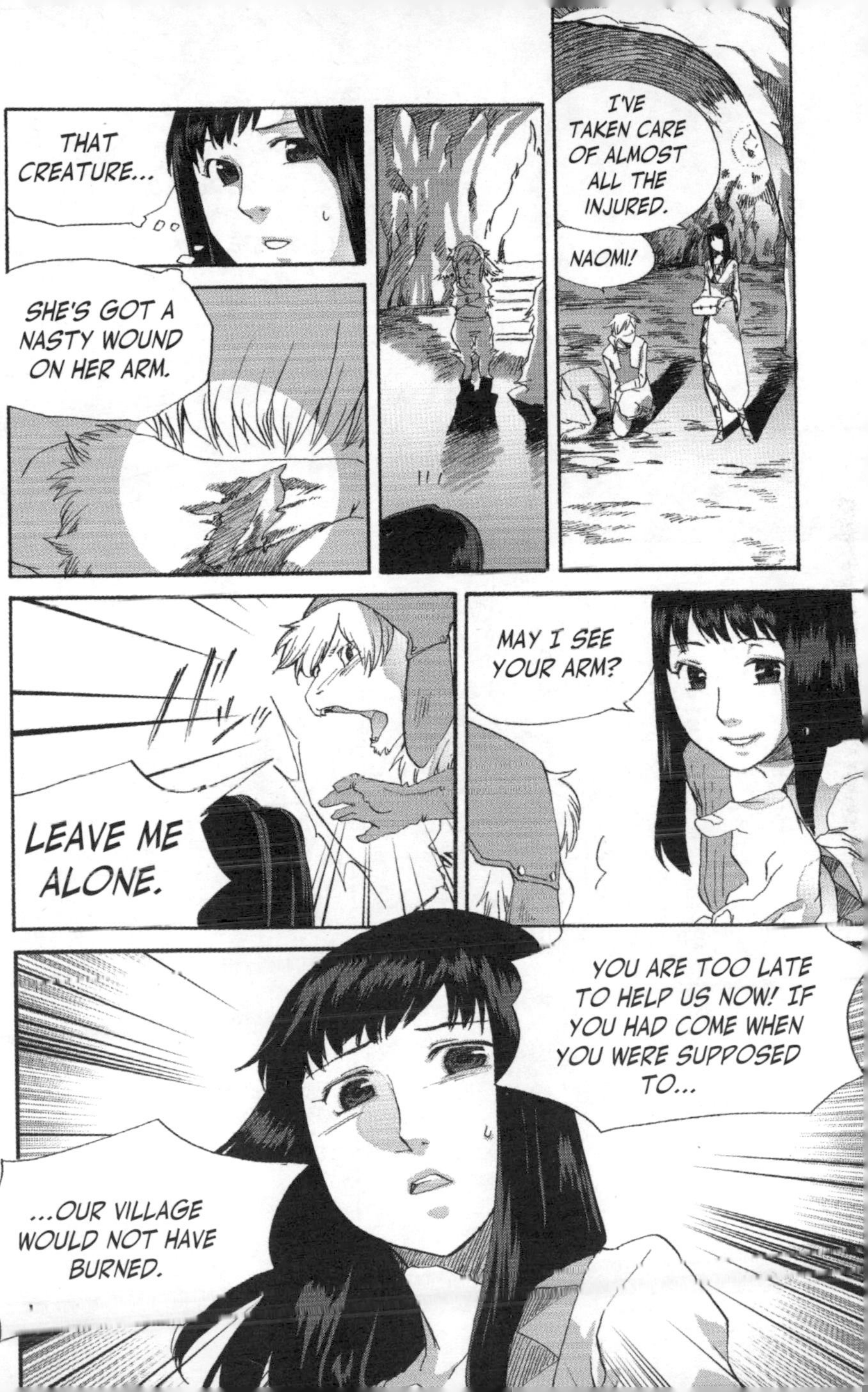
I'VE TAKEN CARE OF ALMOST ALL THE INJURED.
NAOMI!
THAT CREATURE...
SHE'S GOT A NASTY WOUND ON HER ARM.
MAY I SEE YOUR ARM?
LEAVE ME ALONE.
YOU ARE TOO LATE TO HELP US NOW! IF YOU HAD COME WHEN YOU WERE SUPPOSED TO...
...OUR VILLAGE WOULD NOT HAVE BURNED.

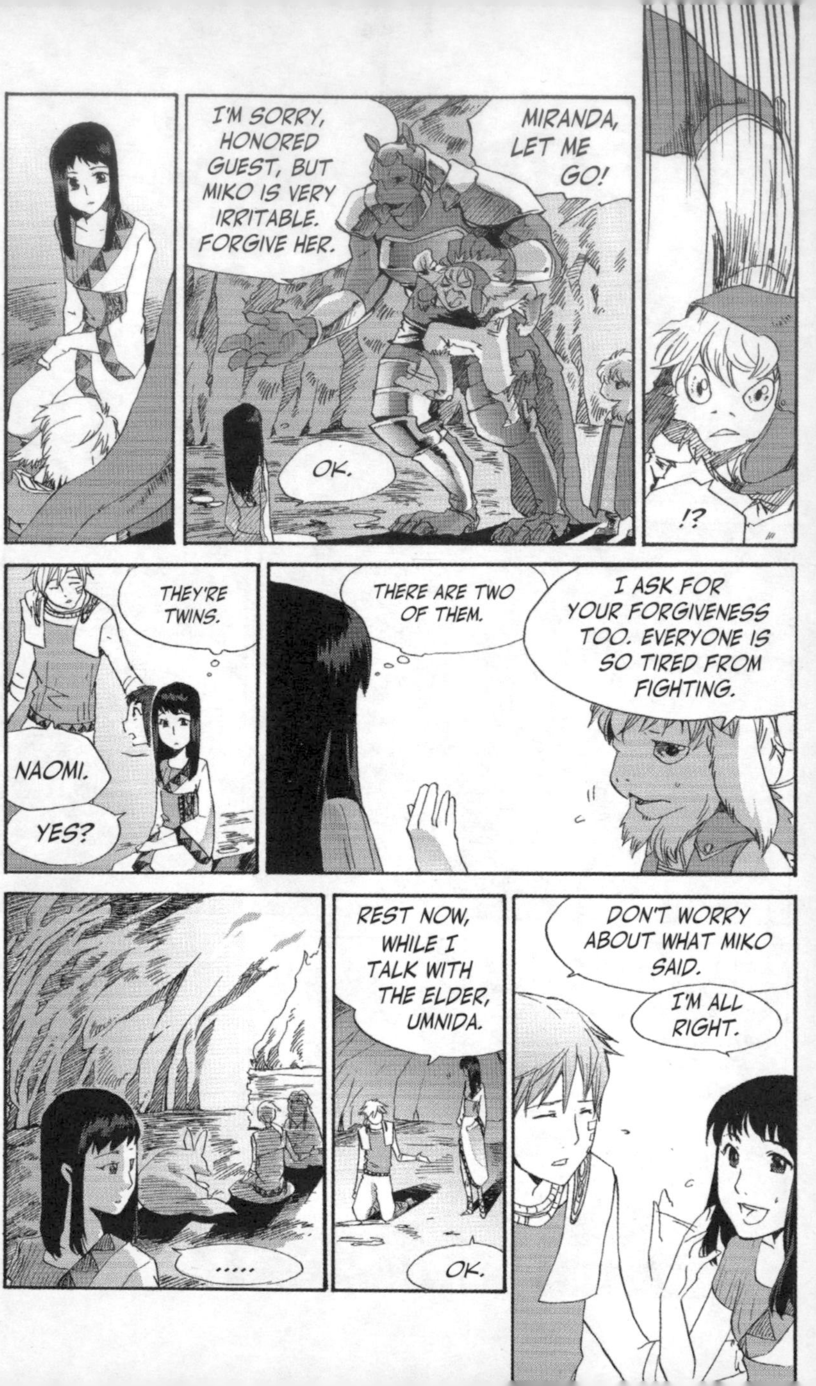
MIRANDA, LET ME GO!
I'M SORRY, HONORED GUEST, BUT MIKO IS VERY IRRITABLE. FORGIVE HER.
OK.
!?
THEY'RE TWINS.
NAOMI.
YES?
THERE ARE TWO OF THEM.
I ASK FOR YOUR FORGIVENESS TOO. EVERYONE IS SO TIRED FROM FIGHTING.
DON'T WORRY ABOUT WHAT MIKO SAID.
I'M ALL RIGHT.
REST NOW, WHILE I TALK WITH THE ELDER, UMNIDA.
OK.
.....

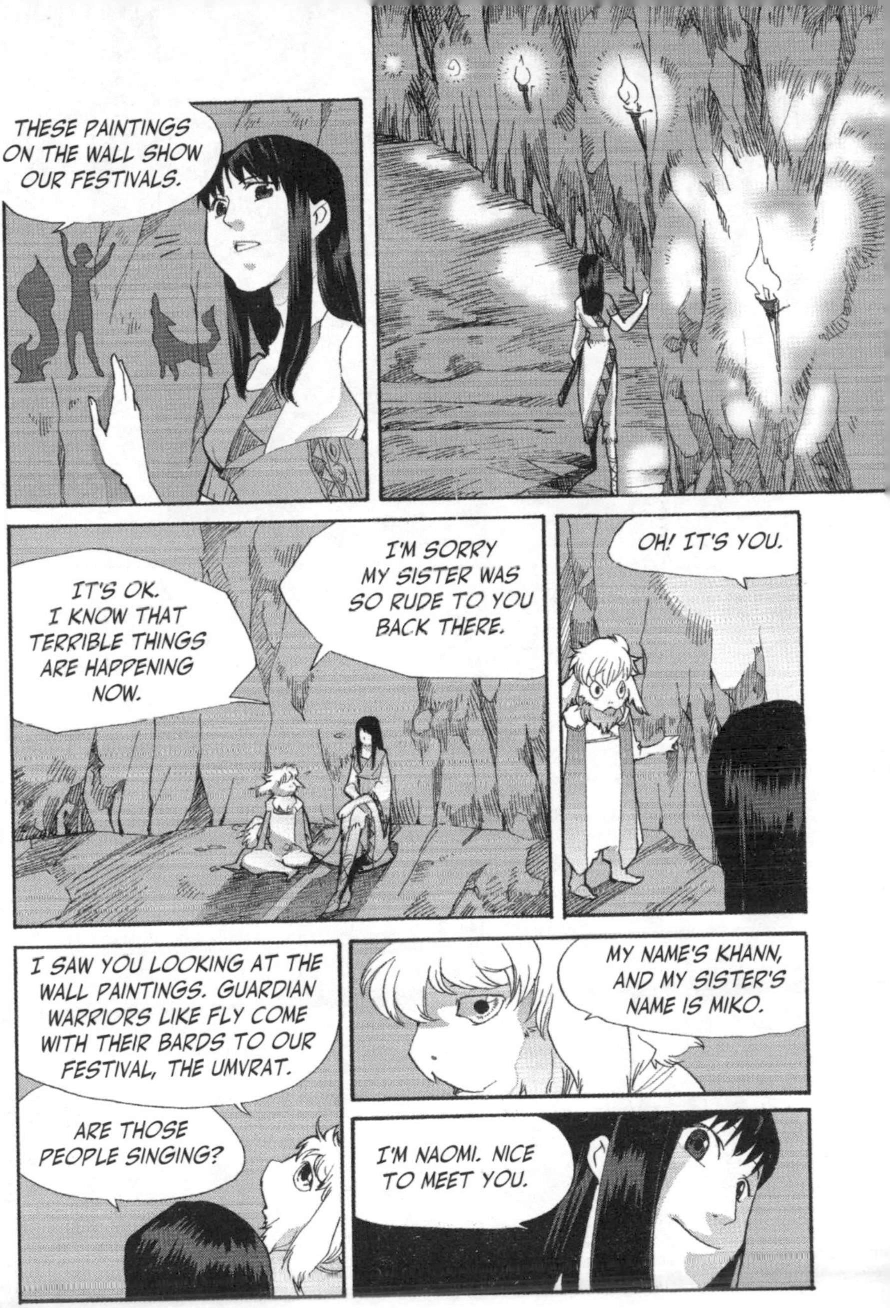
THESE PAINTINGS ON THE WALL SHOW OUR FESTIVALS.
I'M SORRY MY SISTER WAS SO RUDE TO YOU BACK THERE.
IT'S OK. I KNOW THAT TERRIBLE THINGS ARE HAPPENING NOW.
OH! IT'S YOU.
I SAW YOU LOOKING AT THE WALL PAINTINGS. GUARDIAN WARRIORS LIKE FLY COME WITH THEIR BARDS TO OUR FESTIVAL, THE UMVRAT.
ARE THOSE PEOPLE SINGING?
MY NAME'S KHANN, AND MY SISTER'S NAME IS MIKO.
I'M NAOMI. NICE TO MEET YOU.

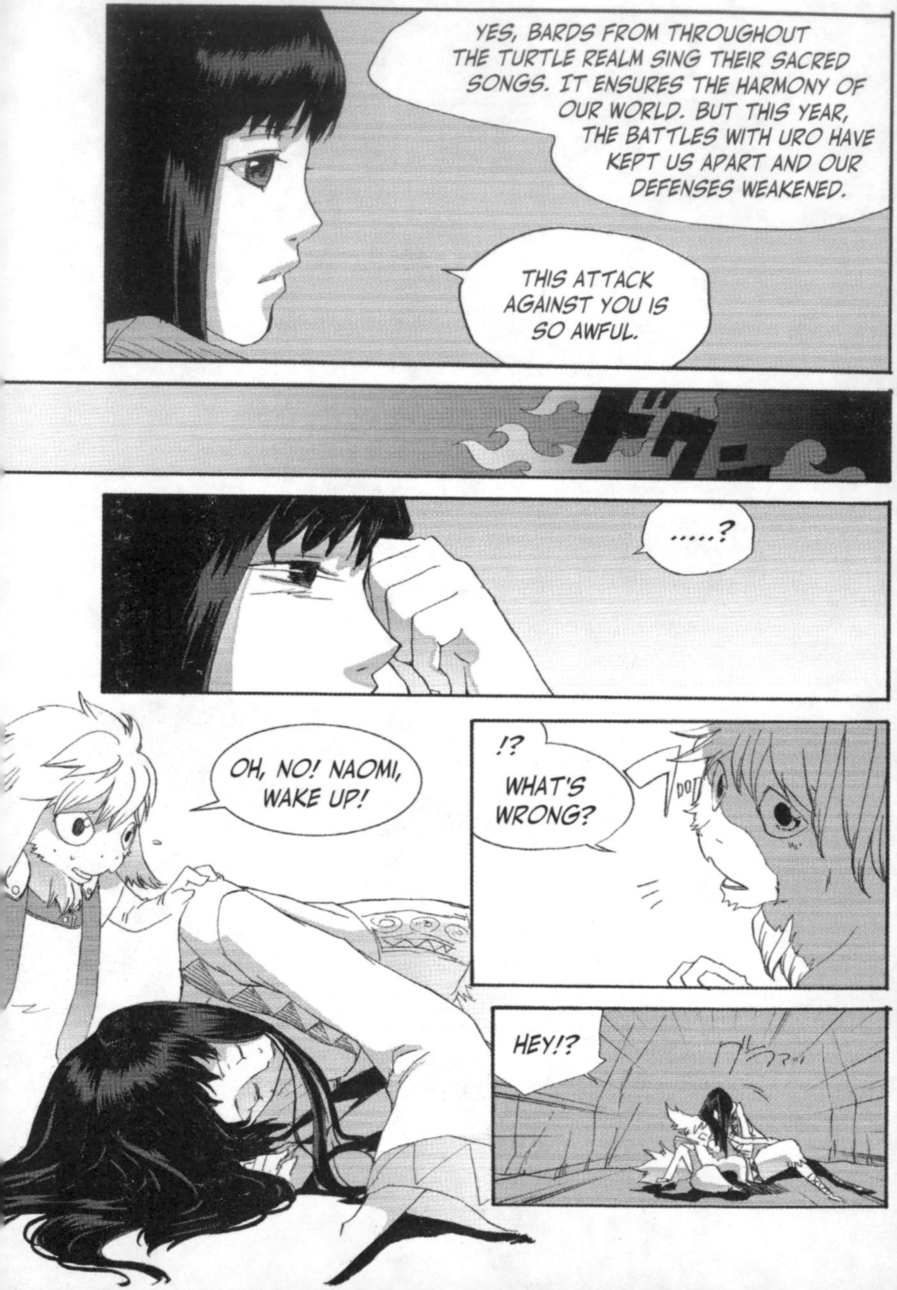

YES, BARDS FROM THROUGHOUT THE TURTLE REALM SING THEIR SACRED SONGS. IT ENSURES THE HARMONY OF OUR WORLD. BUT THIS YEAR, THE BATTLES WITH URO HAVE KEPT US APART AND OUR DEFENSES WEAKENED.
THIS ATTACK AGAINST YOU IS SO AWFUL.
.....?
OH, NO! NAOMI, WAKE UP!
!? WHAT'S WRONG?
DO
HEY!?

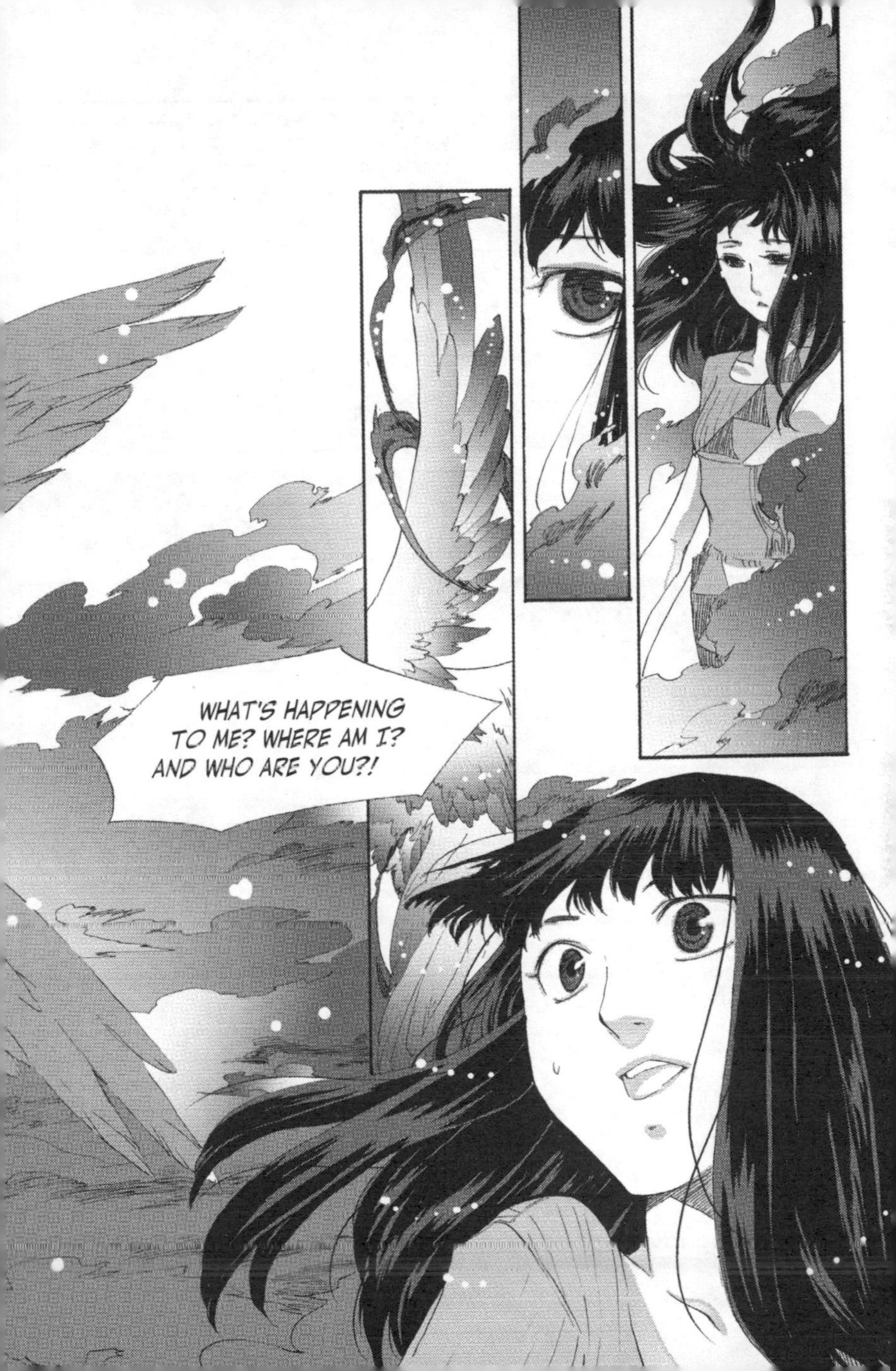
WHAT'S HAPPENING TO ME? WHERE AM I? AND WHO ARE YOU?!

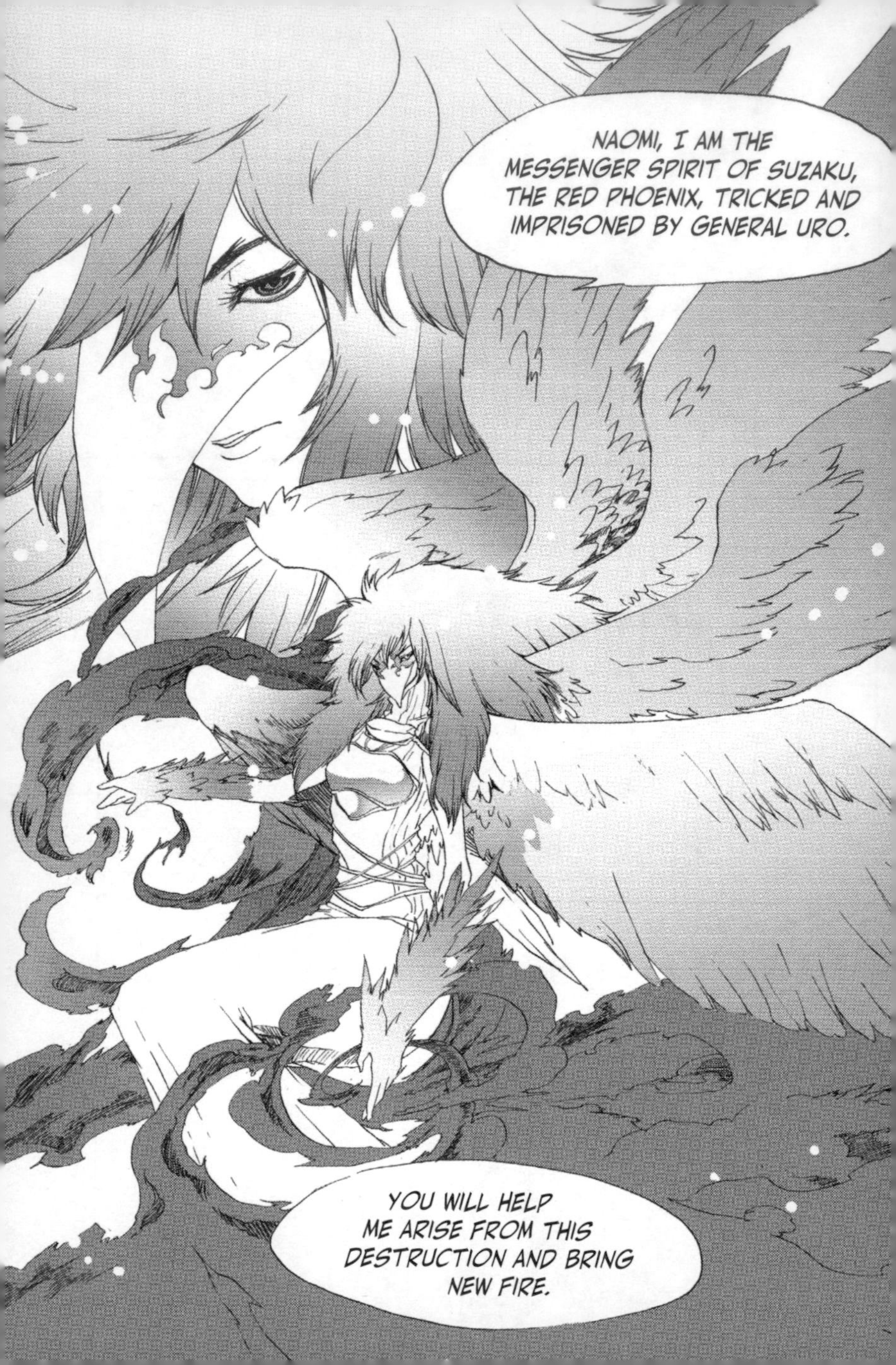
NAOMI, I AM THE MESSENGER SPIRIT OF SUZAKU, THE RED PHOENIX, TRICKED AND IMPRISONED BY GENERAL URO.
YOU WILL HELP ME ARISE FROM THIS DESTRUCTION AND BRING NEW FIRE.

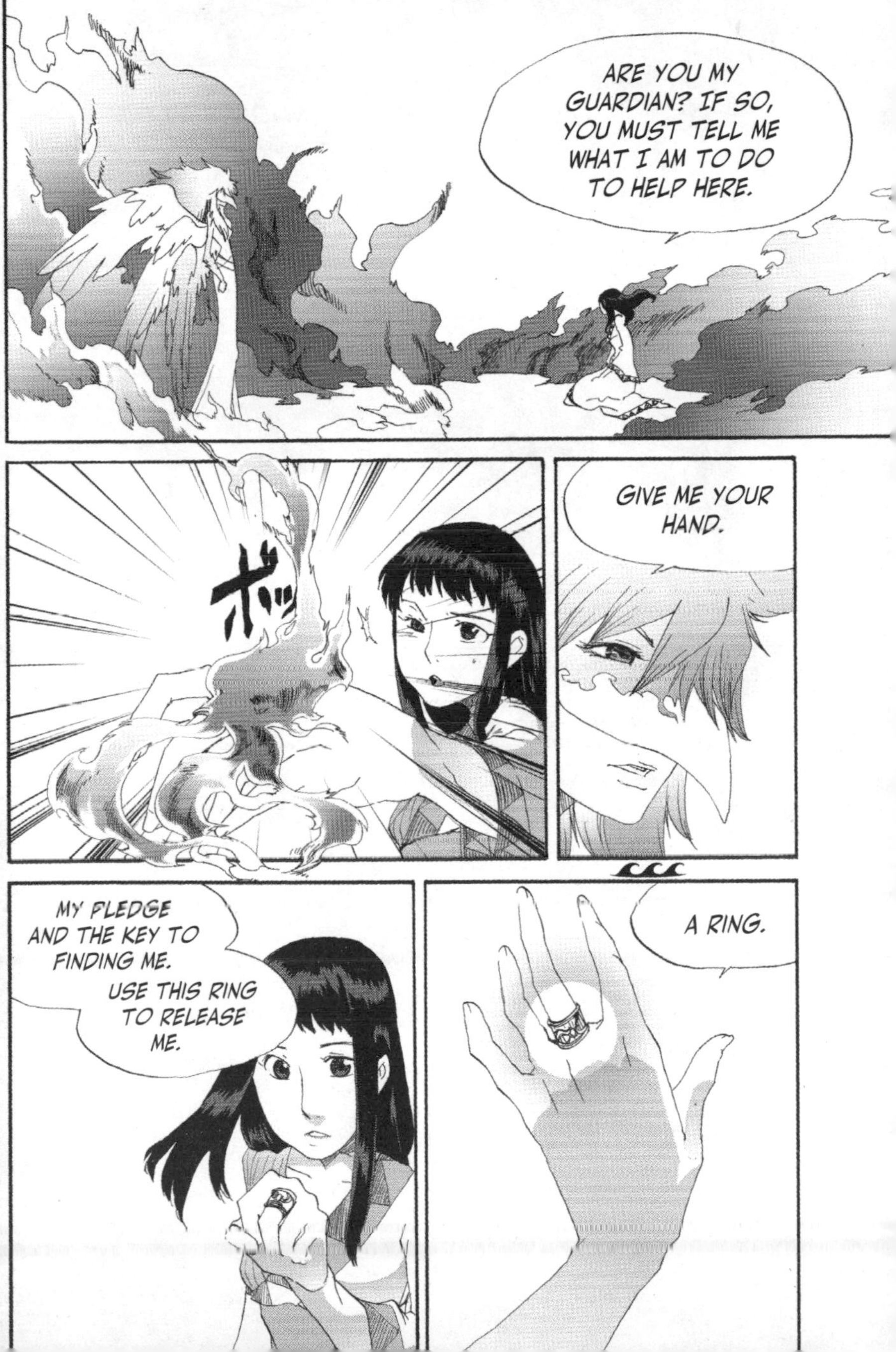
ARE YOU MY GUARDIAN? IF SO, YOU MUST TELL ME WHAT I AM TO DO TO HELP HERE.
ボッ
GIVE ME YOUR HAND.
A RING.
MY PLEDGE AND THE KEY TO FINDING ME.
USE THIS RING TO RELEASE ME.

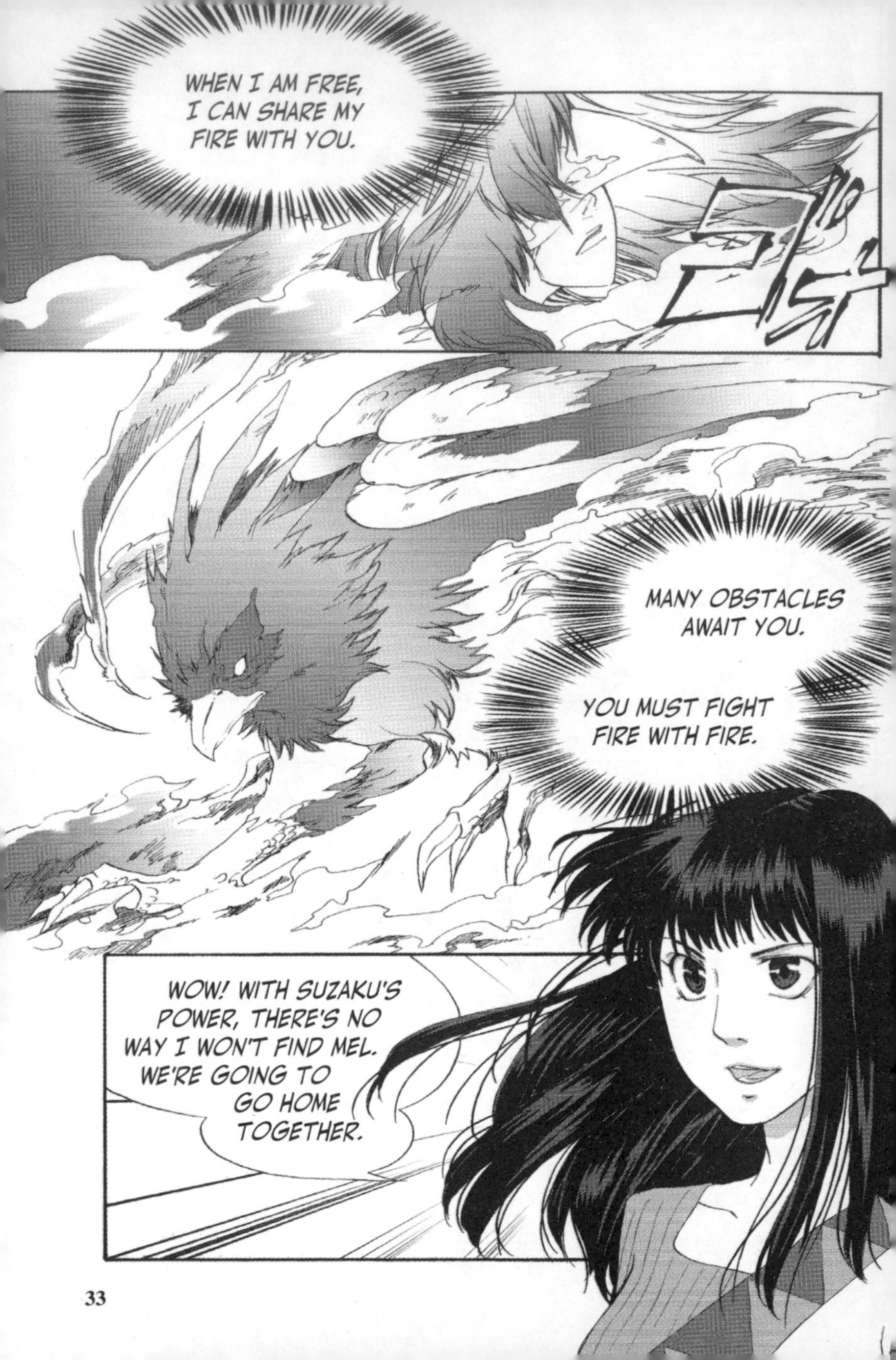
WHEN I AM FREE, I CAN SHARE MY FIRE WITH YOU.
MANY OBSTACLES AWAIT YOU.
YOU MUST FIGHT FIRE WITH FIRE.
WOW! WITH SUZAKU'S POWER, THERE'S NO WAY I WON'T FIND MEL. WE'RE GOING TO GO HOME TOGETHER.

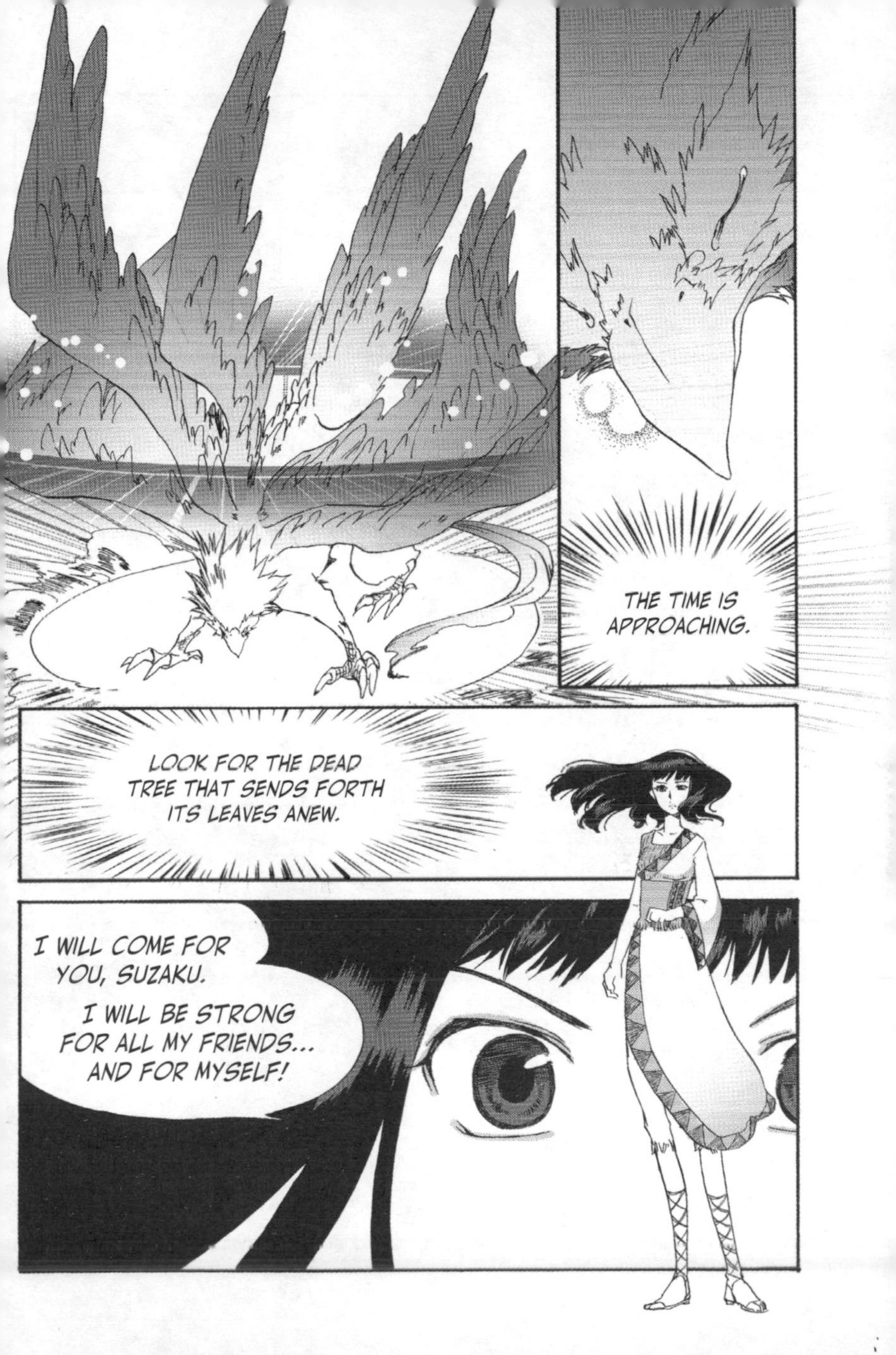
THE TIME IS APPROACHING.
LOOK FOR THE DEAD TREE THAT SENDS FORTH ITS LEAVES ANEW.
I WILL COME FOR YOU, SUZAKU.
I WILL BE STRONG FOR ALL MY FRIENDS... AND FOR MYSELF!

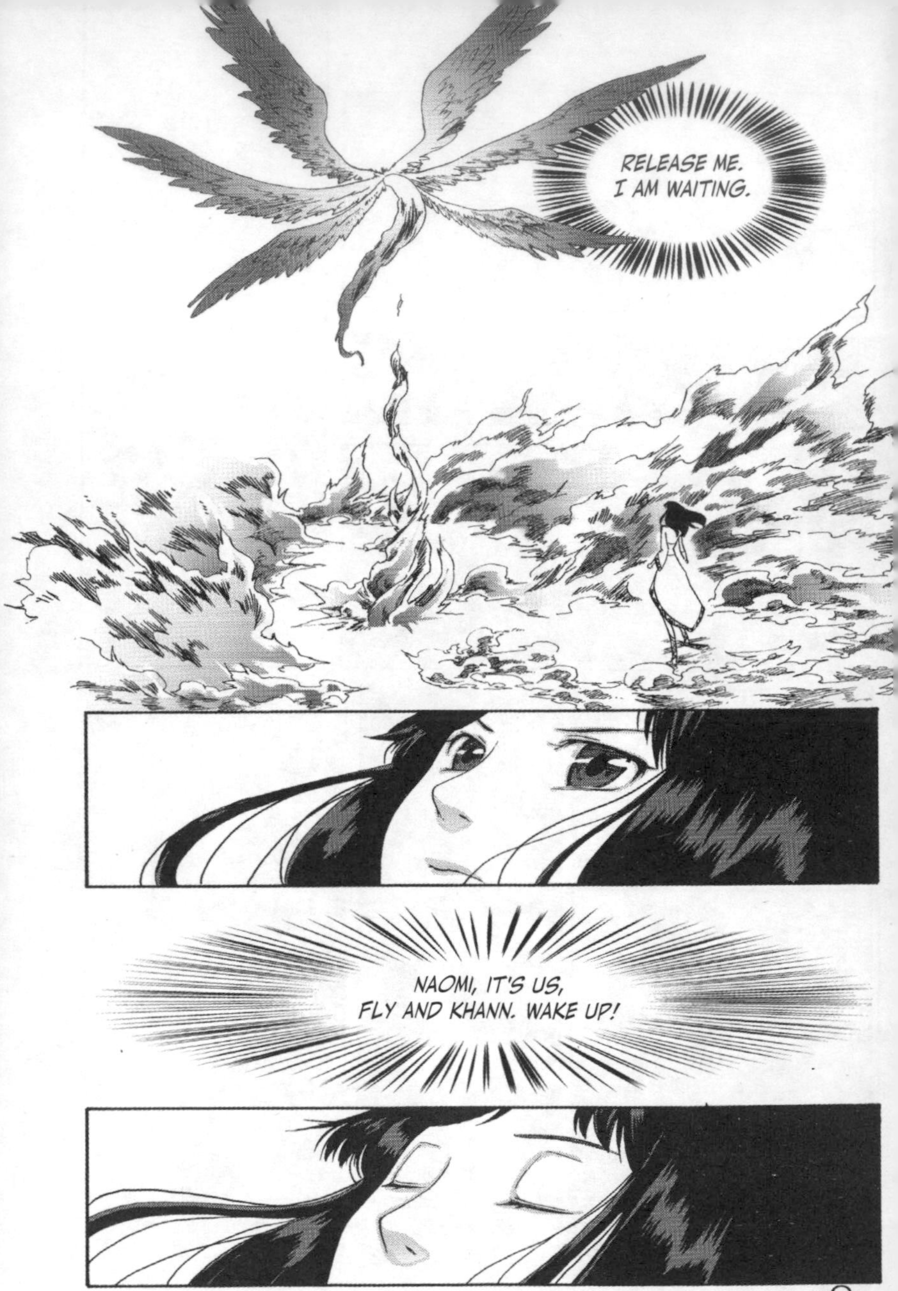
RELEASE ME.
I AM WAITING.
NAOMI, IT'S US,
FLY AND KHANN. WAKE UP!

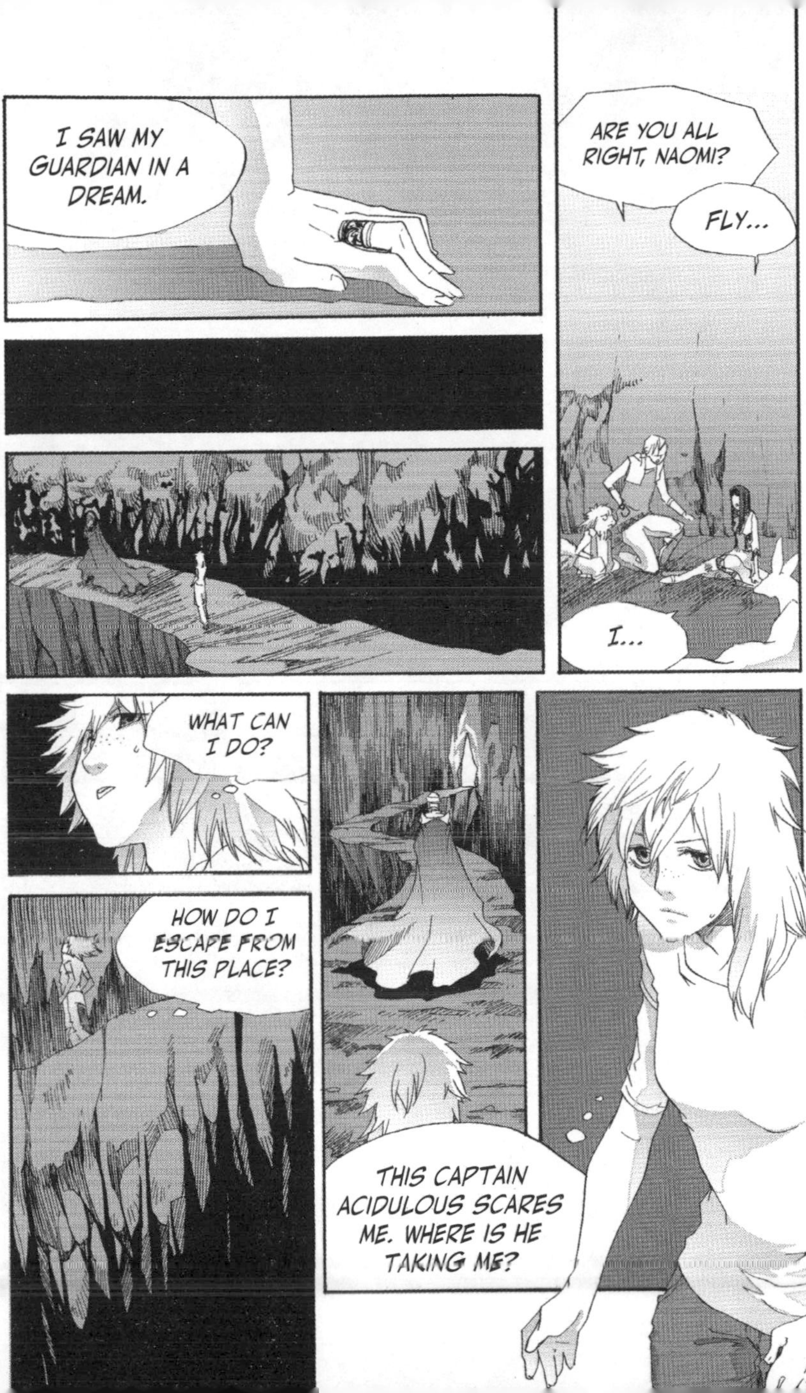
I SAW MY GUARDIAN IN A DREAM.
ARE YOU ALL RIGHT, NAOMI?
FLY...
I...
WHAT CAN I DO?
HOW DO I ESCAPE FROM THIS PLACE?
THIS CAPTAIN ACIDULOUS SCARES ME. WHERE IS HE TAKING ME?

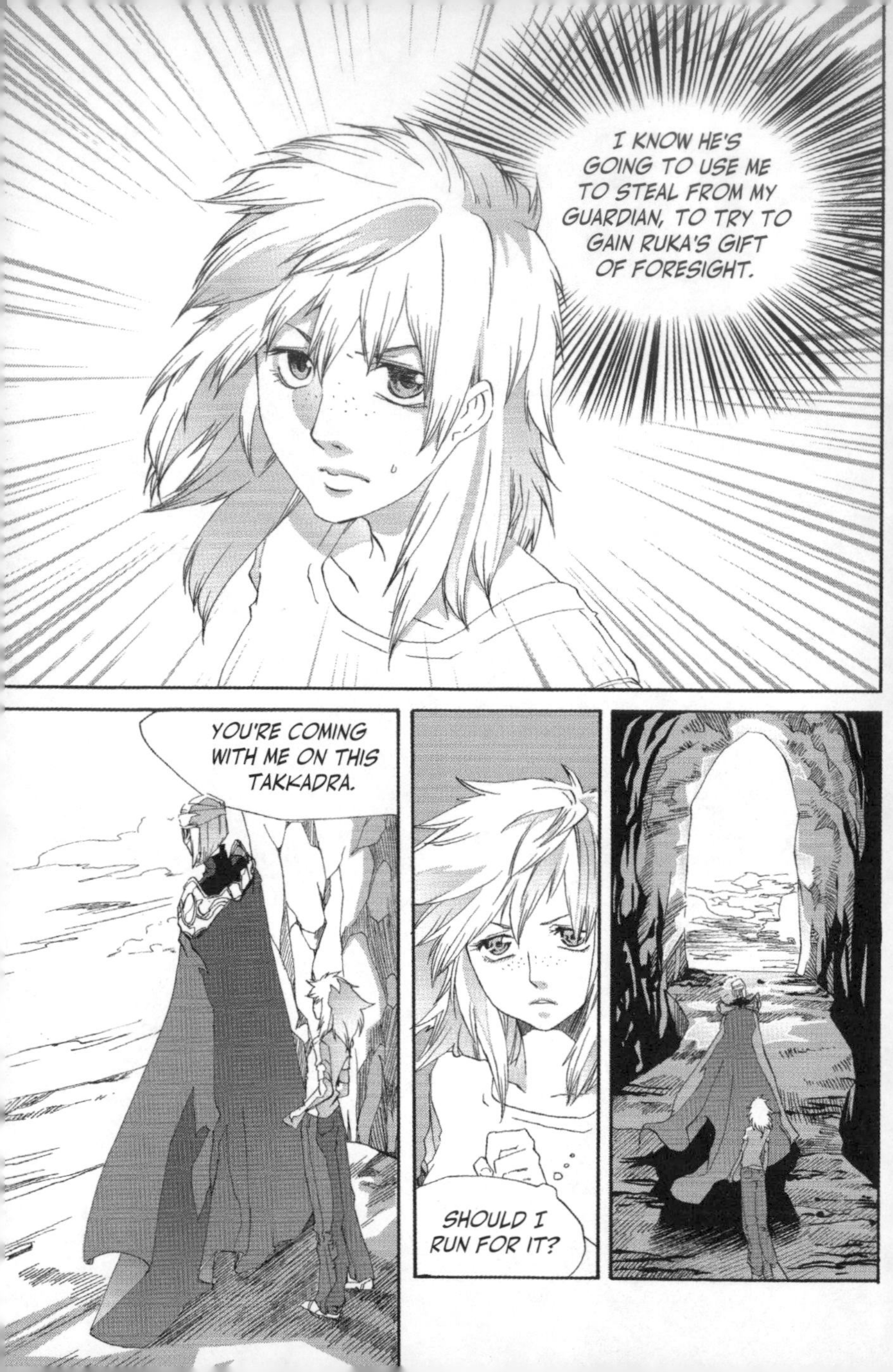
I KNOW HE'S GOING TO USE ME TO STEAL FROM MY GUARDIAN, TO TRY TO GAIN RUKA'S GIFT OF FORESIGHT.
YOU'RE COMING WITH ME ON THIS TAKKADRA.
SHOULD I RUN FOR IT?

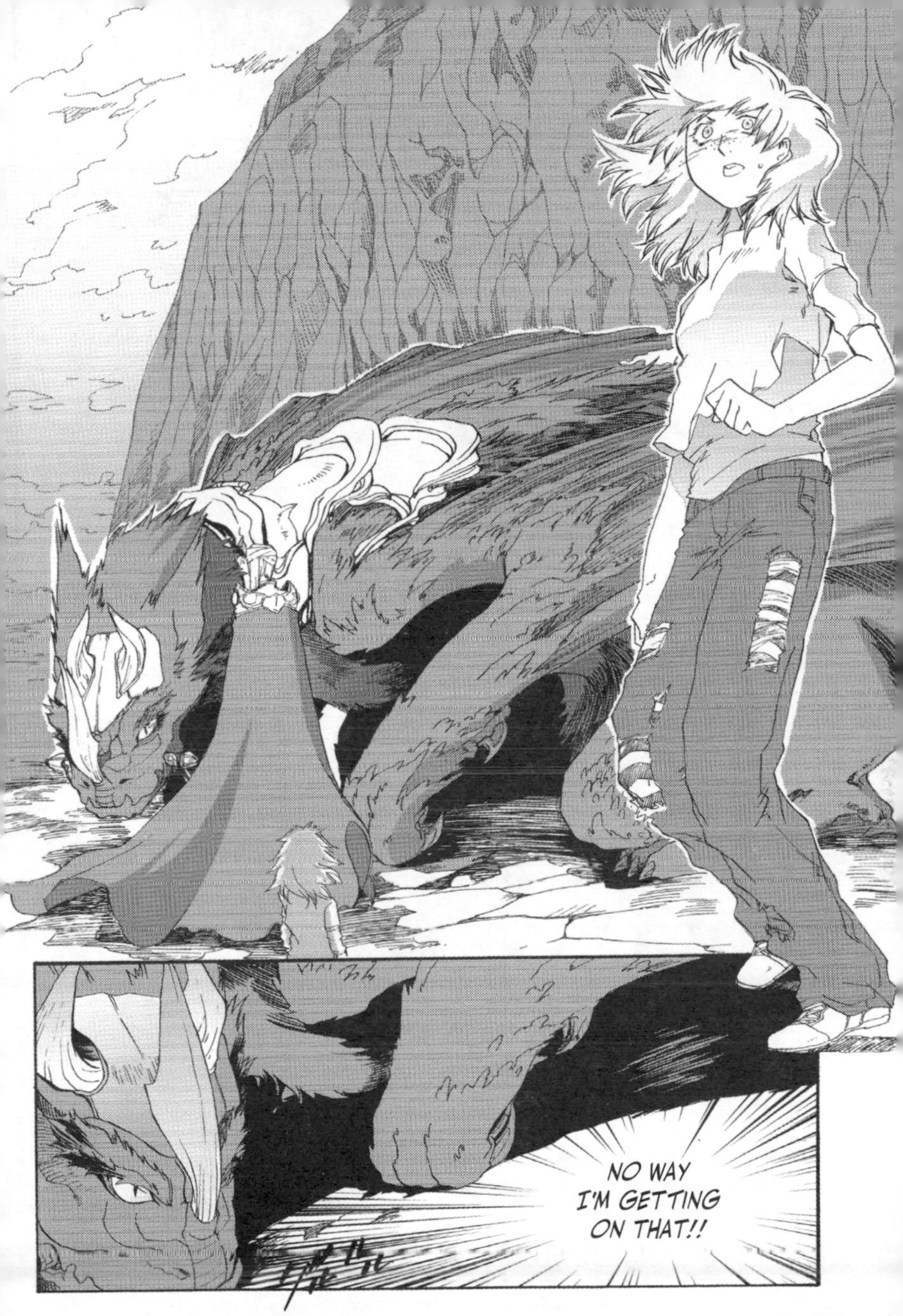
NO WAY I'M GETTING ON THAT!!

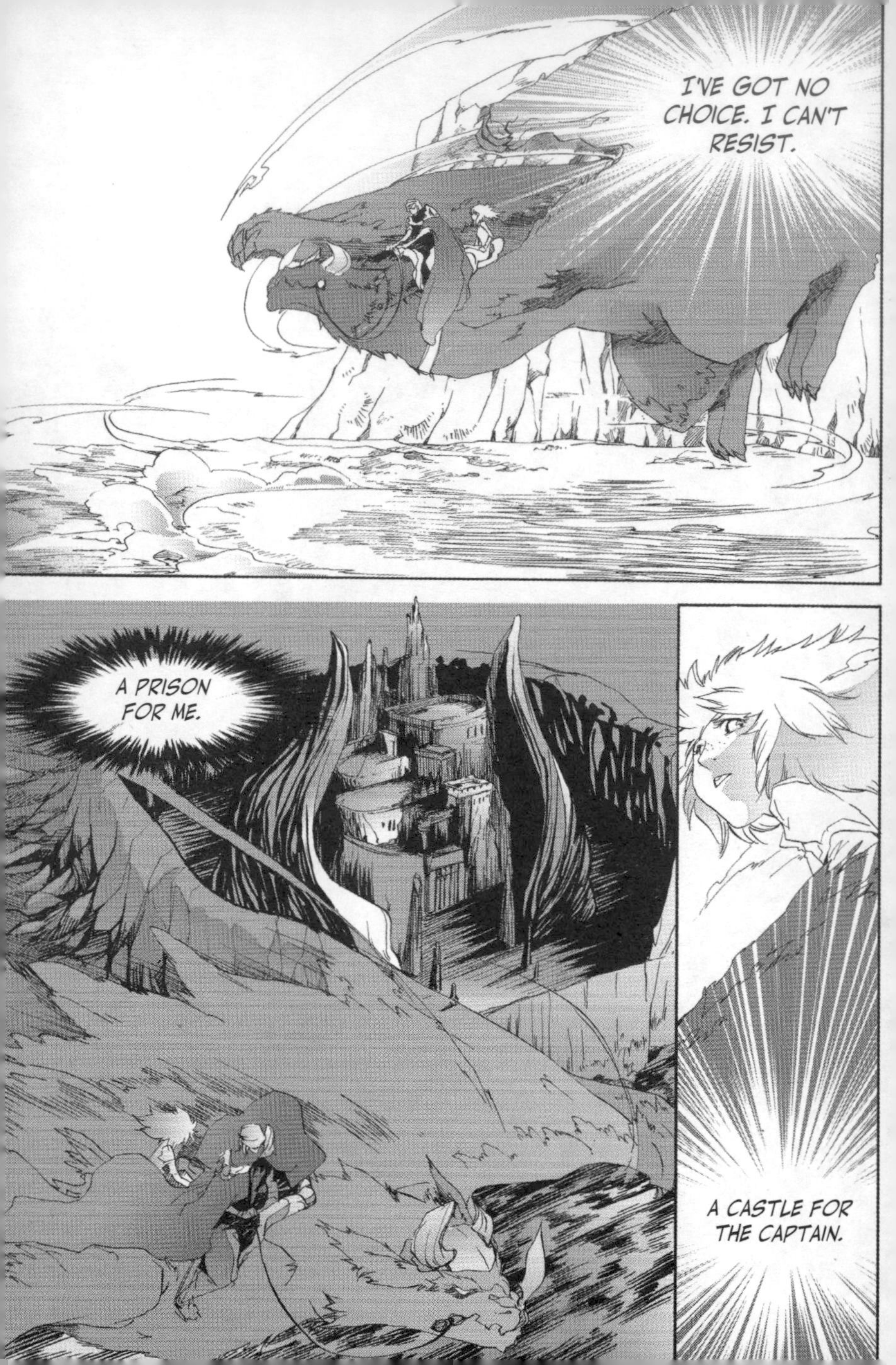

I'VE GOT NO CHOICE. I CAN'T RESIST.
A CASTLE FOR THE CAPTAIN.
A PRISON FOR ME.

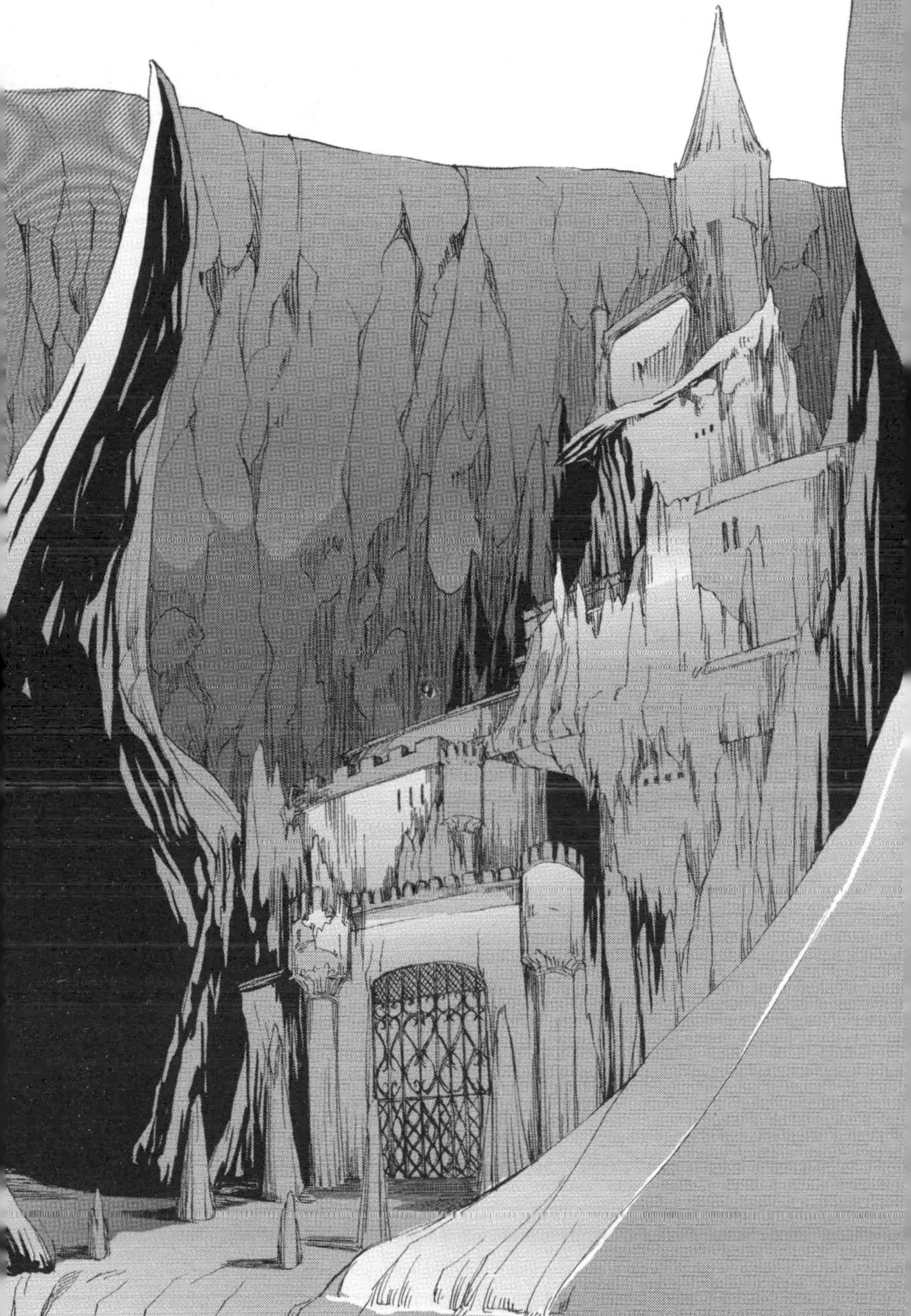

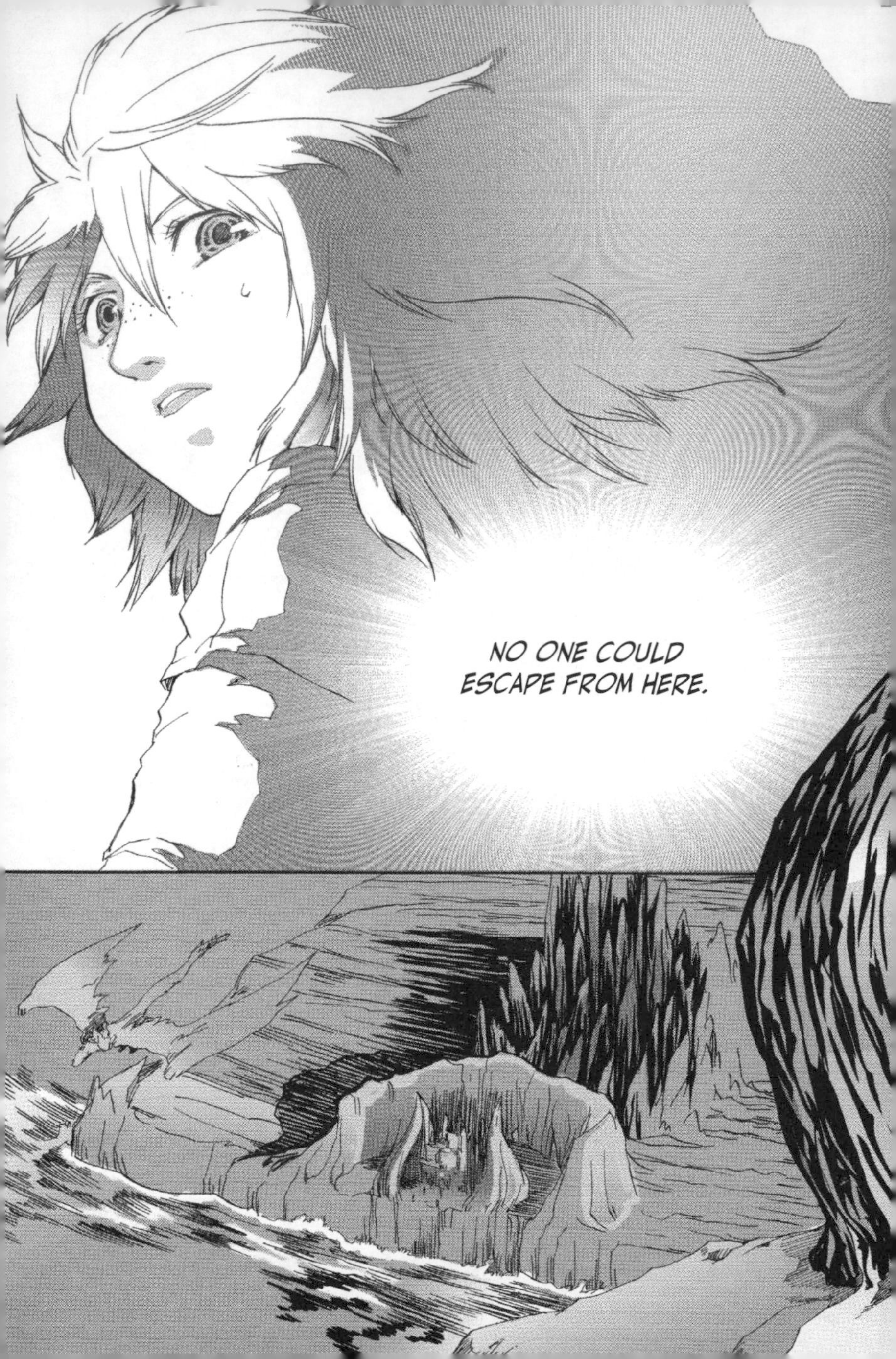
NO ONE COULD
ESCAPE FROM HERE.

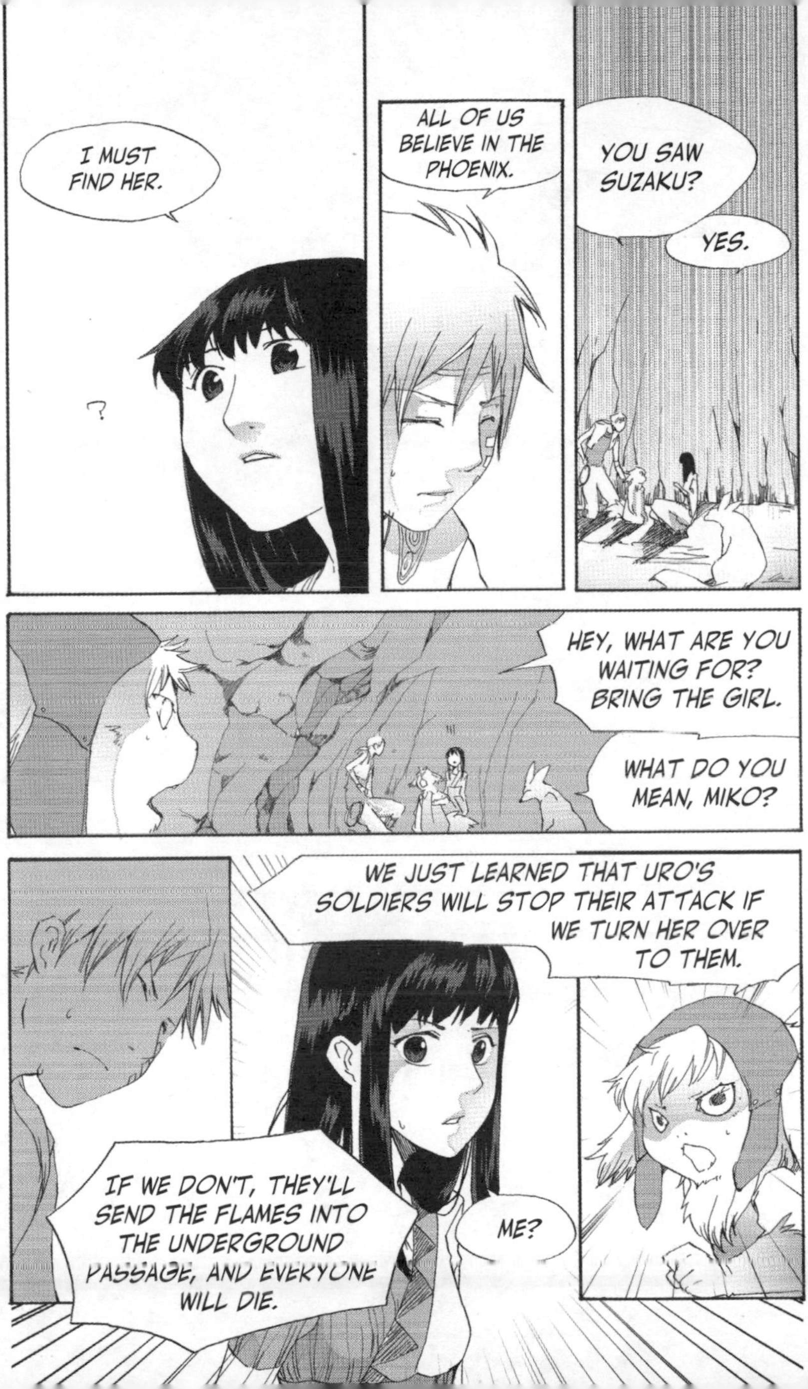
I MUST FIND HER.
?
ALL OF US BELIEVE IN THE PHOENIX.
YOU SAW SUZAKU?
YES.
HEY, WHAT ARE YOU WAITING FOR? BRING THE GIRL.
WHAT DO YOU MEAN, MIKO?
WE JUST LEARNED THAT URO'S SOLDIERS WILL STOP THEIR ATTACK IF WE TURN HER OVER TO THEM.
IF WE DON'T, THEY'LL SEND THE FLAMES INTO THE UNDERGROUND PASSAGE, AND EVERYONE WILL DIE.
ME?

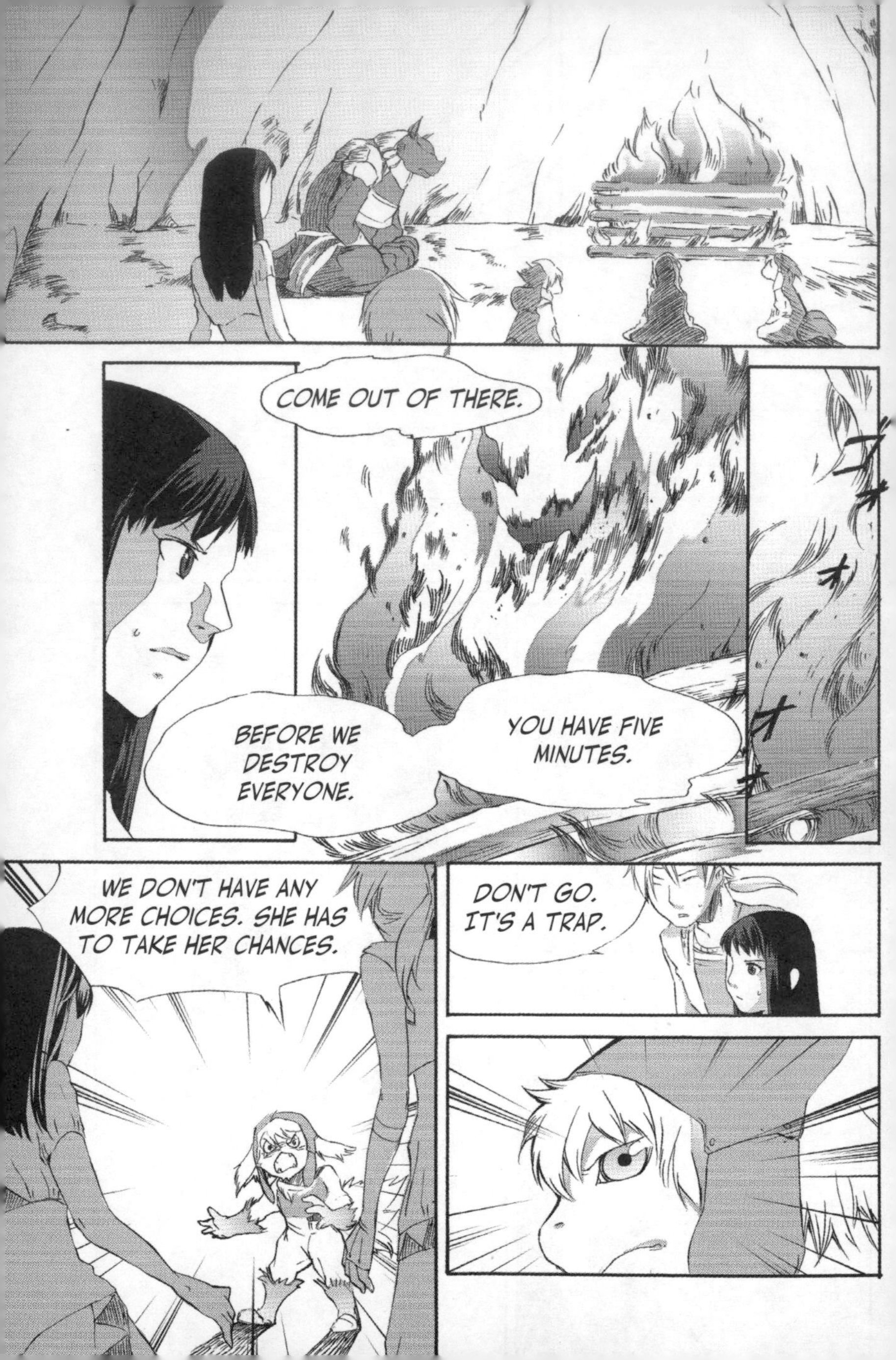
COME OUT OF THERE.
YOU HAVE FIVE MINUTES.
BEFORE WE DESTROY EVERYONE.
DON'T GO. IT'S A TRAP.
WE DON'T HAVE ANY MORE CHOICES. SHE HAS TO TAKE HER CHANCES.

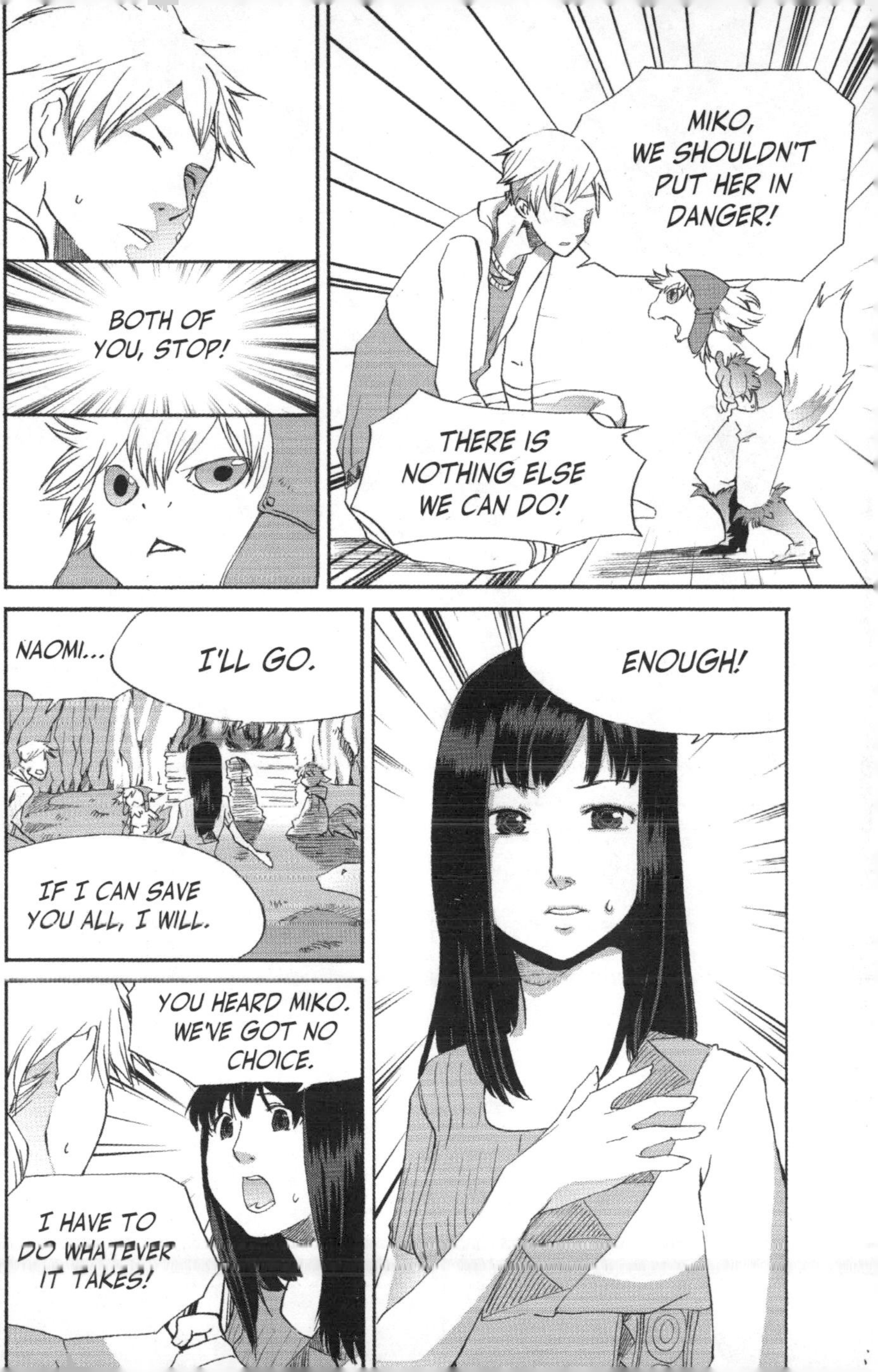
MIKO, WE SHOULDN'T PUT HER IN DANGER!
THERE IS NOTHING ELSE WE CAN DO!
BOTH OF YOU, STOP!
YOU HEARD MIKO. WE'VE GOT NO CHOICE.
I HAVE TO DO WHATEVER IT TAKES!
ENOUGH!
NAOMI...
I'LL GO.
IF I CAN SAVE YOU ALL, I WILL.

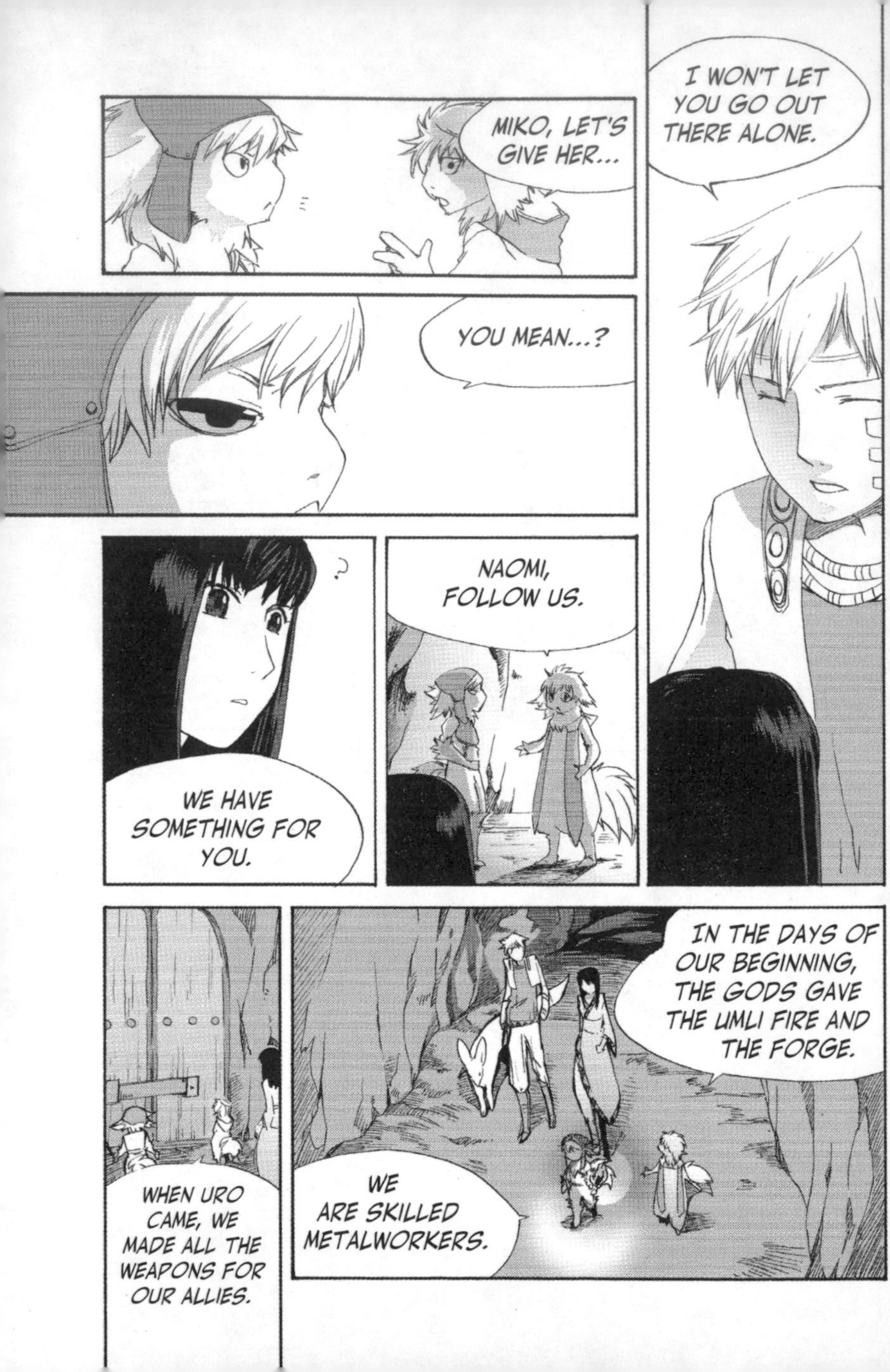
MIKO, LET'S GIVE HER...
I WON'T LET YOU GO OUT THERE ALONE.
YOU MEAN...?
WE HAVE SOMETHING FOR YOU.
NAOMI, FOLLOW US.
WHEN URO CAME, WE MADE ALL THE WEAPONS FOR OUR ALLIES.
WE ARE SKILLED METALWORKERS.
IN THE DAYS OF OUR BEGINNING, THE GODS GAVE THE UMLI FIRE AND THE FORGE.

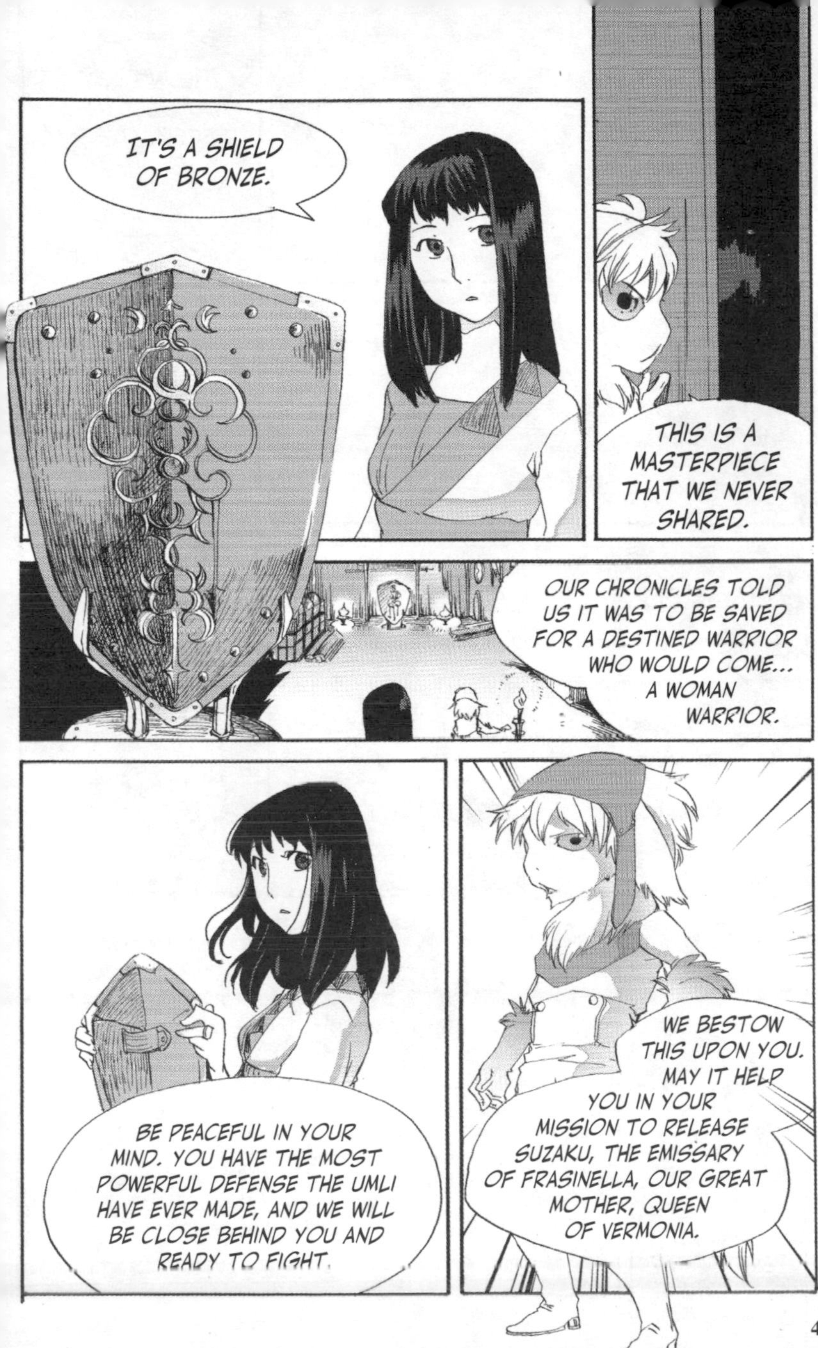
IT'S A SHIELD OF BRONZE.
THIS IS A MASTERPIECE THAT WE NEVER SHARED.
OUR CHRONICLES TOLD US IT WAS TO BE SAVED FOR A DESTINED WARRIOR WHO WOULD COME... A WOMAN WARRIOR.
BE PEACEFUL IN YOUR MIND. YOU HAVE THE MOST POWERFUL DEFENSE THE UMLI HAVE EVER MADE, AND WE WILL BE CLOSE BEHIND YOU AND READY TO FIGHT.
WE BESTOW THIS UPON YOU. MAY IT HELP YOU IN YOUR MISSION TO RELEASE SUZAKU, THE EMISSARY OF FRASINELLA, OUR GREAT MOTHER, QUEEN OF VERMONIA.

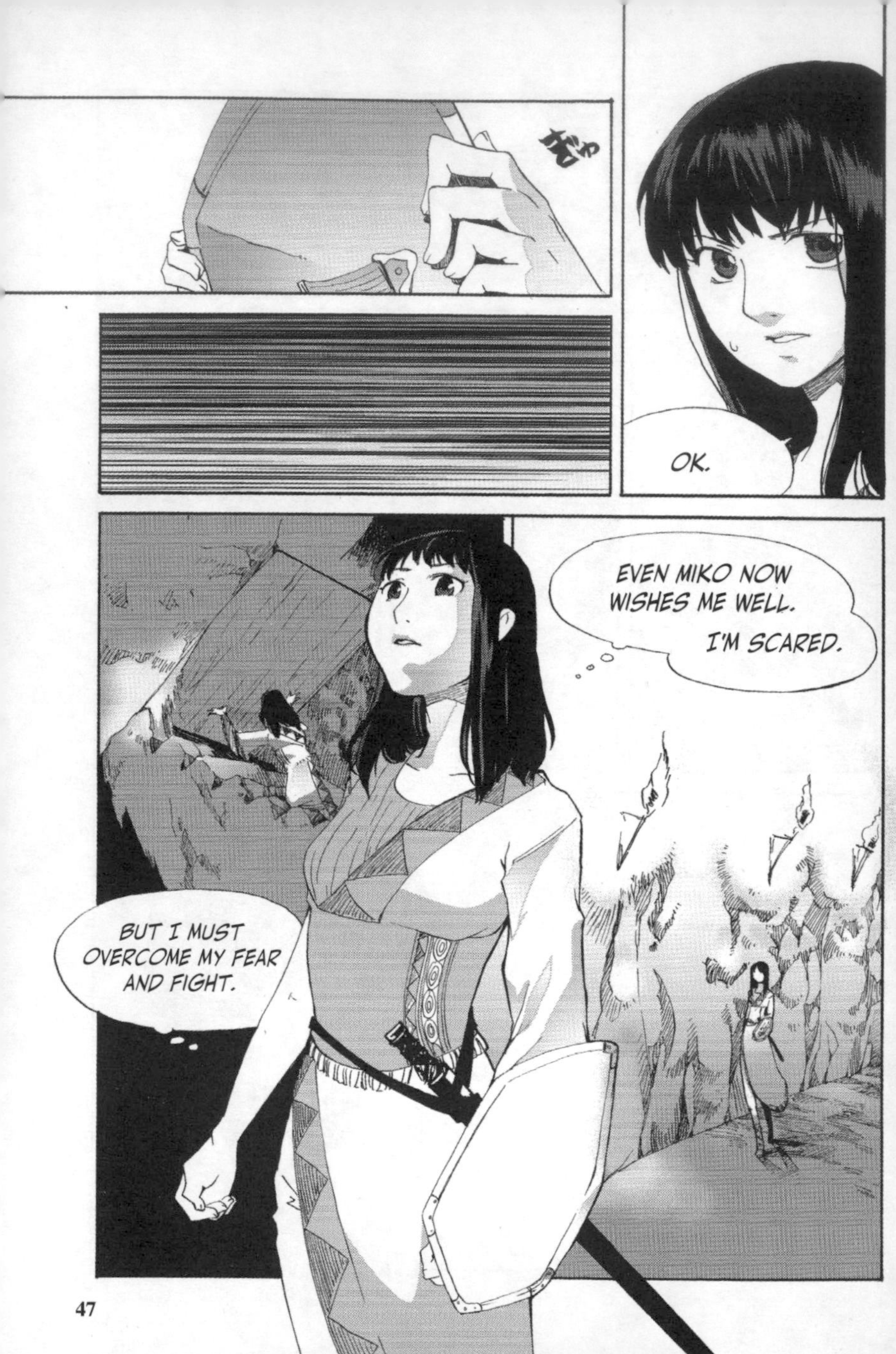
ぎゅ
OK.
EVEN MIKO NOW WISHES ME WELL.
I'M SCARED.
BUT I MUST OVERCOME MY FEAR AND FIGHT.

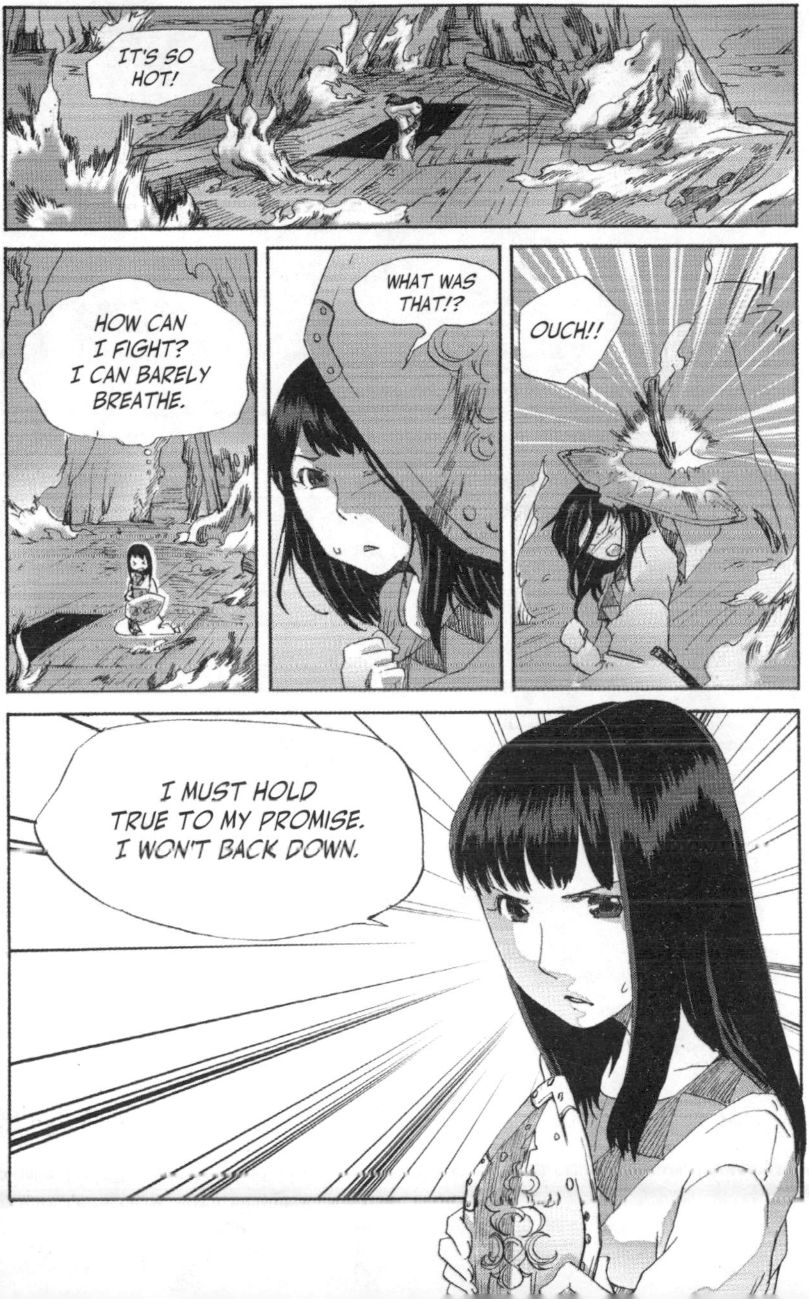
IT'S SO HOT!
HOW CAN I FIGHT? I CAN BARELY BREATHE.
WHAT WAS THAT!?
OUCH!!
I MUST HOLD TRUE TO MY PROMISE. I WON'T BACK DOWN.

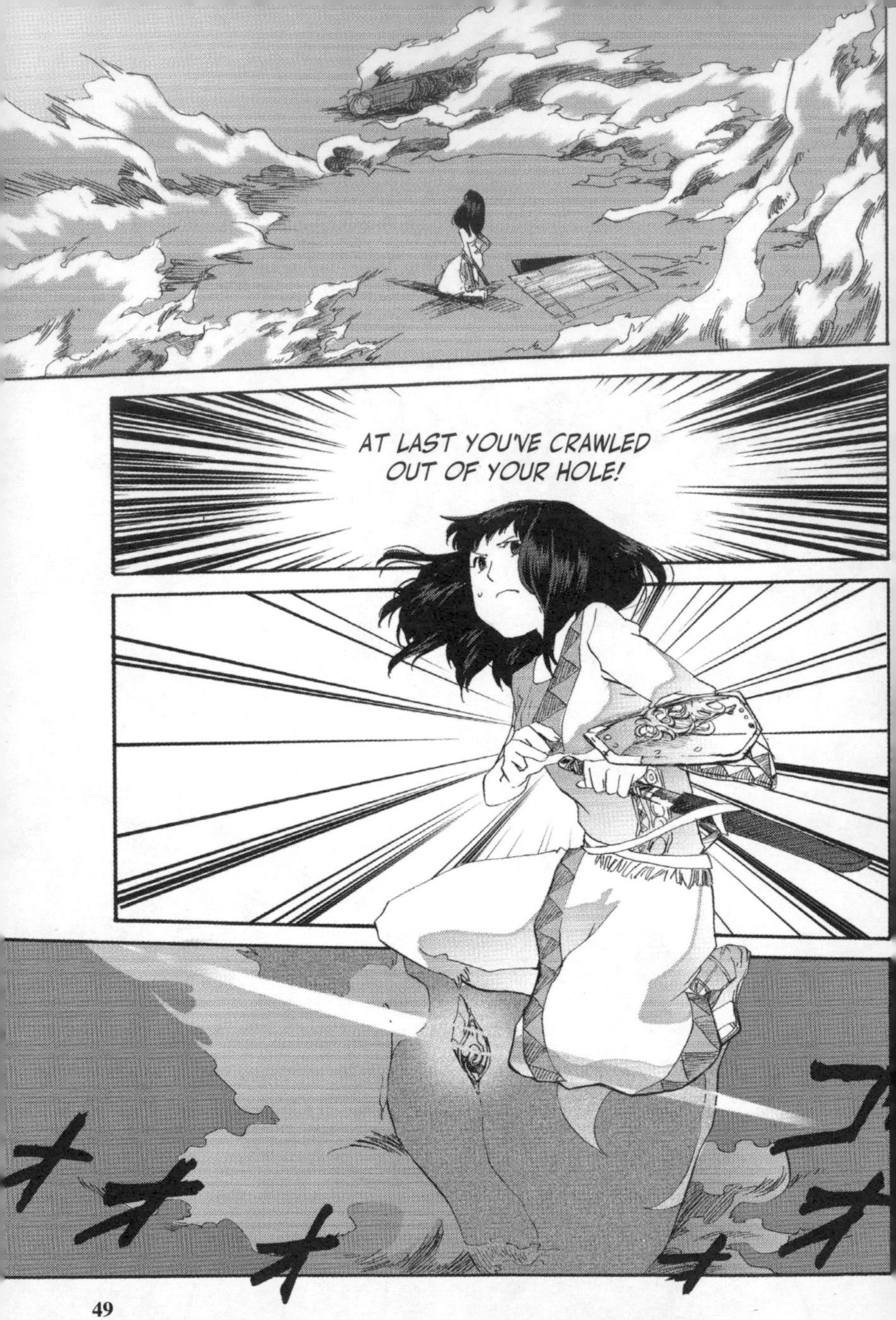
AT LAST YOU'VE CRAWLED OUT OF YOUR HOLE!

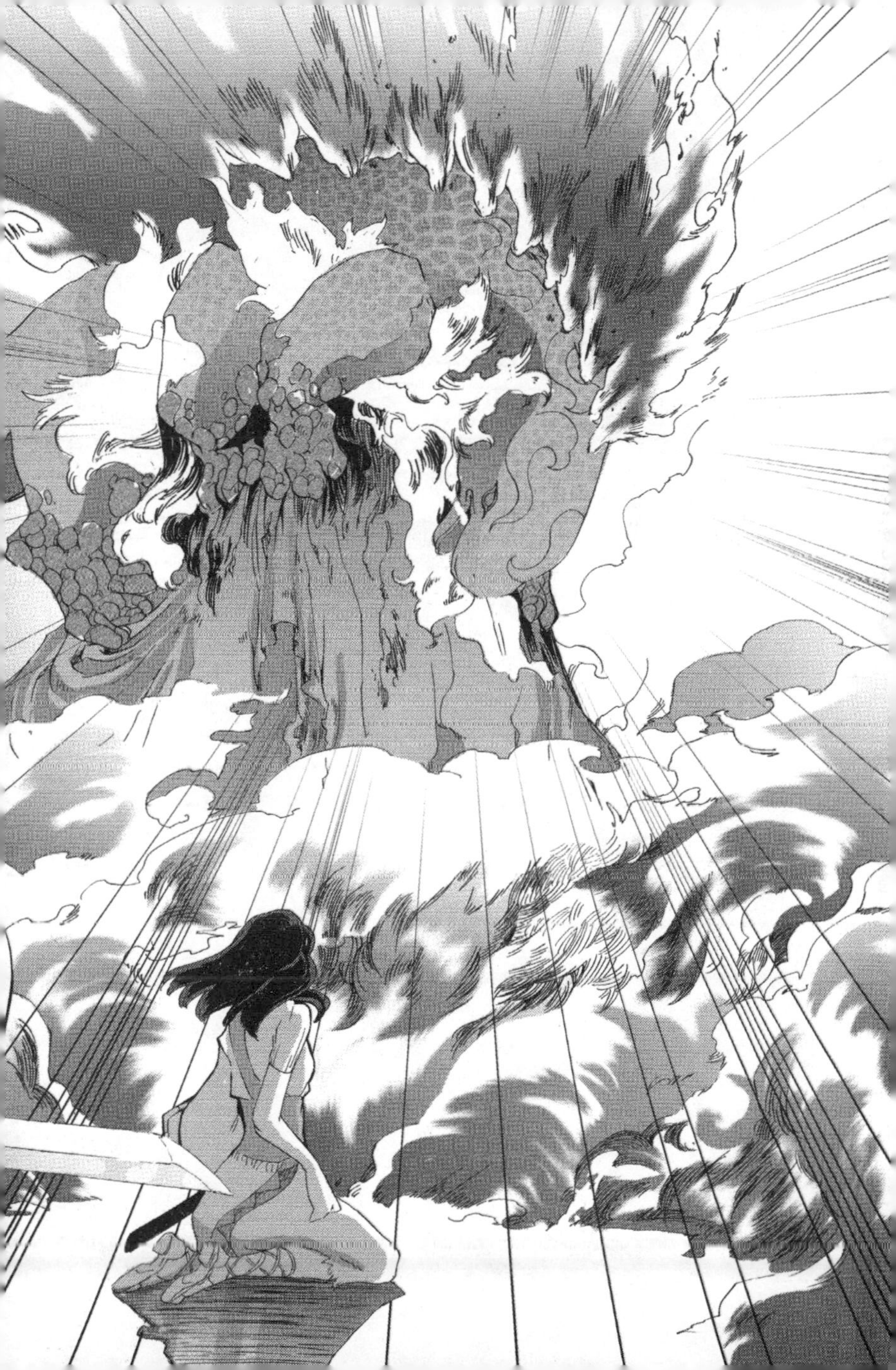

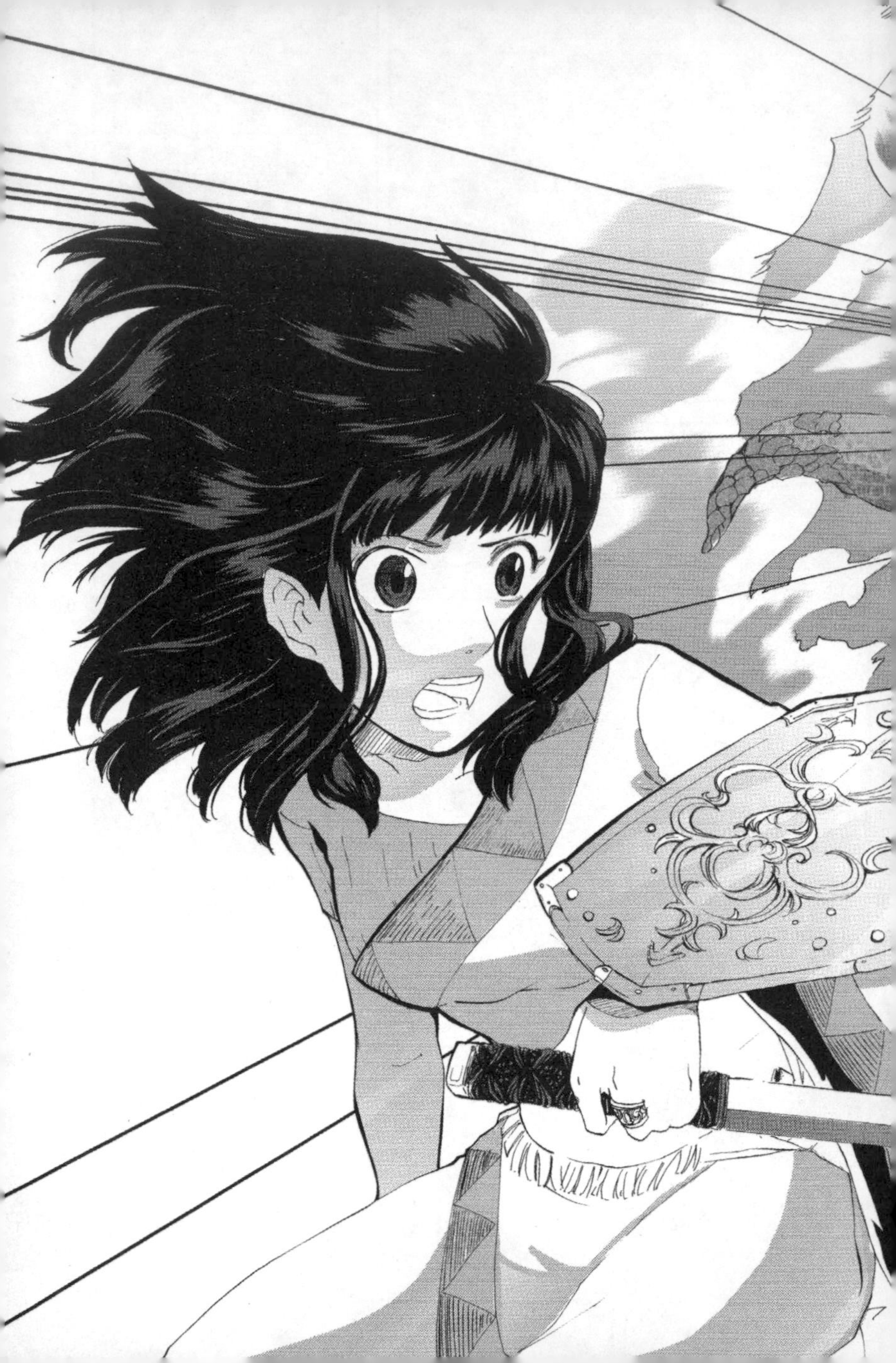

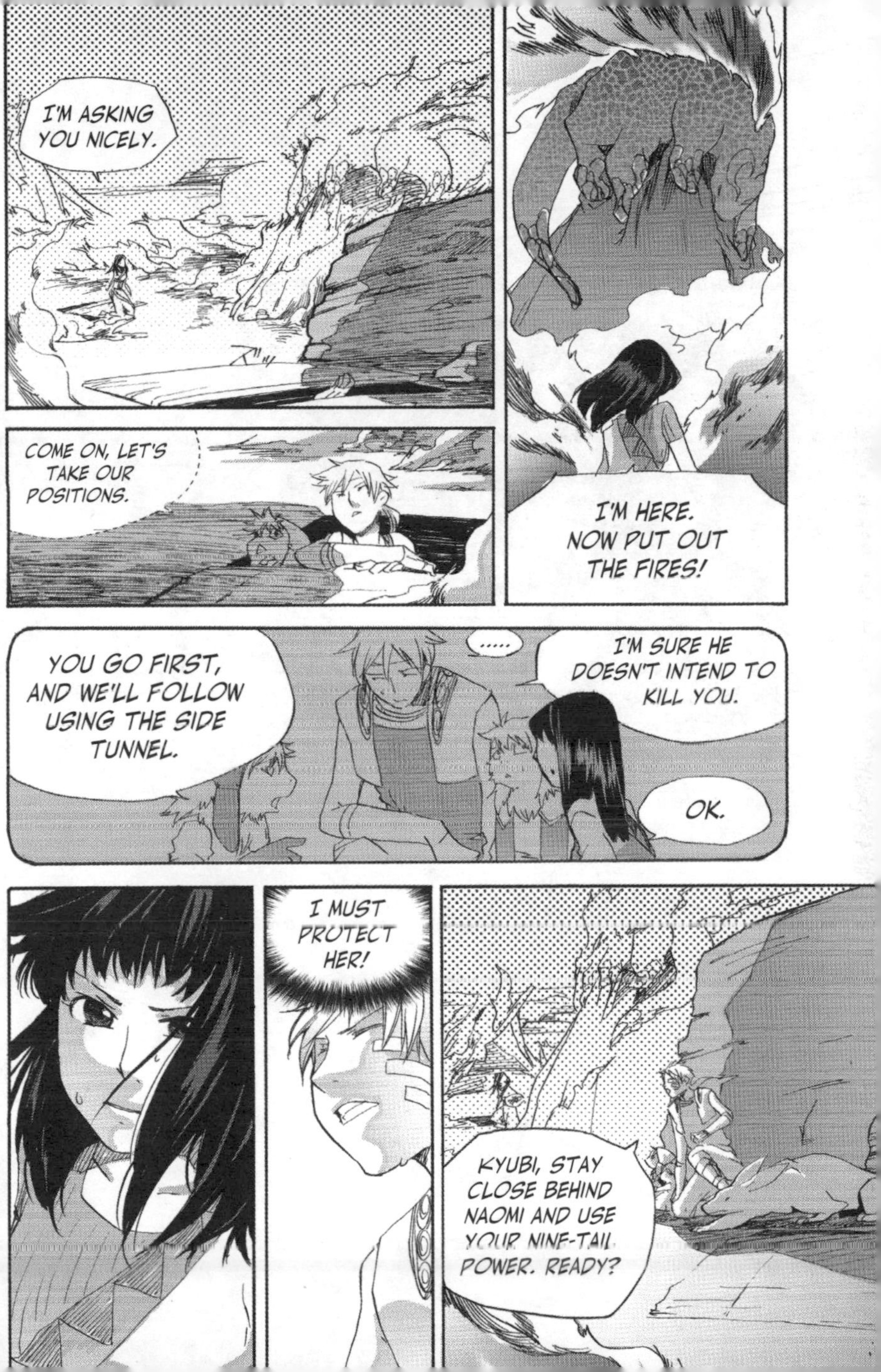
I'M ASKING YOU NICELY.
I'M HERE. NOW PUT OUT THE FIRES!
COME ON, LET'S TAKE OUR POSITIONS.
YOU GO FIRST, AND WE'LL FOLLOW USING THE SIDE TUNNEL.
......
I'M SURE HE DOESN'T INTEND TO KILL YOU.
OK.
I MUST PROTECT HER!
KYUBI, STAY CLOSE BEHIND NAOMI AND USE YOUR NINE-TAIL POWER. READY?

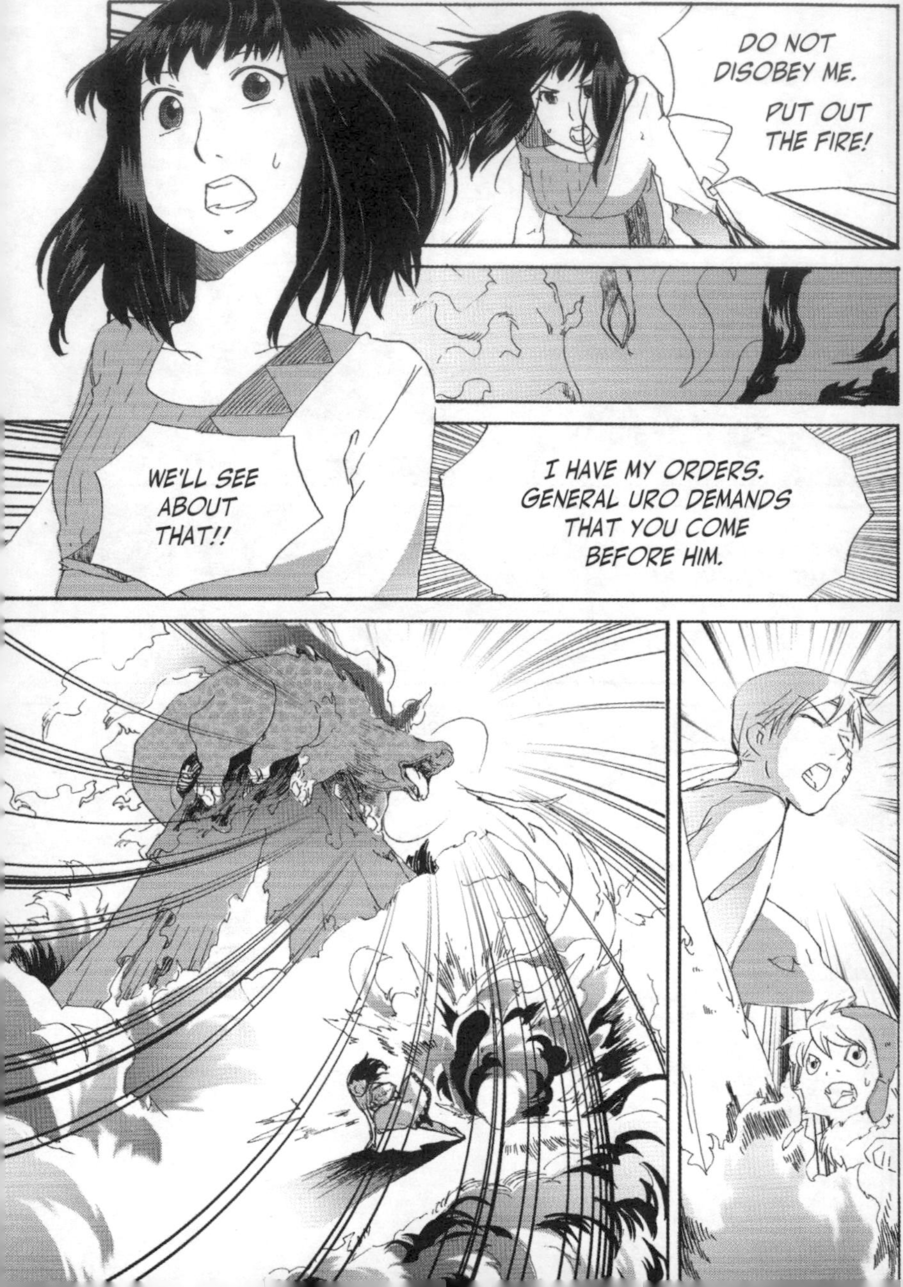
DO NOT DISOBEY ME.
PUT OUT THE FIRE!
I HAVE MY ORDERS. GENERAL URO DEMANDS THAT YOU COME BEFORE HIM.
WE'LL SEE ABOUT THAT!!

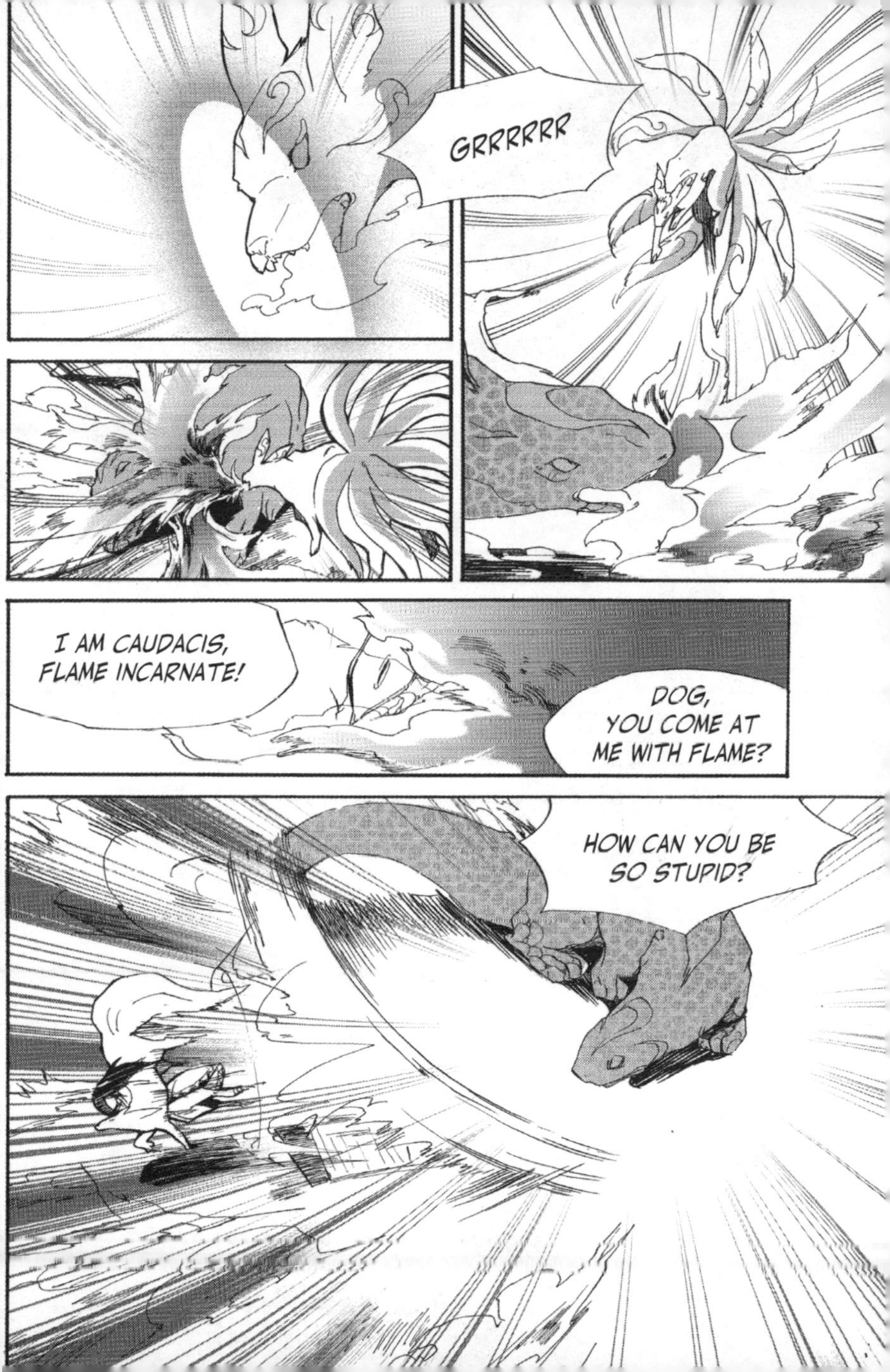
GRRRRRR
I AM CAUDACIS, FLAME INCARNATE!
DOG, YOU COME AT ME WITH FLAME?
HOW CAN YOU BE SO STUPID?

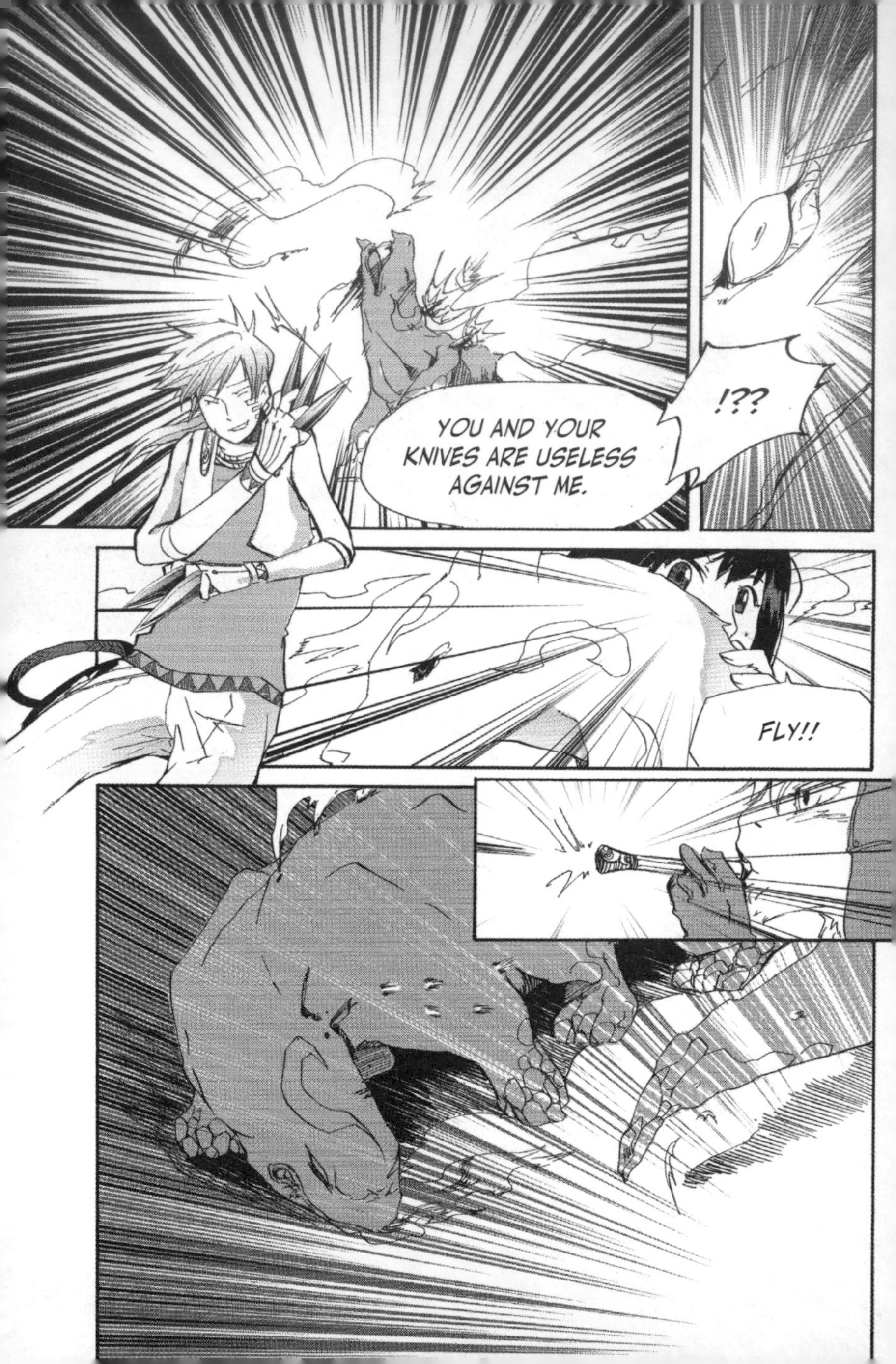
!??
YOU AND YOUR KNIVES ARE USELESS AGAINST ME.
FLY!!

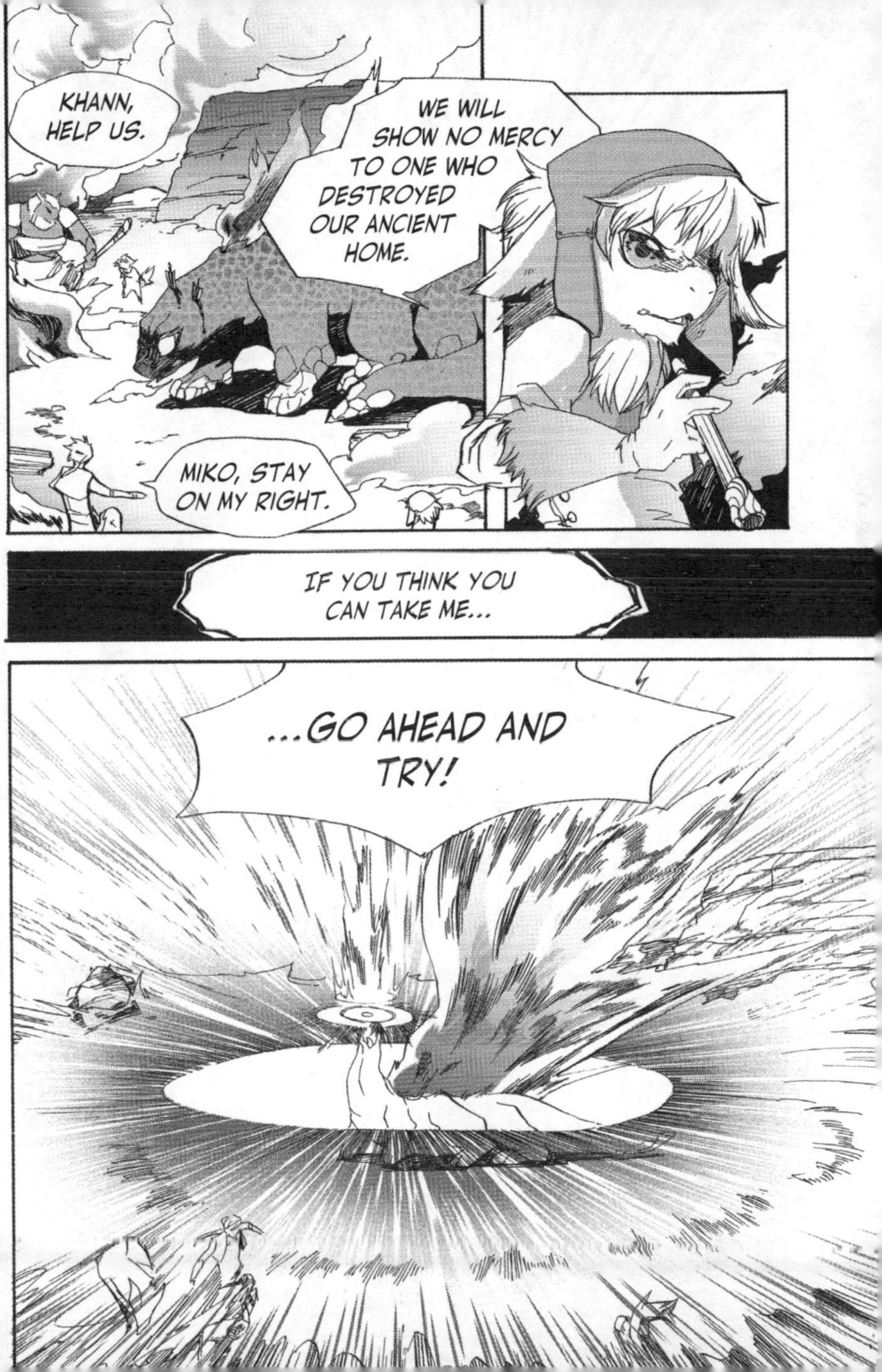
KHANN, HELP US.
WE WILL SHOW NO MERCY TO ONE WHO DESTROYED OUR ANCIENT HOME.
MIKO, STAY ON MY RIGHT.
IF YOU THINK YOU CAN TAKE ME...
...GO AHEAD AND TRY!

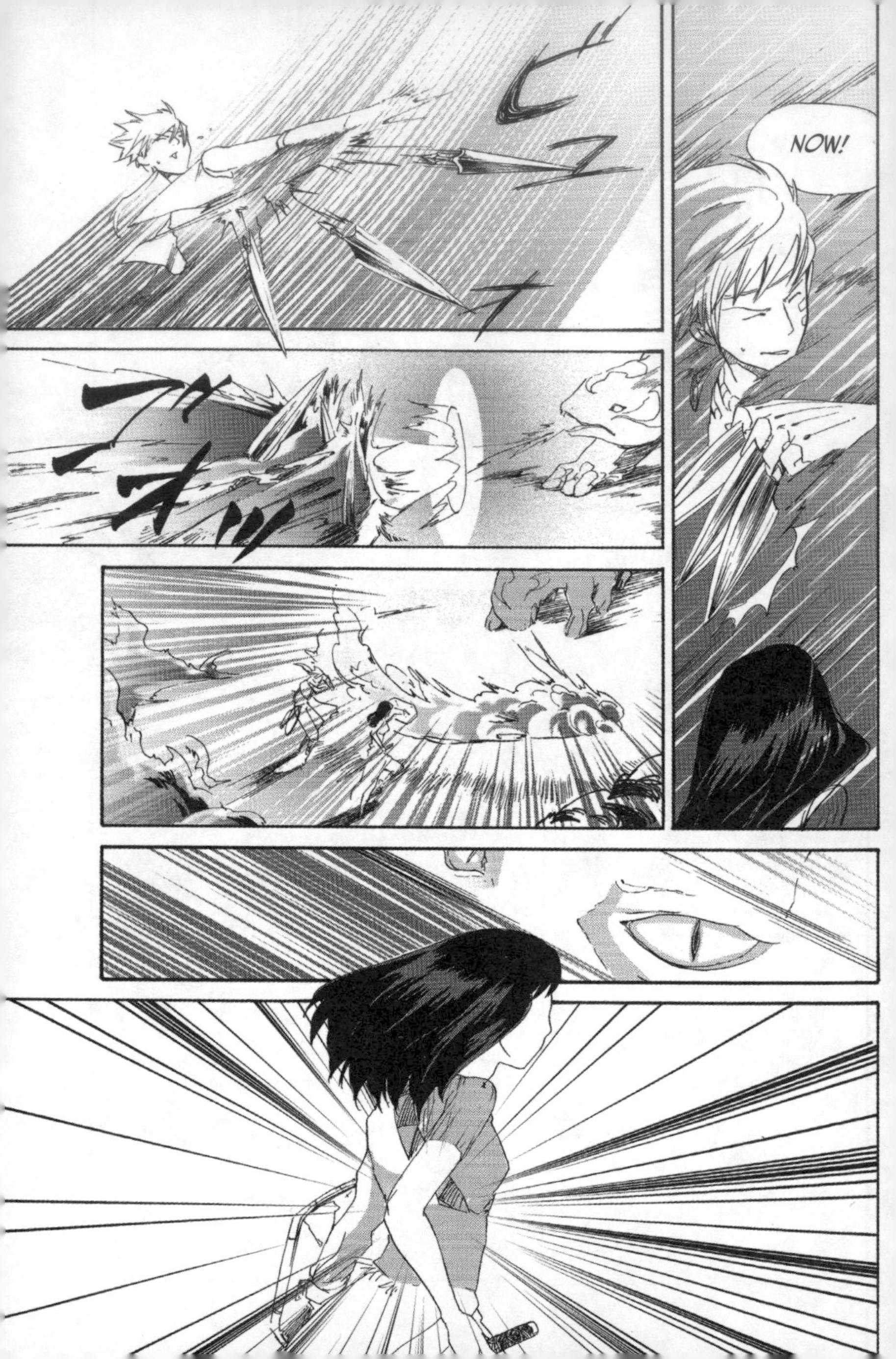
NOW!

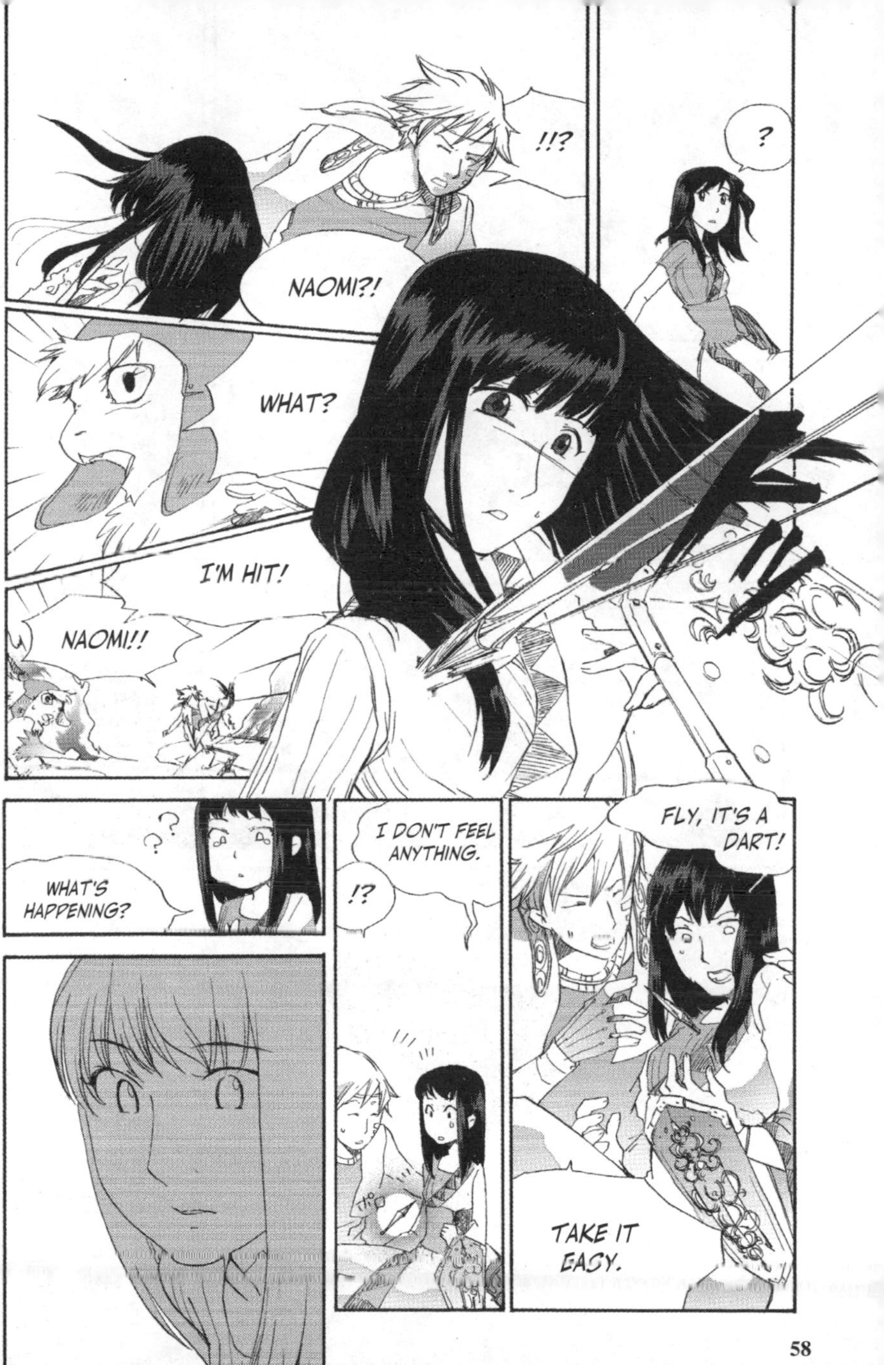

!!?
NAOMI?!
?
WHAT?
I'M HIT!
NAOMI!!
WHAT'S HAPPENING?
I DON'T FEEL ANYTHING.
!?
FLY, IT'S A DART!
TAKE IT EASY.

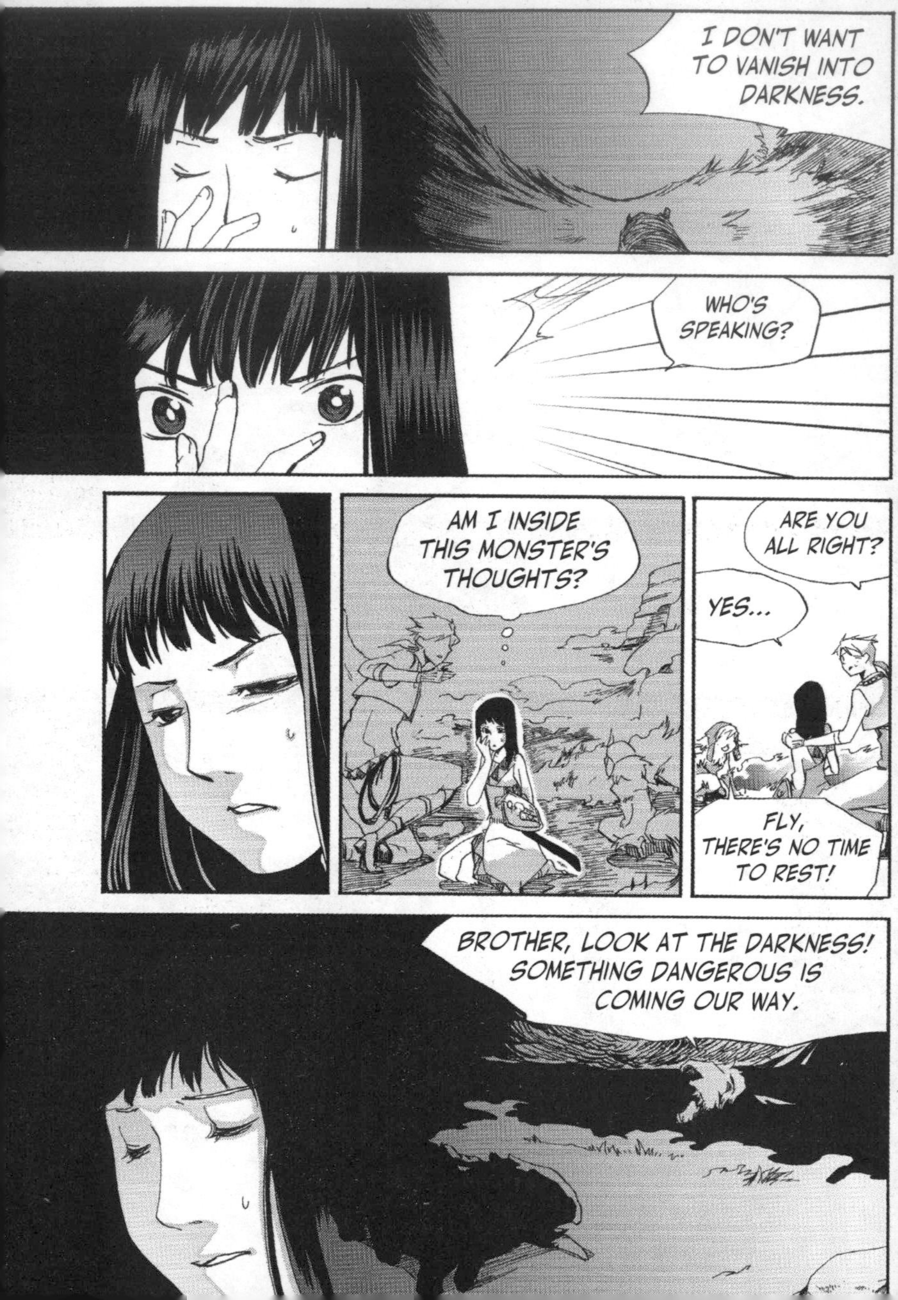
I DON'T WANT TO VANISH INTO DARKNESS.
WHO'S SPEAKING?
AM I INSIDE THIS MONSTER'S THOUGHTS?
ARE YOU ALL RIGHT?
YES...
FLY, THERE'S NO TIME TO REST!
BROTHER, LOOK AT THE DARKNESS! SOMETHING DANGEROUS IS COMING OUR WAY.

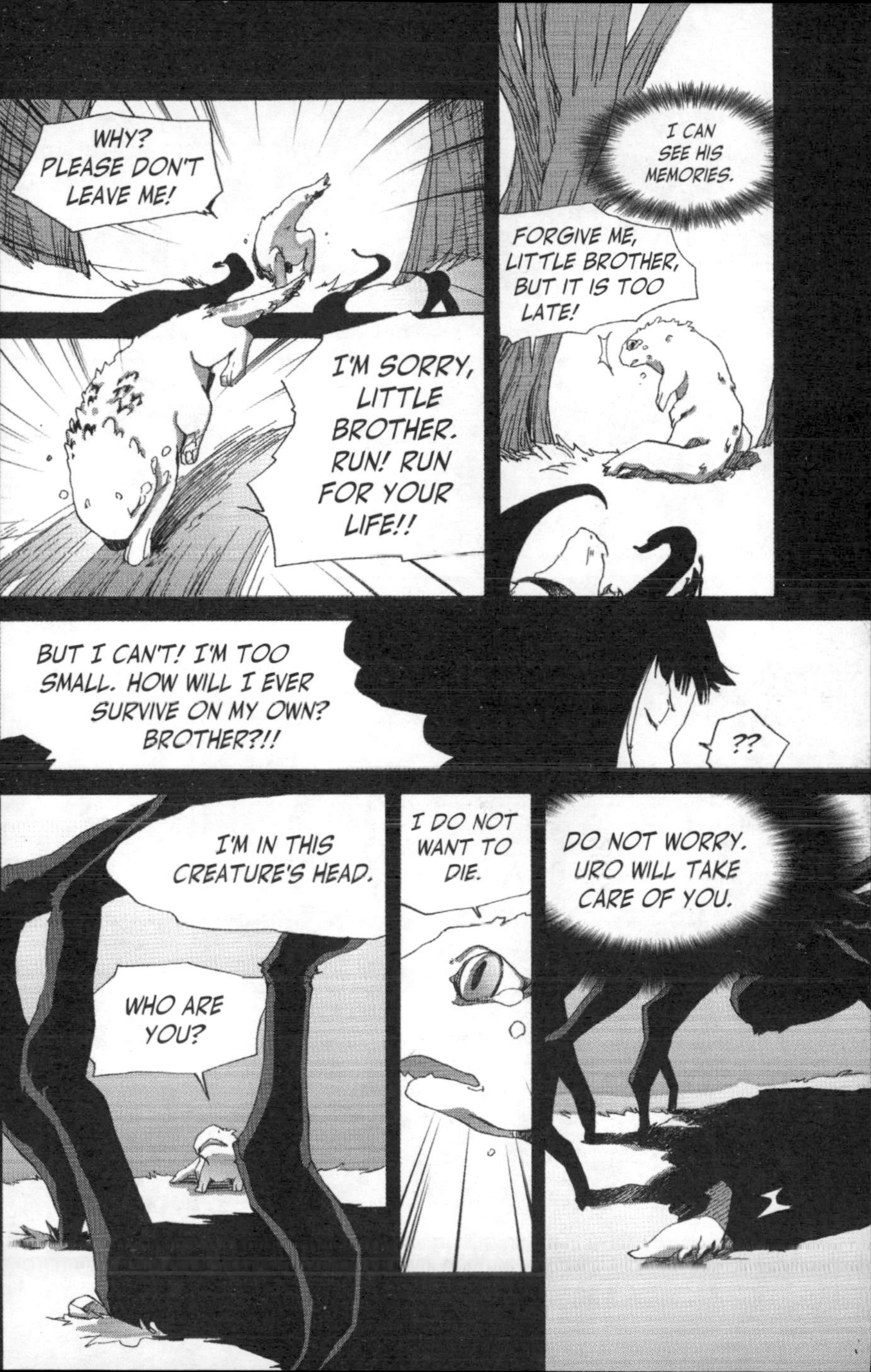
WHY? PLEASE DON'T LEAVE ME!
I CAN SEE HIS MEMORIES.
FORGIVE ME, LITTLE BROTHER, BUT IT IS TOO LATE!
I'M SORRY, LITTLE BROTHER. RUN! RUN FOR YOUR LIFE!!
BUT I CAN'T! I'M TOO SMALL. HOW WILL I EVER SURVIVE ON MY OWN? BROTHER?!!
??
I'M IN THIS CREATURE'S HEAD.
WHO ARE YOU?
I DO NOT WANT TO DIE.
DO NOT WORRY. URO WILL TAKE CARE OF YOU.

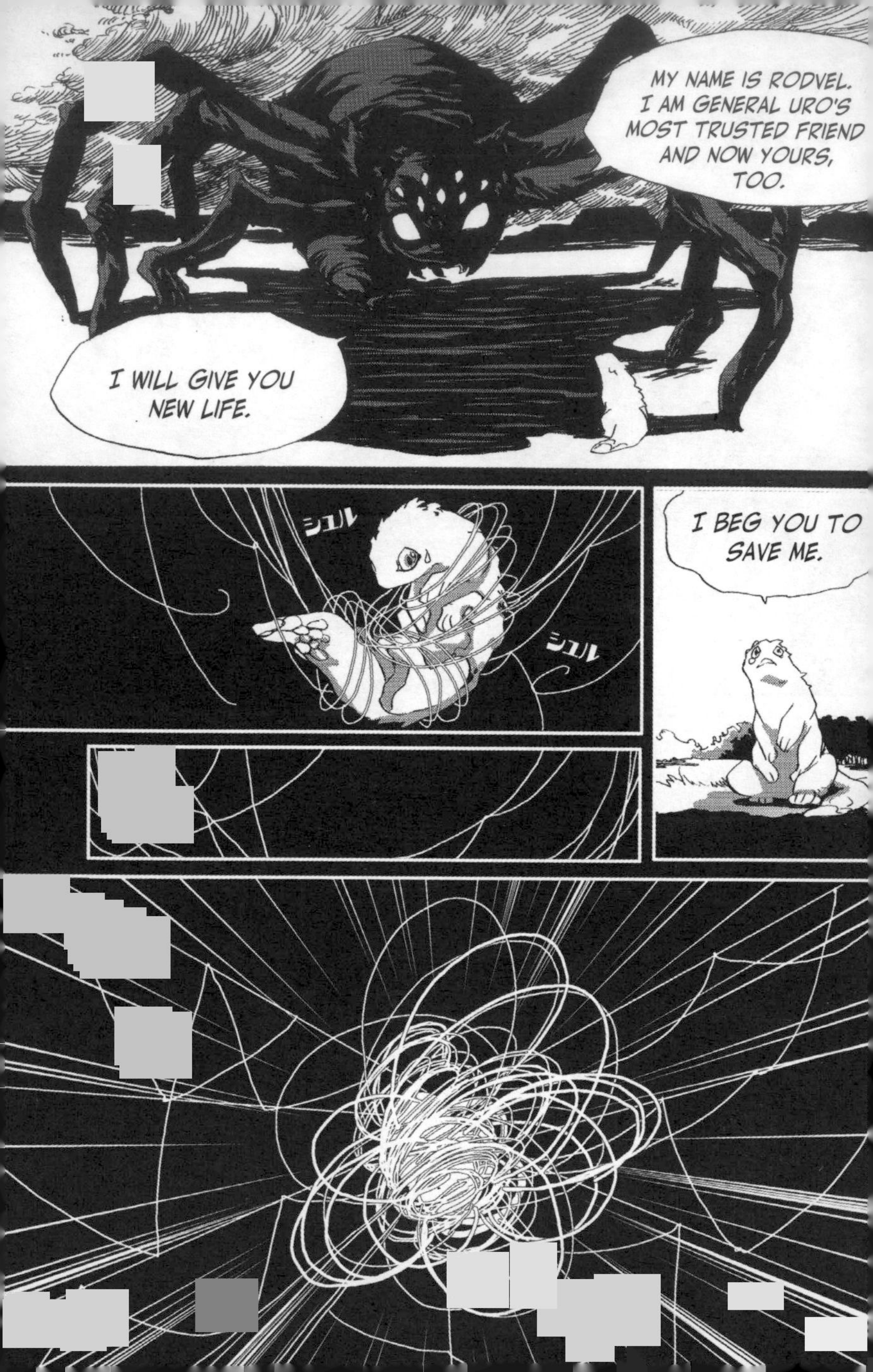
MY NAME IS RODVEL. I AM GENERAL URO'S MOST TRUSTED FRIEND AND NOW YOURS, TOO.
I WILL GIVE YOU NEW LIFE.
I BEG YOU TO SAVE ME.
シュル
シュル

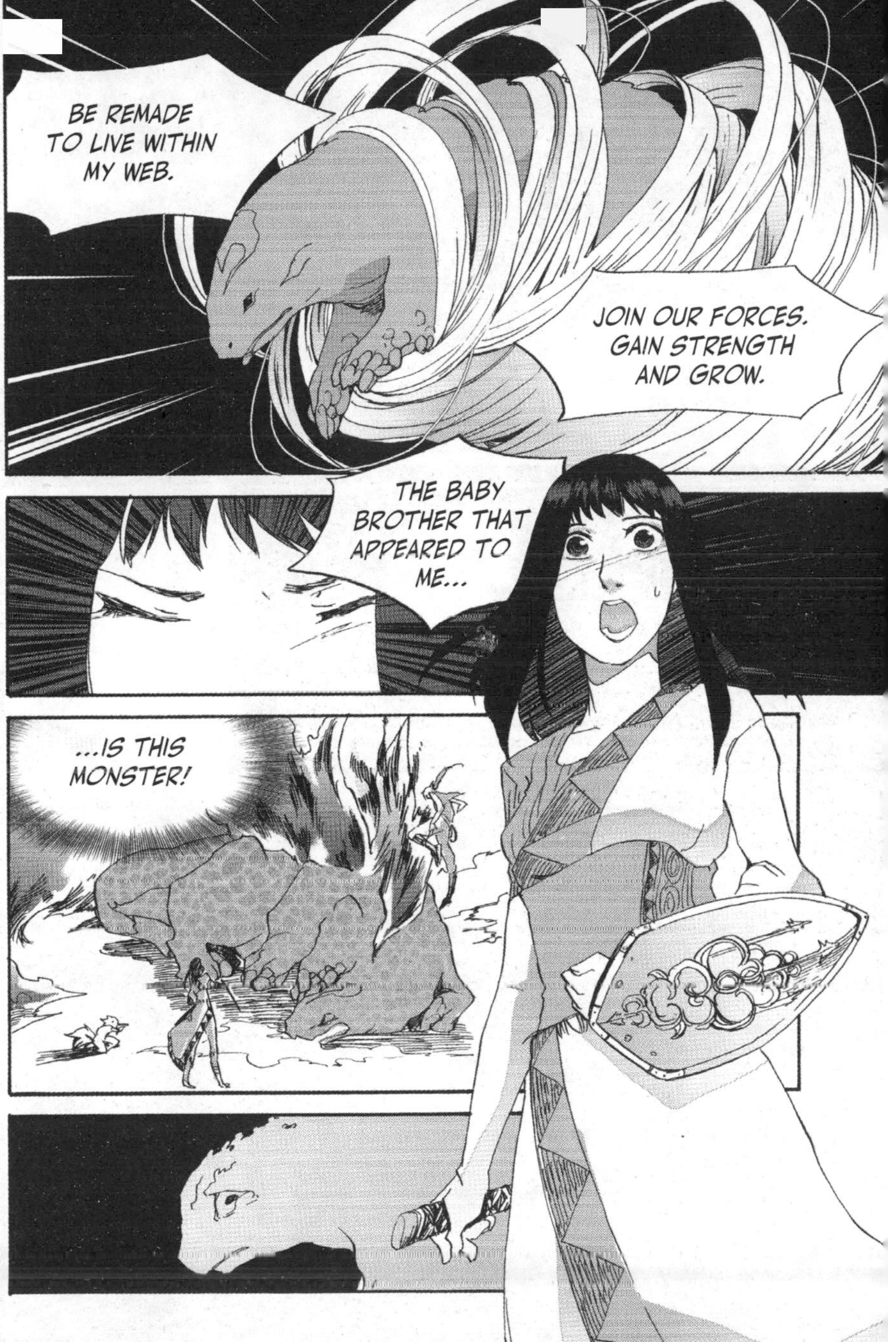
BE REMADE TO LIVE WITHIN MY WEB.
JOIN OUR FORCES. GAIN STRENGTH AND GROW.
THE BABY BROTHER THAT APPEARED TO ME...
...IS THIS MONSTER!

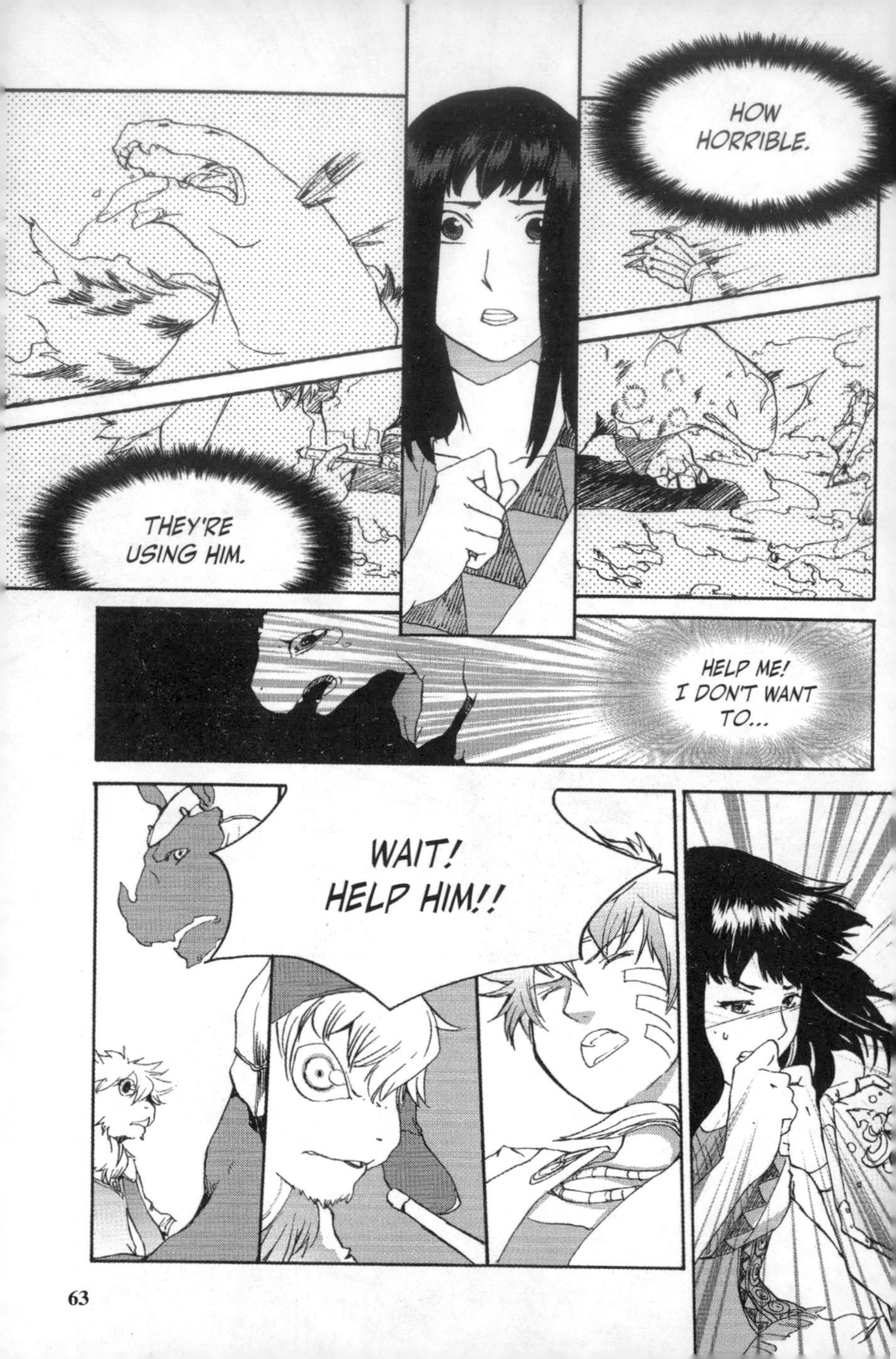
HOW HORRIBLE.
THEY'RE USING HIM.
HELP ME! I DON'T WANT TO...
WAIT! HELP HIM!!

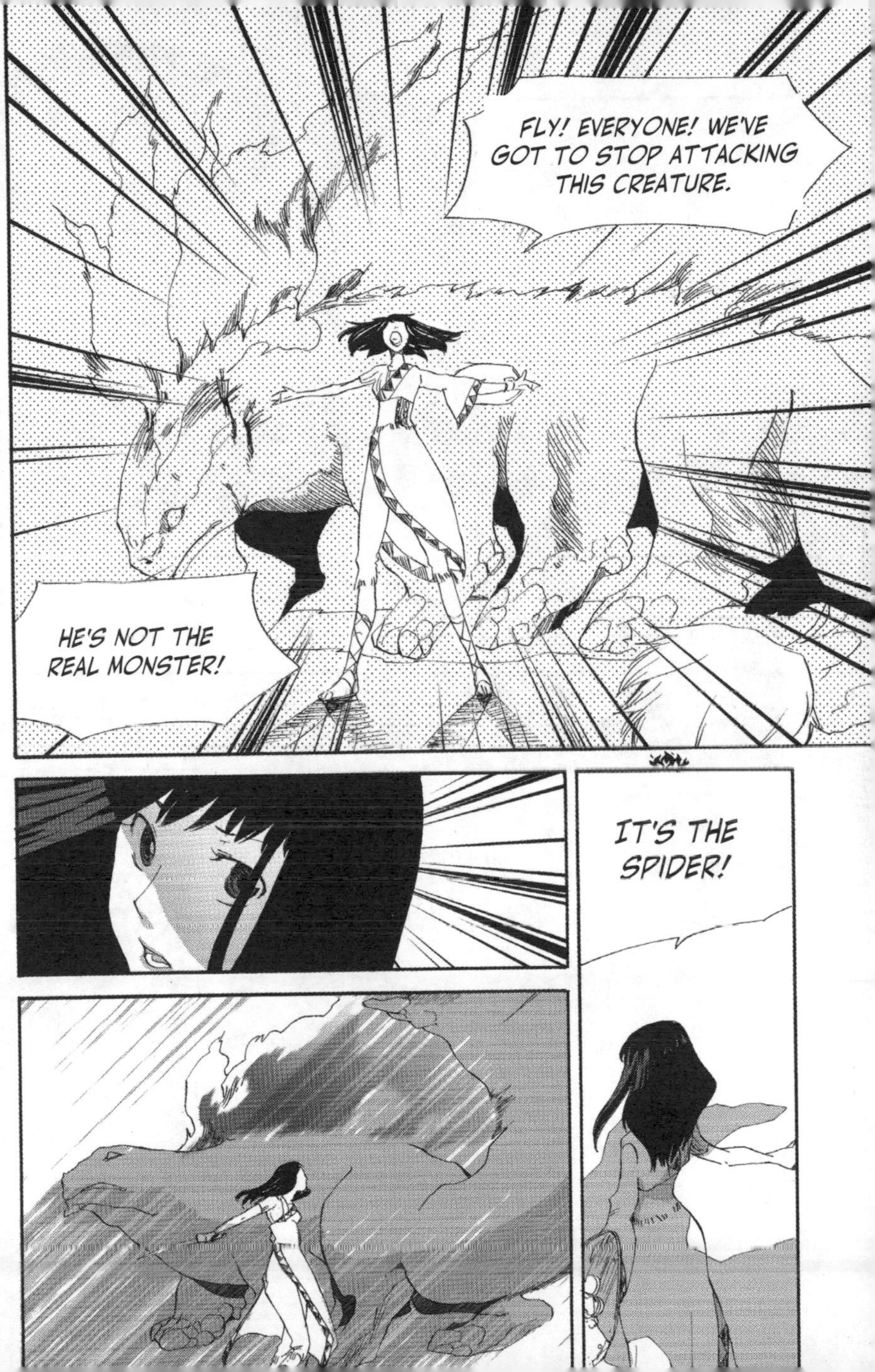
FLY! EVERYONE! WE'VE GOT TO STOP ATTACKING THIS CREATURE.
HE'S NOT THE REAL MONSTER!
IT'S THE SPIDER!

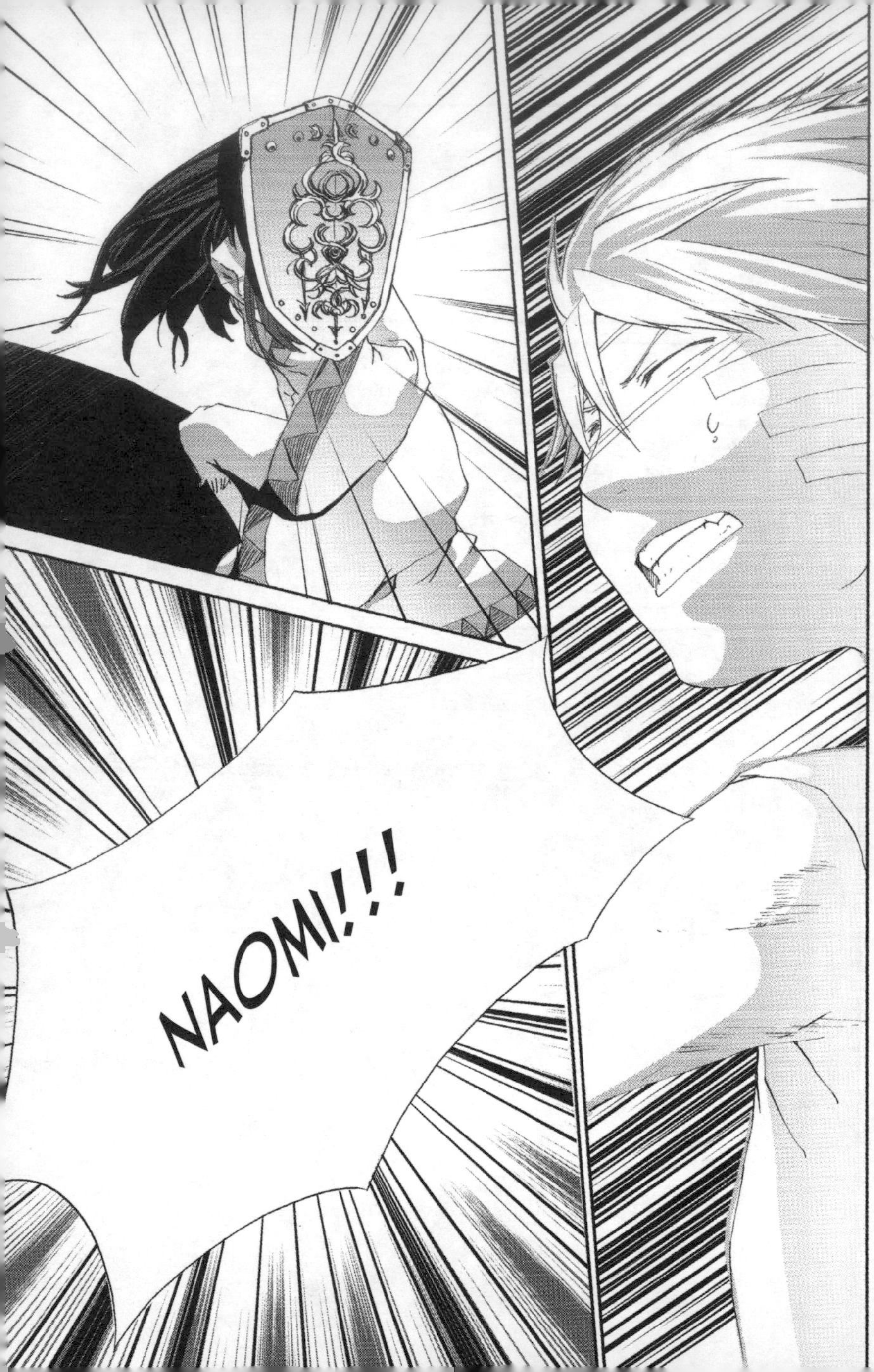
NAOMI!!!

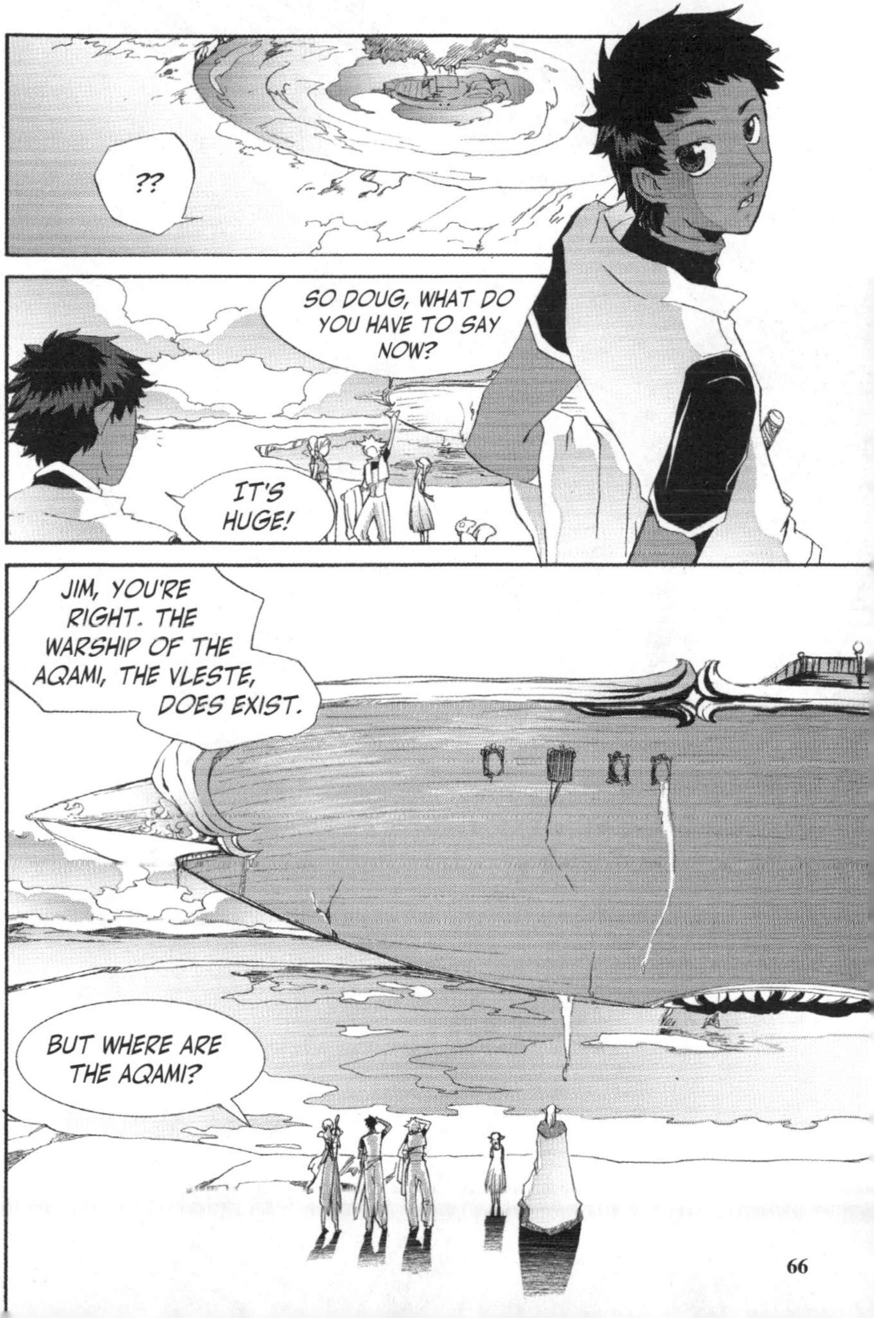
??
SO DOUG, WHAT DO YOU HAVE TO SAY NOW?
IT'S HUGE!
JIM, YOU'RE RIGHT. THE WARSHIP OF THE AQAMI, THE VLESTE, DOES EXIST.
BUT WHERE ARE THE AQAMI?

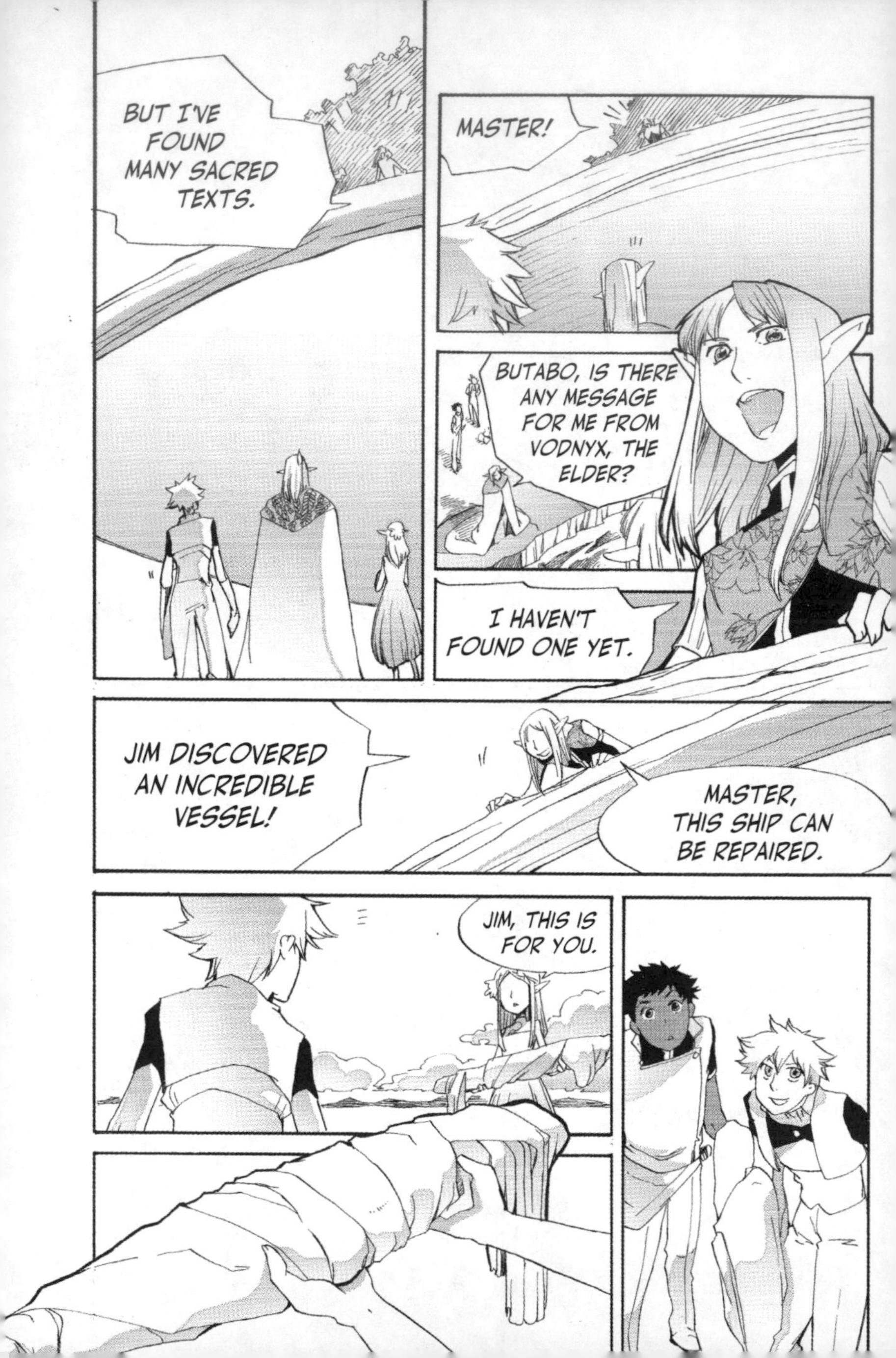
BUT I'VE FOUND MANY SACRED TEXTS.
MASTER!
BUTABO, IS THERE ANY MESSAGE FOR ME FROM VODNYX, THE ELDER?
I HAVEN'T FOUND ONE YET.
JIM DISCOVERED AN INCREDIBLE VESSEL!
MASTER, THIS SHIP CAN BE REPAIRED.
JIM, THIS IS FOR YOU.

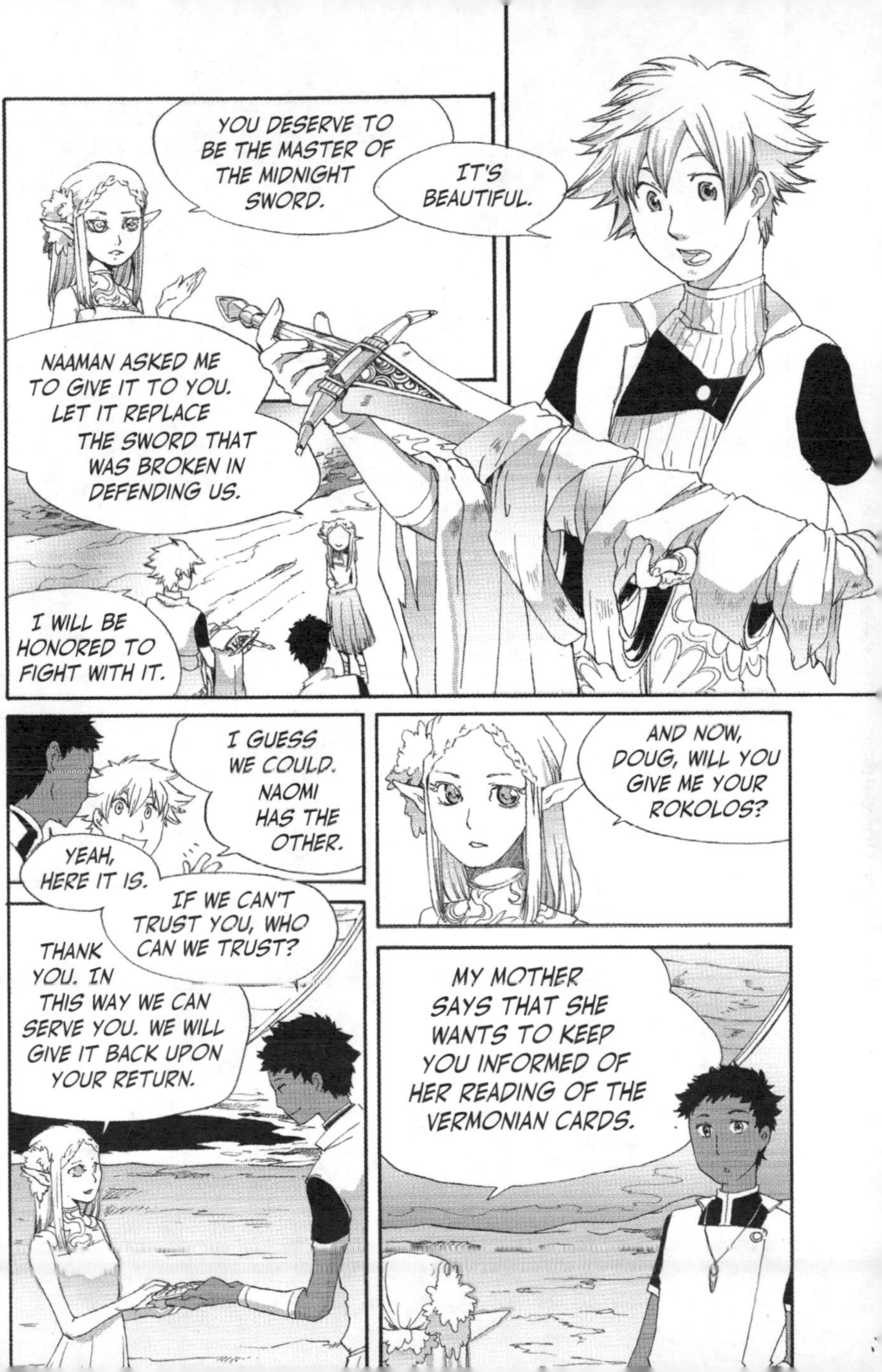
YOU DESERVE TO BE THE MASTER OF THE MIDNIGHT SWORD.
IT'S BEAUTIFUL.
NAAMAN ASKED ME TO GIVE IT TO YOU. LET IT REPLACE THE SWORD THAT WAS BROKEN IN DEFENDING US.
I WILL BE HONORED TO FIGHT WITH IT.
AND NOW, DOUG, WILL YOU GIVE ME YOUR ROKOLOS?
I GUESS WE COULD. NAOMI HAS THE OTHER.
YEAH, HERE IT IS.
IF WE CAN'T TRUST YOU, WHO CAN WE TRUST?
THANK YOU. IN THIS WAY WE CAN SERVE YOU. WE WILL GIVE IT BACK UPON YOUR RETURN.
MY MOTHER SAYS THAT SHE WANTS TO KEEP YOU INFORMED OF HER READING OF THE VERMONIAN CARDS.

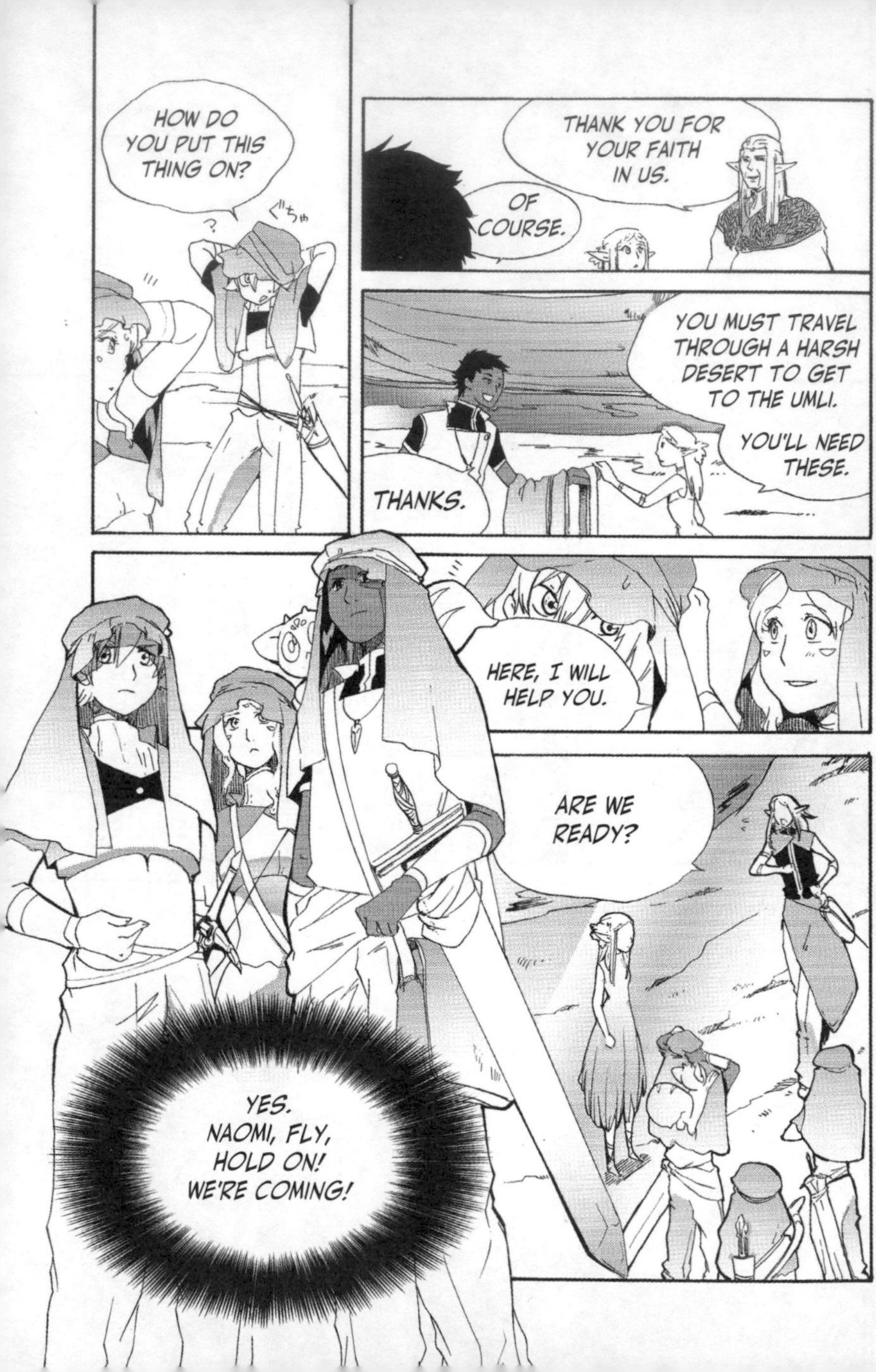
HOW DO YOU PUT THIS THING ON?
?
ぐちゃ
THANK YOU FOR YOUR FAITH IN US.
OF COURSE.
YOU MUST TRAVEL THROUGH A HARSH DESERT TO GET TO THE UMLI.
YOU'LL NEED THESE.
THANKS.
HERE, I WILL HELP YOU.
ARE WE READY?
YES. NAOMI, FLY, HOLD ON! WE'RE COMING!

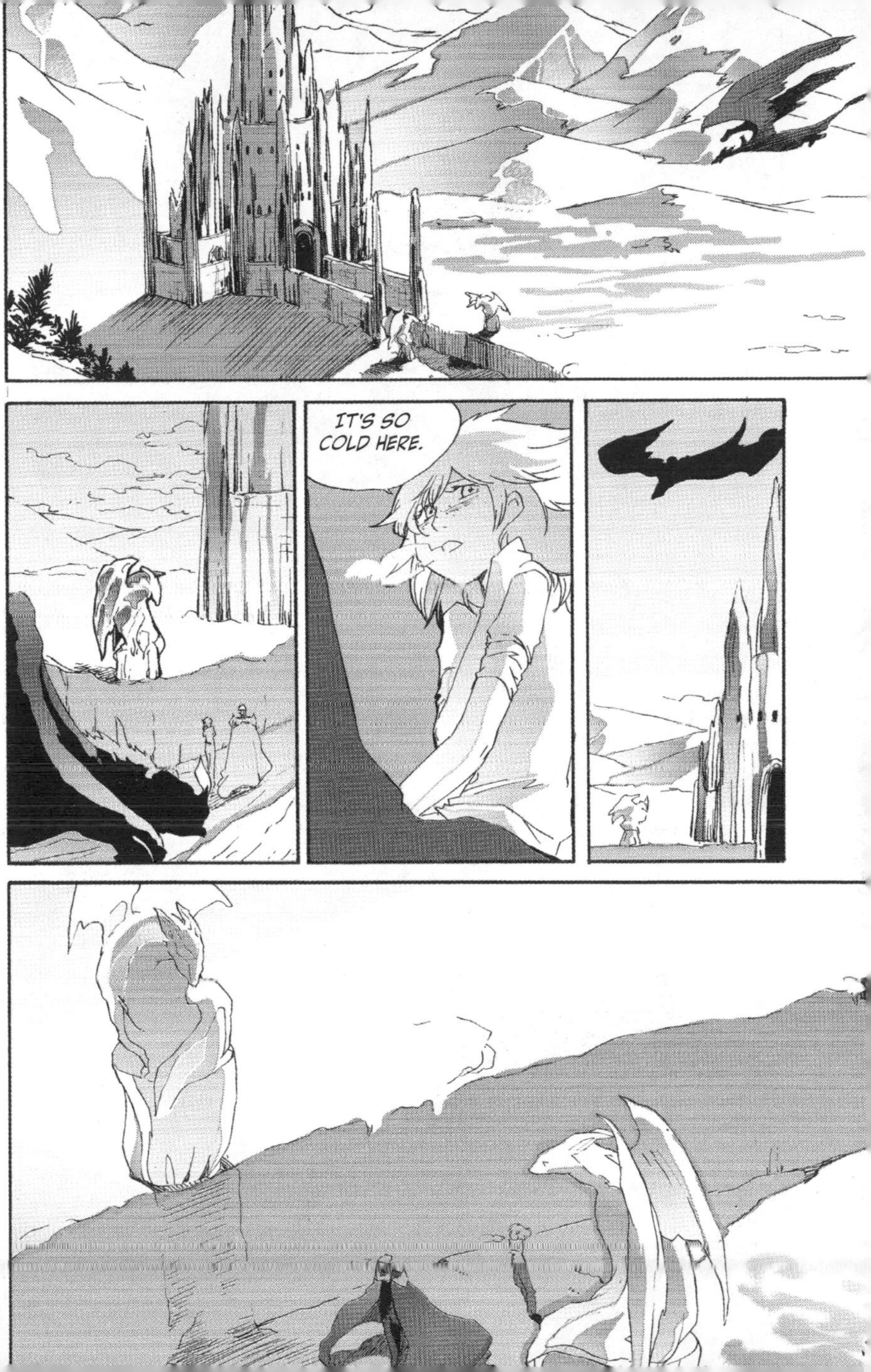
IT'S SO COLD HERE.

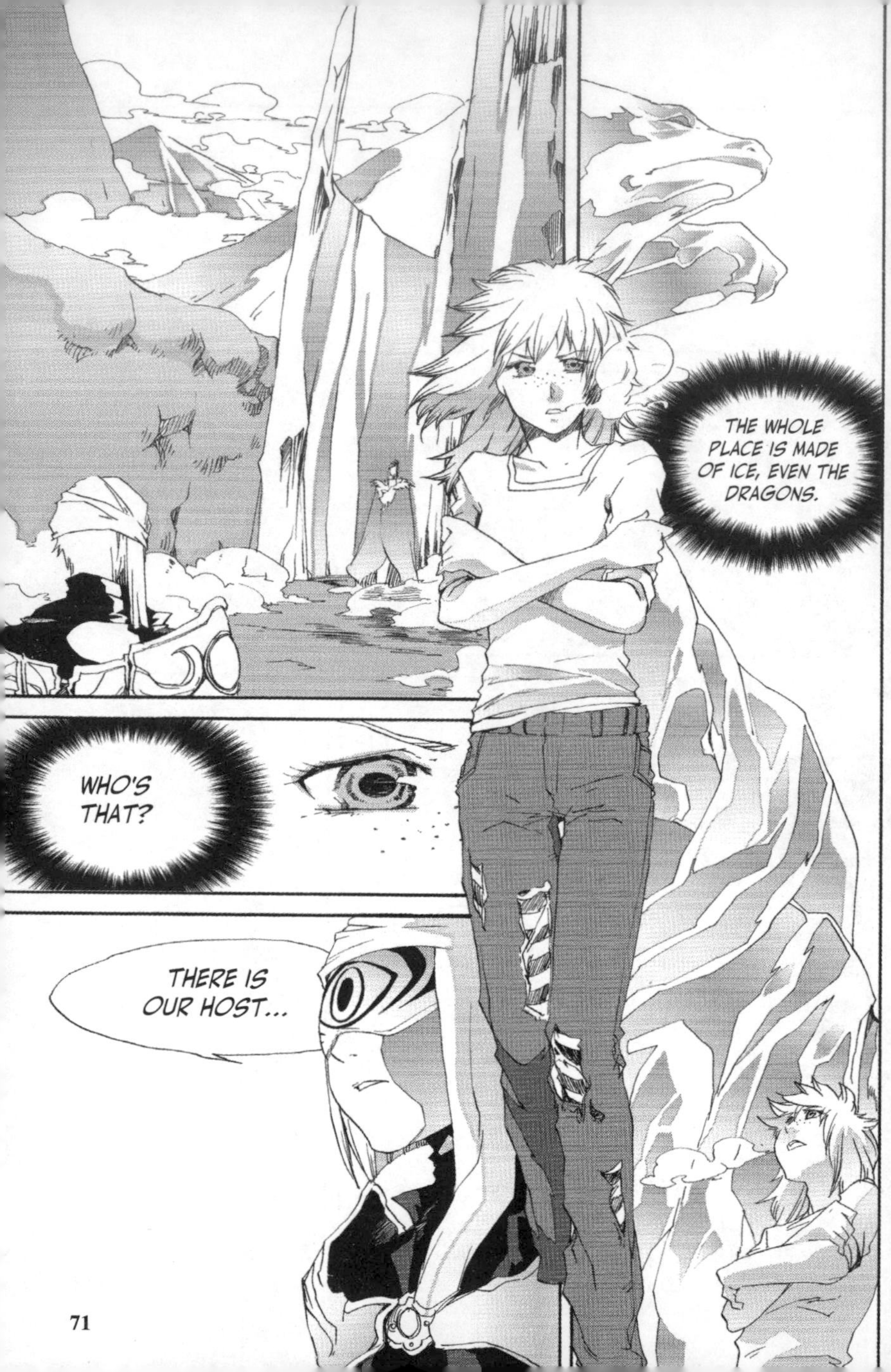
THE WHOLE PLACE IS MADE OF ICE, EVEN THE DRAGONS.
WHO'S THAT?
THERE IS OUR HOST...

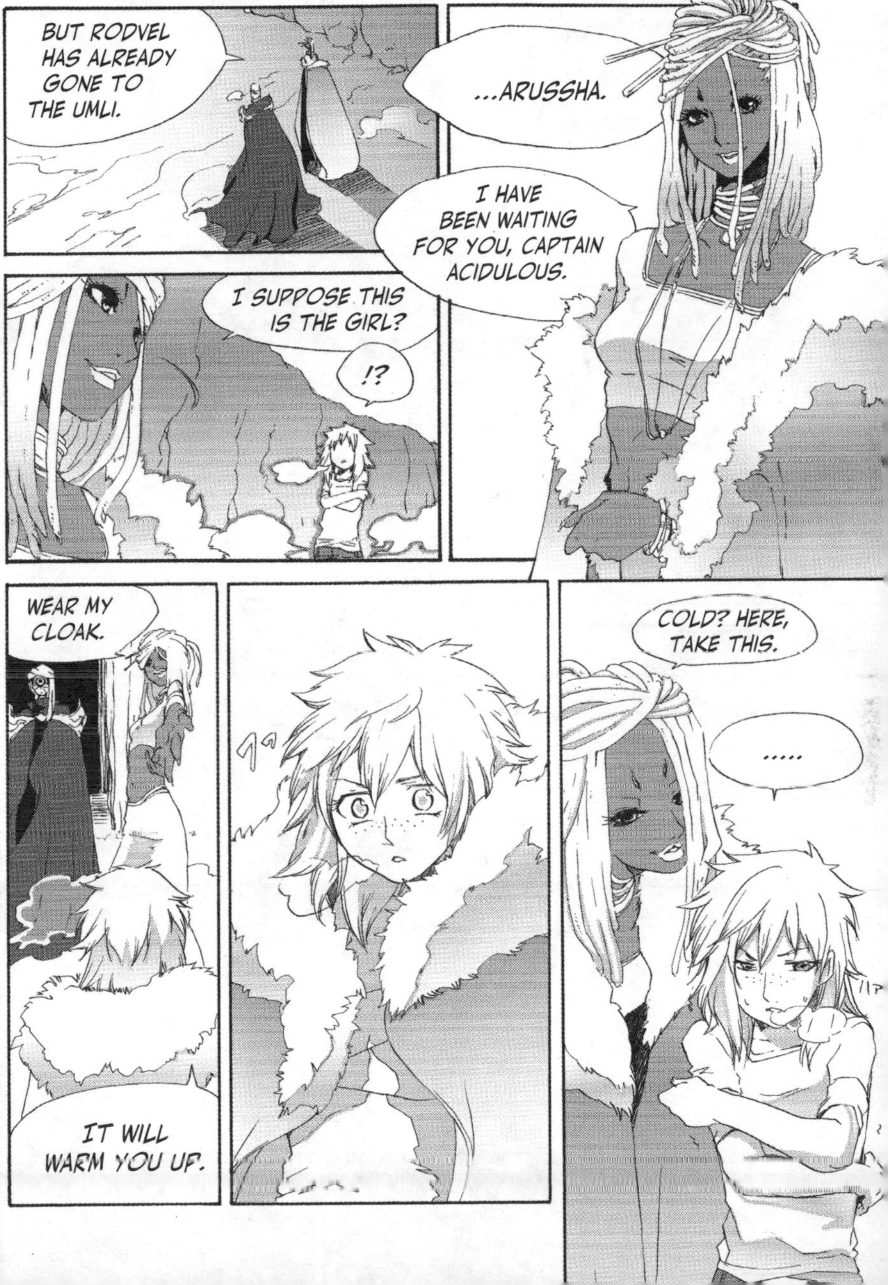
BUT RODVEL HAS ALREADY GONE TO THE UMLI.
...ARUSSHA.
I HAVE BEEN WAITING FOR YOU, CAPTAIN ACIDULOUS.
I SUPPOSE THIS IS THE GIRL?
!?
WEAR MY CLOAK.
IT WILL WARM YOU UP.
COLD? HERE, TAKE THIS.
.....

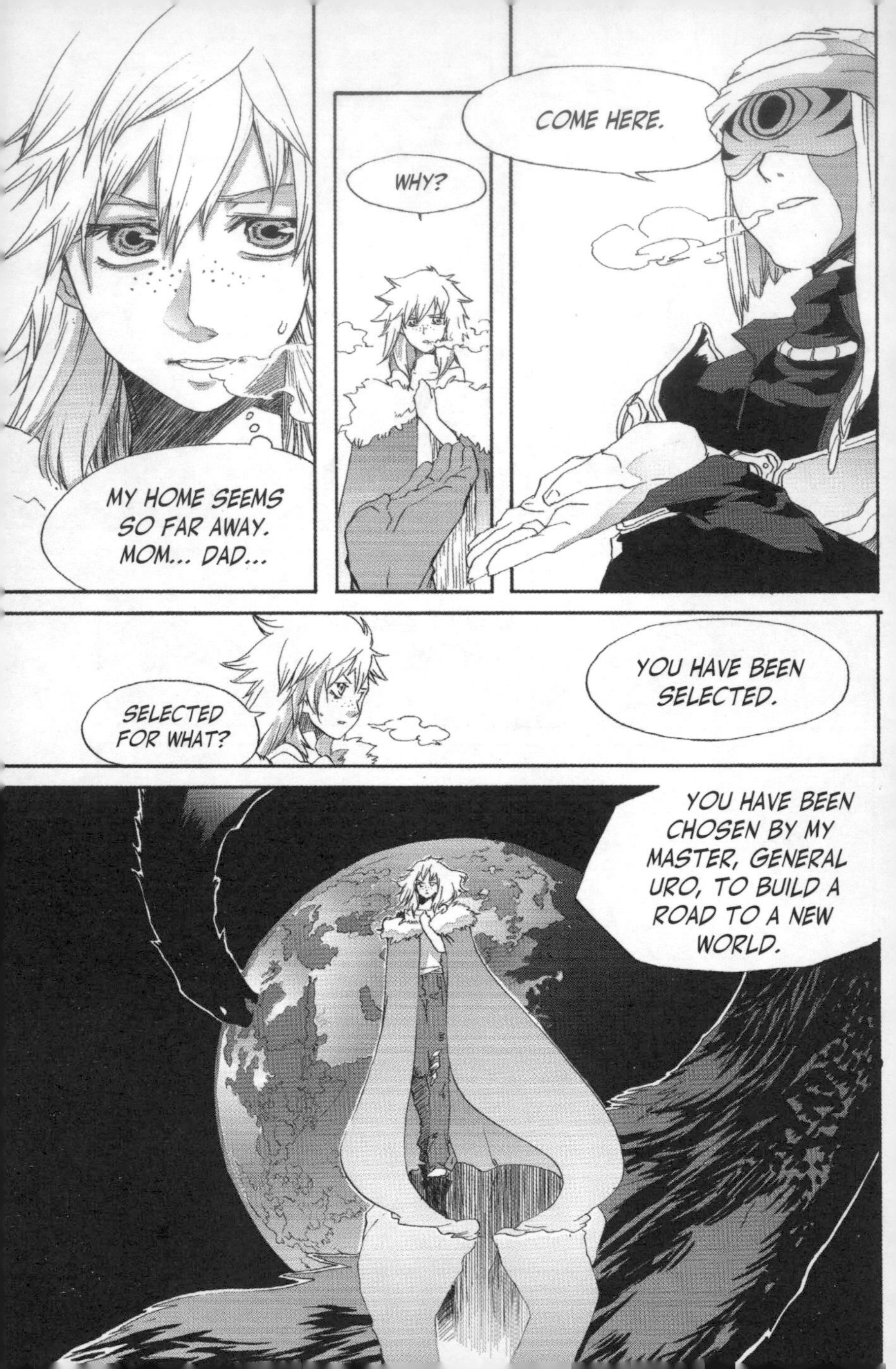
MY HOME SEEMS SO FAR AWAY. MOM... DAD...
WHY?
COME HERE.
SELECTED FOR WHAT?
YOU HAVE BEEN SELECTED.
YOU HAVE BEEN CHOSEN BY MY MASTER, GENERAL URO, TO BUILD A ROAD TO A NEW WORLD.

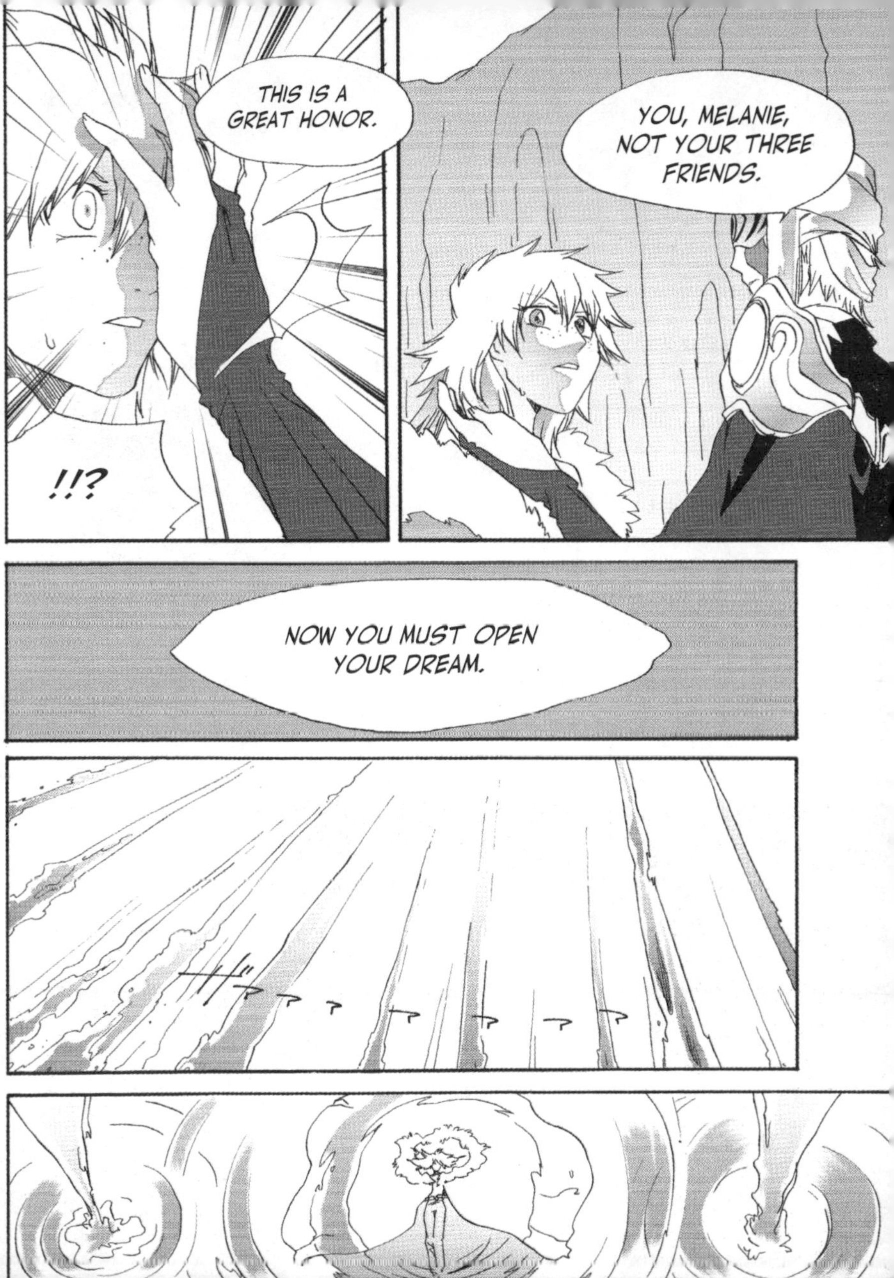
THIS IS A GREAT HONOR.
!!?
YOU, MELANIE, NOT YOUR THREE FRIENDS.
NOW YOU MUST OPEN YOUR DREAM.

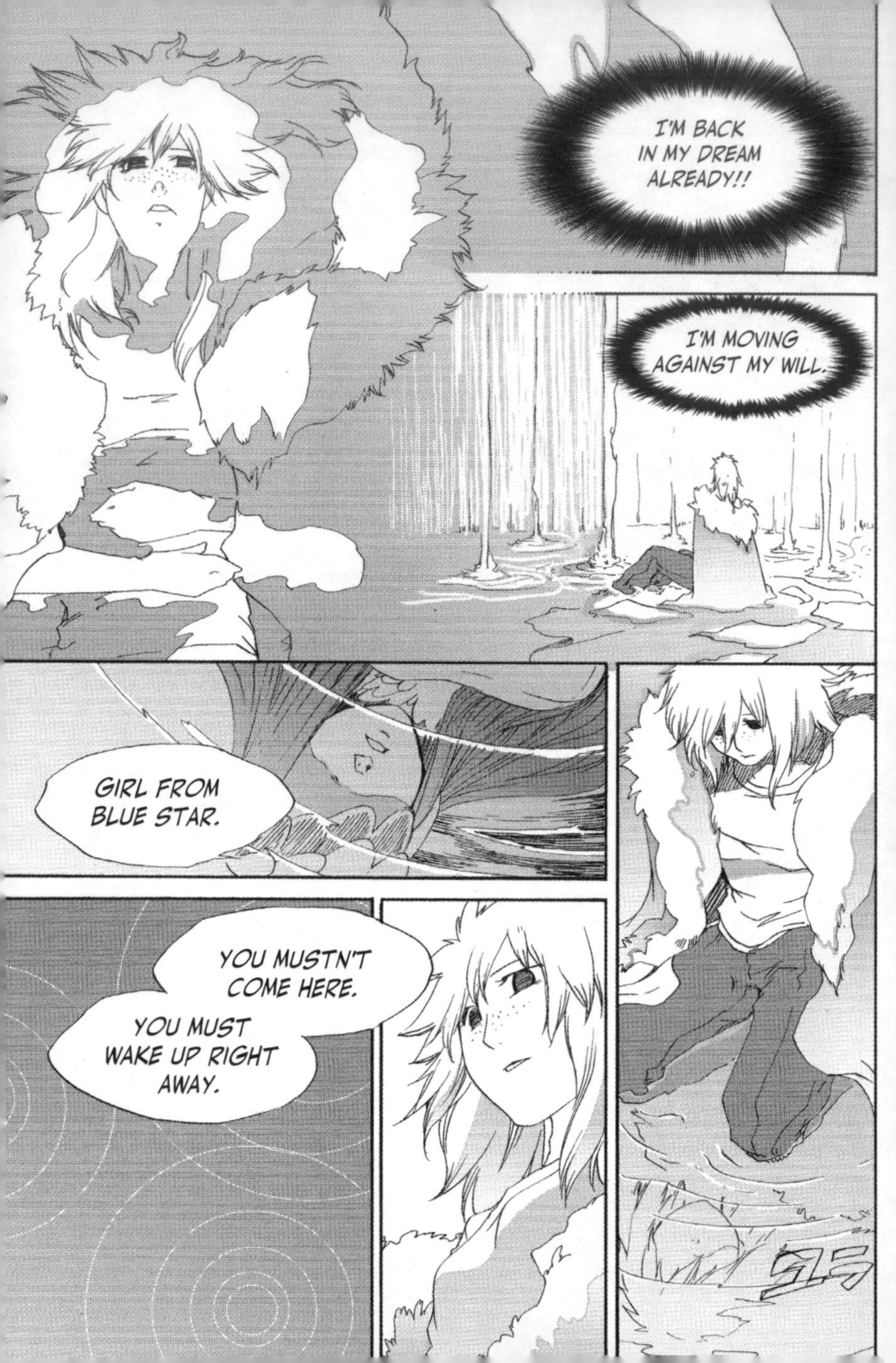

I'M BACK IN MY DREAM ALREADY!!
I'M MOVING AGAINST MY WILL.
GIRL FROM BLUE STAR.
YOU MUSTN'T COME HERE.
YOU MUST WAKE UP RIGHT AWAY.

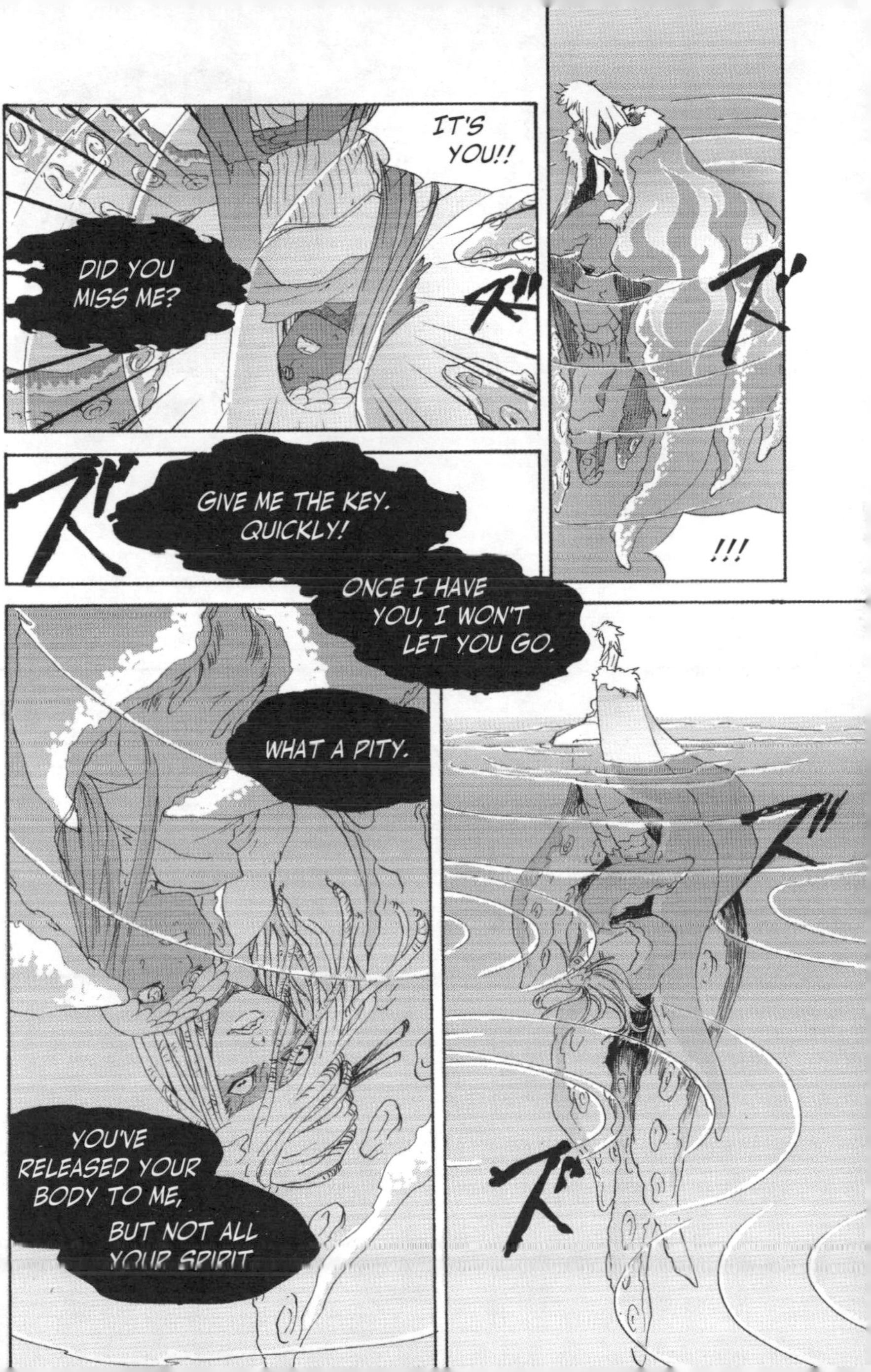
IT'S YOU!!
DID YOU MISS ME?
ズ
ズ
!!!
ズ
GIVE ME THE KEY. QUICKLY!
ONCE I HAVE YOU, I WON'T LET YOU GO.
WHAT A PITY.
ズ
YOU'VE RELEASED YOUR BODY TO ME,
BUT NOT ALL YOUR SPIRIT
ズ

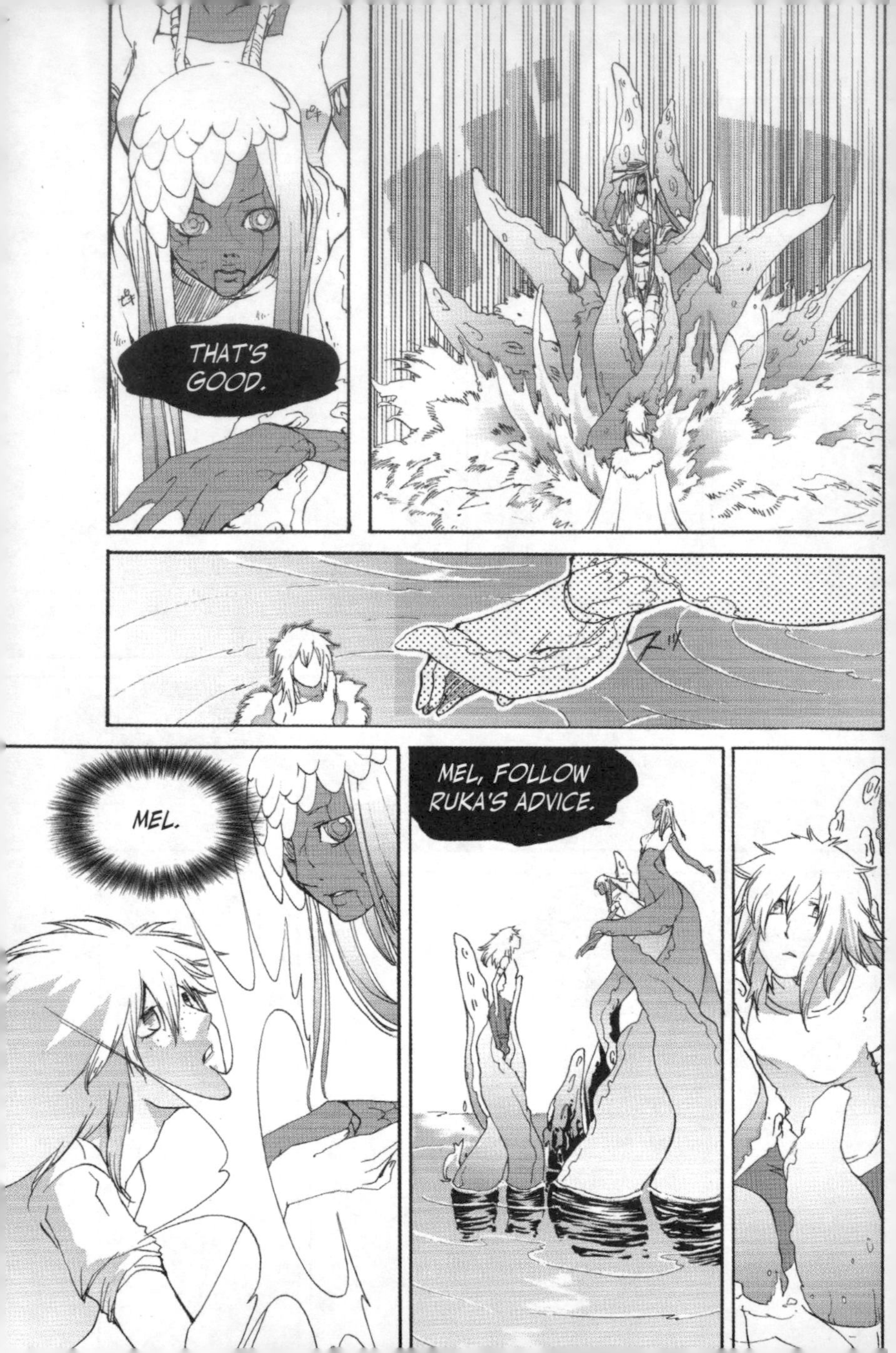
THAT'S GOOD.
MEL.
MEL, FOLLOW RUKA'S ADVICE.

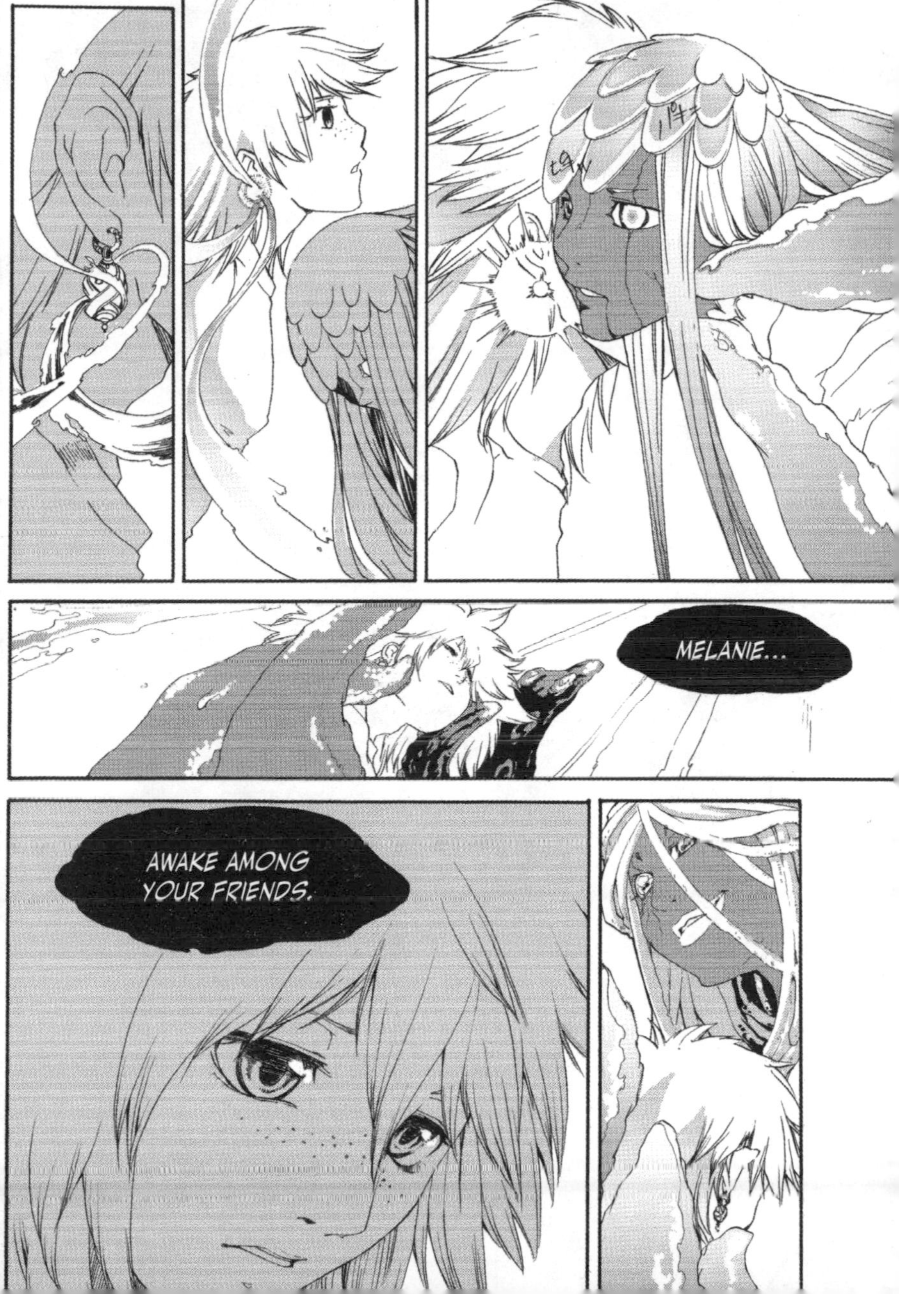
MELANIE...
AWAKE AMONG YOUR FRIENDS.

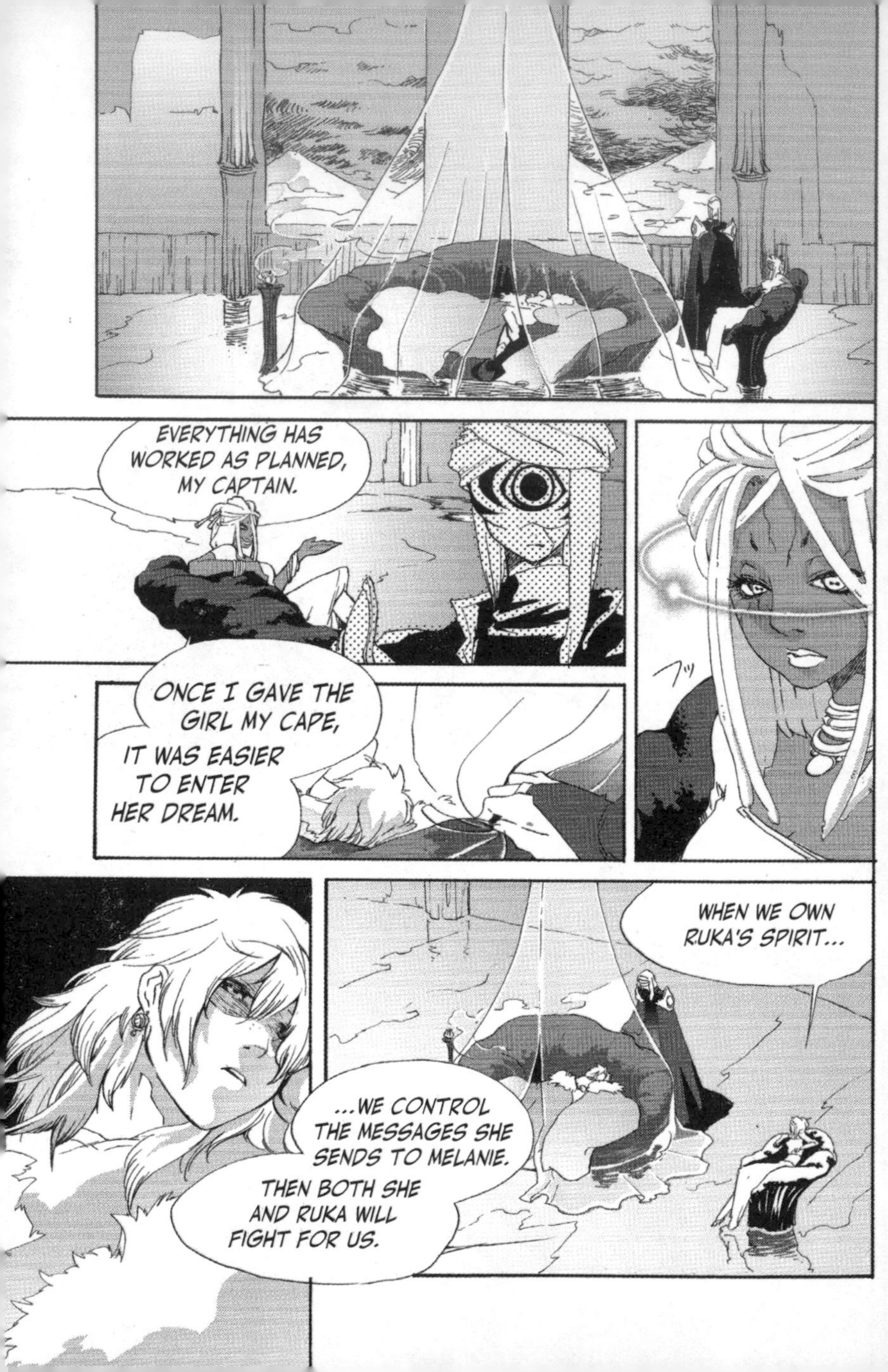
EVERYTHING HAS WORKED AS PLANNED, MY CAPTAIN.
ONCE I GAVE THE GIRL MY CAPE,
IT WAS EASIER TO ENTER HER DREAM.
WHEN WE OWN RUKA'S SPIRIT...
...WE CONTROL THE MESSAGES SHE SENDS TO MELANIE.
THEN BOTH SHE AND RUKA WILL FIGHT FOR US.

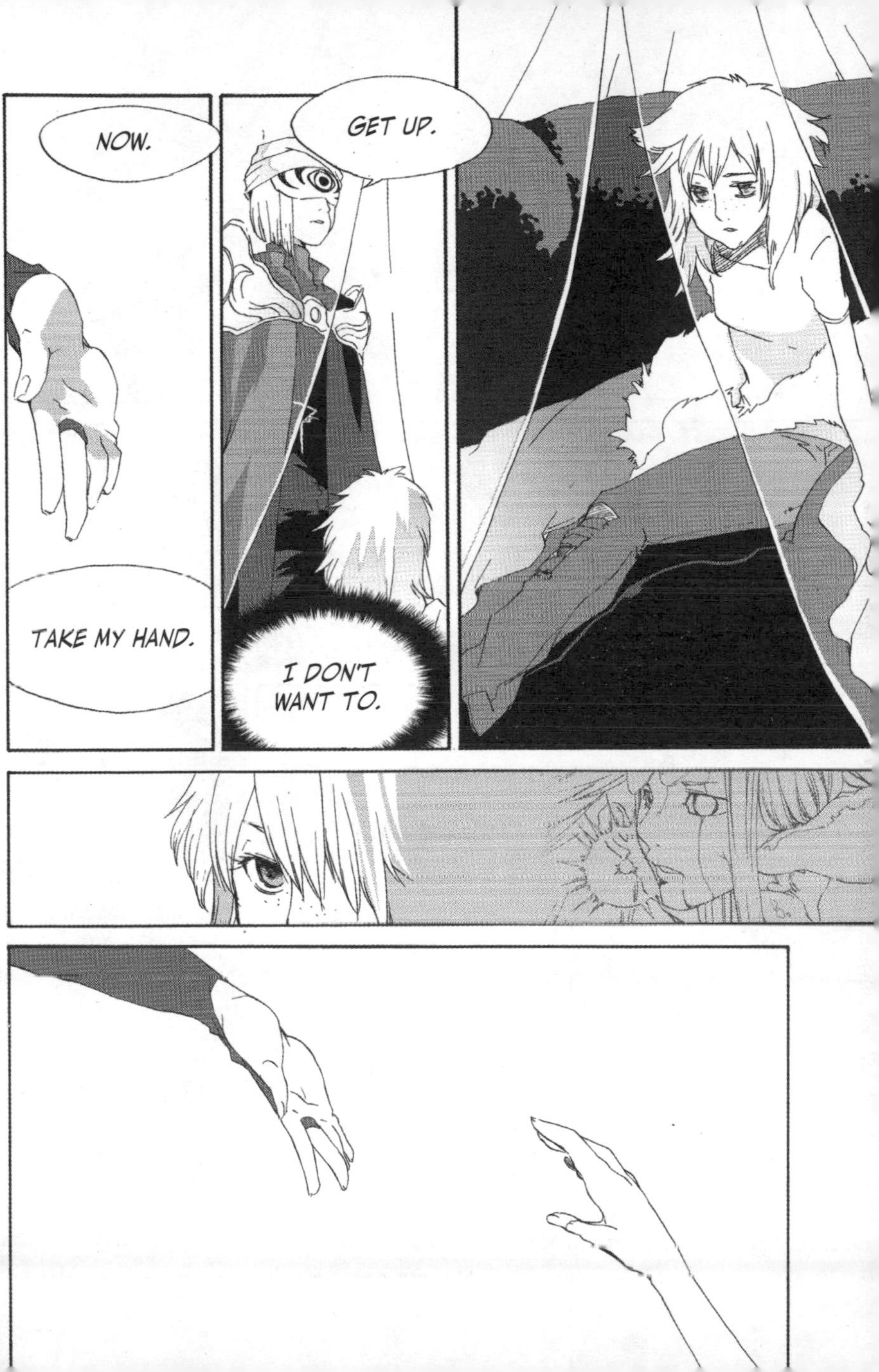
GET UP.
NOW.
TAKE MY HAND.
I DON'T
WANT TO.

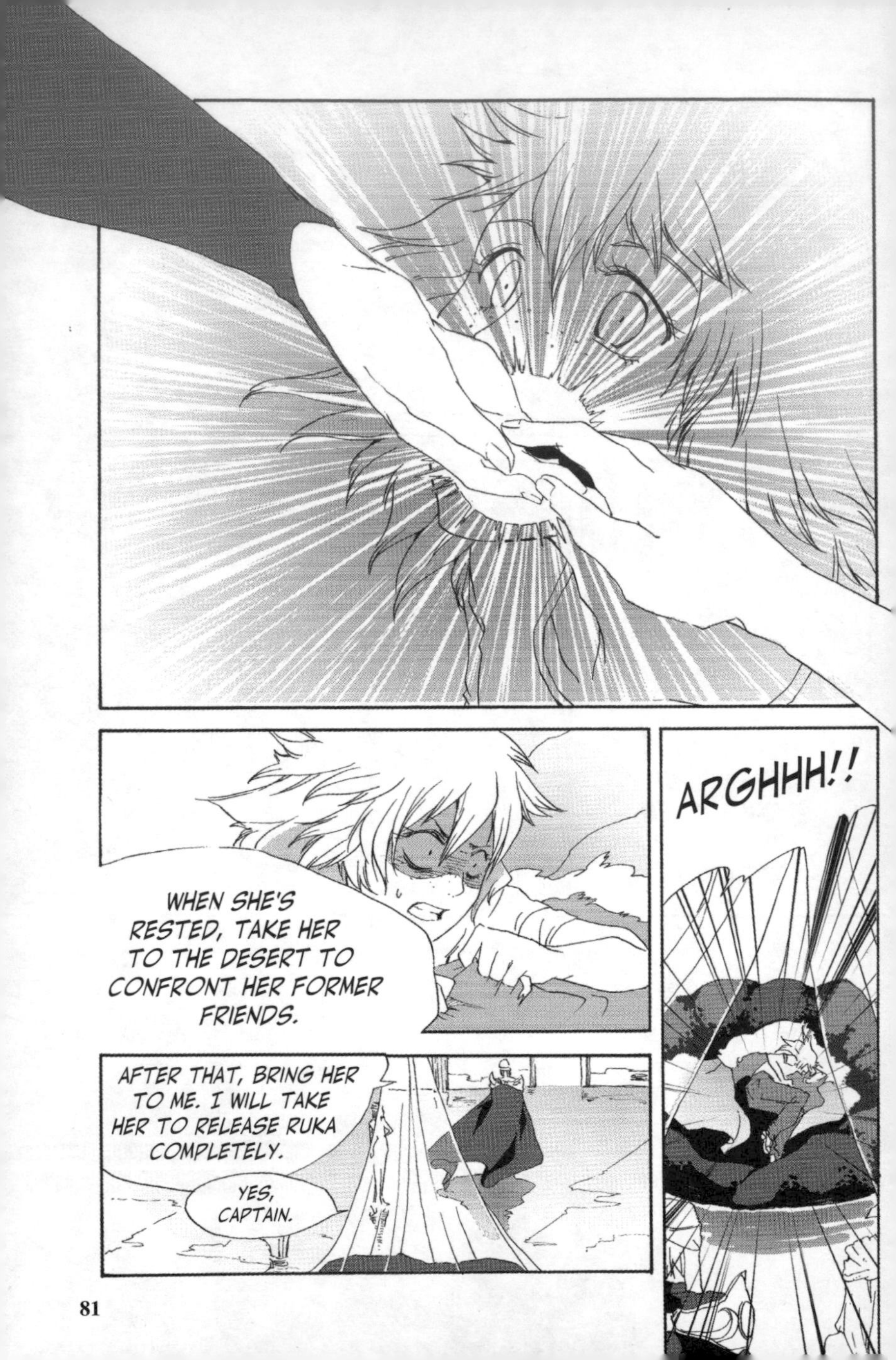
ARGHHH!!
WHEN SHE'S RESTED, TAKE HER TO THE DESERT TO CONFRONT HER FORMER FRIENDS.
AFTER THAT, BRING HER TO ME. I WILL TAKE HER TO RELEASE RUKA COMPLETELY.
YES, CAPTAIN.

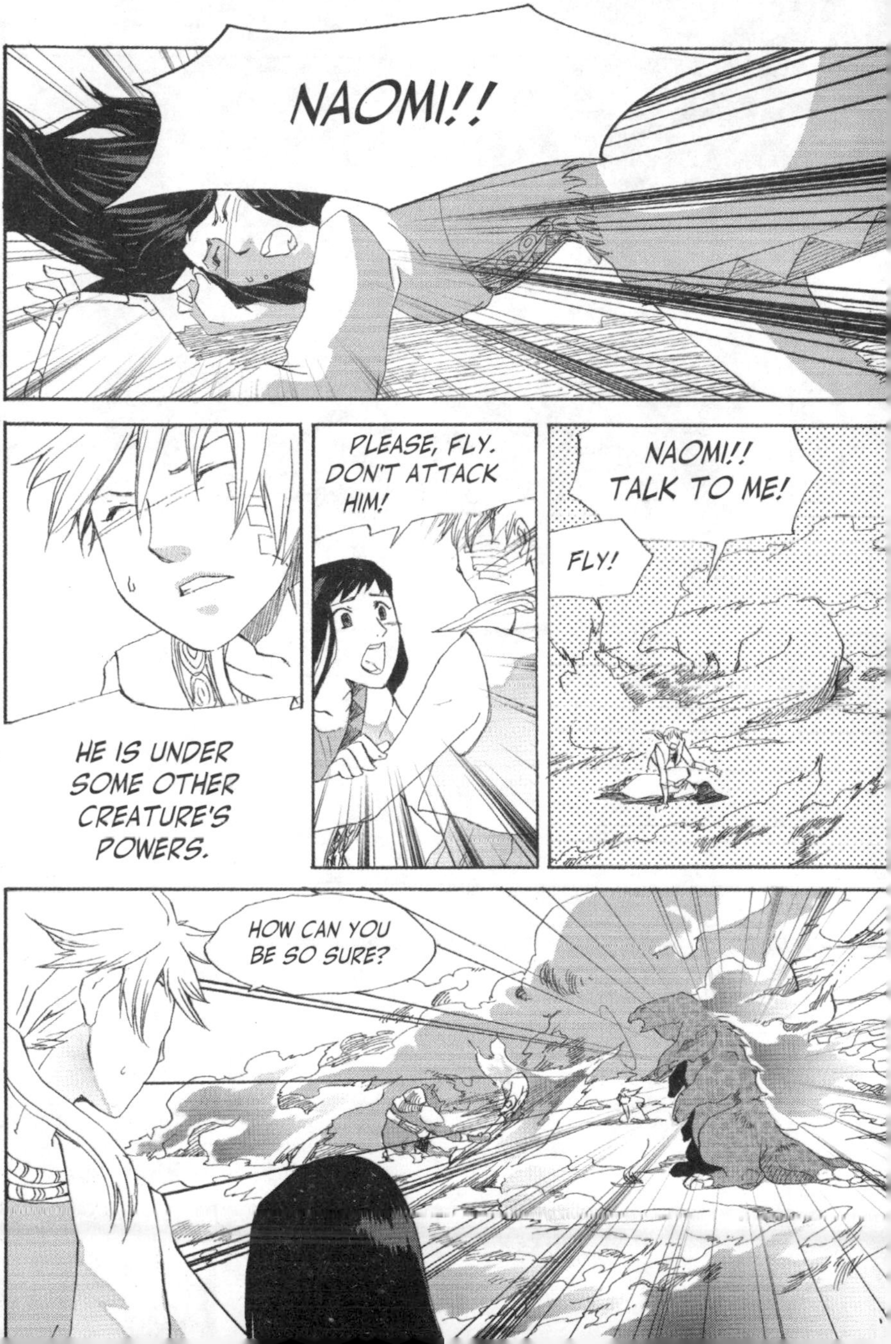
NAOMI!!
PLEASE, FLY. DON'T ATTACK HIM!
NAOMI!! TALK TO ME!
FLY!
HE IS UNDER SOME OTHER CREATURE'S POWERS.
HOW CAN YOU BE SO SURE?

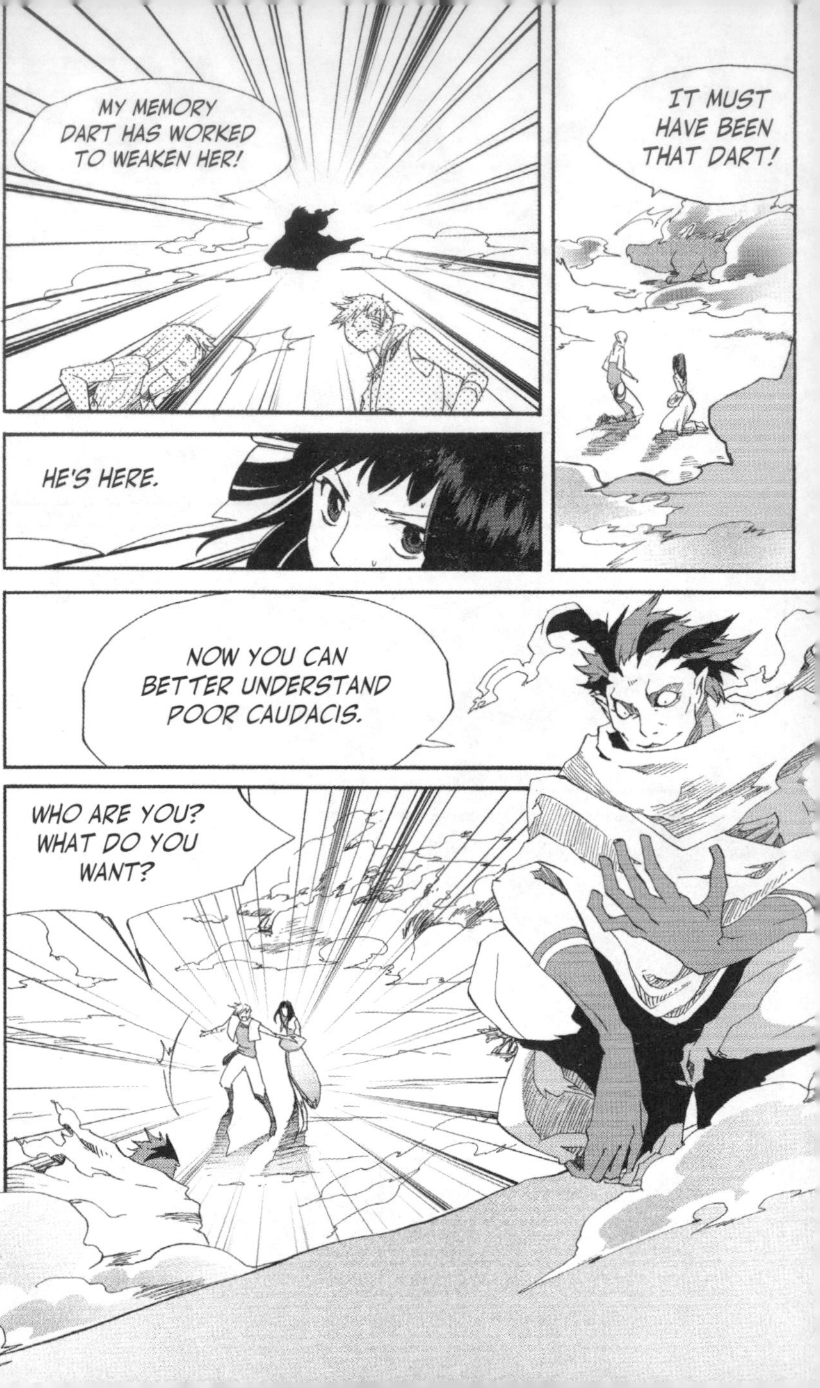
IT MUST HAVE BEEN THAT DART!
MY MEMORY DART HAS WORKED TO WEAKEN HER!
HE'S HERE.
NOW YOU CAN BETTER UNDERSTAND POOR CAUDACIS.
WHO ARE YOU? WHAT DO YOU WANT?

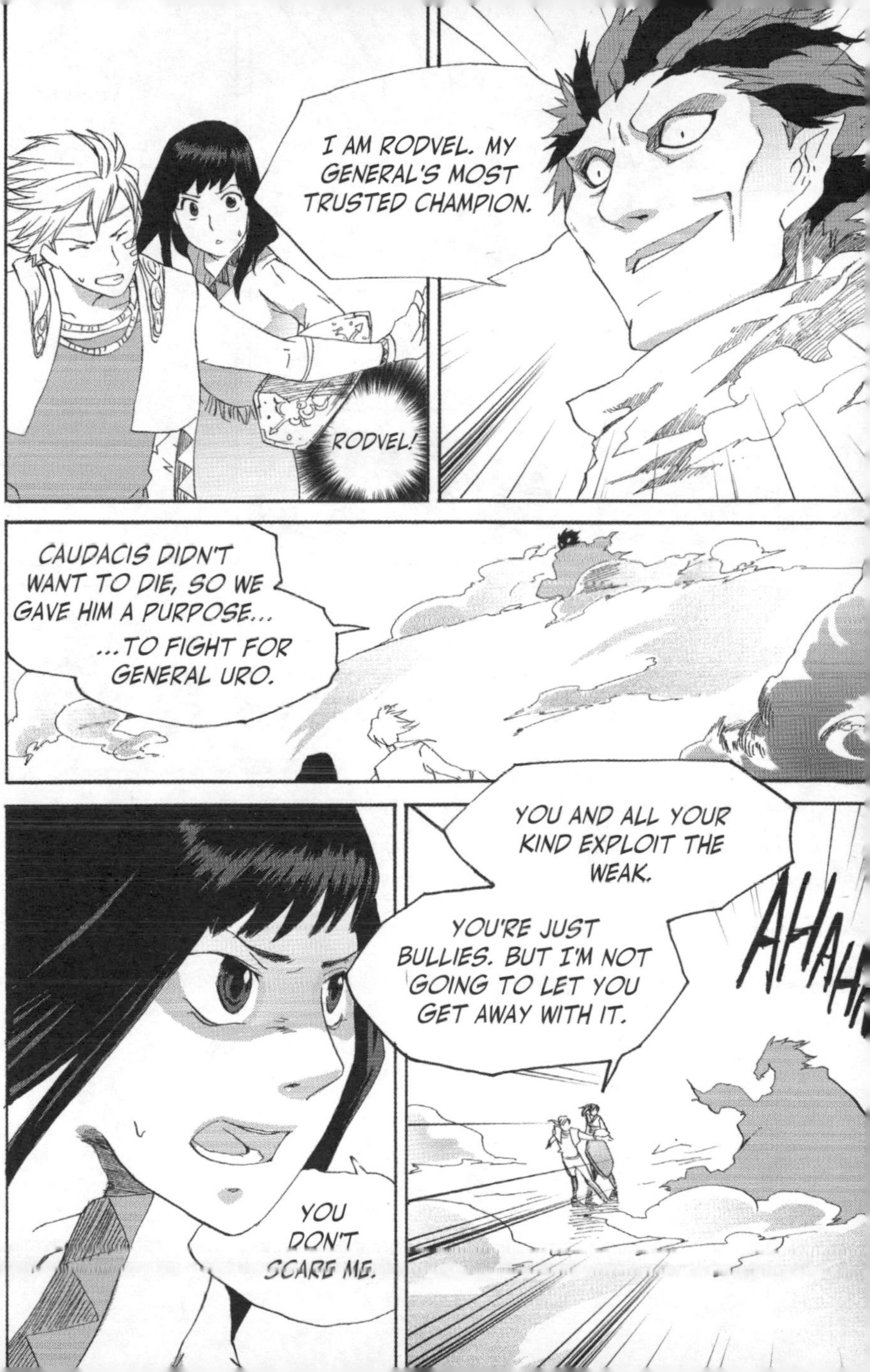
I AM RODVEL. MY GENERAL'S MOST TRUSTED CHAMPION.
RODVEL!
CAUDACIS DIDN'T WANT TO DIE, SO WE GAVE HIM A PURPOSE...
...TO FIGHT FOR GENERAL URO.
YOU AND ALL YOUR KIND EXPLOIT THE WEAK.
YOU'RE JUST BULLIES. BUT I'M NOT GOING TO LET YOU GET AWAY WITH IT.
YOU DON'T SCARE ME.

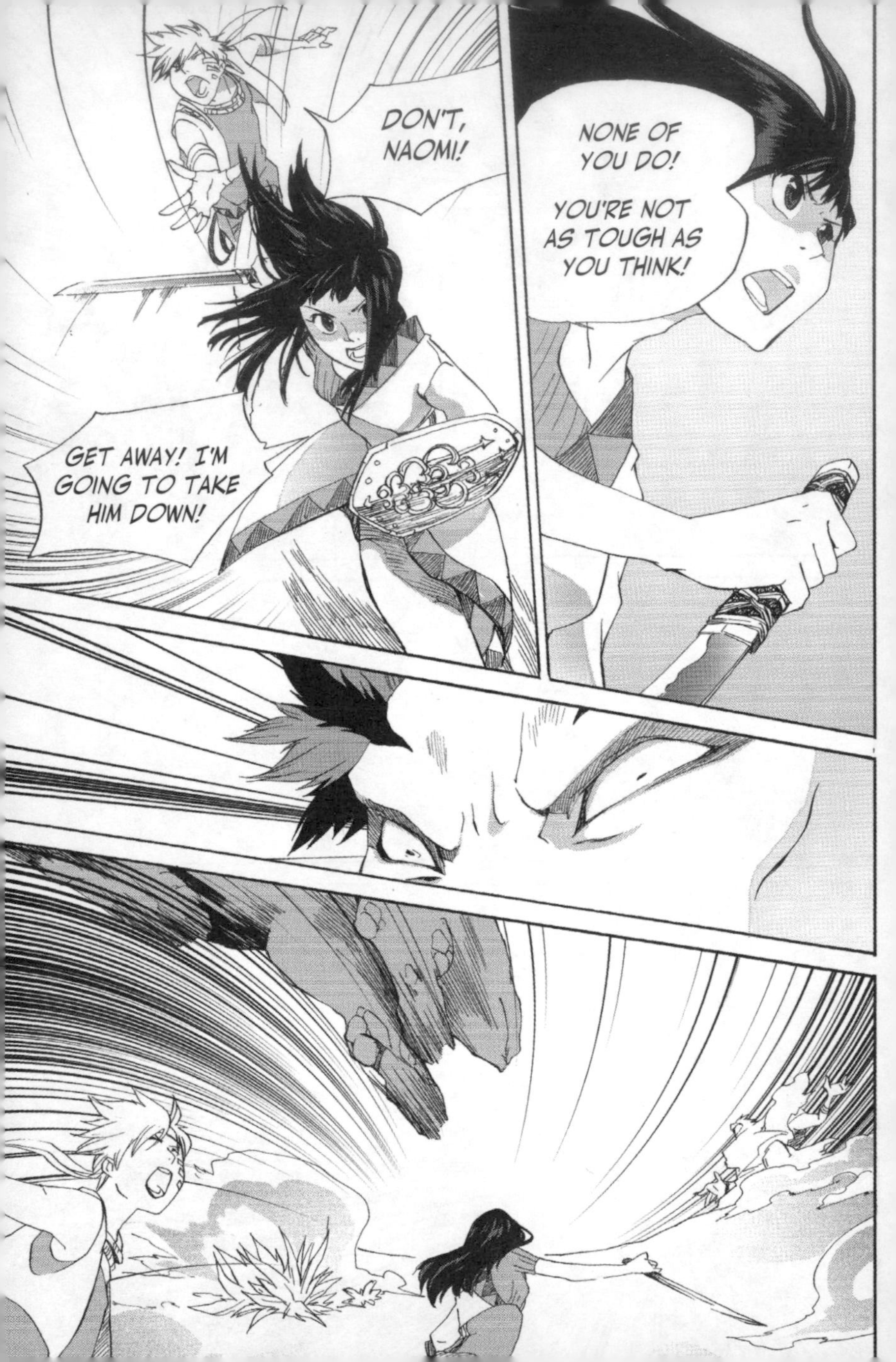
NONE OF YOU DO!
YOU'RE NOT AS TOUGH AS YOU THINK!
DON'T, NAOMI!
GET AWAY! I'M GOING TO TAKE HIM DOWN!

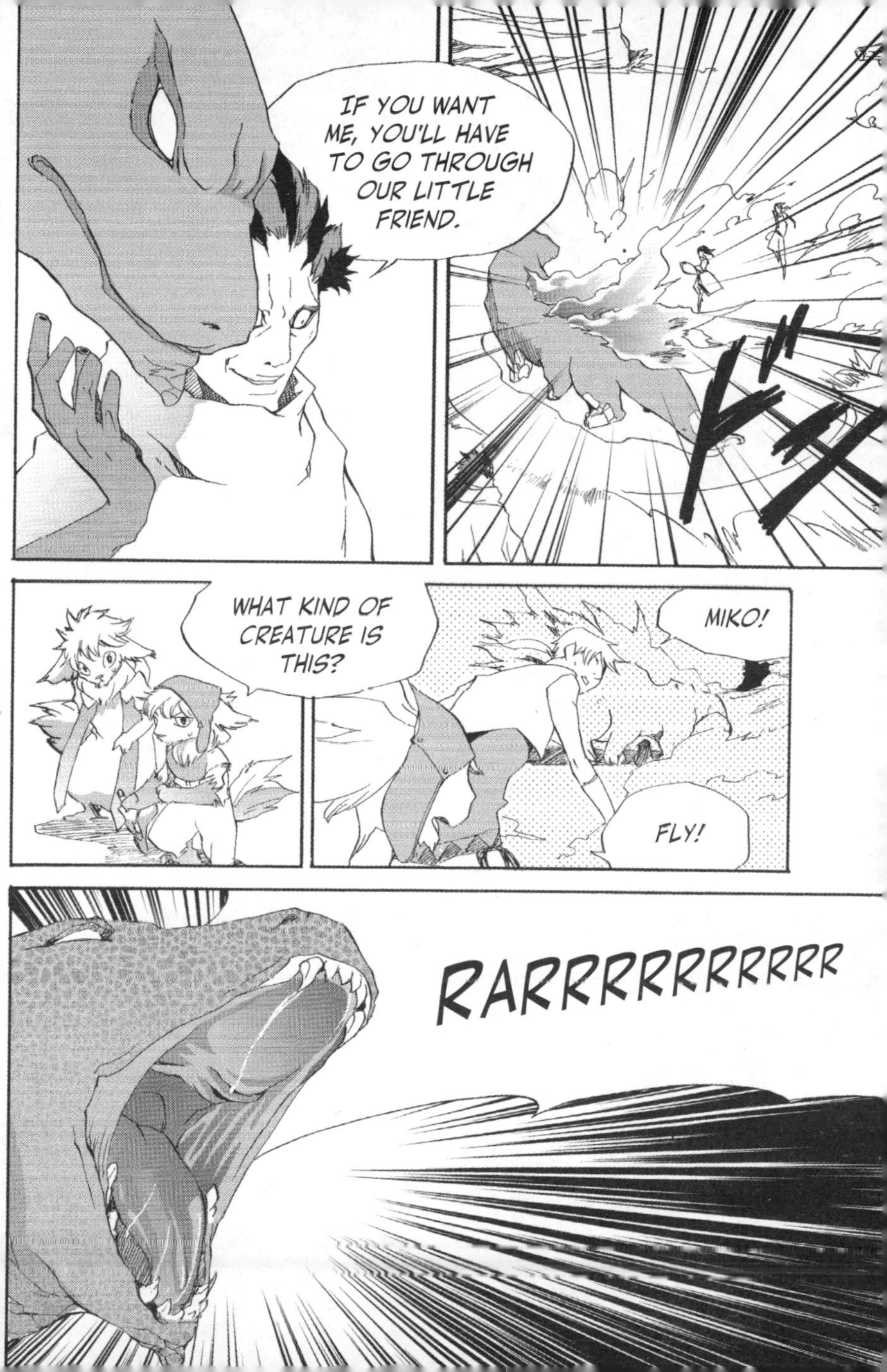
IF YOU WANT ME, YOU'LL HAVE TO GO THROUGH OUR LITTLE FRIEND.
WHAT KIND OF CREATURE IS THIS?
MIKO!
FLY!
RARRRRRRRRRR

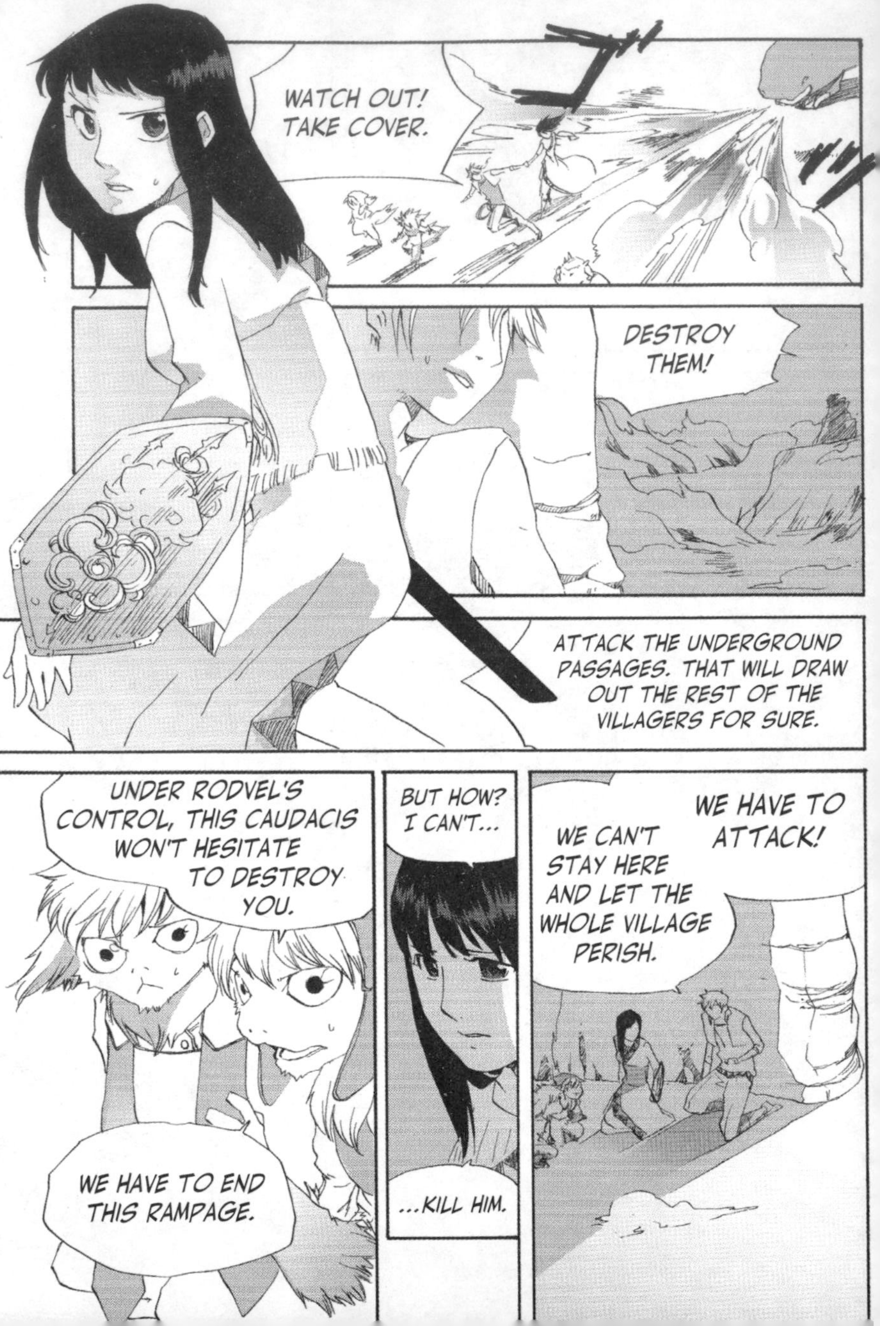
WATCH OUT! TAKE COVER.
DESTROY THEM!
ATTACK THE UNDERGROUND PASSAGES. THAT WILL DRAW OUT THE REST OF THE VILLAGERS FOR SURE.
UNDER RODVEL'S CONTROL, THIS CAUDACIS WON'T HESITATE TO DESTROY YOU.
WE HAVE TO END THIS RAMPAGE.
BUT HOW? I CAN'T...
...KILL HIM.
WE HAVE TO ATTACK!
WE CAN'T STAY HERE AND LET THE WHOLE VILLAGE PERISH.

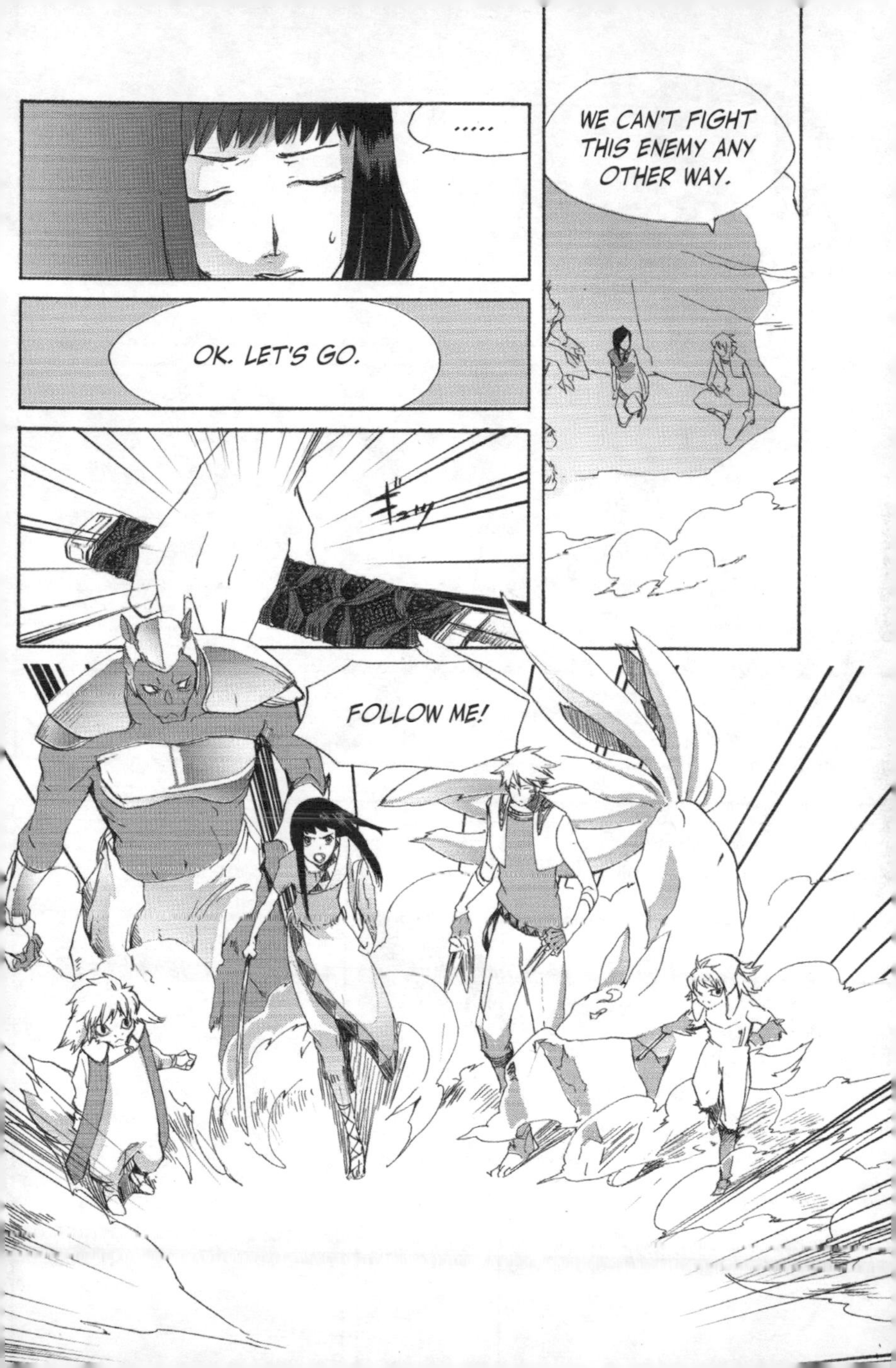
WE CAN'T FIGHT THIS ENEMY ANY OTHER WAY.
......
OK. LET'S GO.
FOLLOW ME!

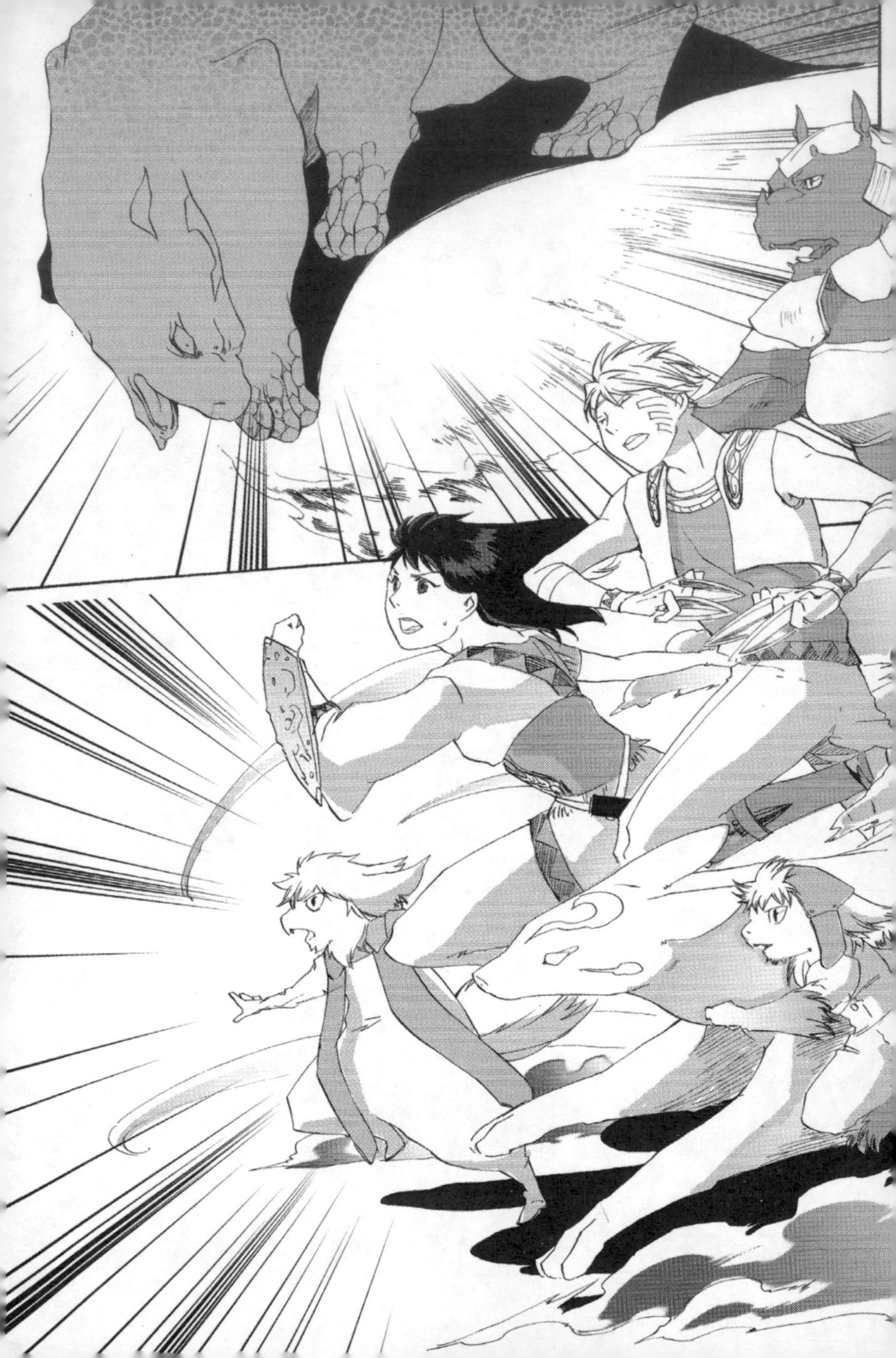

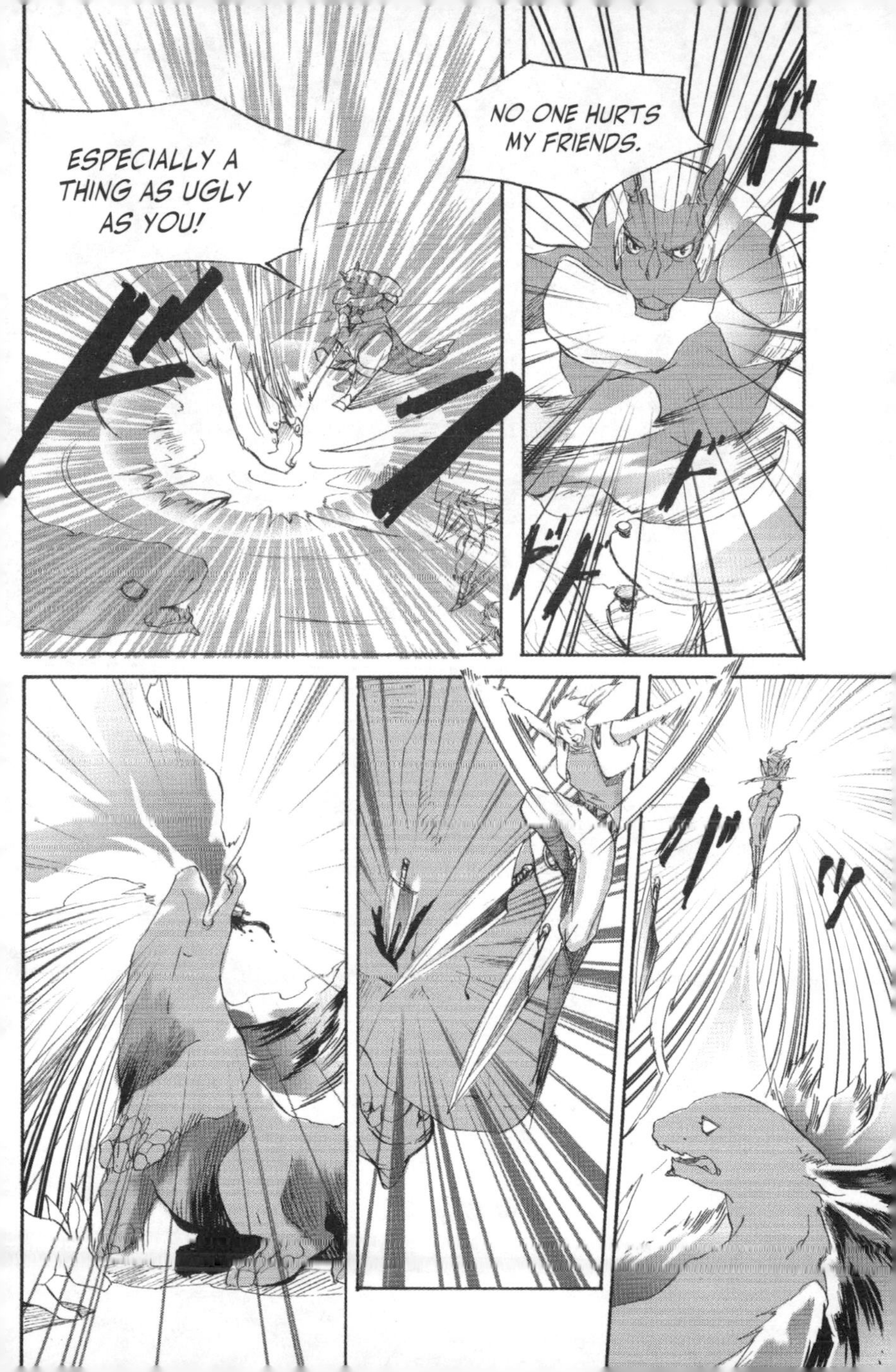
NO ONE HURTS MY FRIENDS.
ESPECIALLY A THING AS UGLY AS YOU!

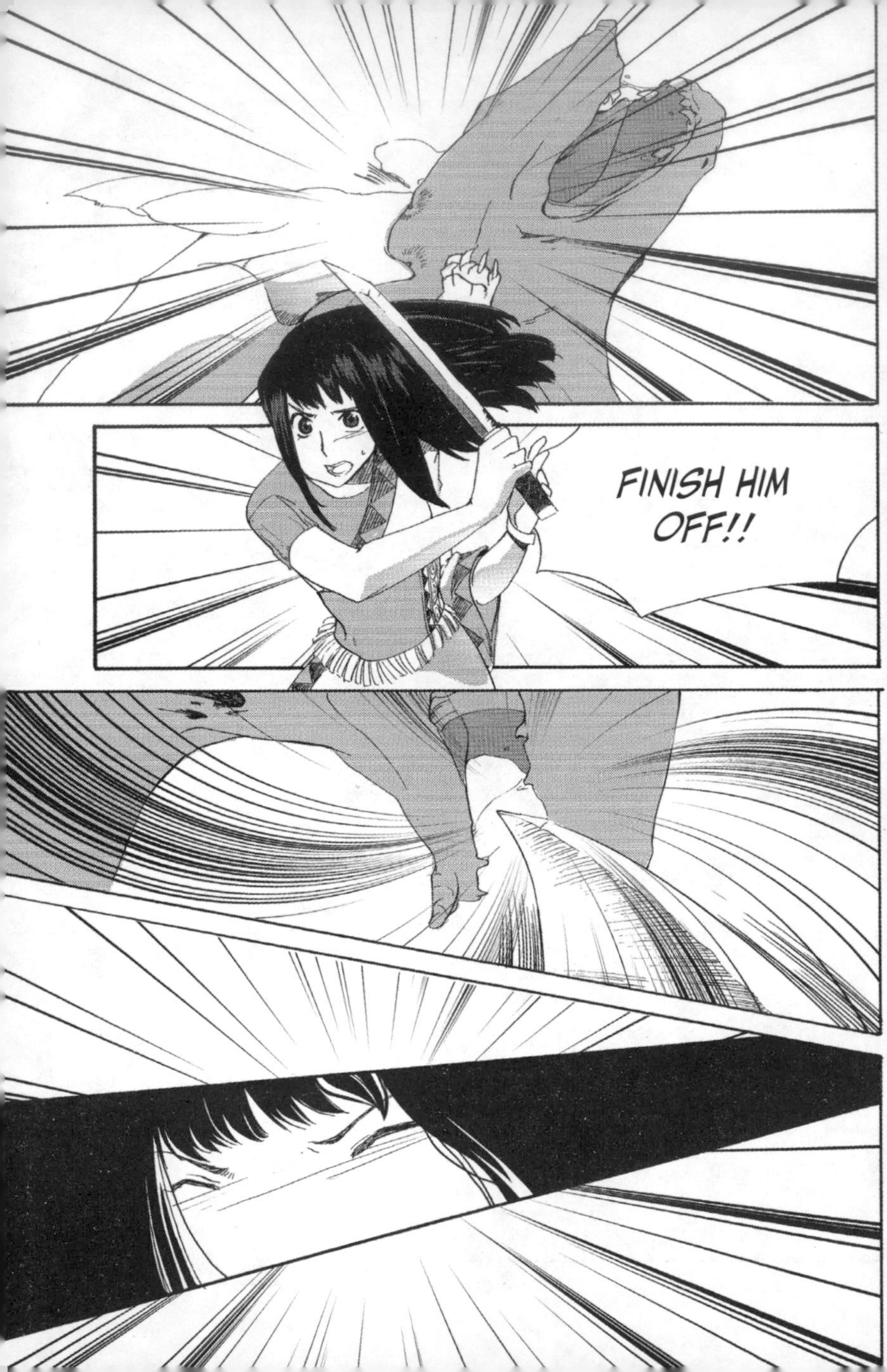
FINISH HIM OFF!!

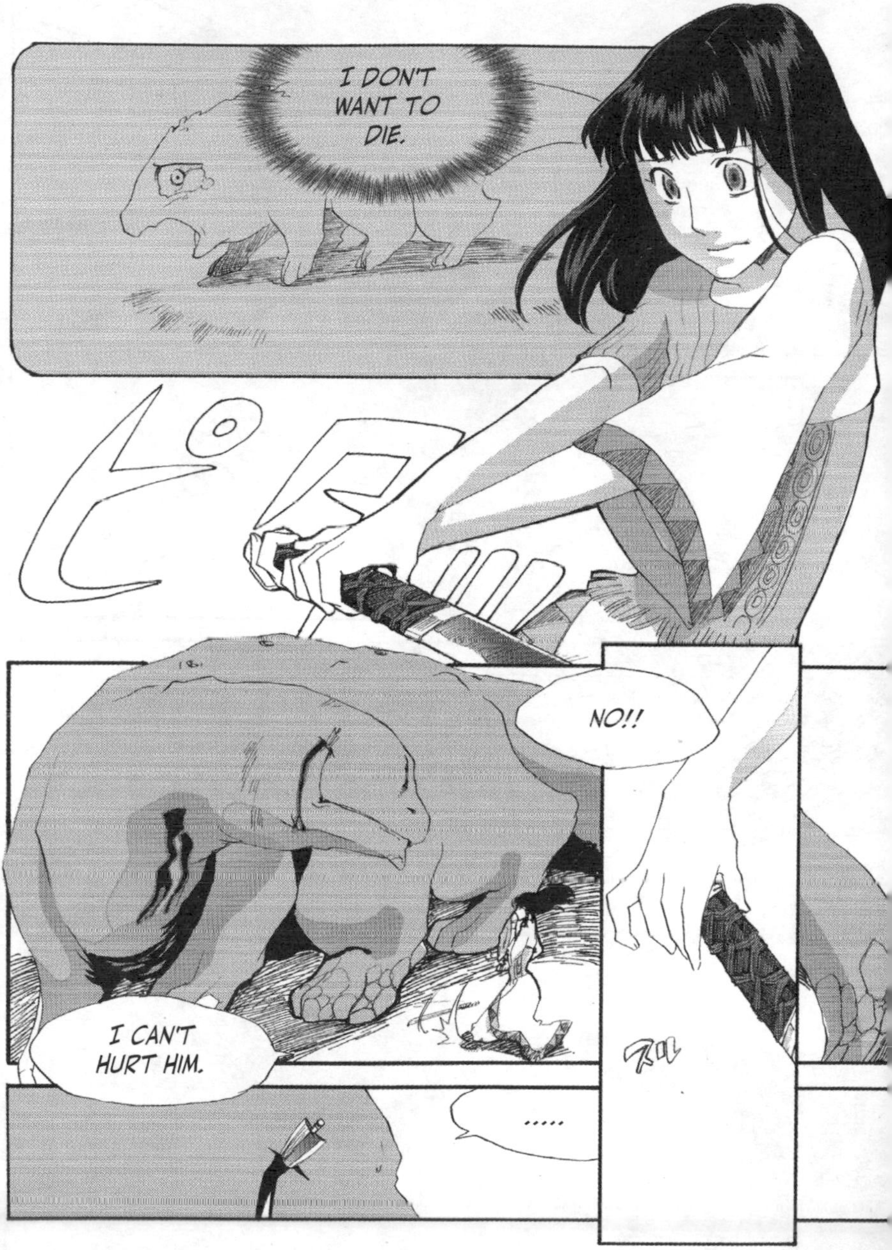
I DON'T WANT TO DIE.
ピョ
NO!!
I CAN'T HURT HIM.
スル
.....

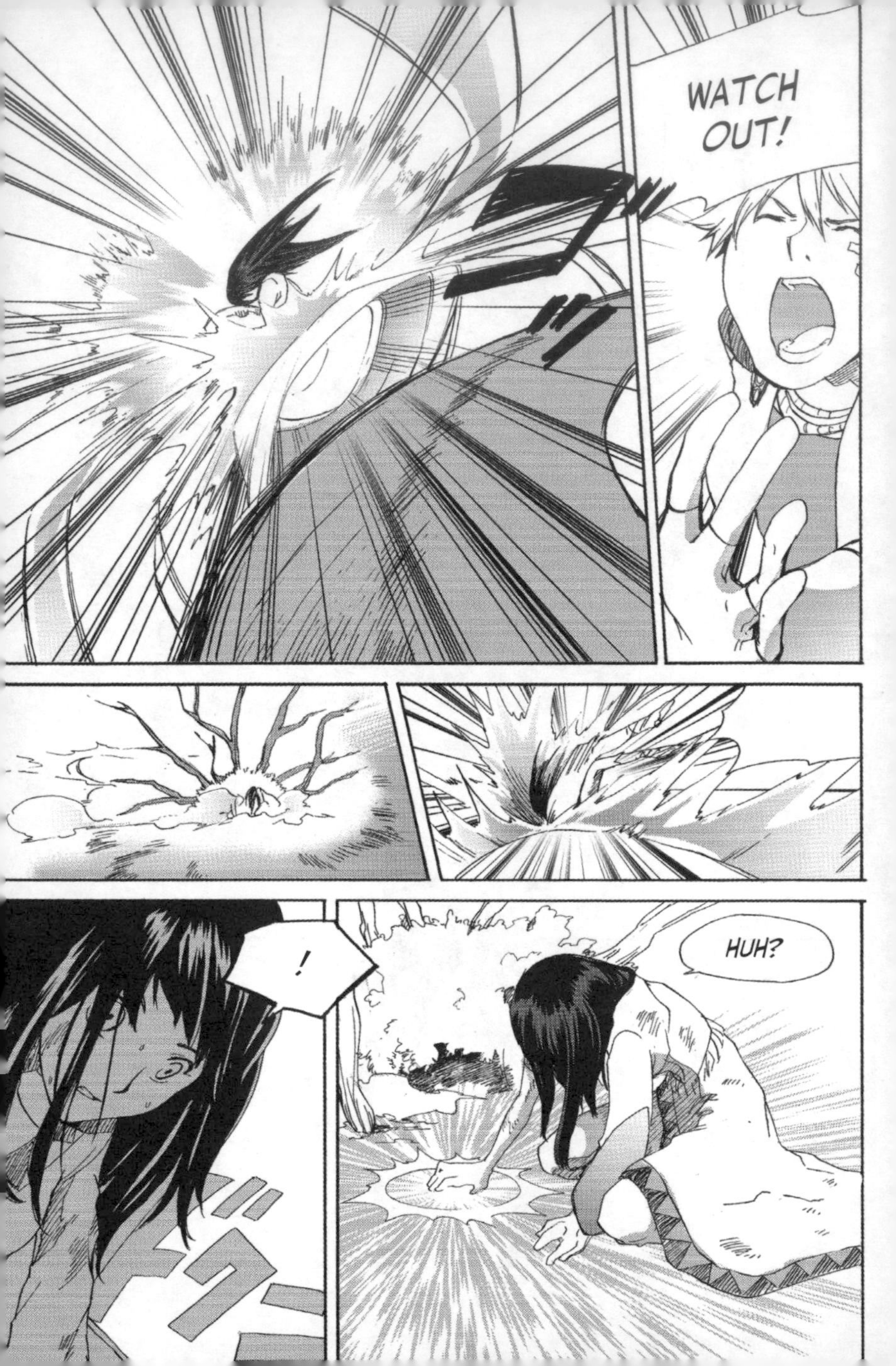
WATCH OUT!
!
HUH?

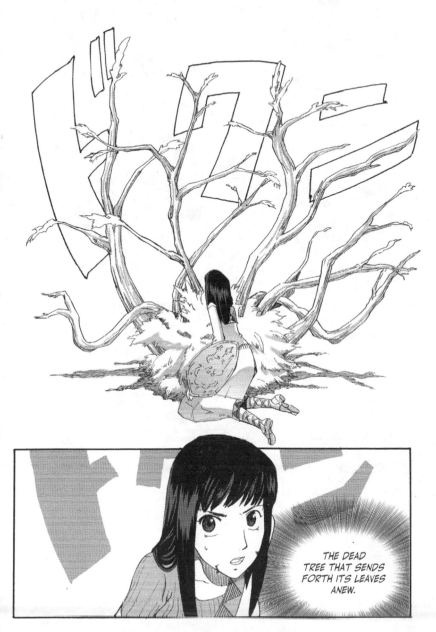

THE DEAD
TREE THAT SENDS
FORTH ITS LEAVES
ANEW.

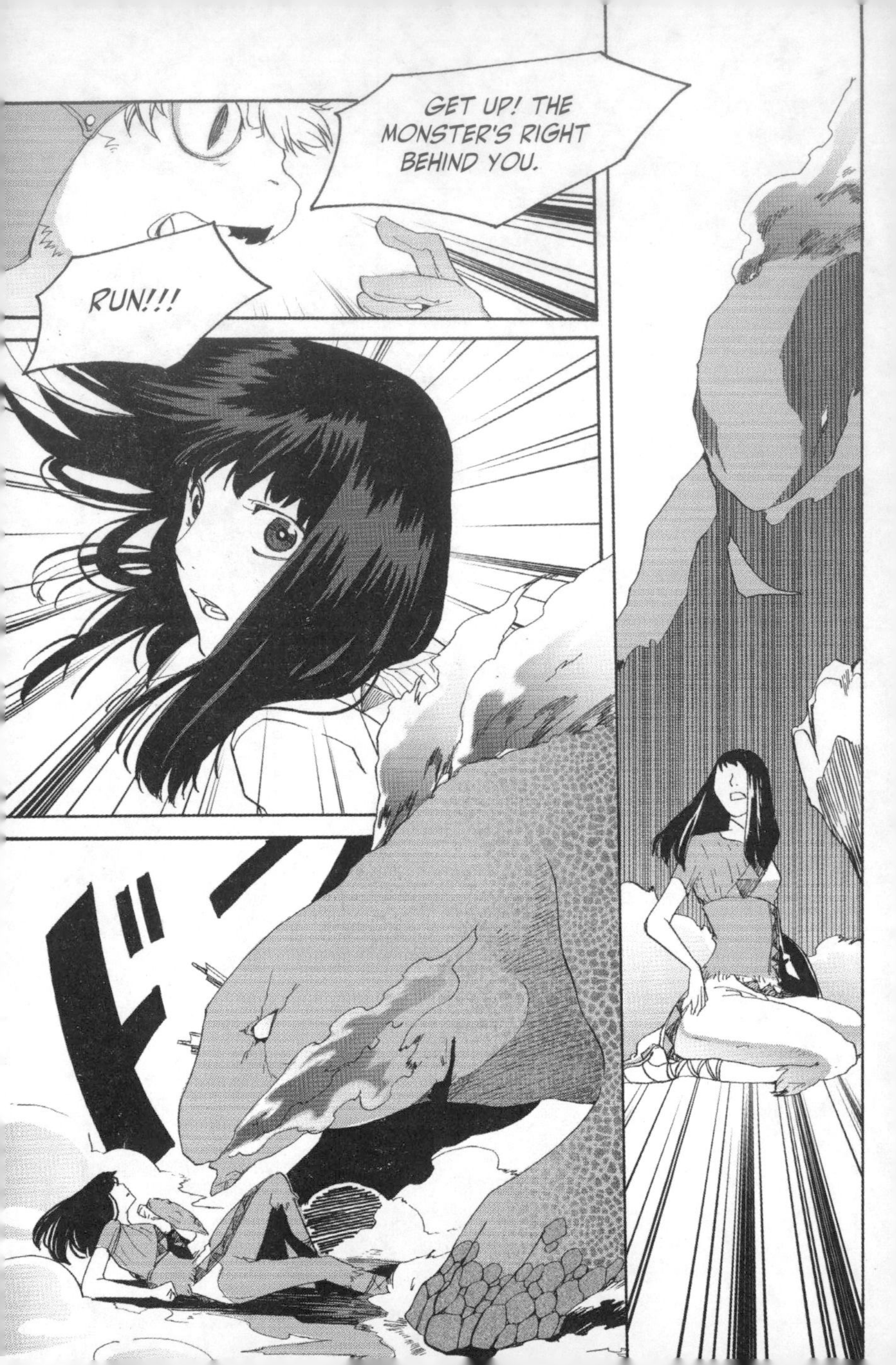
GET UP! THE MONSTER'S RIGHT BEHIND YOU.
RUN!!!

USE THE SHIELD!
YESSSSSS... YOU'RE DONE.
DESTROY HER!
HA HA HA HA HA HA HA
IT CAN'T BE.

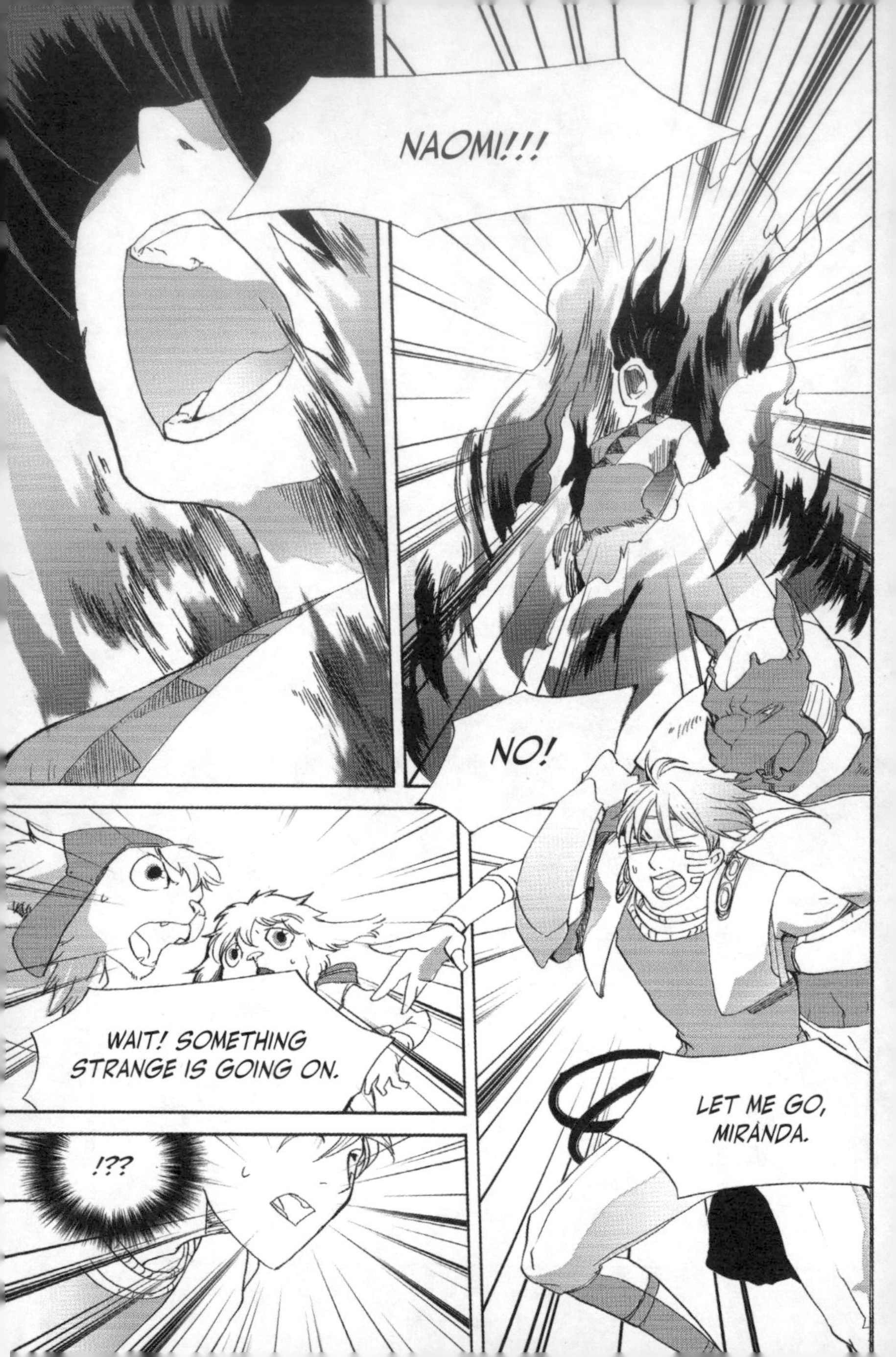
NAOMI!!!
NO!
WAIT! SOMETHING STRANGE IS GOING ON.
LET ME GO, MIRANDA.
!??

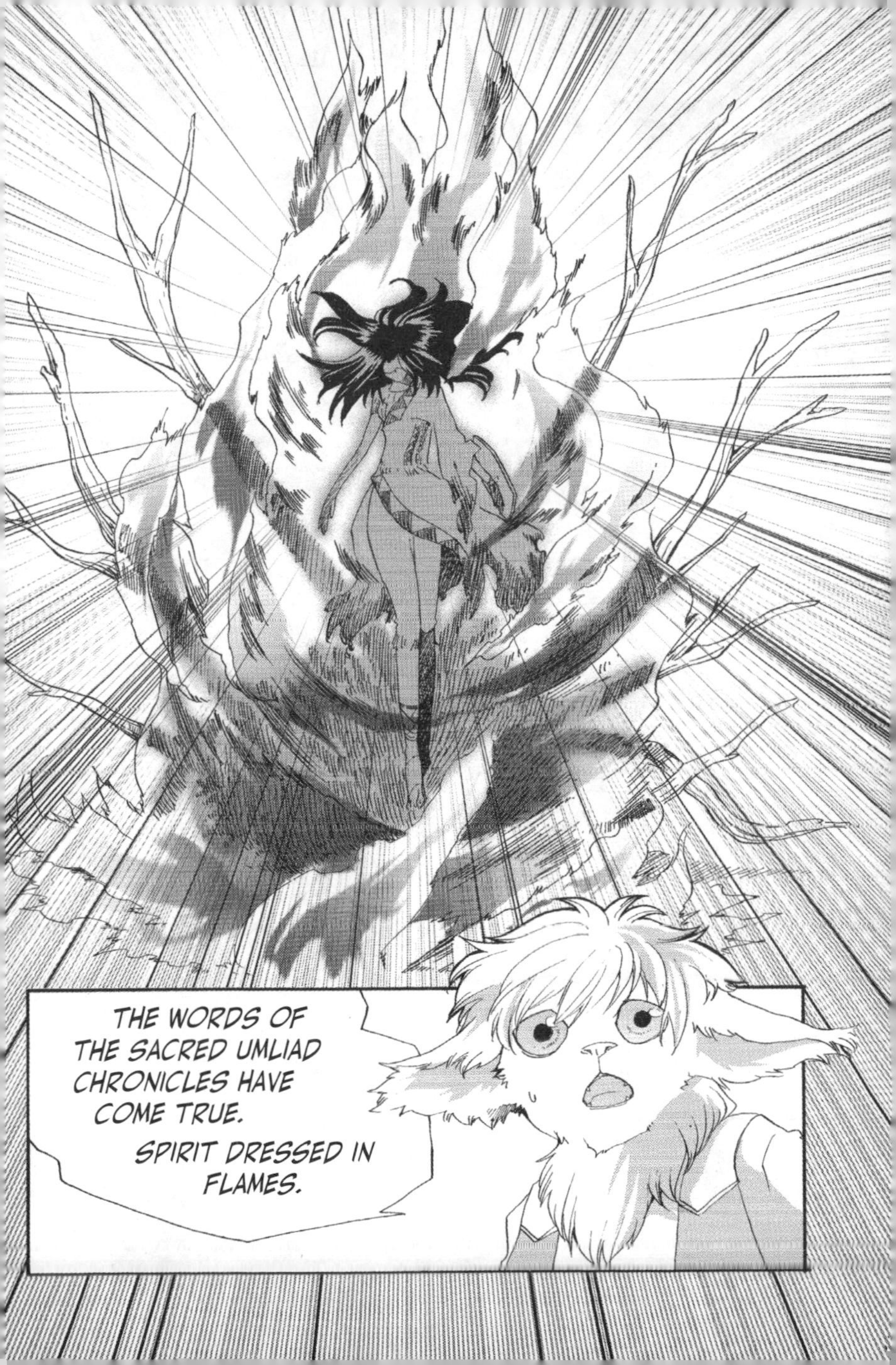
THE WORDS OF THE SACRED UMLIAD CHRONICLES HAVE COME TRUE.
SPIRIT DRESSED IN FLAMES.

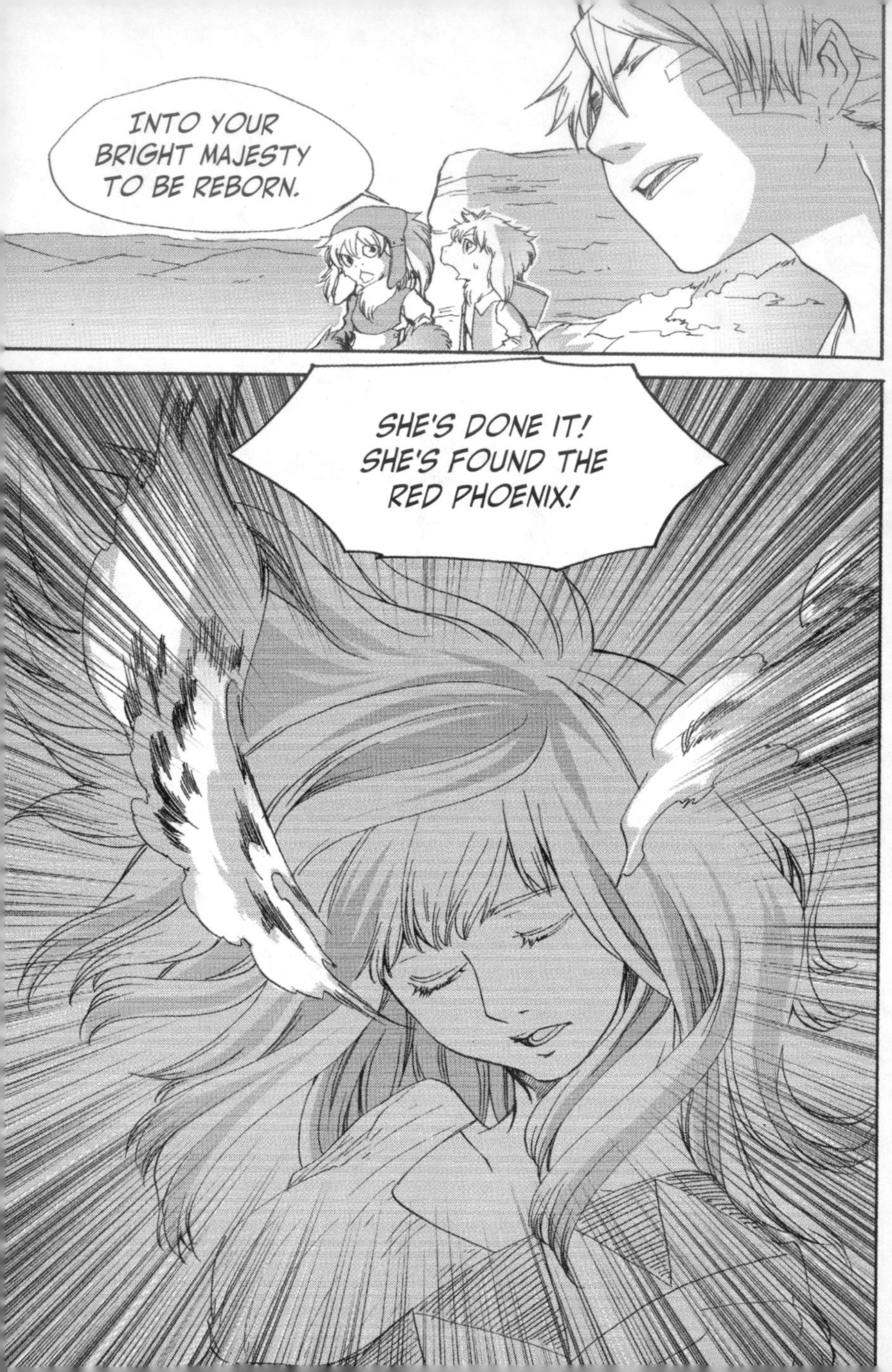
INTO YOUR BRIGHT MAJESTY TO BE REBORN.
SHE'S DONE IT! SHE'S FOUND THE RED PHOENIX!

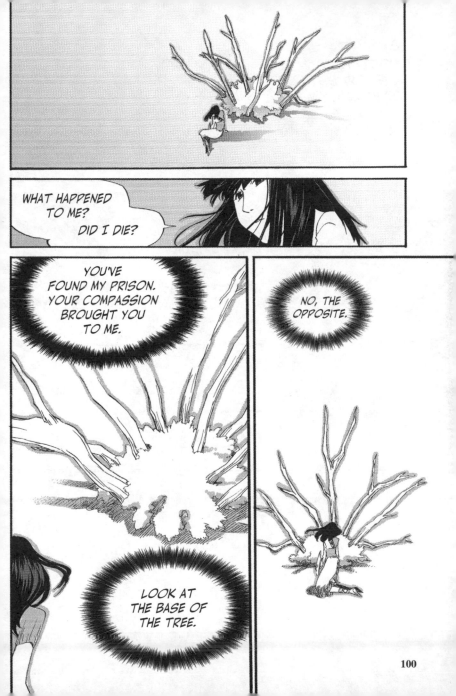

WHAT HAPPENED TO ME? DID I DIE?

YOU'VE FOUND MY PRISON. YOUR COMPASSION BROUGHT YOU TO ME.

NO, THE OPPOSITE.

LOOK AT THE BASE OF THE TREE.

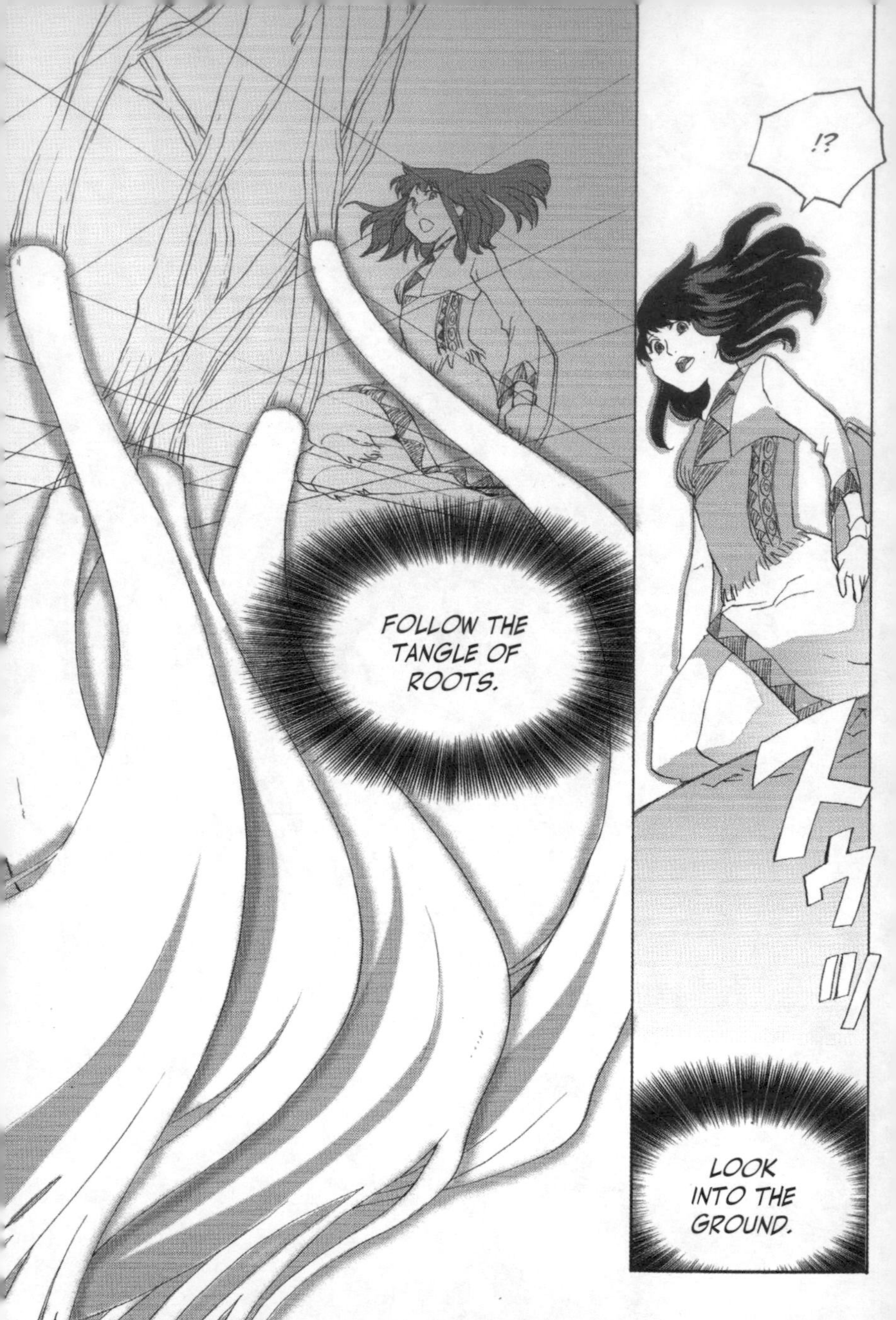
!?
FOLLOW THE TANGLE OF ROOTS.
LOOK INTO THE GROUND.

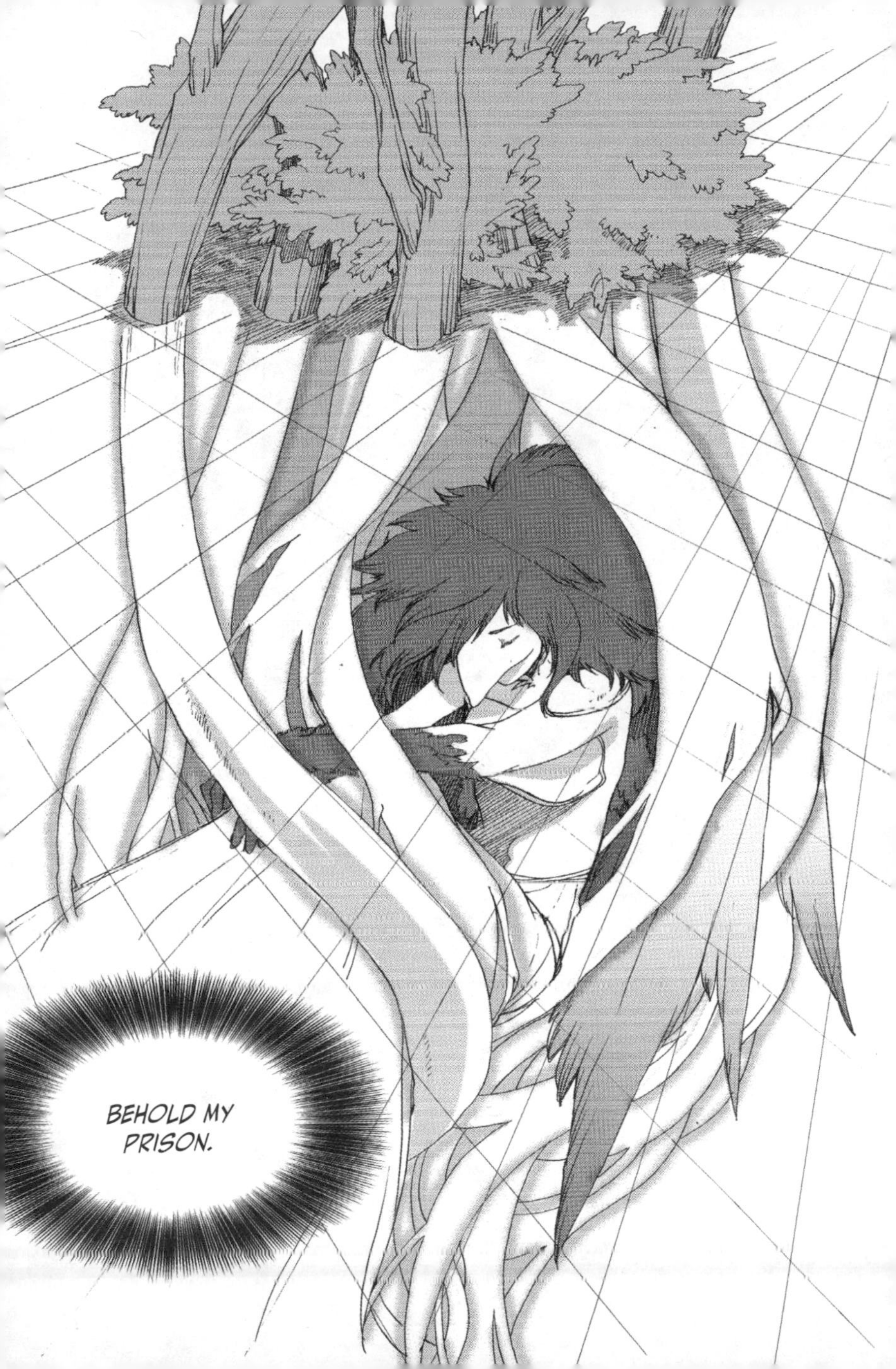
BEHOLD MY PRISON.

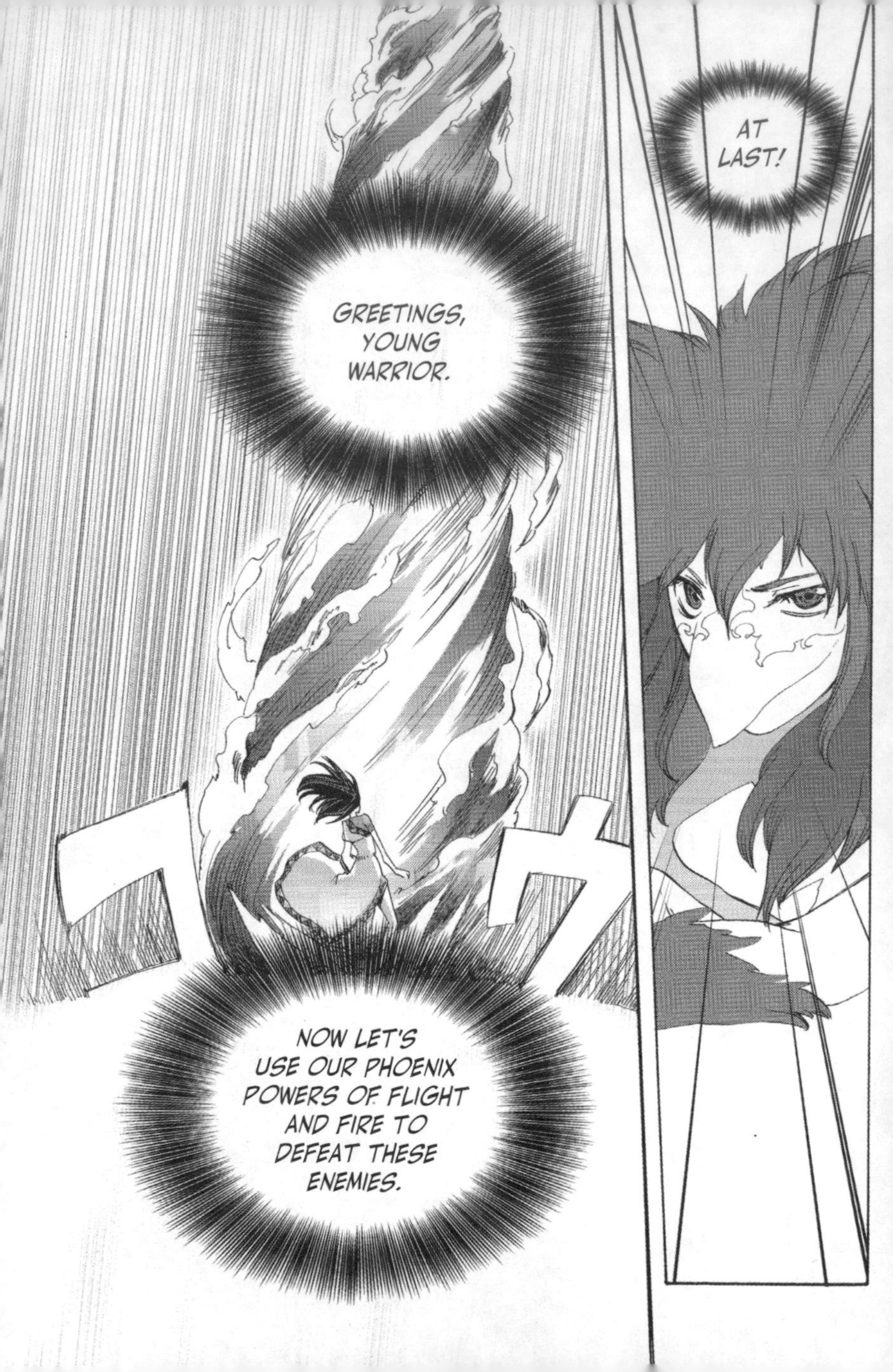
AT LAST!
GREETINGS, YOUNG WARRIOR.
NOW LET'S USE OUR PHOENIX POWERS OF FLIGHT AND FIRE TO DEFEAT THESE ENEMIES.

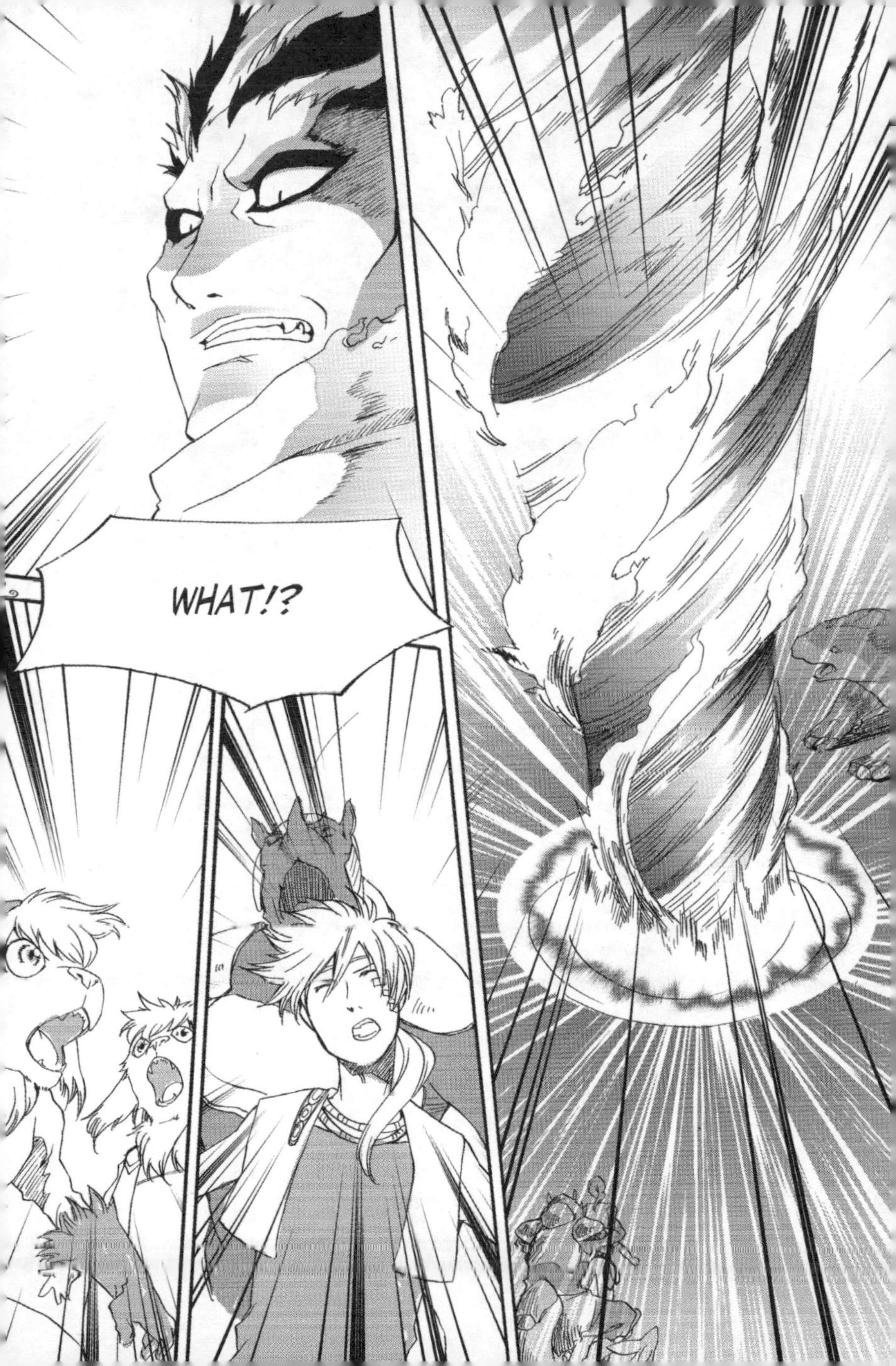
WHAT!?

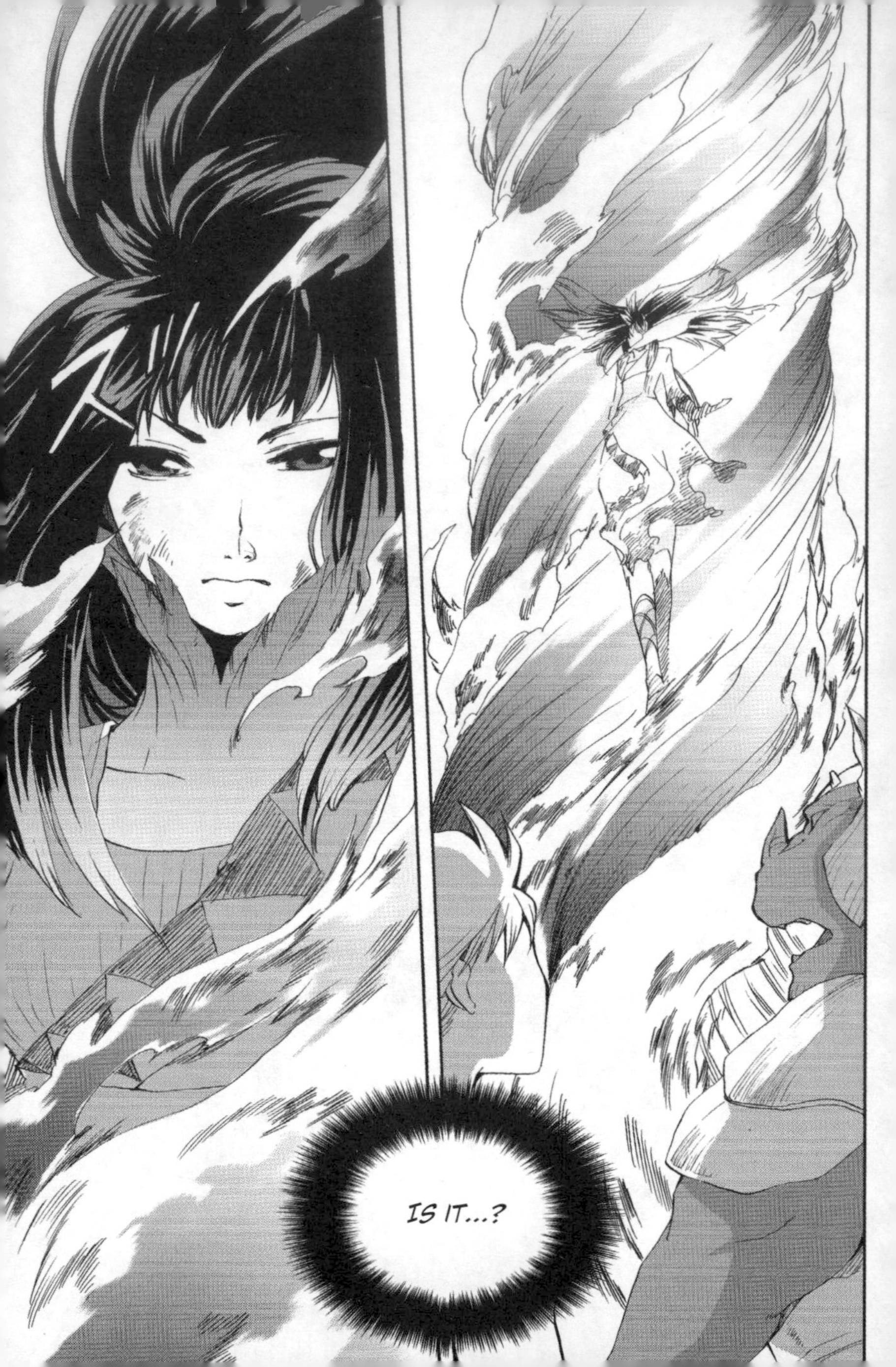
IS IT...?

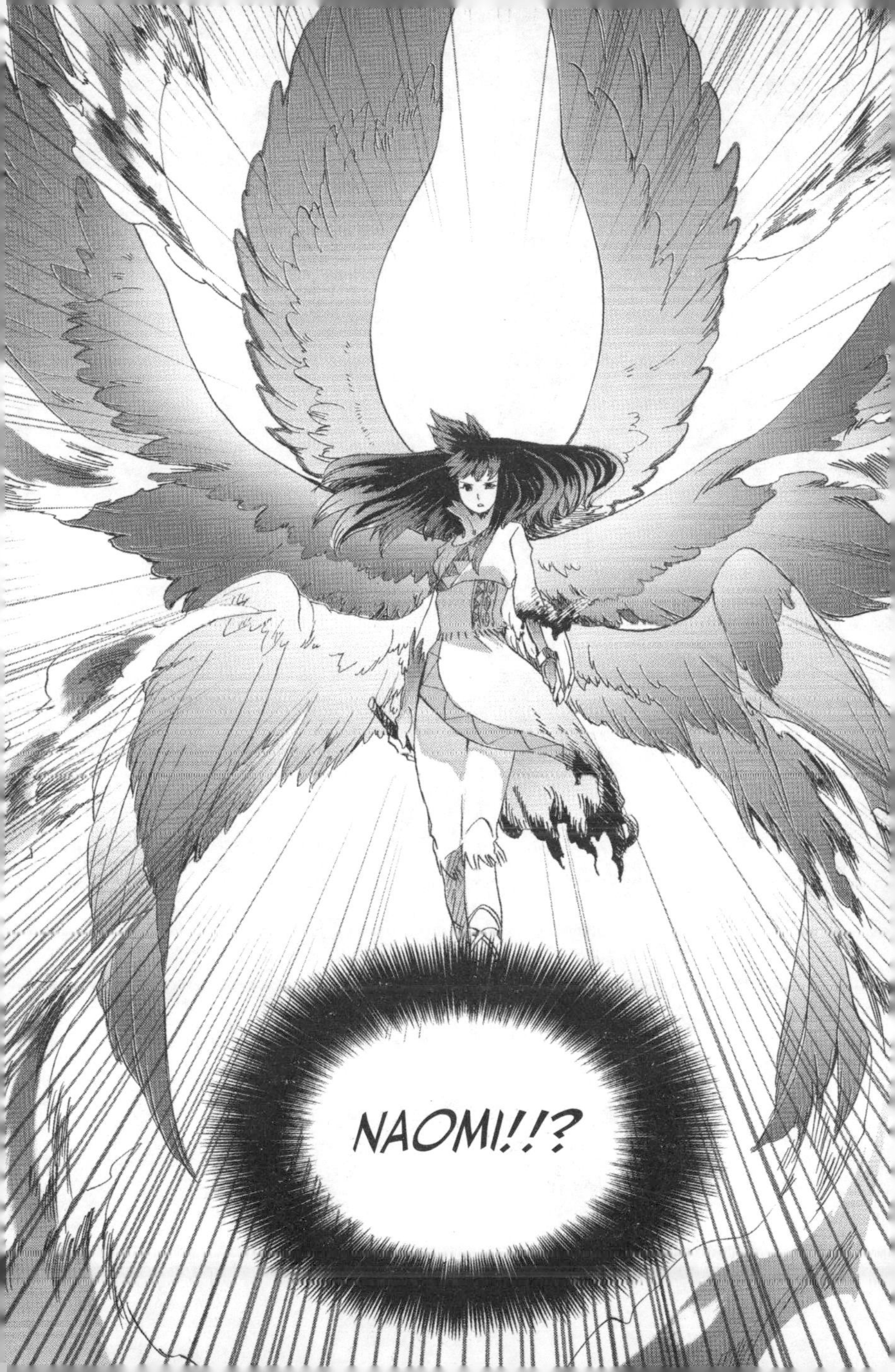
NAOMI!!?

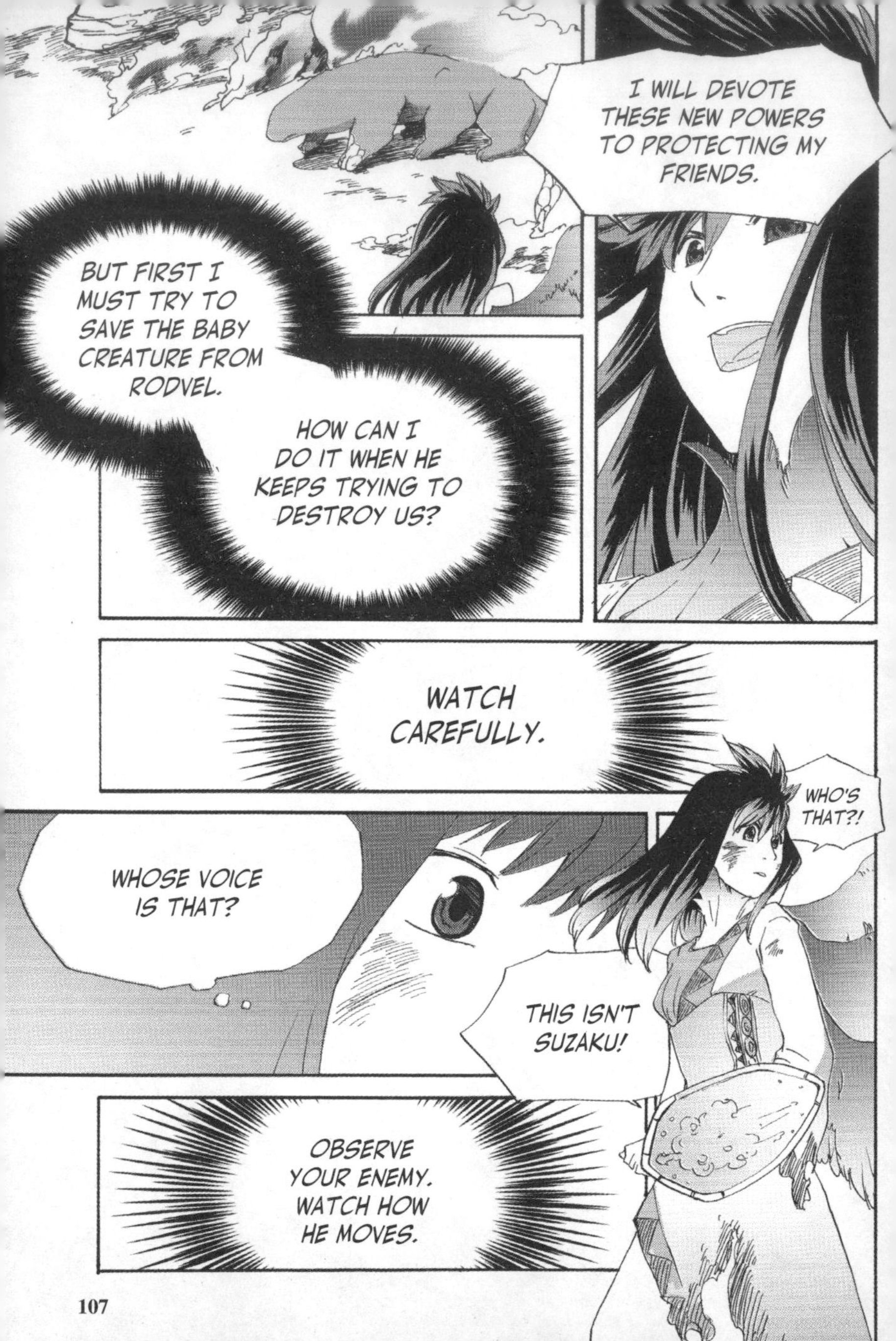
I WILL DEVOTE THESE NEW POWERS TO PROTECTING MY FRIENDS.
BUT FIRST I MUST TRY TO SAVE THE BABY CREATURE FROM RODVEL.
HOW CAN I DO IT WHEN HE KEEPS TRYING TO DESTROY US?
WATCH CAREFULLY.
WHO'S THAT?!
WHOSE VOICE IS THAT?
THIS ISN'T SUZAKU!
OBSERVE YOUR ENEMY. WATCH HOW HE MOVES.

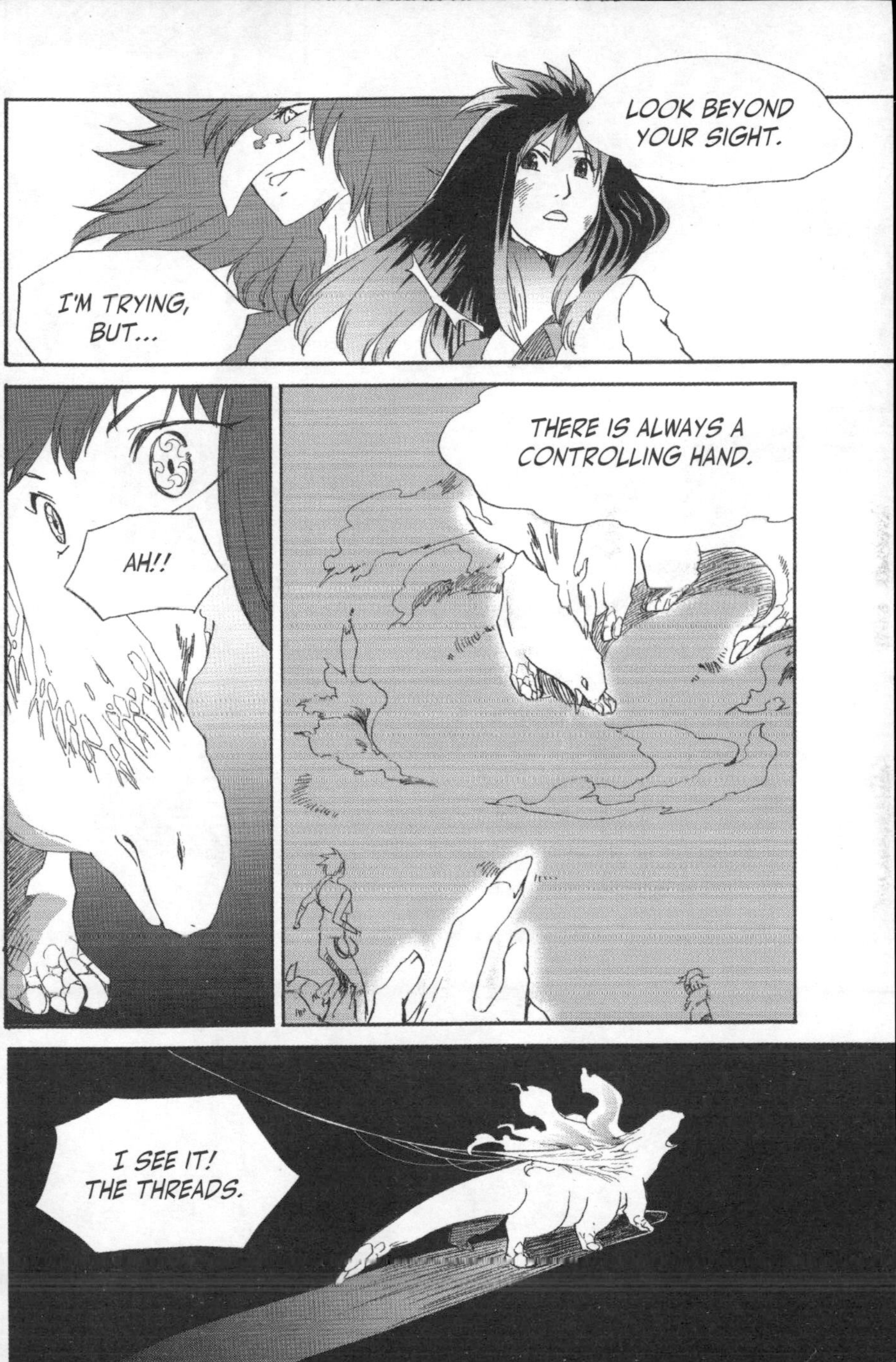
LOOK BEYOND YOUR SIGHT.
I'M TRYING, BUT...
AH!!
THERE IS ALWAYS A CONTROLLING HAND.
I SEE IT! THE THREADS.

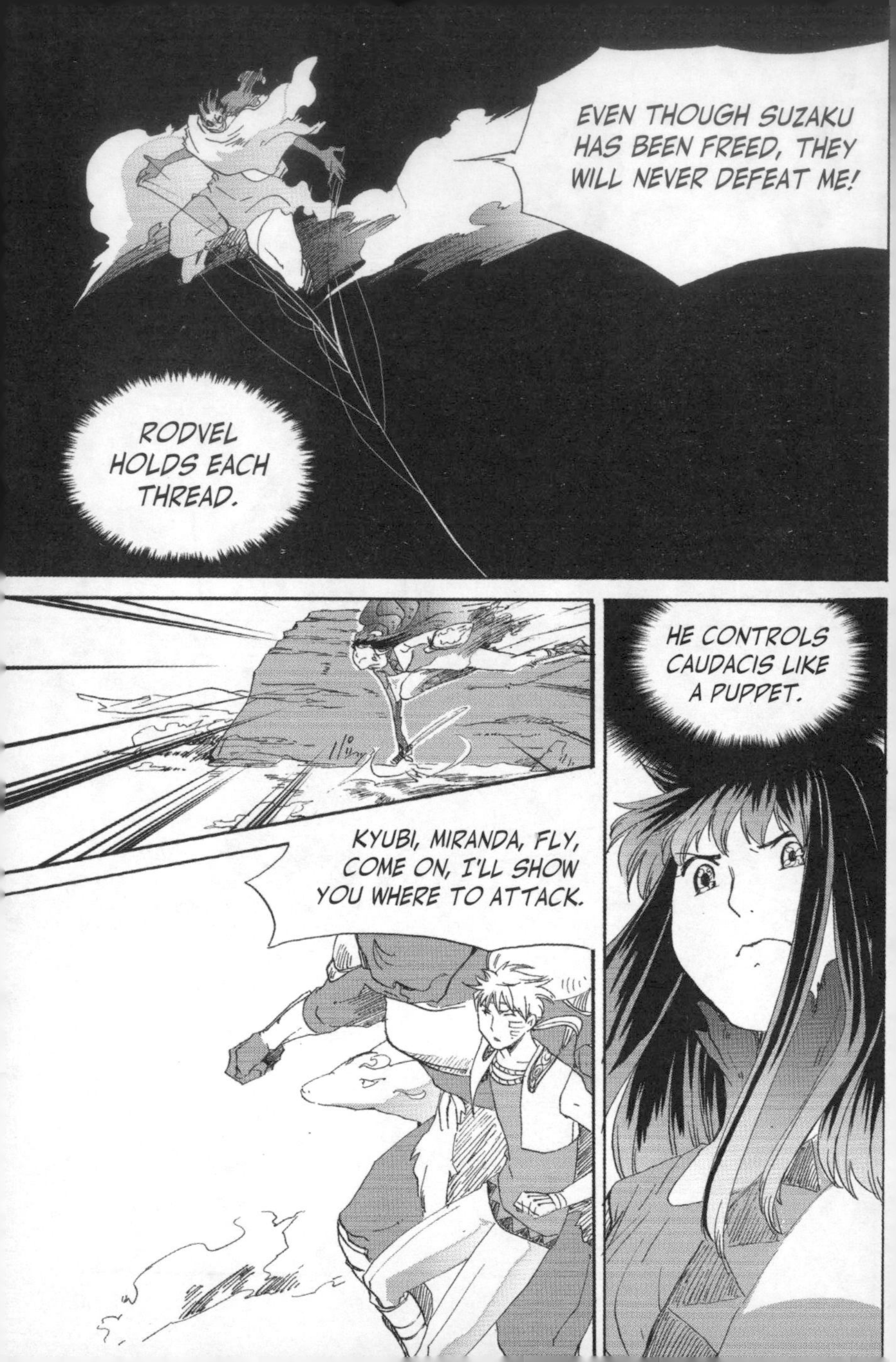
EVEN THOUGH SUZAKU HAS BEEN FREED, THEY WILL NEVER DEFEAT ME!
RODVEL HOLDS EACH THREAD.
KYUBI, MIRANDA, FLY, COME ON, I'LL SHOW YOU WHERE TO ATTACK.
HE CONTROLS CAUDACIS LIKE A PUPPET.

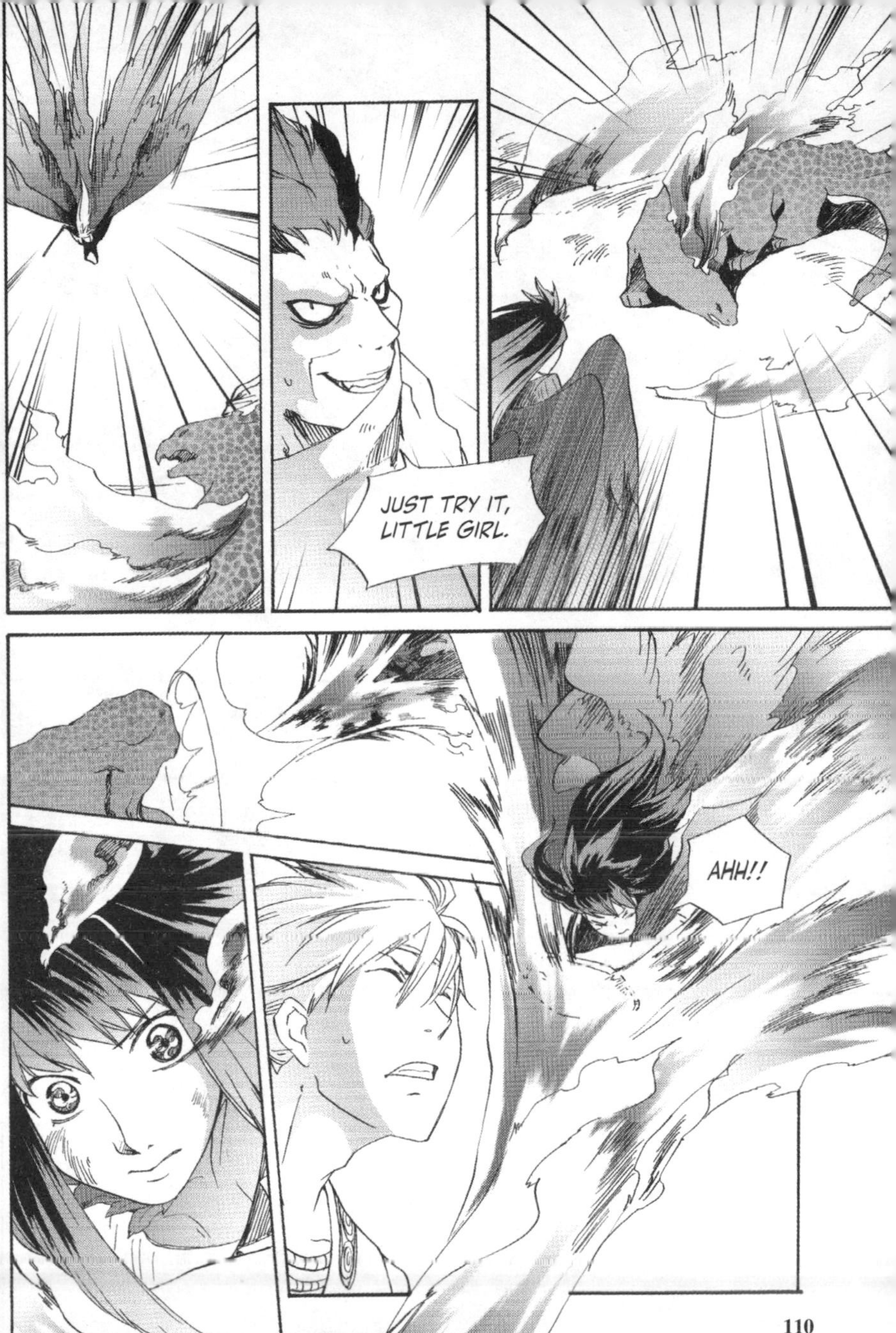
JUST TRY IT, LITTLE GIRL.
AHH!!

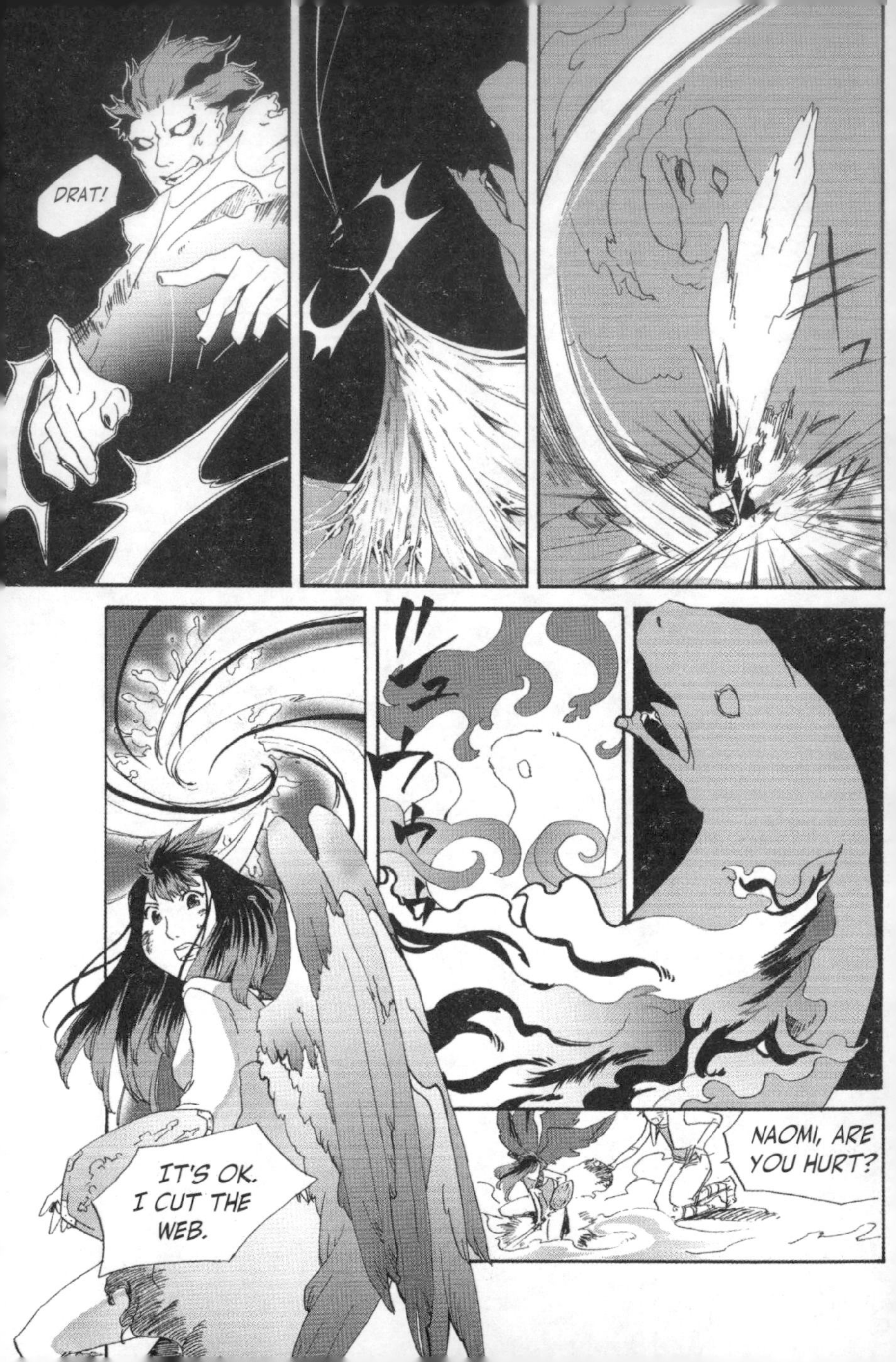
DRAT!
NAOMI, ARE YOU HURT?
IT'S OK. I CUT THE WEB.

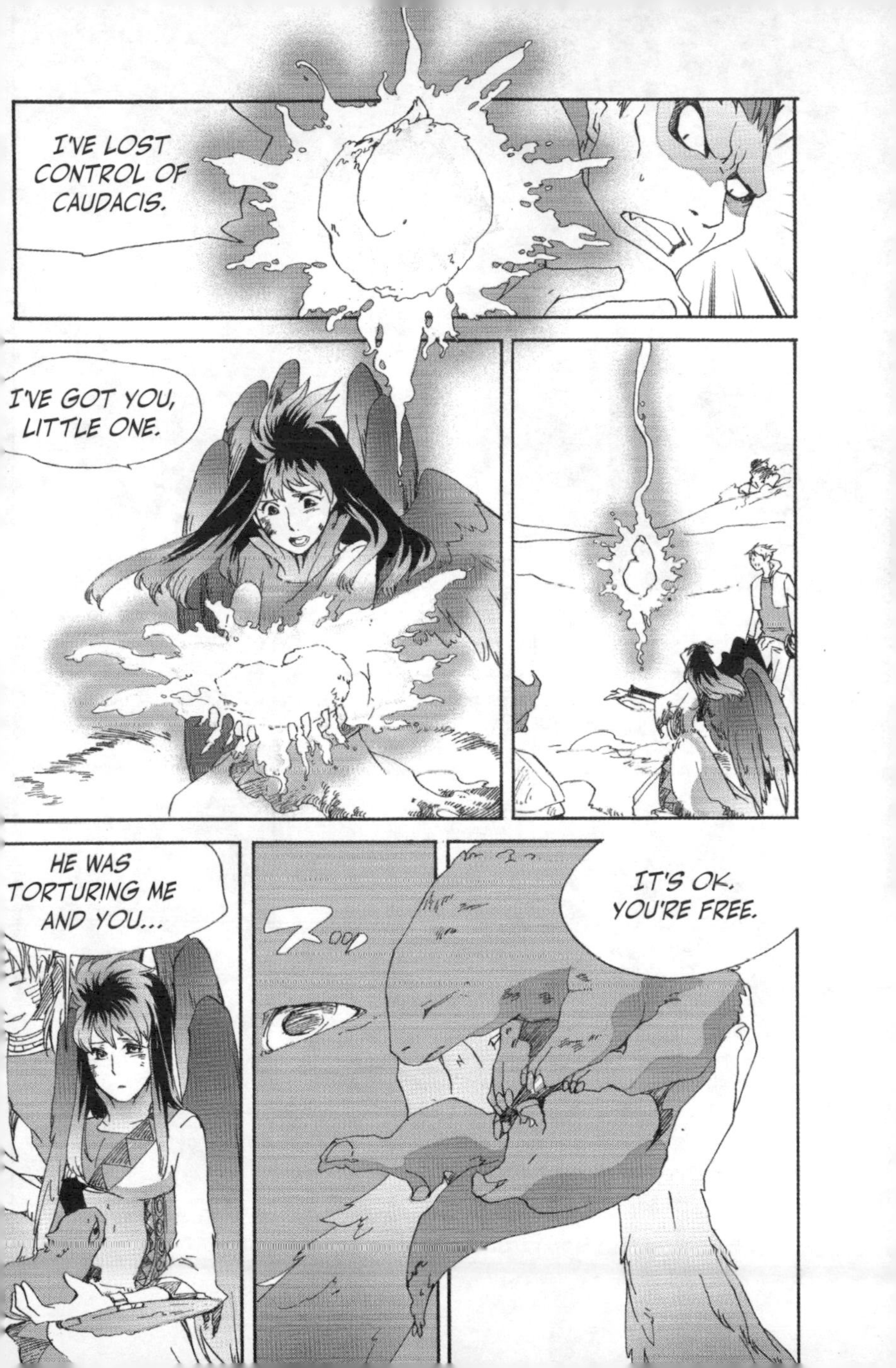
I'VE LOST CONTROL OF CAUDACIS.
I'VE GOT YOU, LITTLE ONE.
HE WAS TORTURING ME AND YOU...
ZOOP
IT'S OK. YOU'RE FREE.

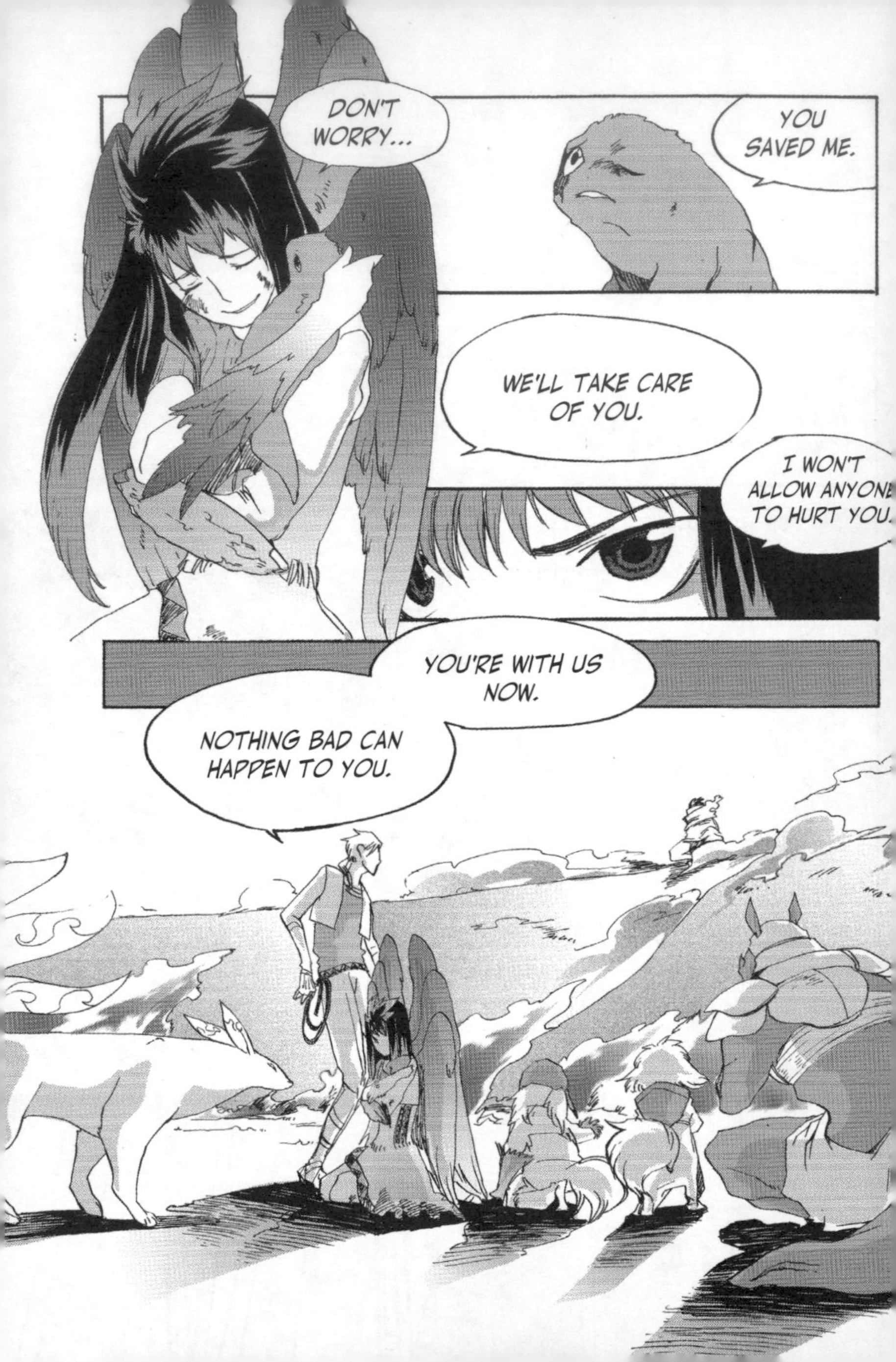
YOU SAVED ME.
DON'T WORRY...
WE'LL TAKE CARE OF YOU.
I WON'T ALLOW ANYONE TO HURT YOU.
YOU'RE WITH US NOW.
NOTHING BAD CAN HAPPEN TO YOU.

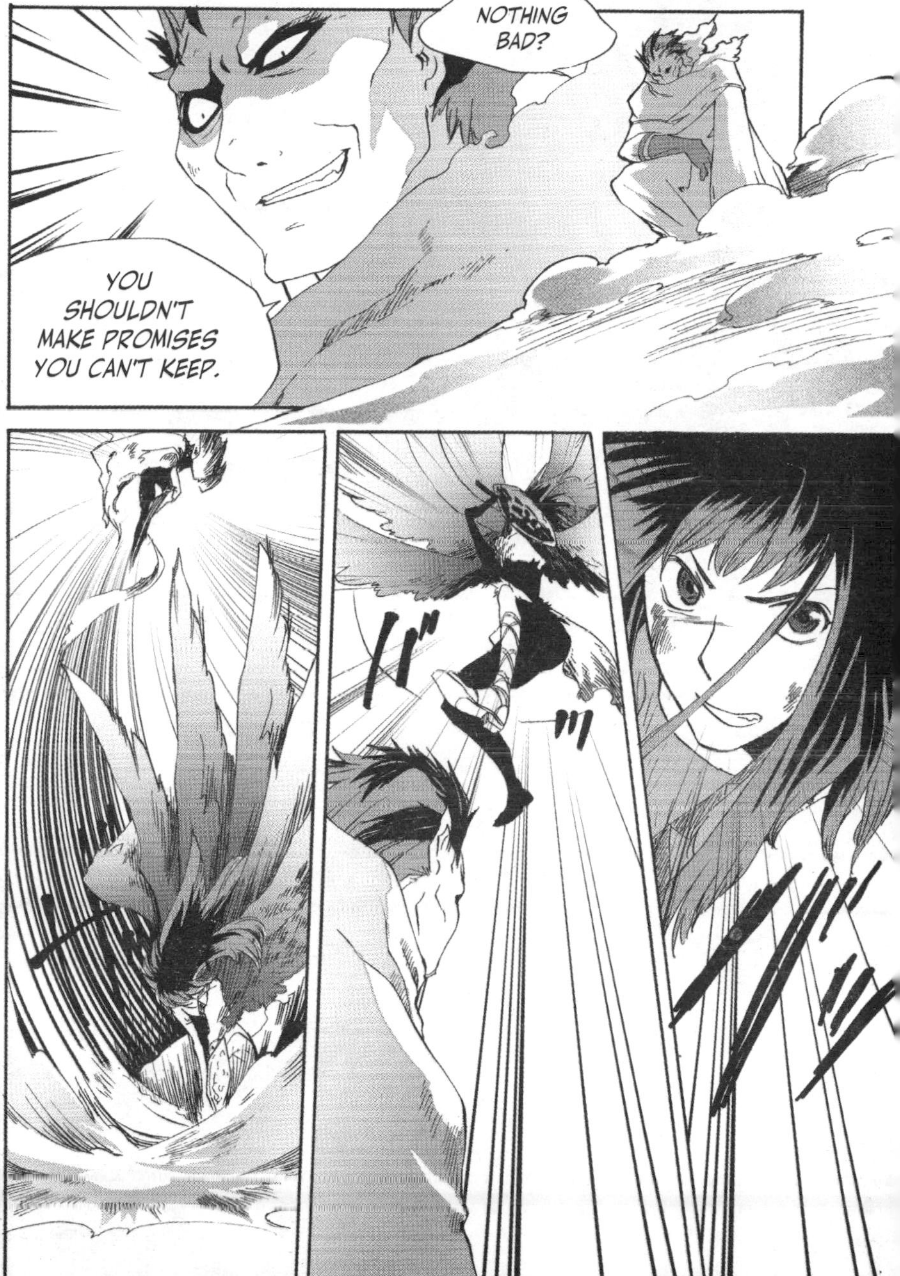
NOTHING BAD?
YOU SHOULDN'T MAKE PROMISES YOU CAN'T KEEP.

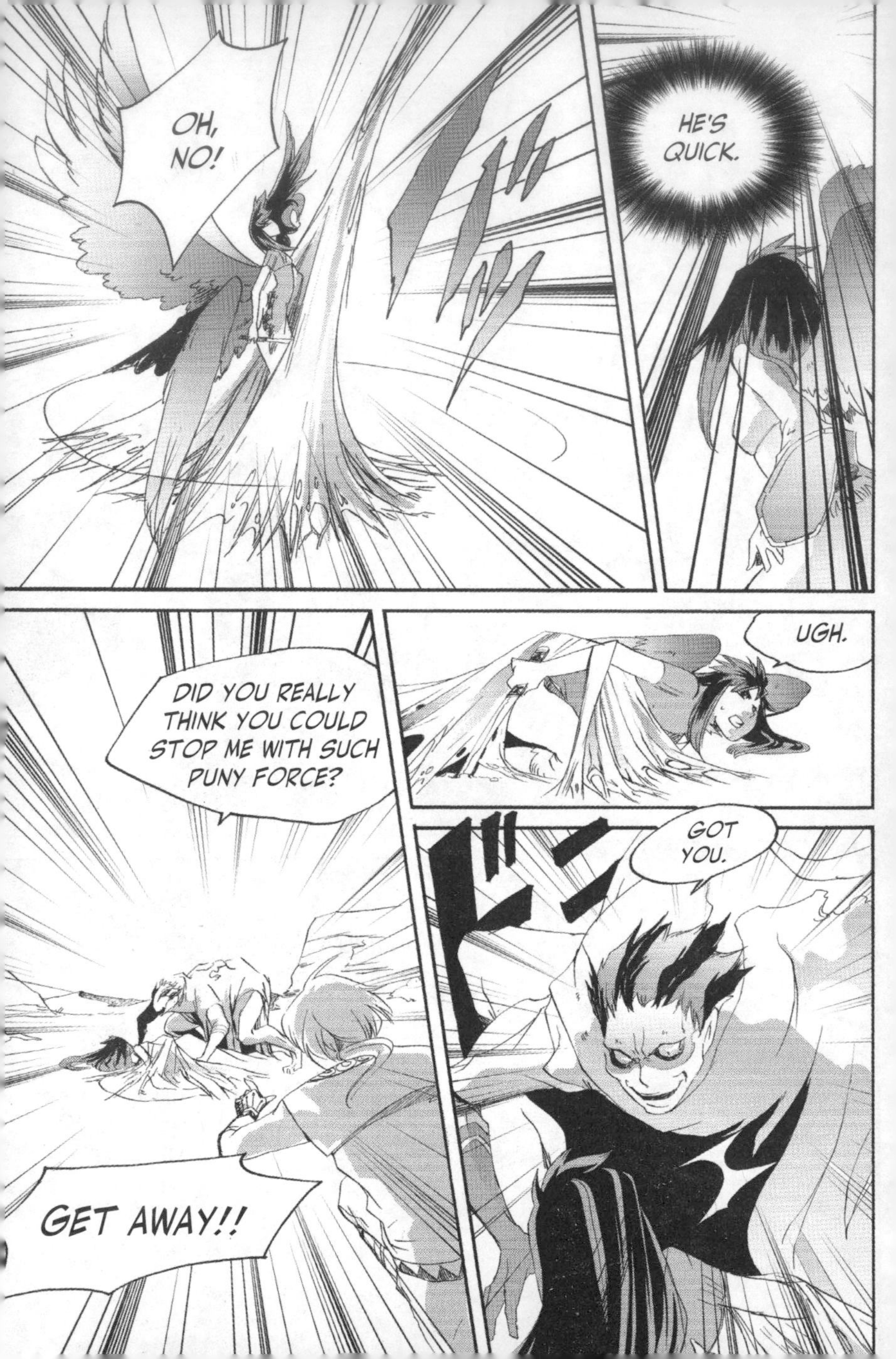
OH, NO!
HE'S QUICK.
DID YOU REALLY THINK YOU COULD STOP ME WITH SUCH PUNY FORCE?
UGH.
ドン
GOT YOU.
GET AWAY!!

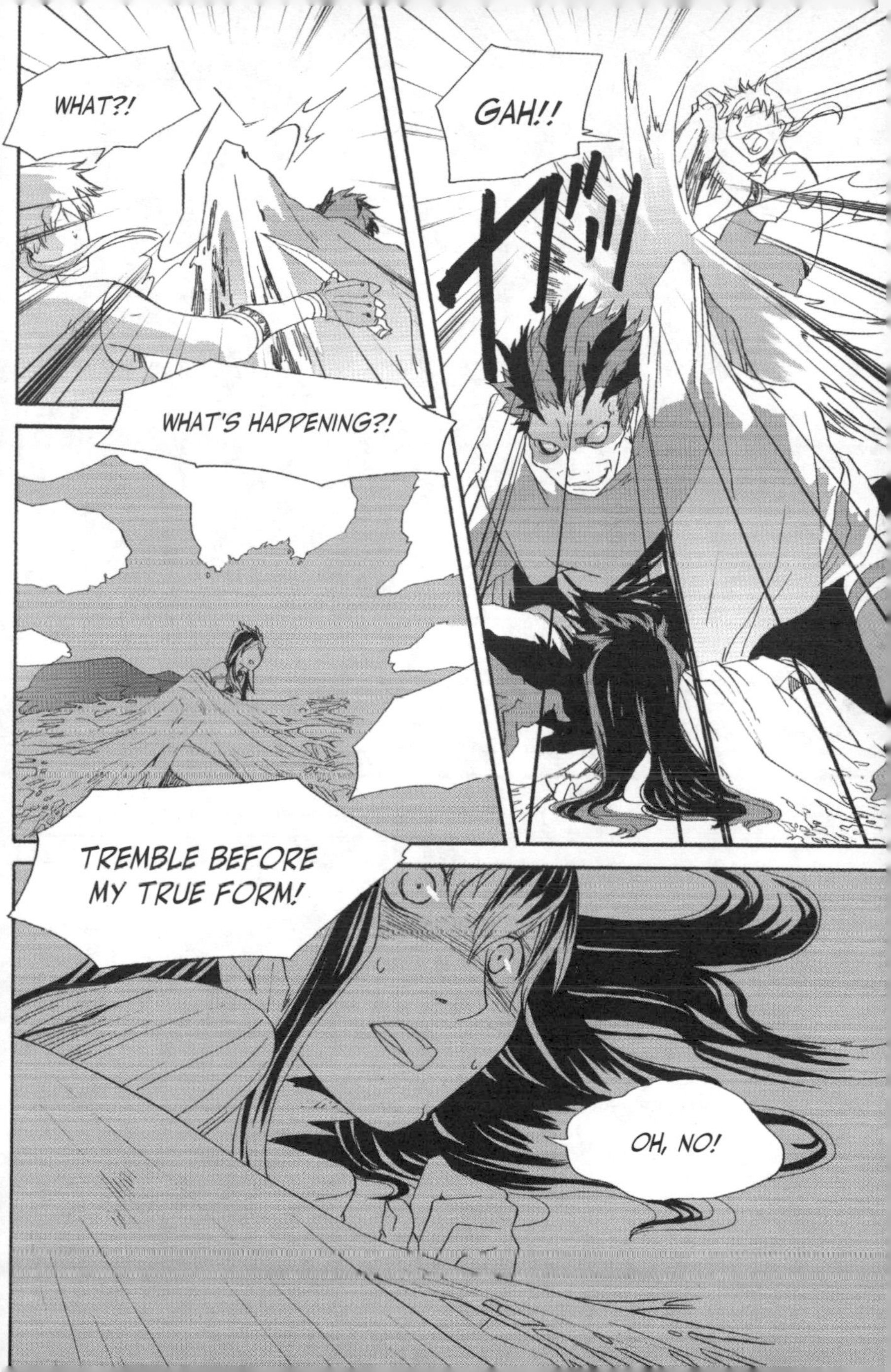
WHAT?!
GAH!!
WHAT'S HAPPENING?!
TREMBLE BEFORE MY TRUE FORM!
OH, NO!

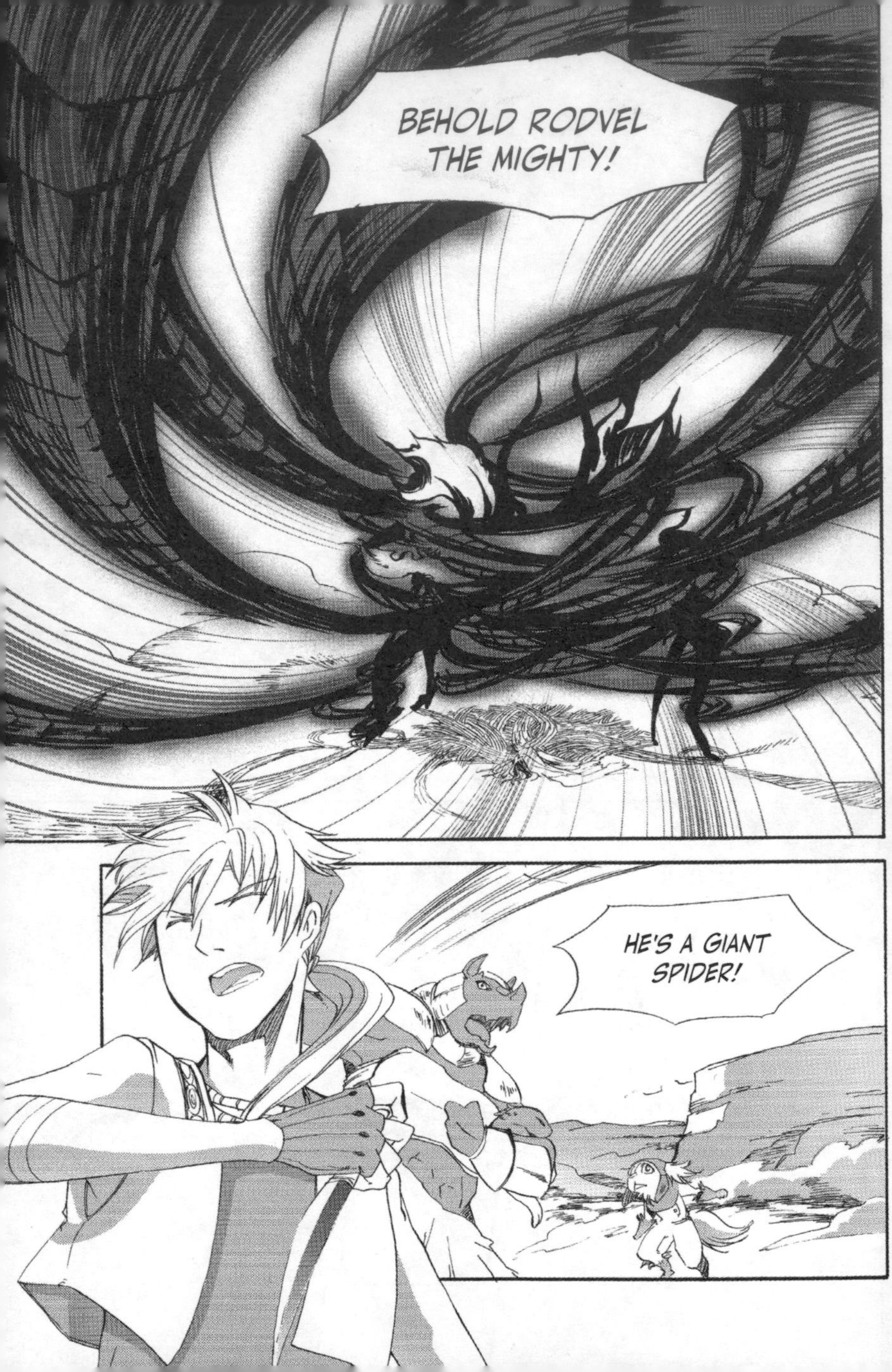
BEHOLD RODVEL THE MIGHTY!
HE'S A GIANT SPIDER!

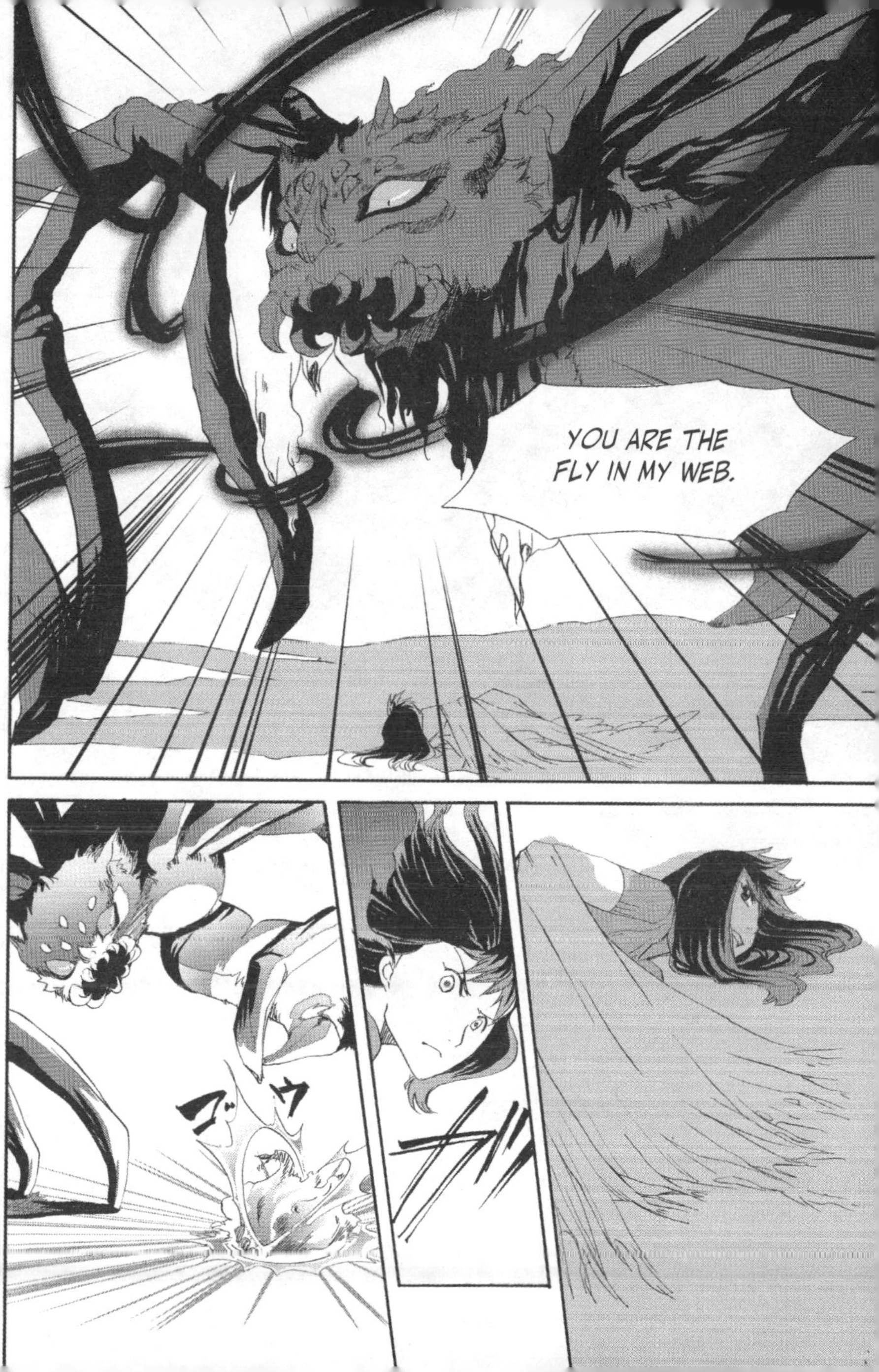
YOU ARE THE
FLY IN MY WEB.

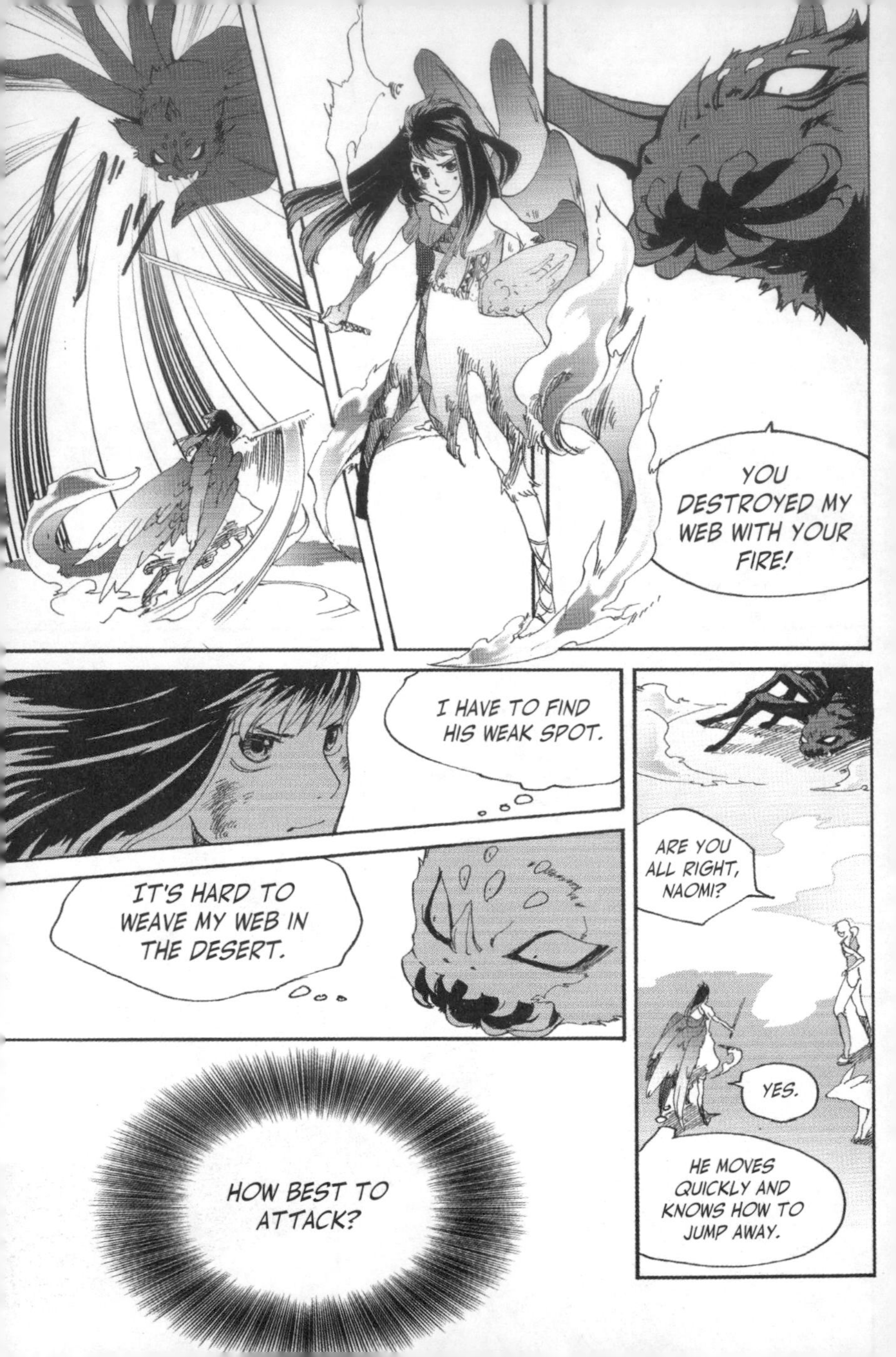
YOU DESTROYED MY WEB WITH YOUR FIRE!
I HAVE TO FIND HIS WEAK SPOT.
IT'S HARD TO WEAVE MY WEB IN THE DESERT.
ARE YOU ALL RIGHT, NAOMI?
YES.
HE MOVES QUICKLY AND KNOWS HOW TO JUMP AWAY.
HOW BEST TO ATTACK?

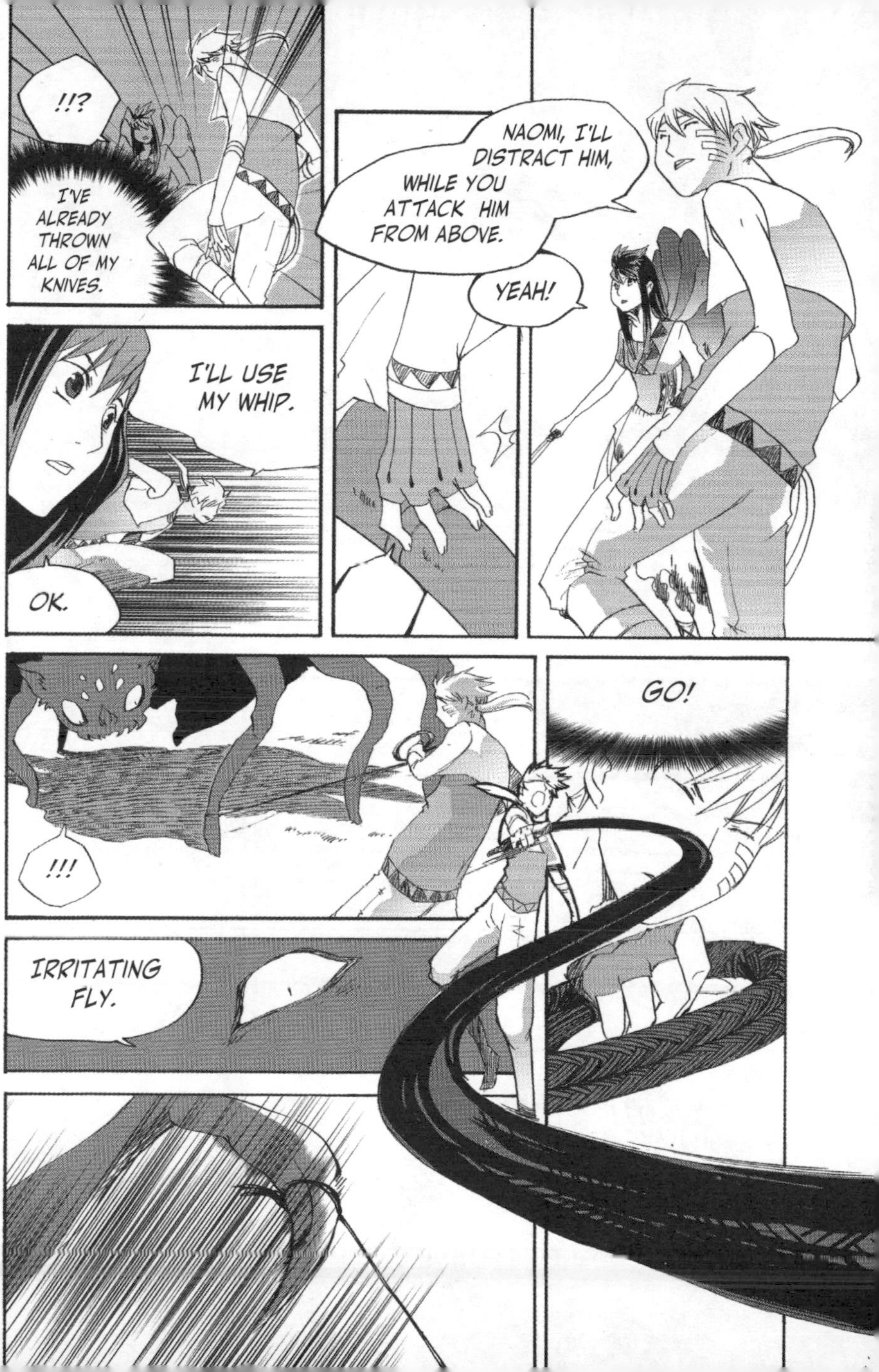
!!?
I'VE ALREADY THROWN ALL OF MY KNIVES.
NAOMI, I'LL DISTRACT HIM, WHILE YOU ATTACK HIM FROM ABOVE.
YEAH!
I'LL USE MY WHIP.
OK.
!!!
GO!
IRRITATING FLY.

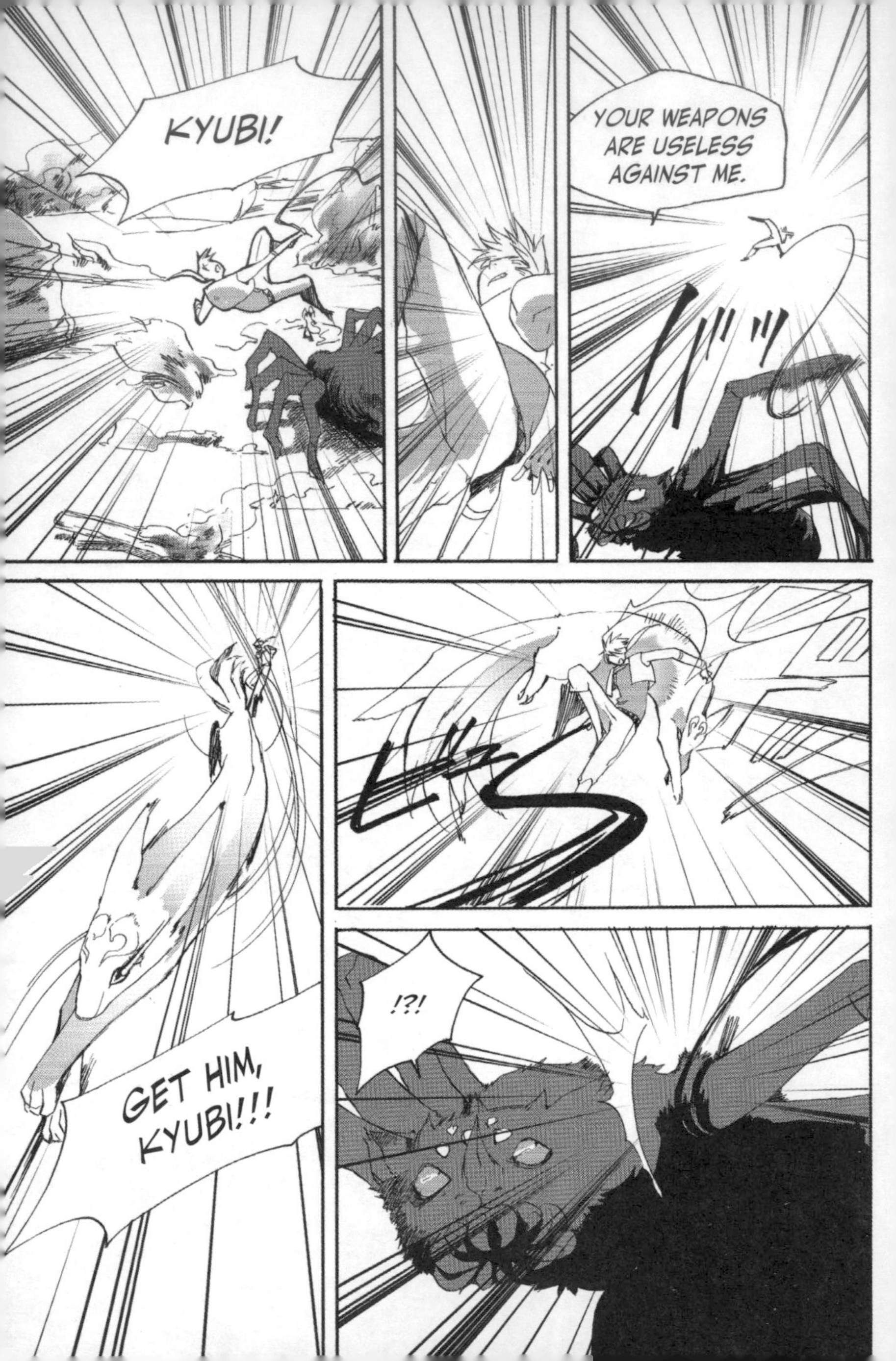
KYUBI!
YOUR WEAPONS ARE USELESS AGAINST ME.
GET HIM, KYUBI!!!
!?!

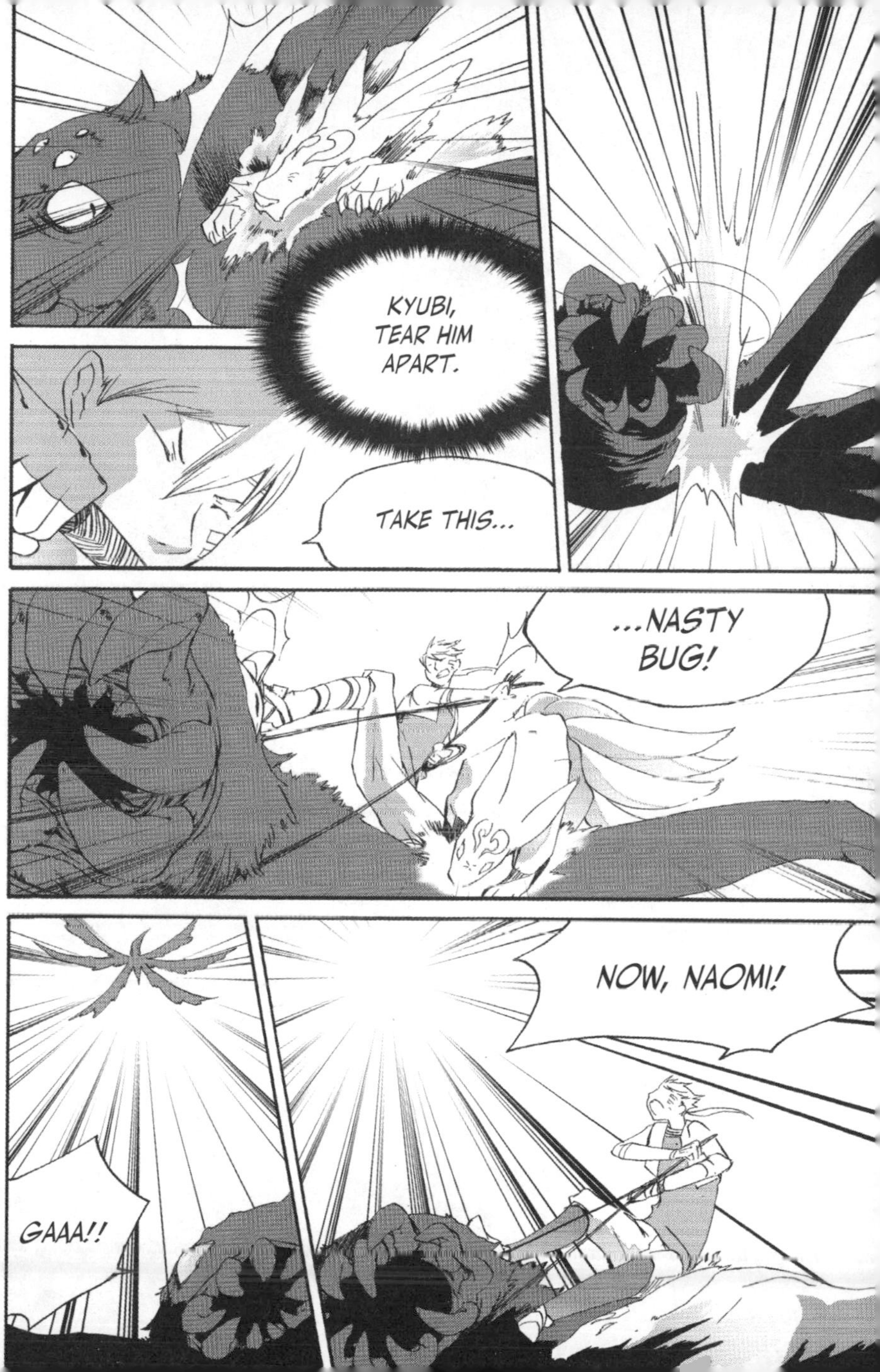
KYUBI, TEAR HIM APART.
TAKE THIS...
...NASTY BUG!
NOW, NAOMI!
GAAA!!

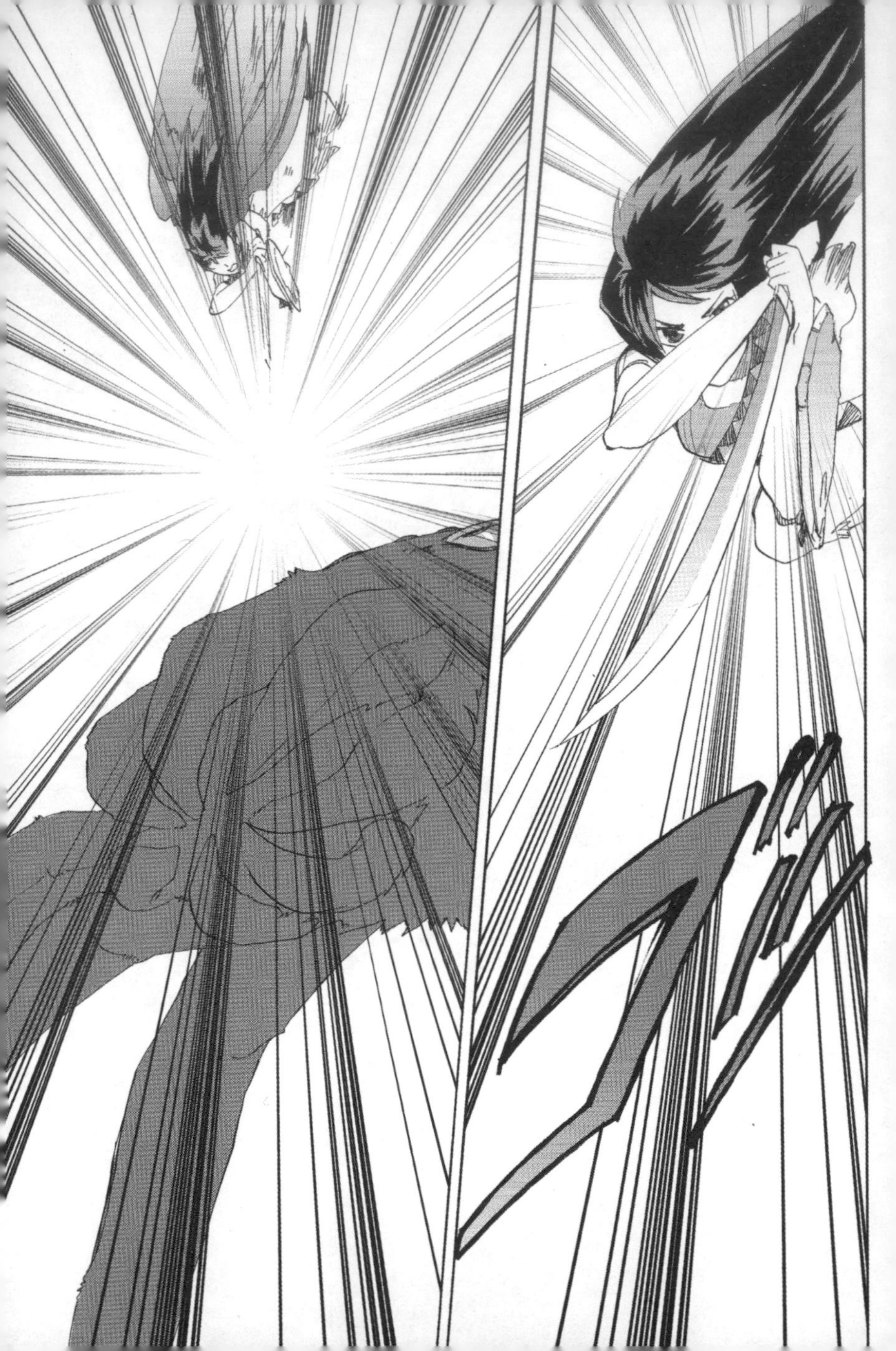

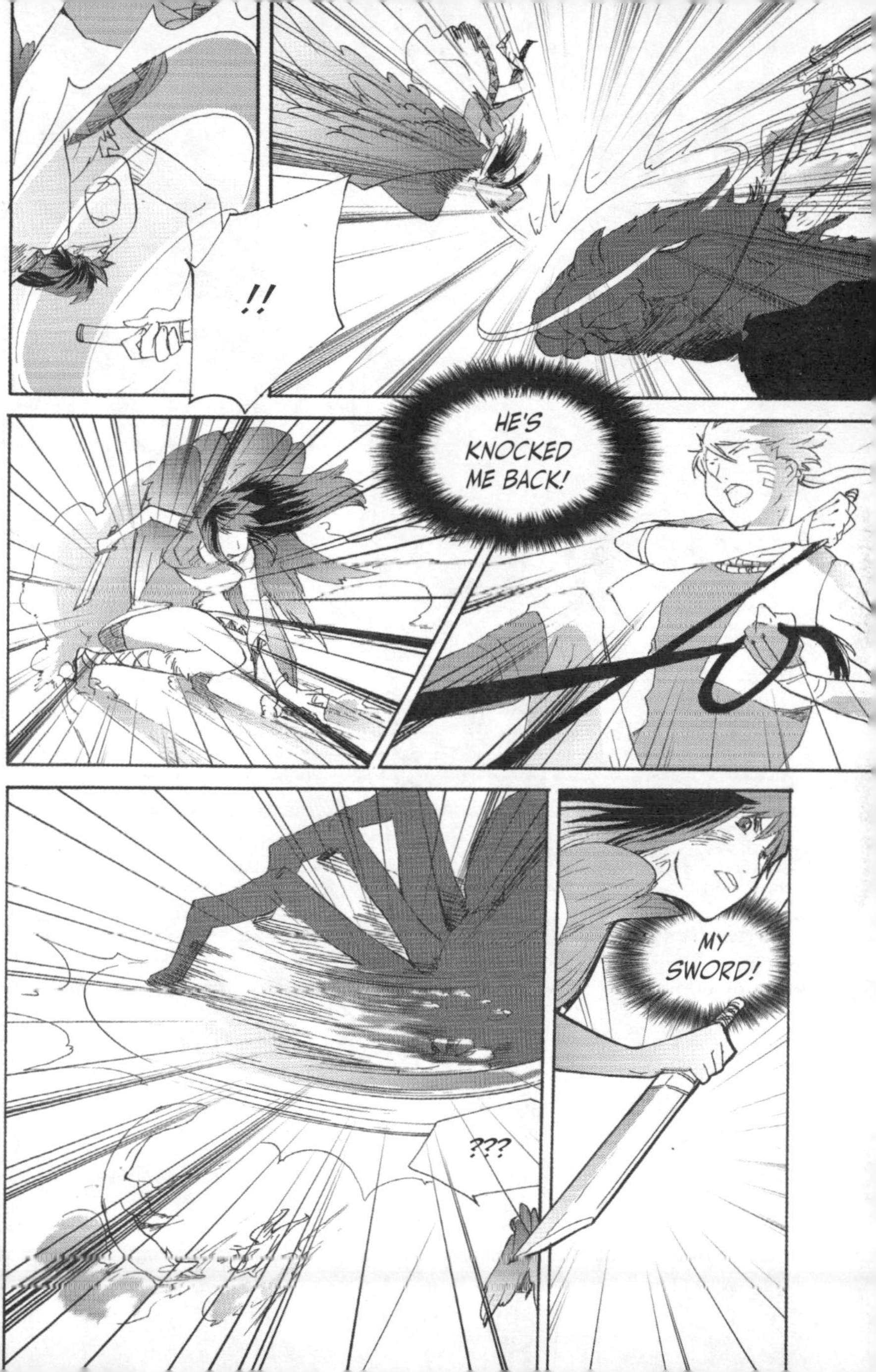
!!
HE'S KNOCKED ME BACK!
MY SWORD!
???

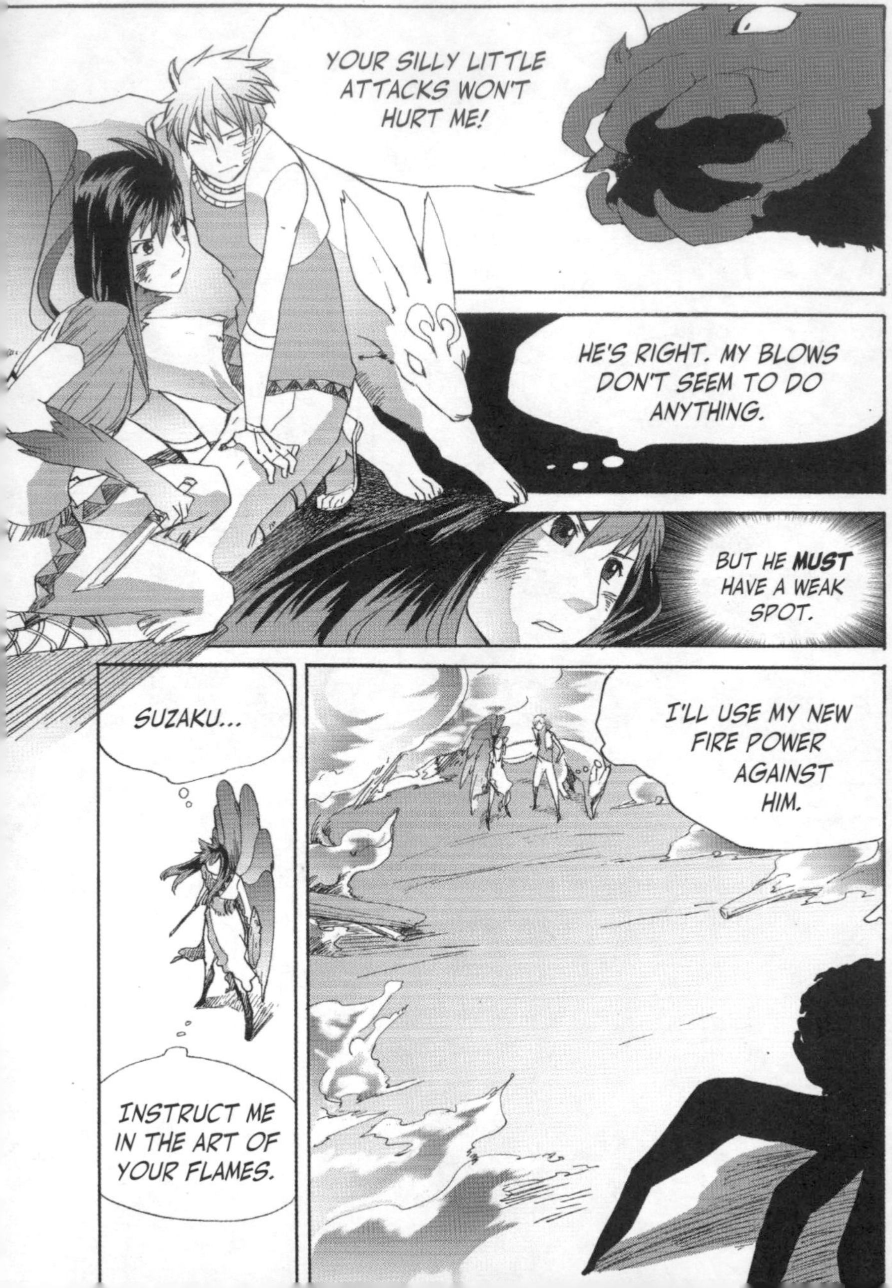

YOUR SILLY LITTLE ATTACKS WON'T HURT ME!
HE'S RIGHT. MY BLOWS DON'T SEEM TO DO ANYTHING.
BUT HE **MUST** HAVE A WEAK SPOT.
I'LL USE MY NEW FIRE POWER AGAINST HIM.
SUZAKU...
INSTRUCT ME IN THE ART OF YOUR FLAMES.

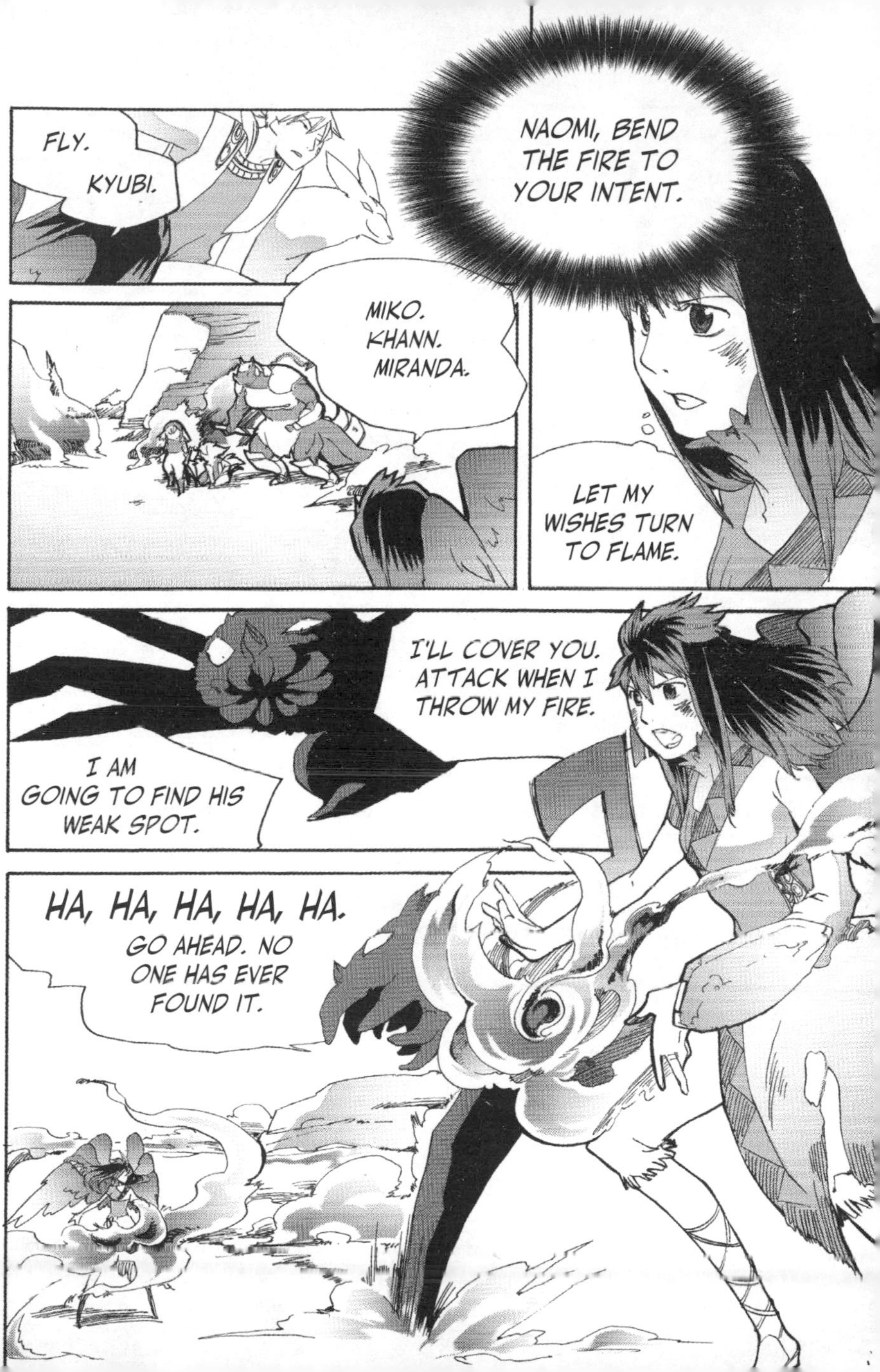
FLY.
KYUBI.
NAOMI, BEND THE FIRE TO YOUR INTENT.
MIKO. KHANN. MIRANDA.
LET MY WISHES TURN TO FLAME.
I'LL COVER YOU. ATTACK WHEN I THROW MY FIRE.
I AM GOING TO FIND HIS WEAK SPOT.
HA, HA, HA, HA, HA.
GO AHEAD. NO ONE HAS EVER FOUND IT.

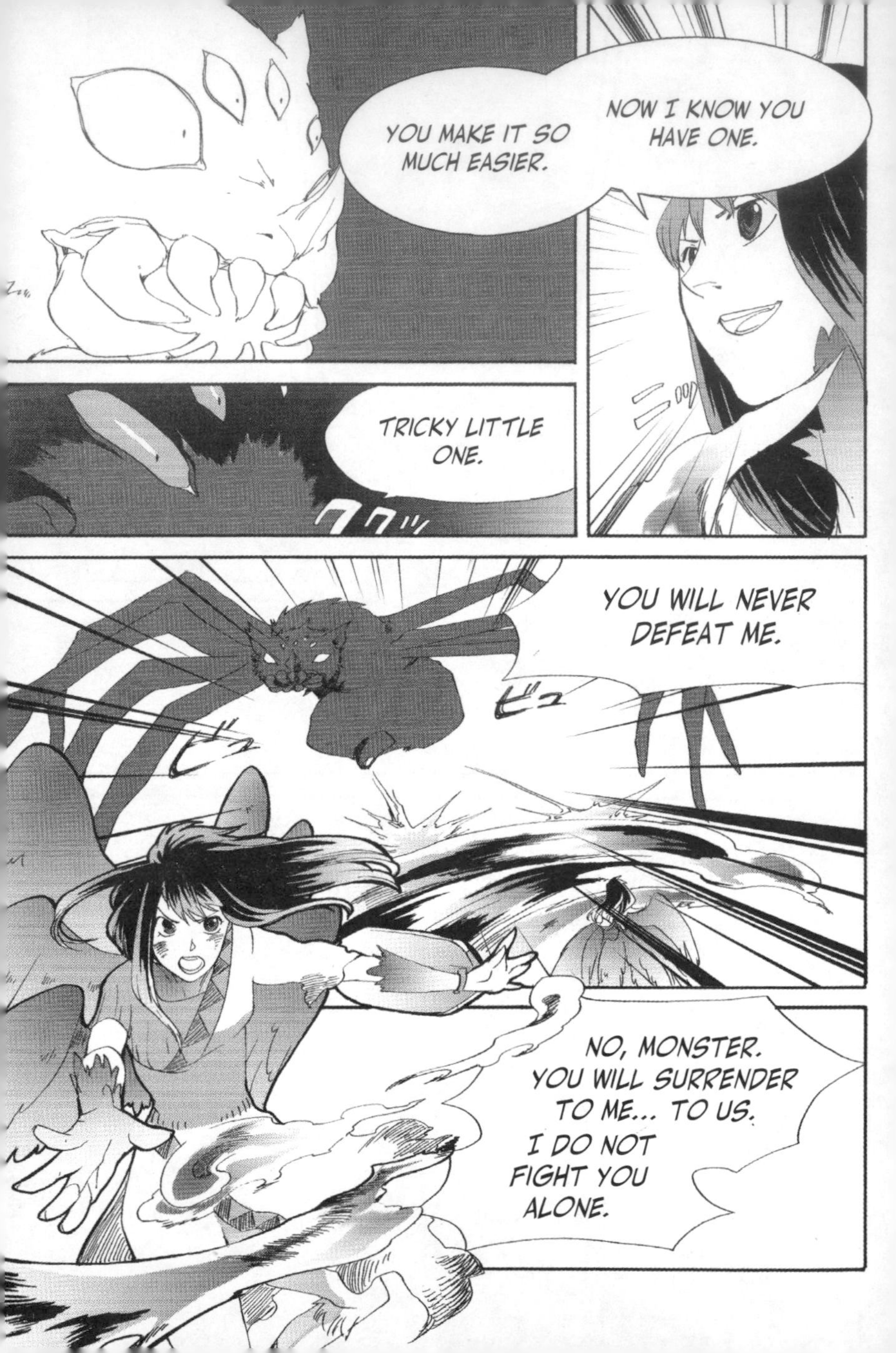
YOU MAKE IT SO MUCH EASIER.
NOW I KNOW YOU HAVE ONE.
TRICKY LITTLE ONE.
YOU WILL NEVER DEFEAT ME.
NO, MONSTER. YOU WILL SURRENDER TO ME... TO US.
I DO NOT FIGHT YOU ALONE.

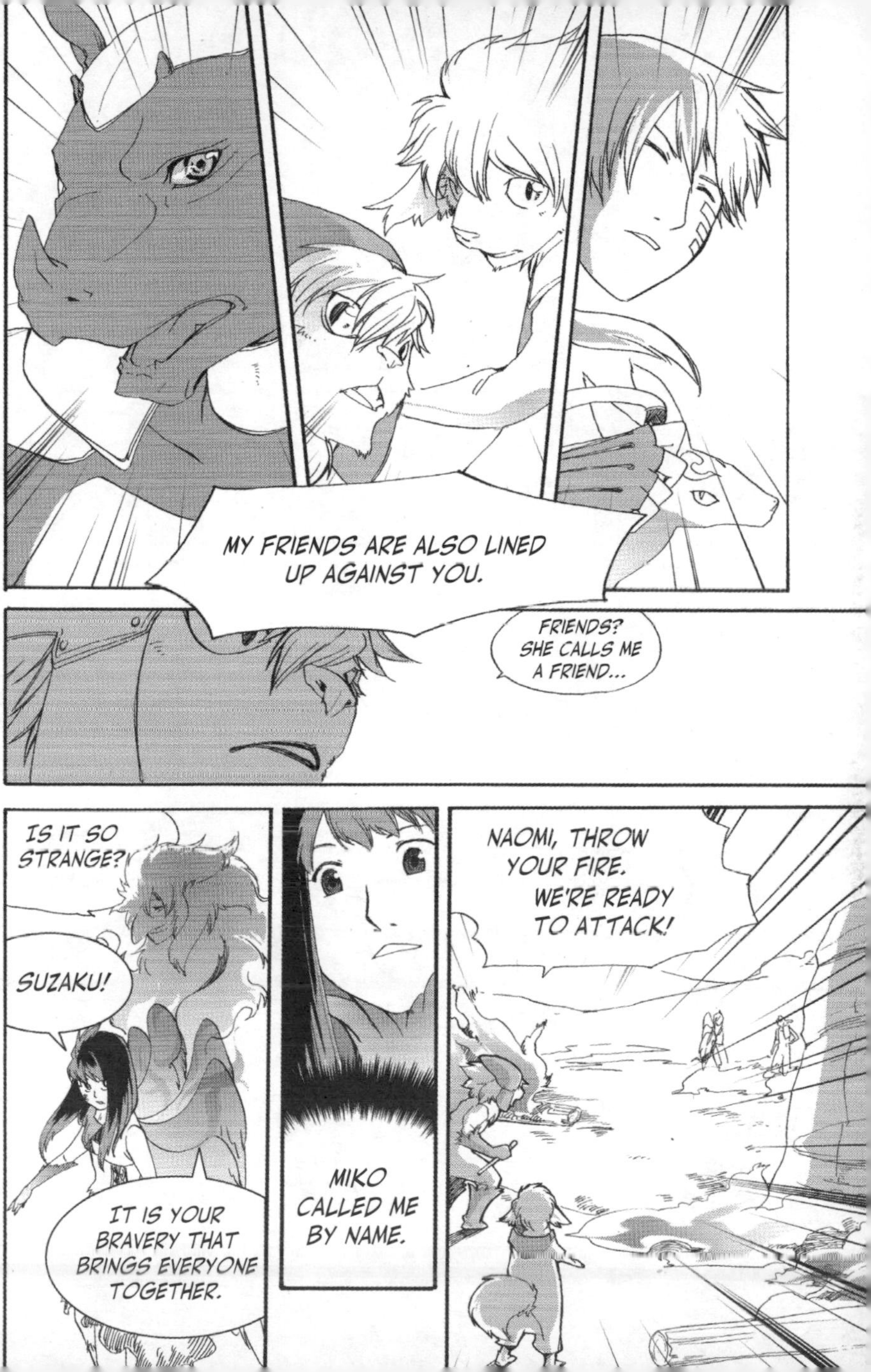
MY FRIENDS ARE ALSO LINED UP AGAINST YOU.
FRIENDS? SHE CALLS ME A FRIEND...
IS IT SO STRANGE?
SUZAKU!
IT IS YOUR BRAVERY THAT BRINGS EVERYONE TOGETHER.
MIKO CALLED ME BY NAME.
NAOMI, THROW YOUR FIRE.
WE'RE READY TO ATTACK!

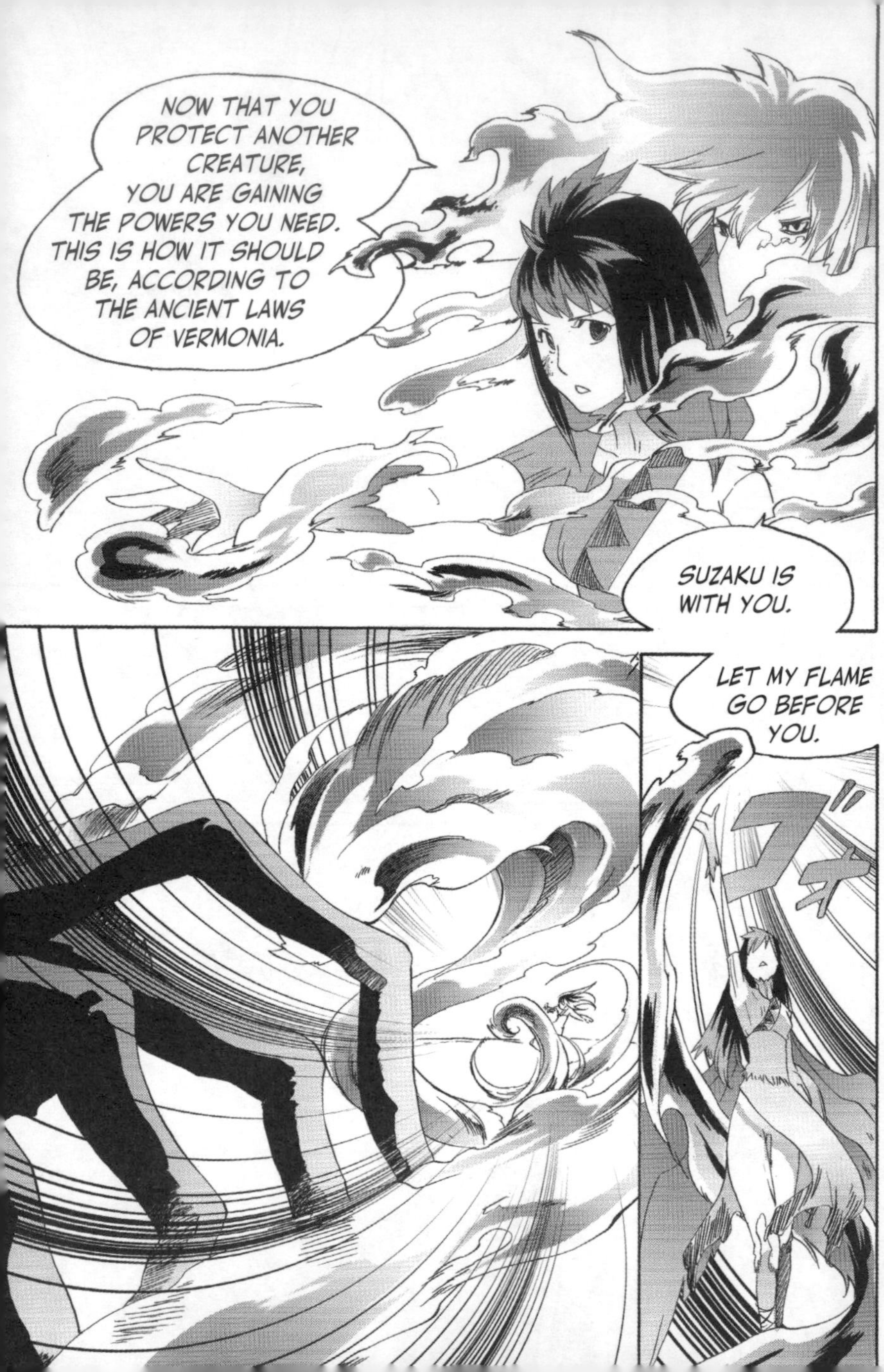
NOW THAT YOU PROTECT ANOTHER CREATURE, YOU ARE GAINING THE POWERS YOU NEED. THIS IS HOW IT SHOULD BE, ACCORDING TO THE ANCIENT LAWS OF VERMONIA.
SUZAKU IS WITH YOU.
LET MY FLAME GO BEFORE YOU.

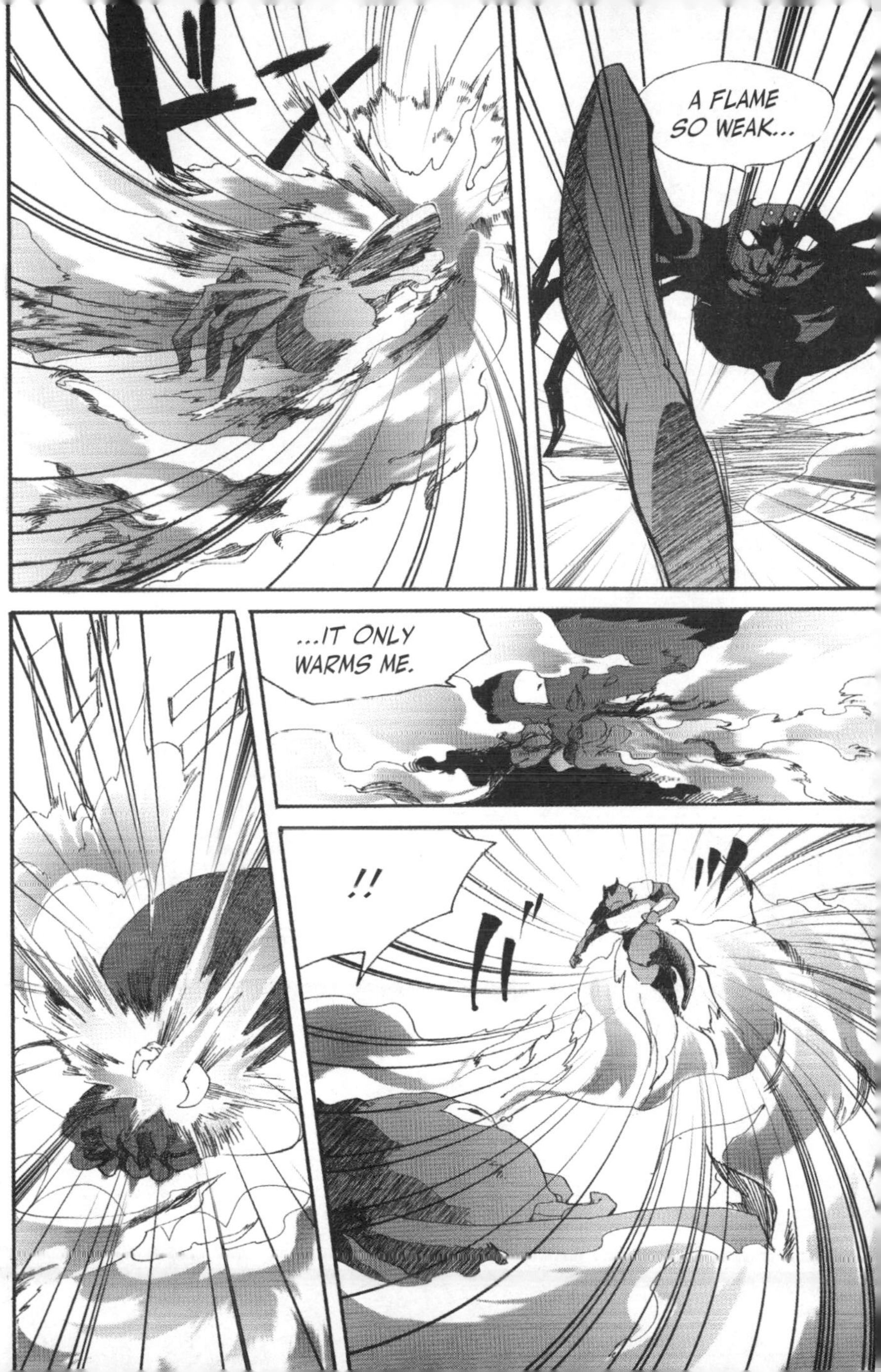
A FLAME SO WEAK...
...IT ONLY WARMS ME.
!!

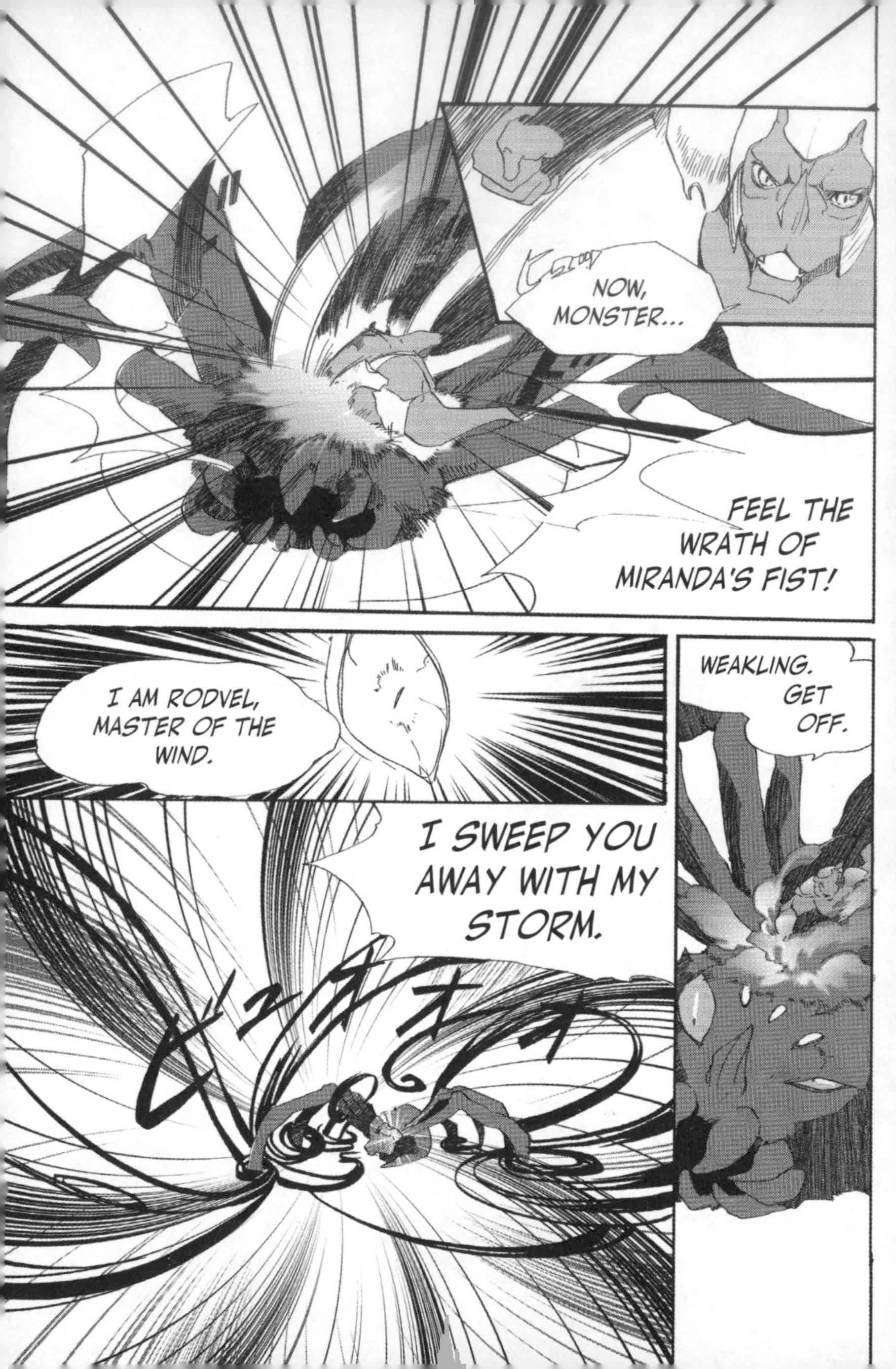
NOW, MONSTER...
FEEL THE WRATH OF MIRANDA'S FIST!
WEAKLING. GET OFF.
I AM RODVEL, MASTER OF THE WIND.
I SWEEP YOU AWAY WITH MY STORM.

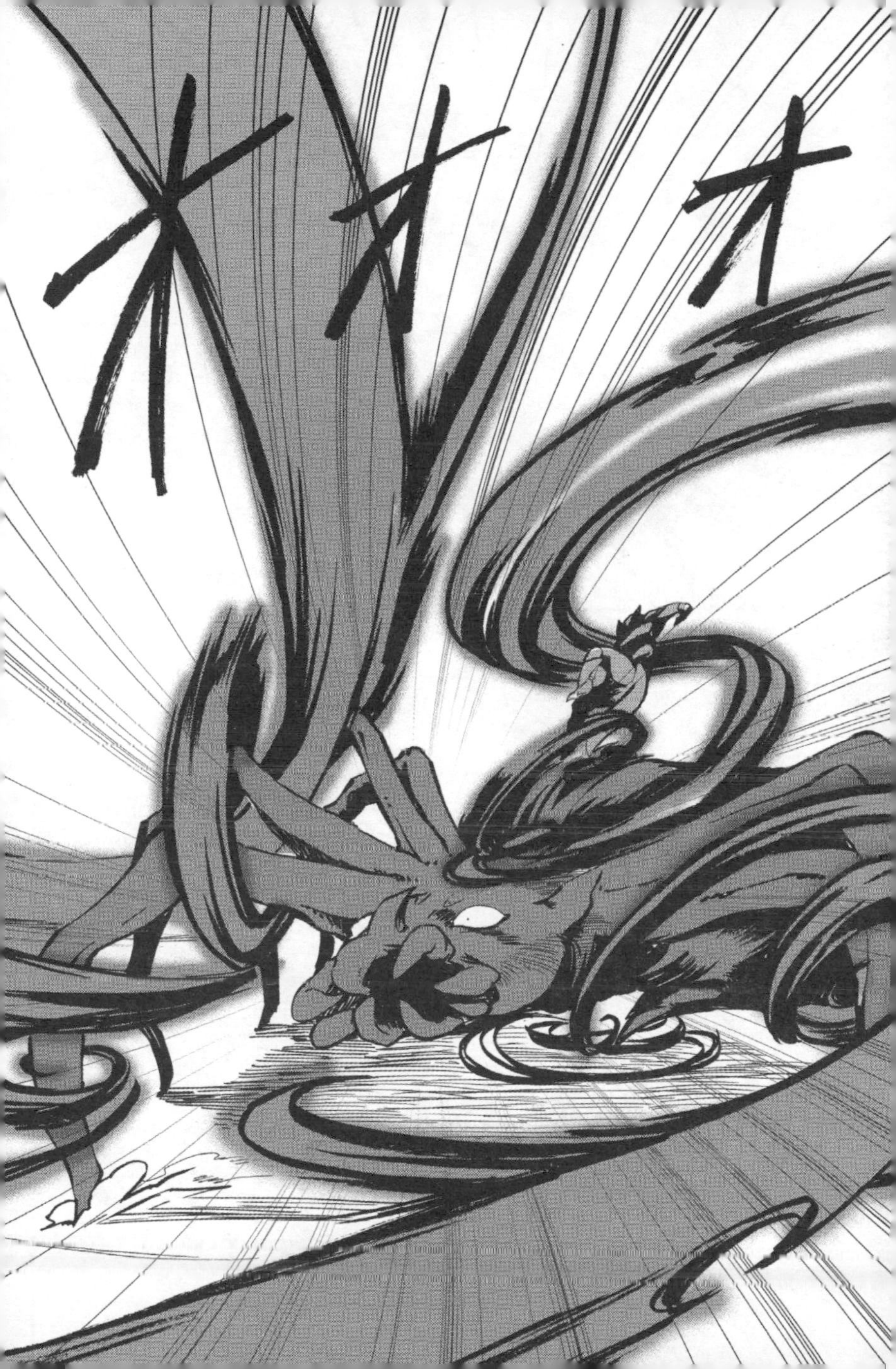
オオオ

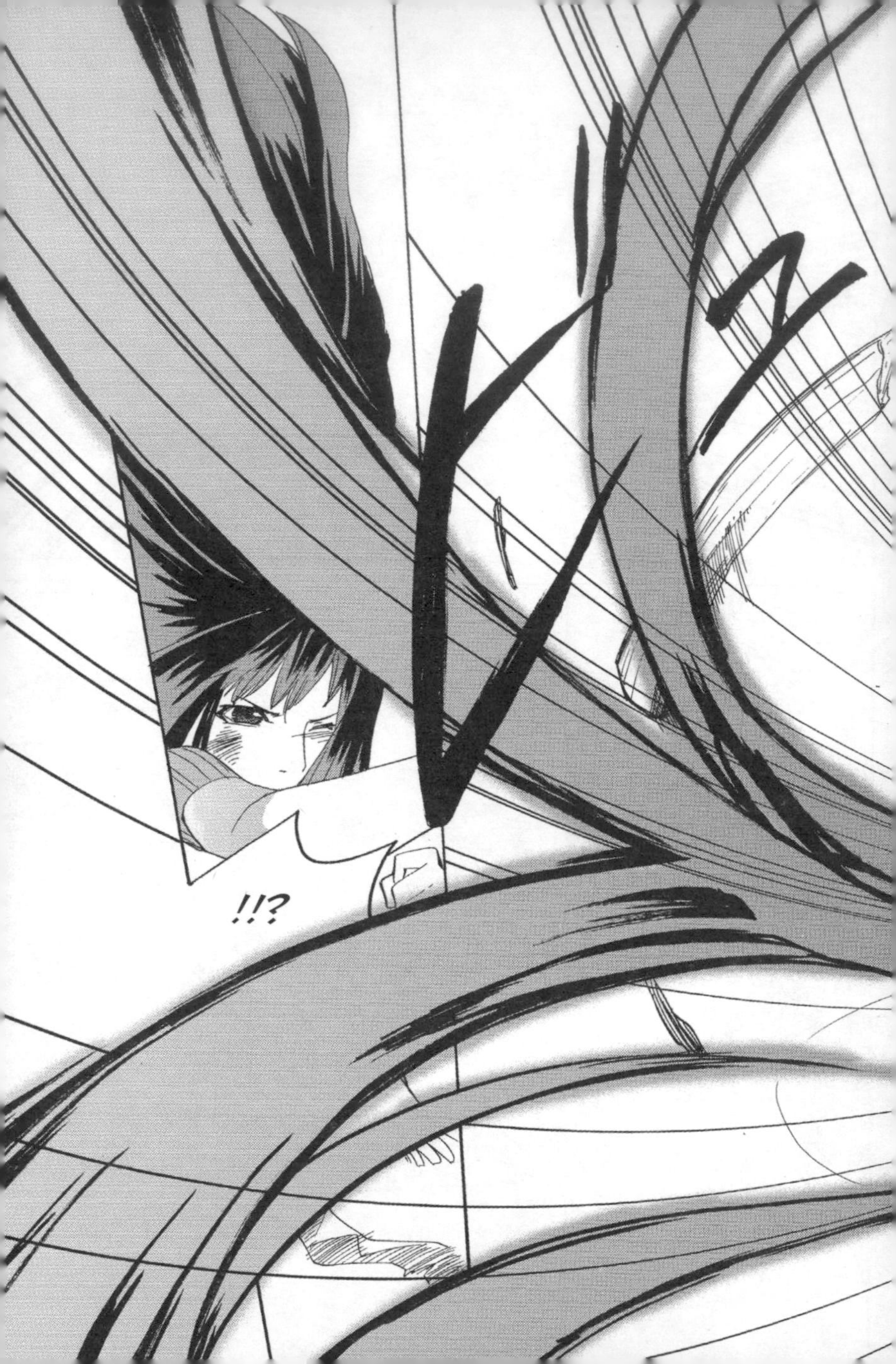
!!?

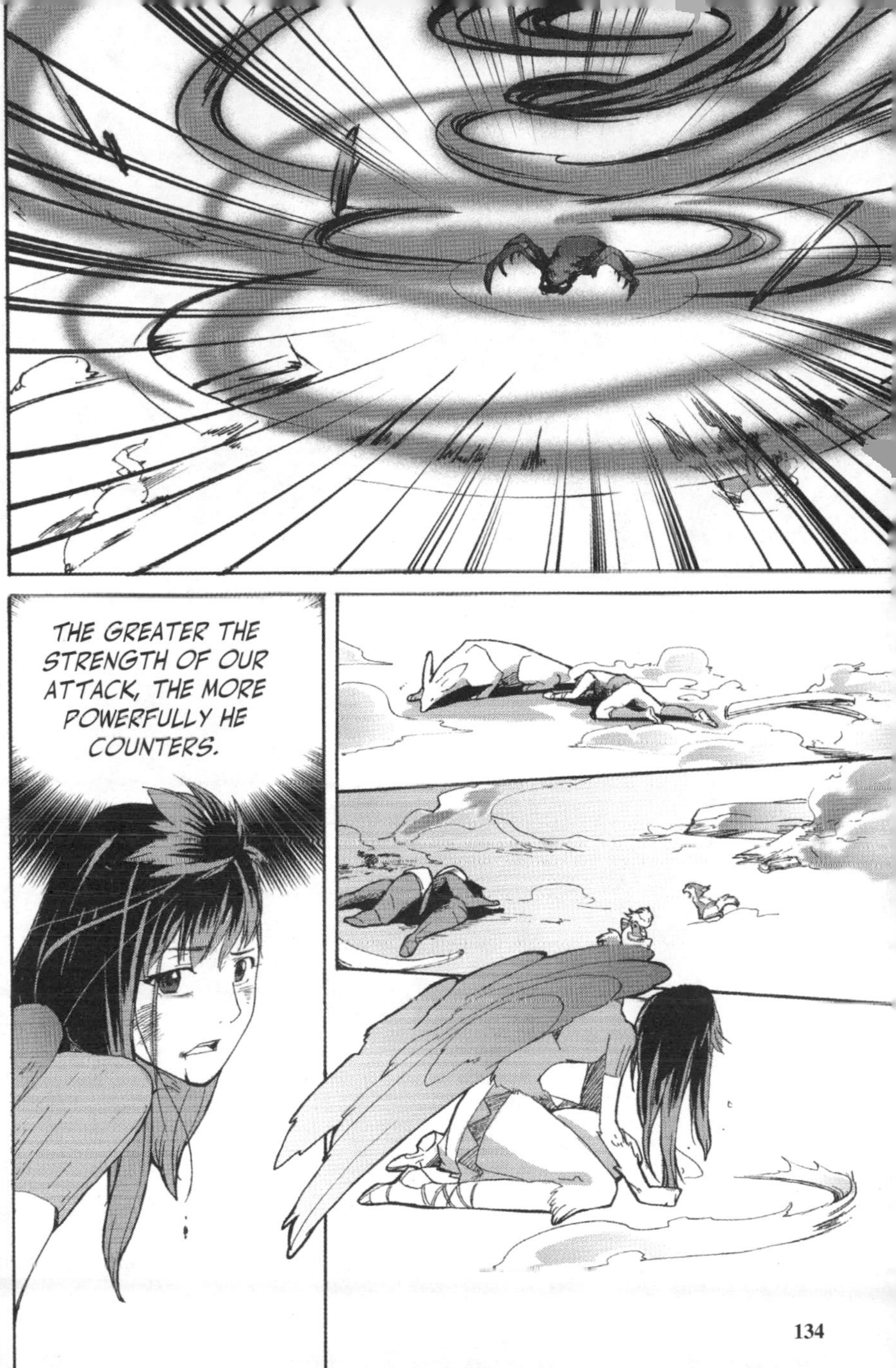
THE GREATER THE STRENGTH OF OUR ATTACK, THE MORE POWERFULLY HE COUNTERS.

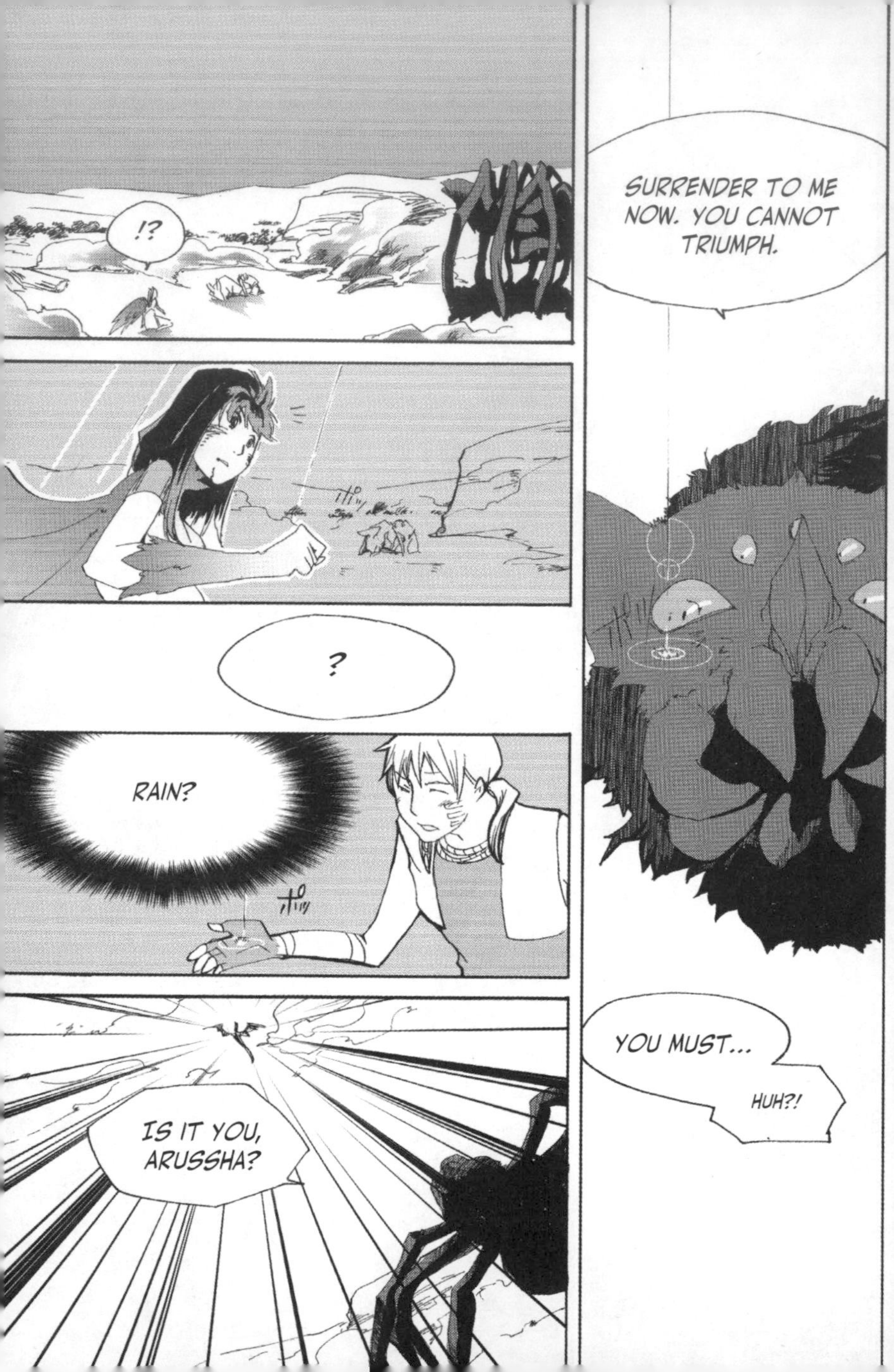
!?
?
RAIN?
IS IT YOU, ARUSSHA?
SURRENDER TO ME NOW. YOU CANNOT TRIUMPH.
YOU MUST...
HUH?!

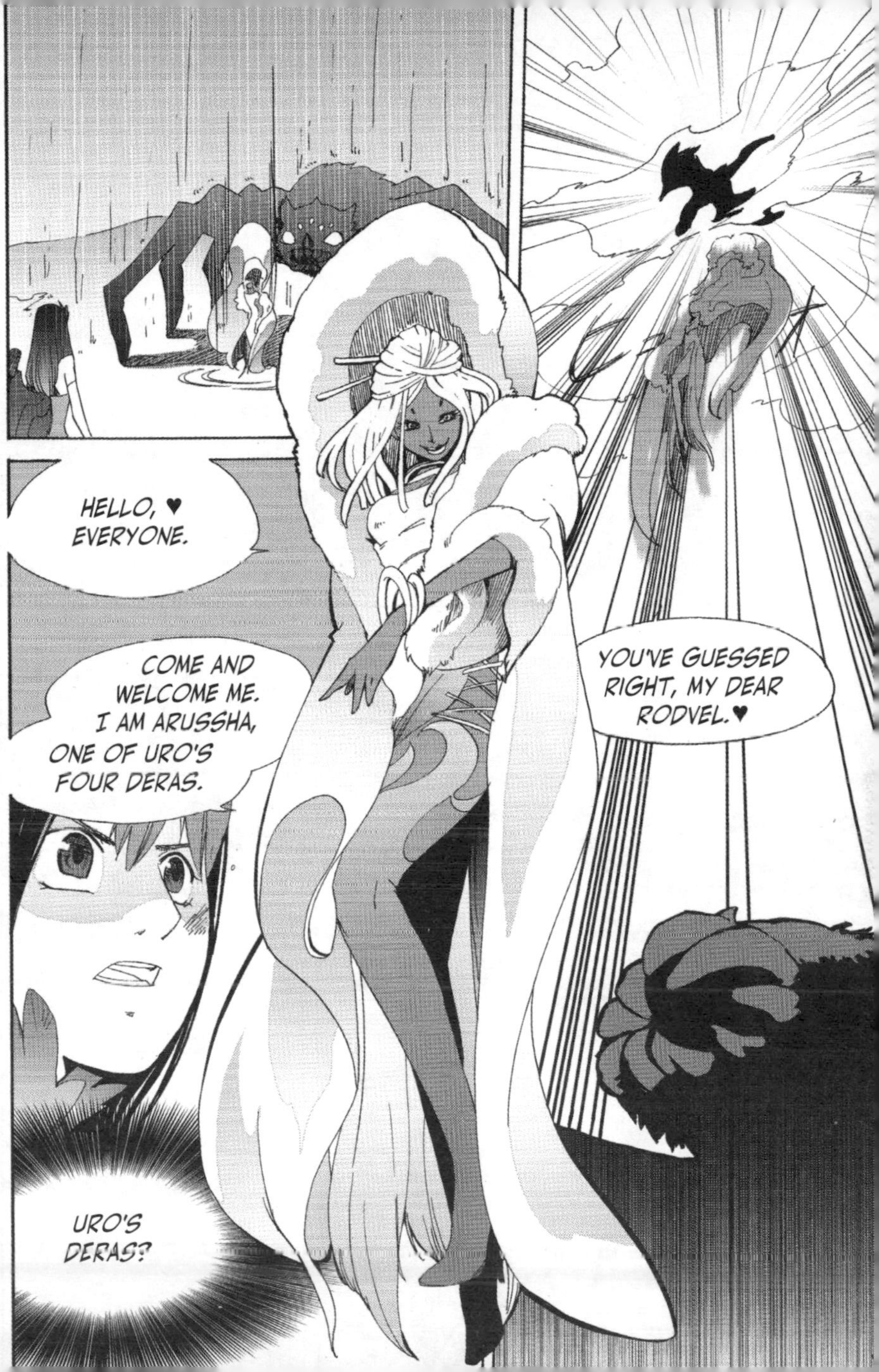
HELLO, ♥ EVERYONE.
COME AND WELCOME ME. I AM ARUSSHA, ONE OF URO'S FOUR DERAS.
YOU'VE GUESSED RIGHT, MY DEAR RODVEL.♥
URO'S DERAS?

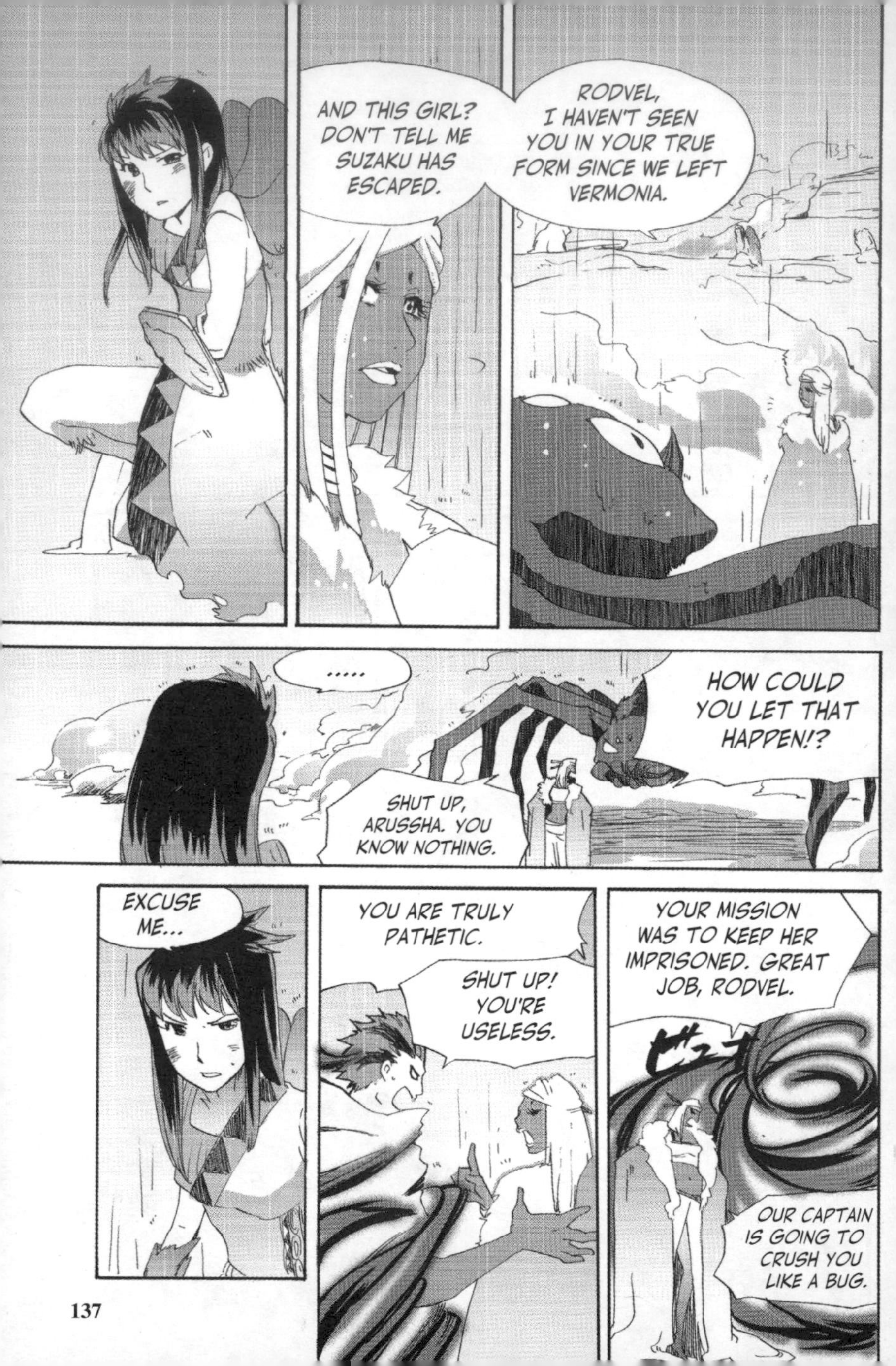
AND THIS GIRL? DON'T TELL ME SUZAKU HAS ESCAPED.
RODVEL, I HAVEN'T SEEN YOU IN YOUR TRUE FORM SINCE WE LEFT VERMONIA.
.....
HOW COULD YOU LET THAT HAPPEN!?
SHUT UP, ARUSSHA. YOU KNOW NOTHING.
EXCUSE ME...
YOU ARE TRULY PATHETIC.
SHUT UP! YOU'RE USELESS.
YOUR MISSION WAS TO KEEP HER IMPRISONED. GREAT JOB, RODVEL.
OUR CAPTAIN IS GOING TO CRUSH YOU LIKE A BUG.

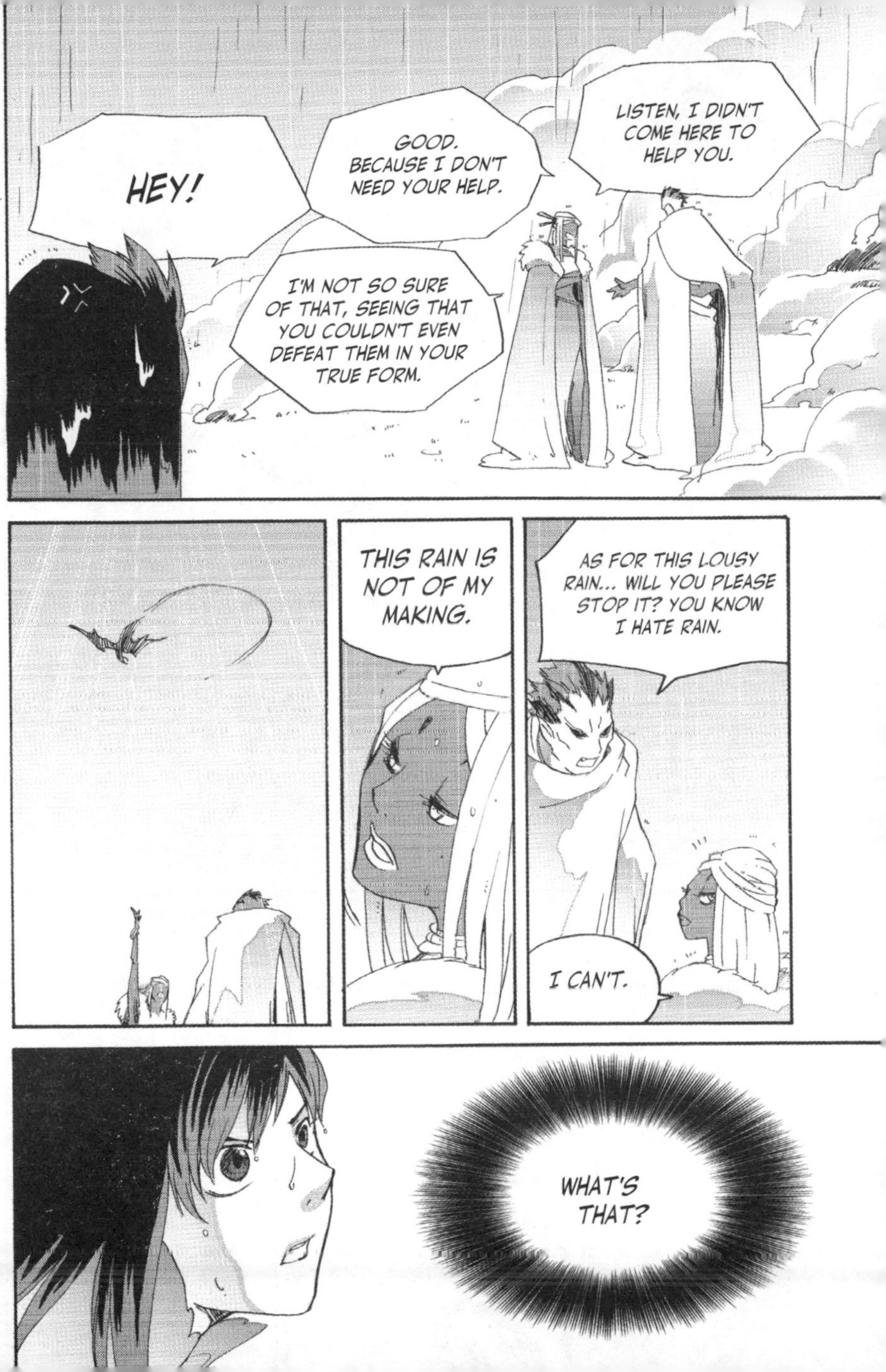

HEY!
GOOD. BECAUSE I DON'T NEED YOUR HELP.
LISTEN, I DIDN'T COME HERE TO HELP YOU.
I'M NOT SO SURE OF THAT, SEEING THAT YOU COULDN'T EVEN DEFEAT THEM IN YOUR TRUE FORM.
THIS RAIN IS NOT OF MY MAKING.
AS FOR THIS LOUSY RAIN... WILL YOU PLEASE STOP IT? YOU KNOW I HATE RAIN.
I CAN'T.
WHAT'S THAT?

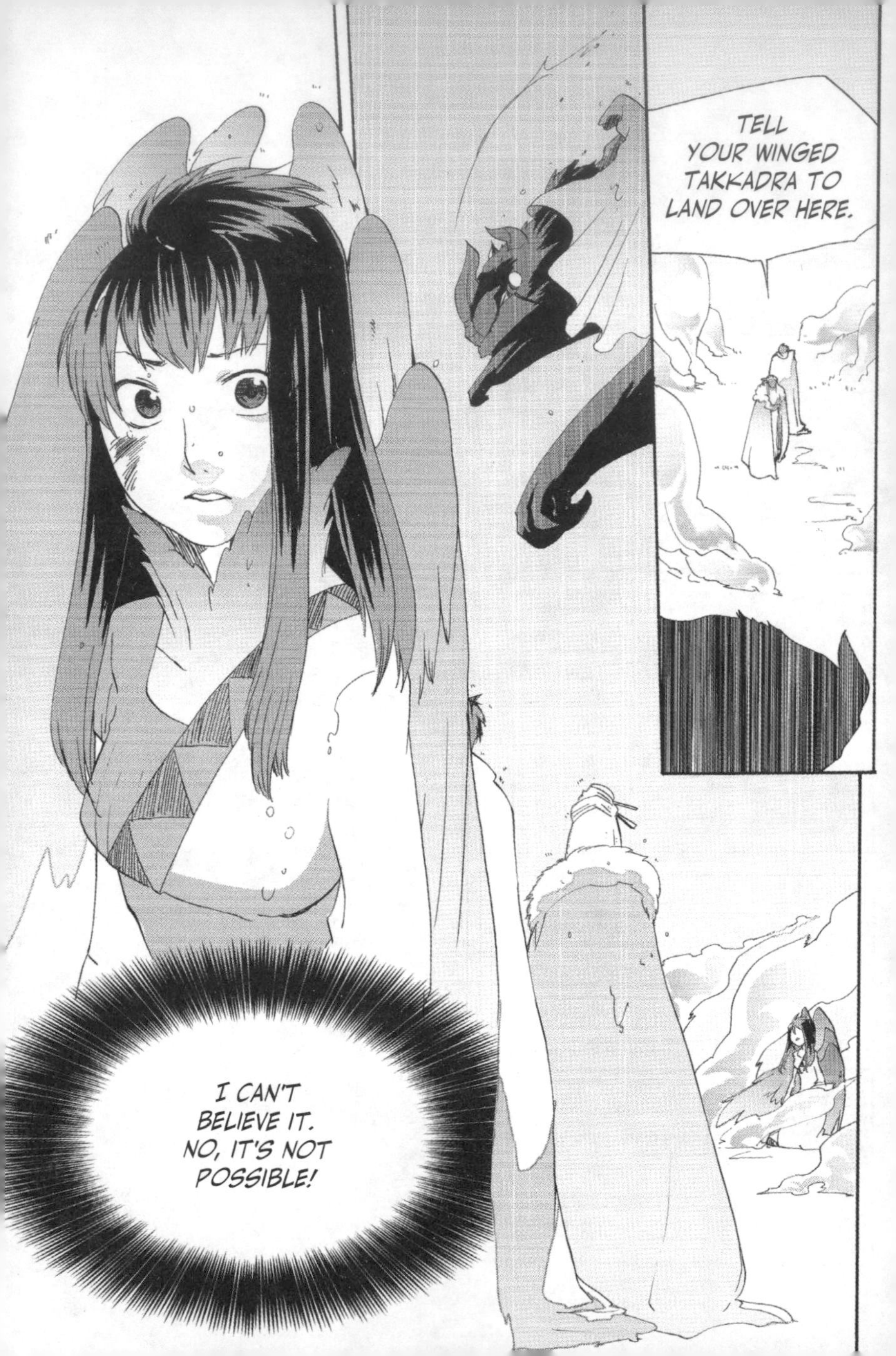
TELL YOUR WINGED TAKKADRA TO LAND OVER HERE.
I CAN'T BELIEVE IT. NO, IT'S NOT POSSIBLE!

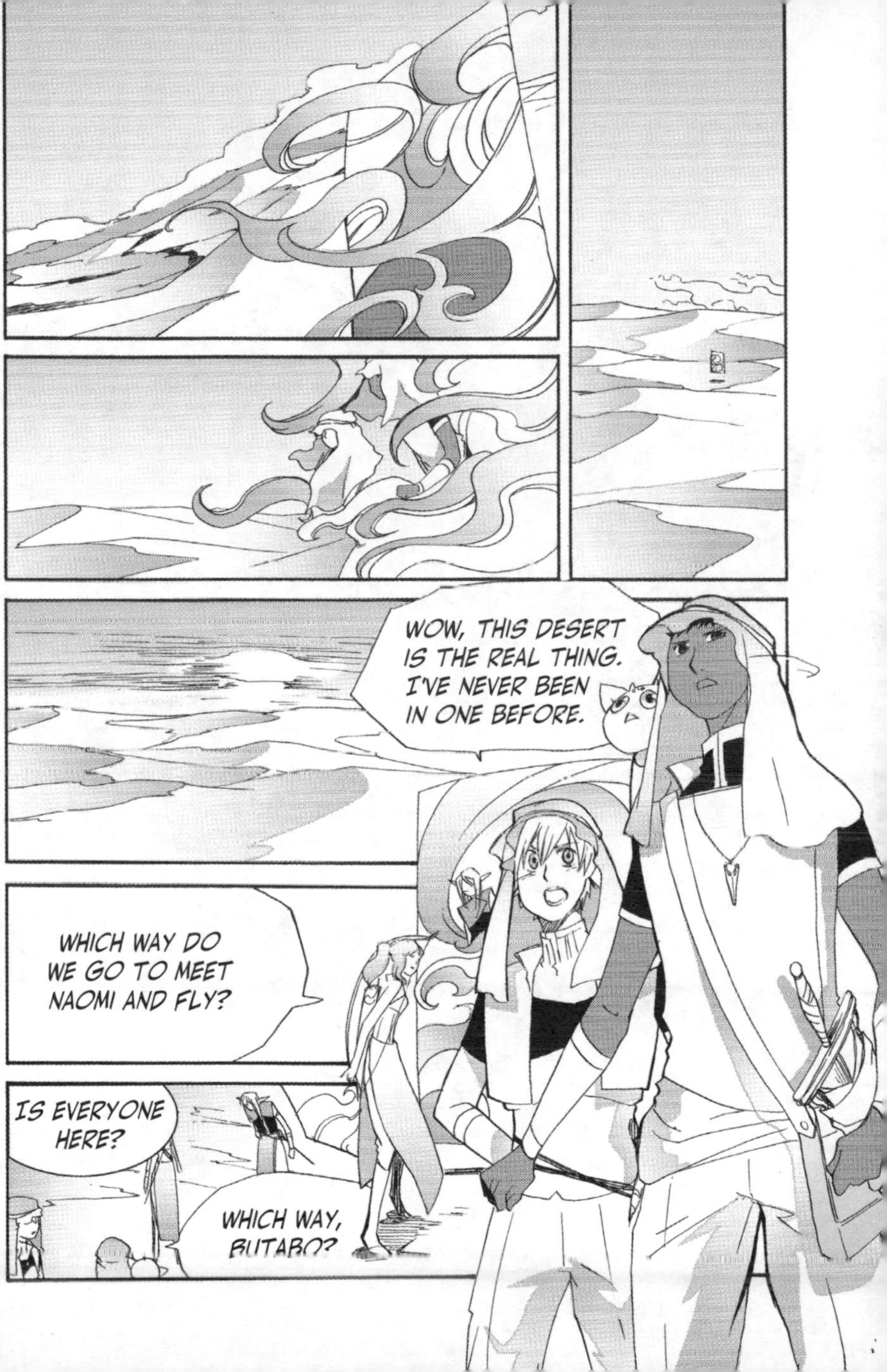

WOW, THIS DESERT IS THE REAL THING. I'VE NEVER BEEN IN ONE BEFORE.
WHICH WAY DO WE GO TO MEET NAOMI AND FLY?
IS EVERYONE HERE?
WHICH WAY, BUTABO?

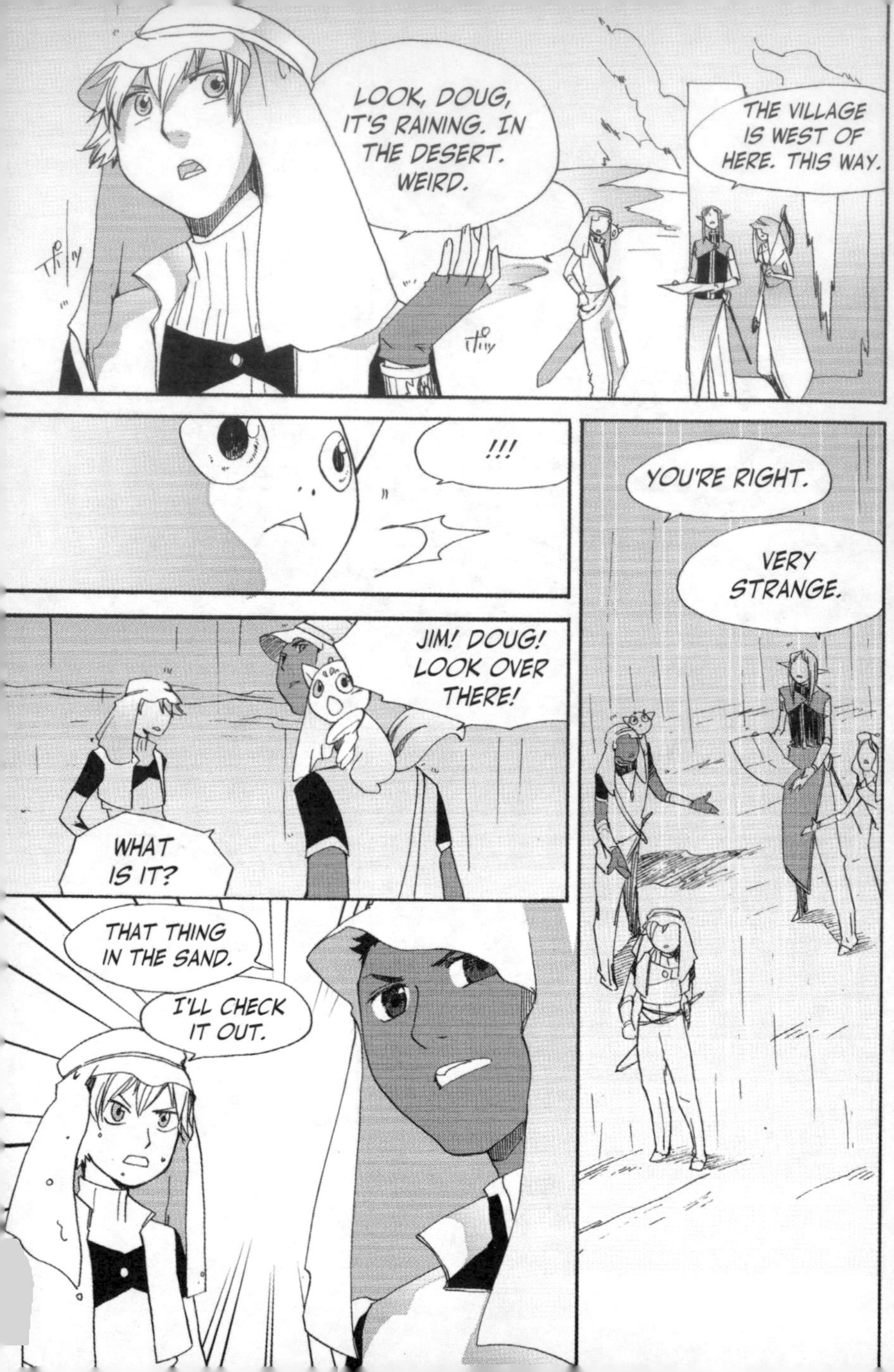
LOOK, DOUG, IT'S RAINING. IN THE DESERT. WEIRD.
THE VILLAGE IS WEST OF HERE. THIS WAY.
!!!
YOU'RE RIGHT.
VERY STRANGE.
JIM! DOUG! LOOK OVER THERE!
WHAT IS IT?
THAT THING IN THE SAND.
I'LL CHECK IT OUT.

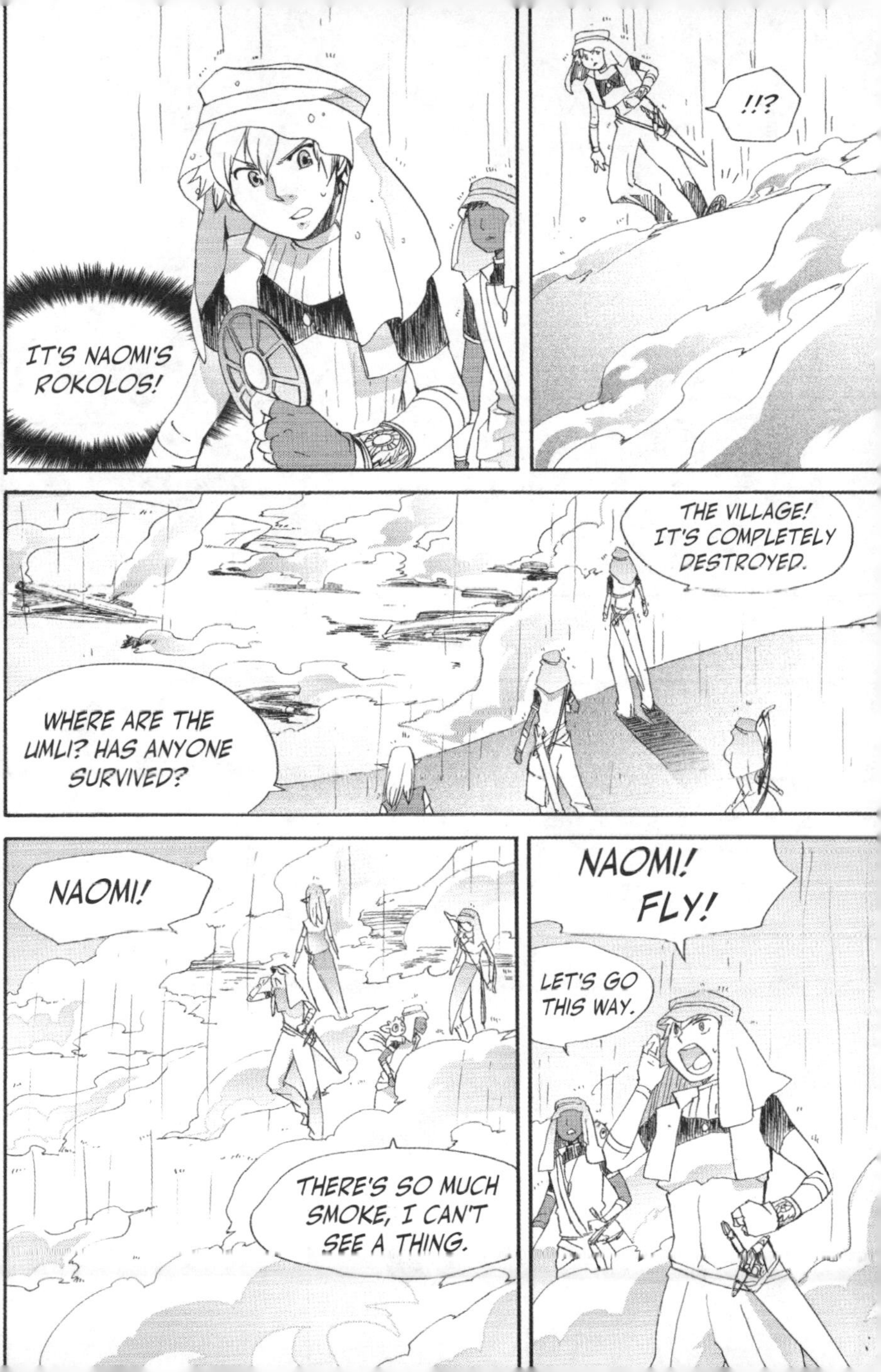
IT'S NAOMI'S ROKOLOS!
!!?
THE VILLAGE! IT'S COMPLETELY DESTROYED.
WHERE ARE THE UMLI? HAS ANYONE SURVIVED?
NAOMI!
THERE'S SO MUCH SMOKE, I CAN'T SEE A THING.
NAOMI! FLY!
LET'S GO THIS WAY.

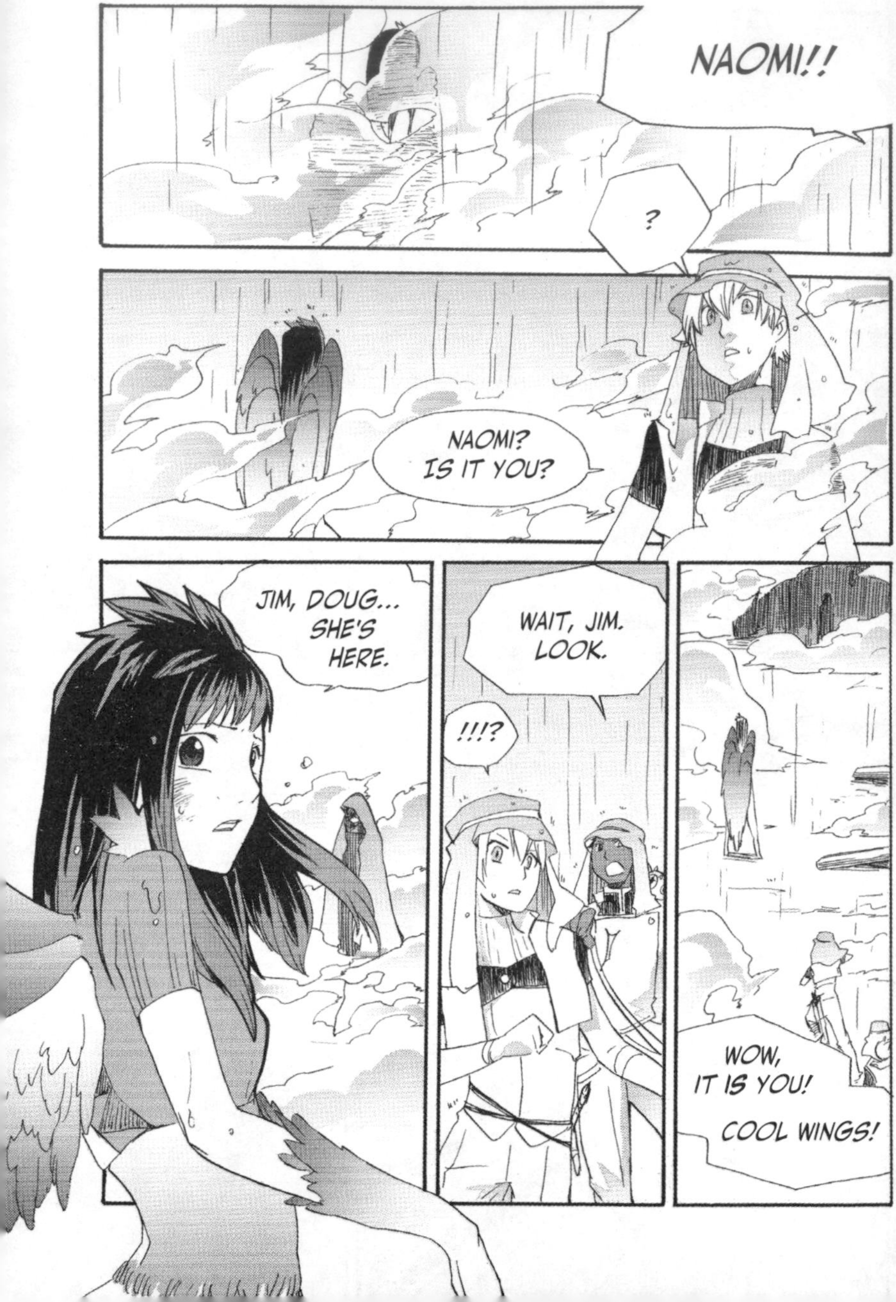
NAOMI!!
?
NAOMI?
IS IT YOU?
JIM, DOUG...
SHE'S
HERE.
WAIT, JIM.
LOOK.
!!!?
WOW,
IT IS YOU!
COOL WINGS!

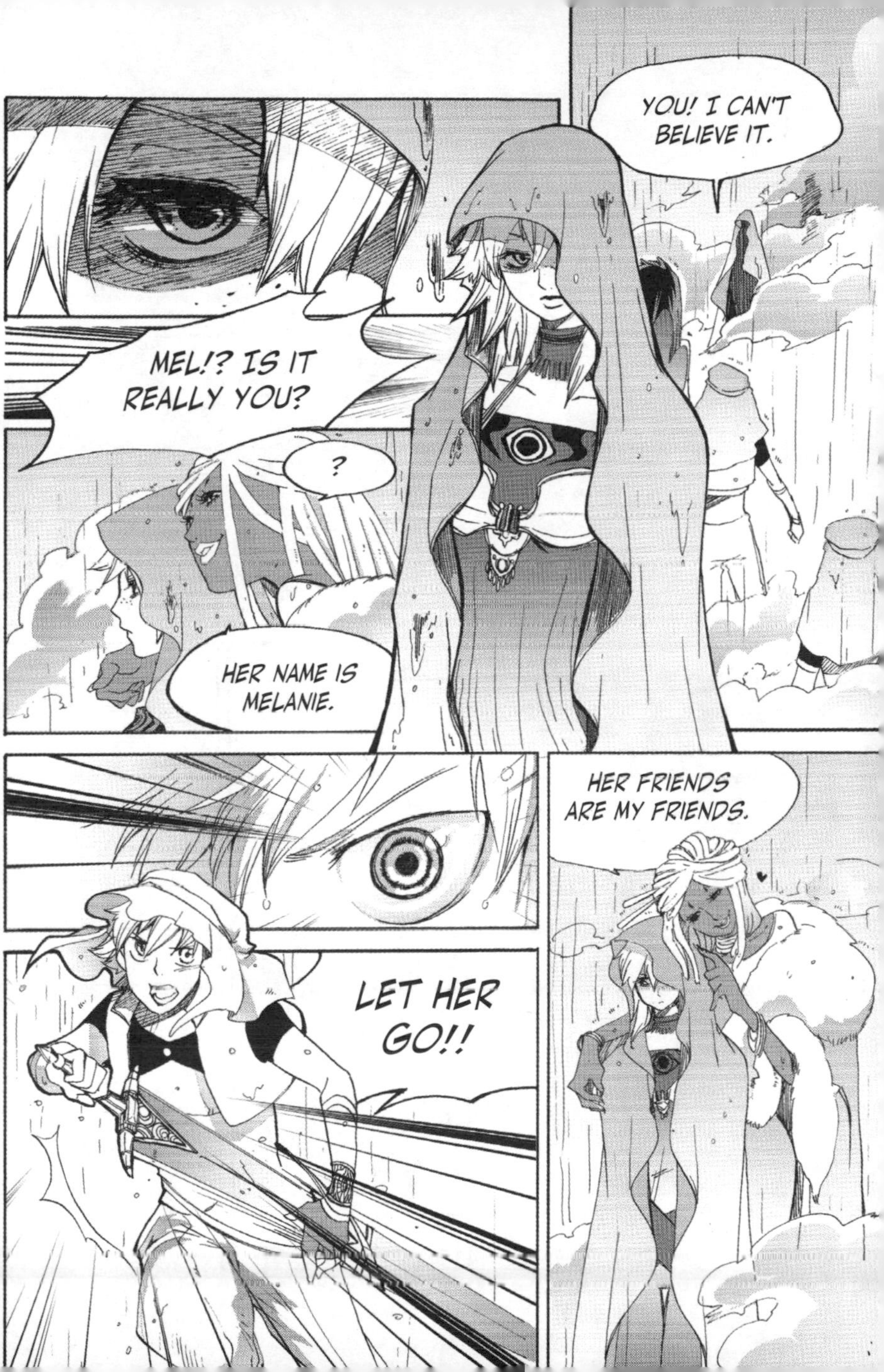
YOU! I CAN'T BELIEVE IT.
MEL!? IS IT REALLY YOU?
?
HER NAME IS MELANIE.
HER FRIENDS ARE MY FRIENDS.
LET HER GO!!

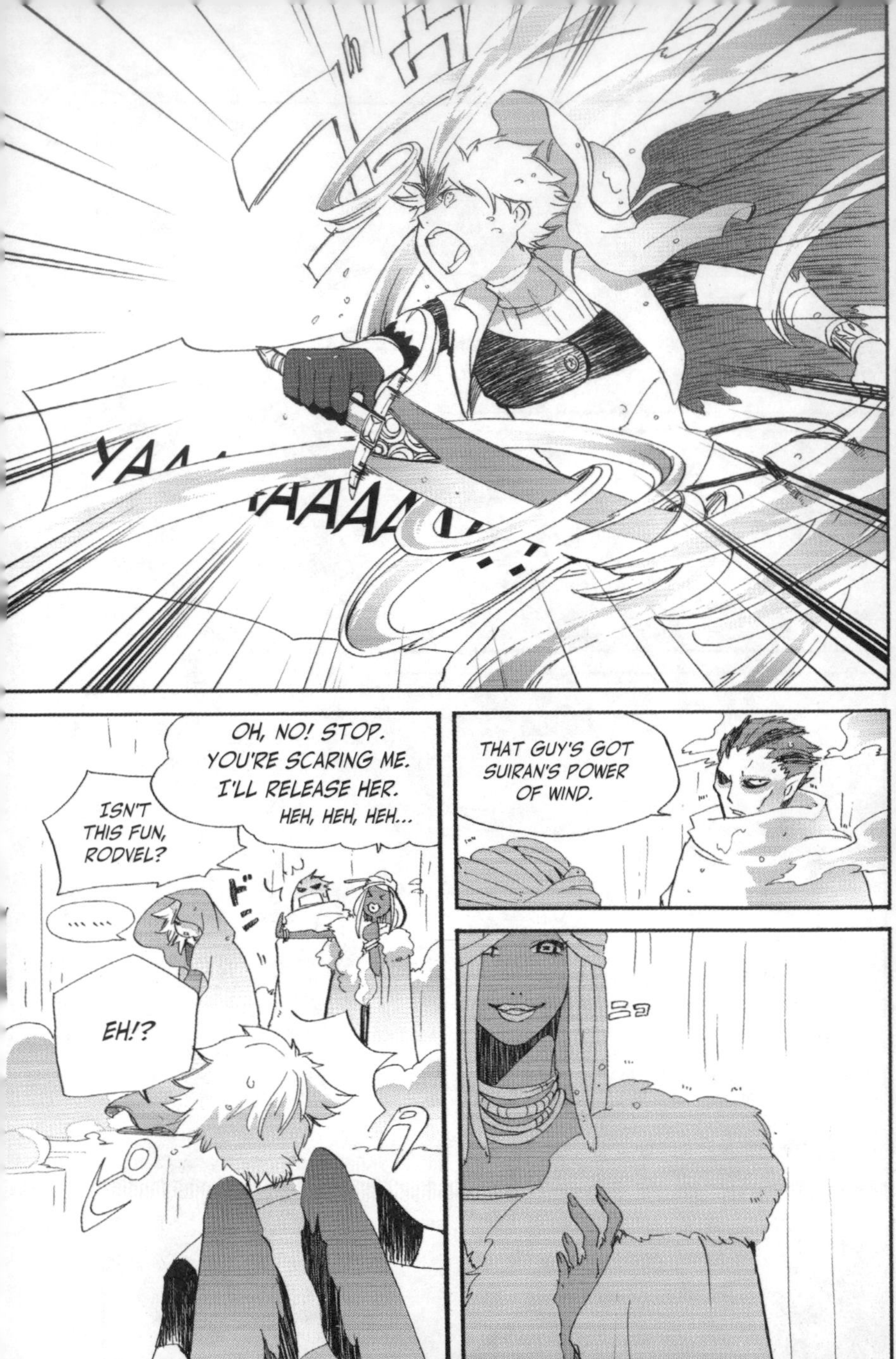

YAA
AAAAA
THAT GUY'S GOT SUIRAN'S POWER OF WIND.
ニコ
ISN'T THIS FUN, RODVEL?
OH, NO! STOP. YOU'RE SCARING ME. I'LL RELEASE HER.
HEH, HEH, HEH...
... ...
EH!?

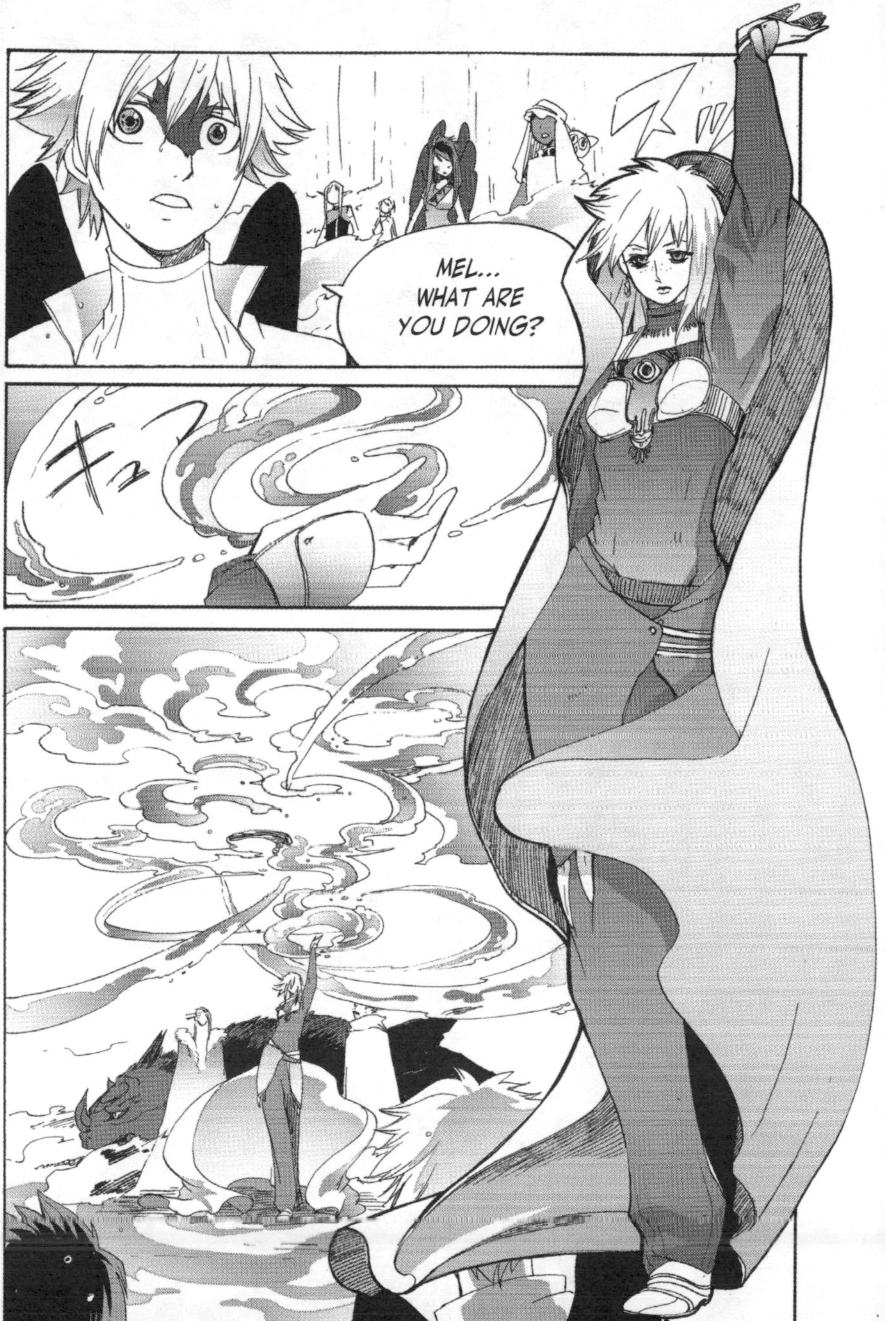
MEL... WHAT ARE YOU DOING?

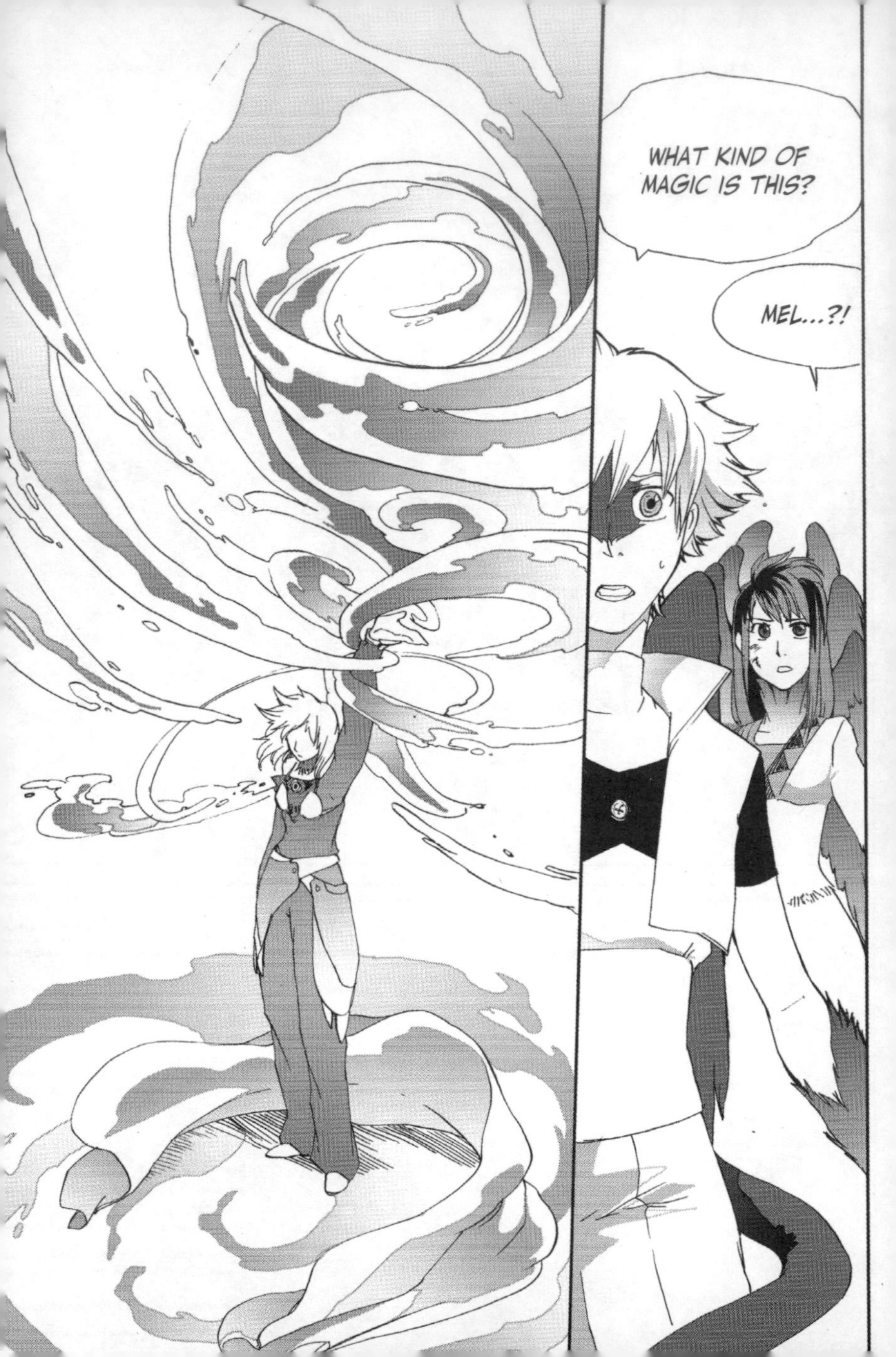
WHAT KIND OF MAGIC IS THIS?
MEL...?!

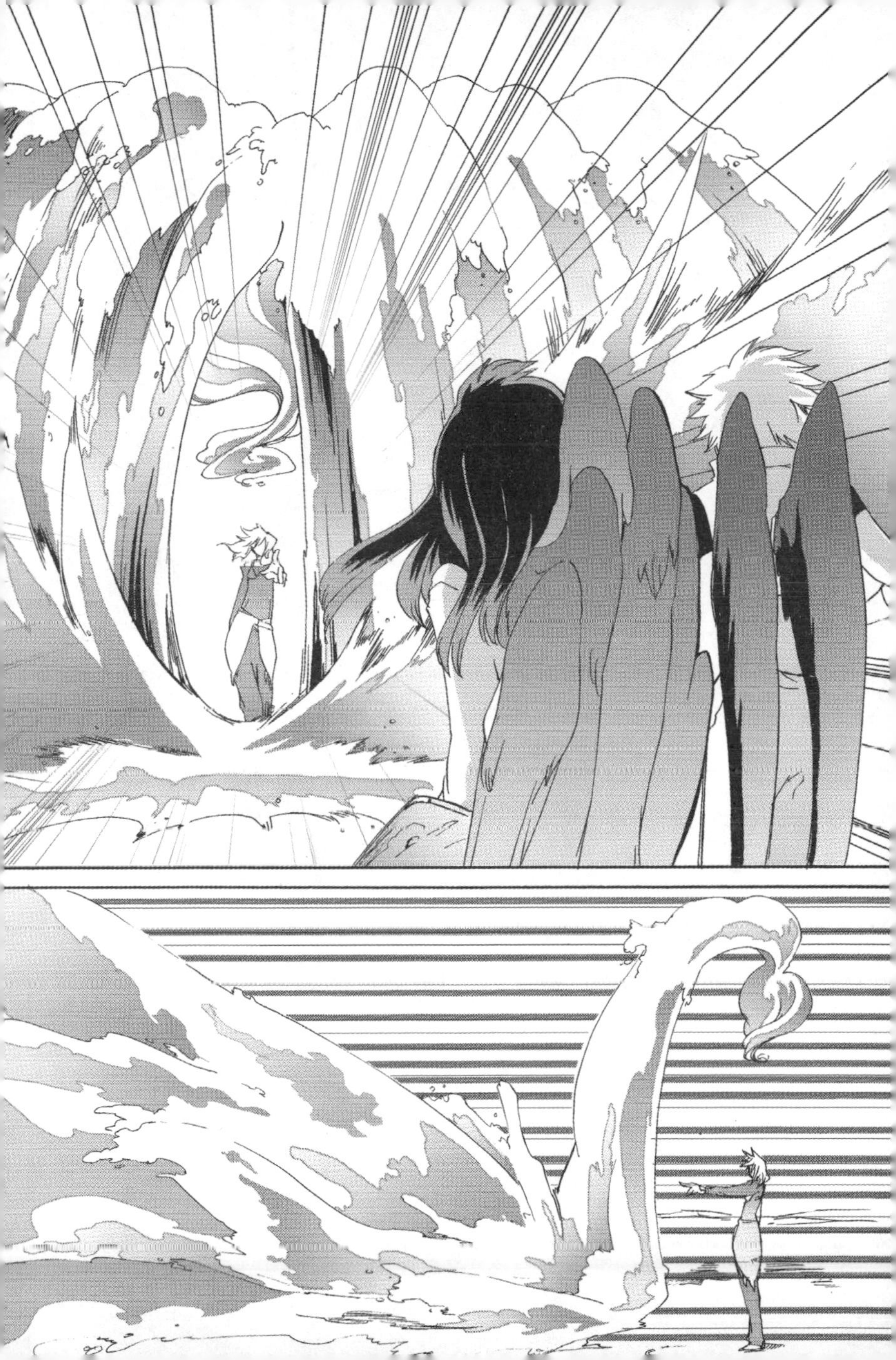

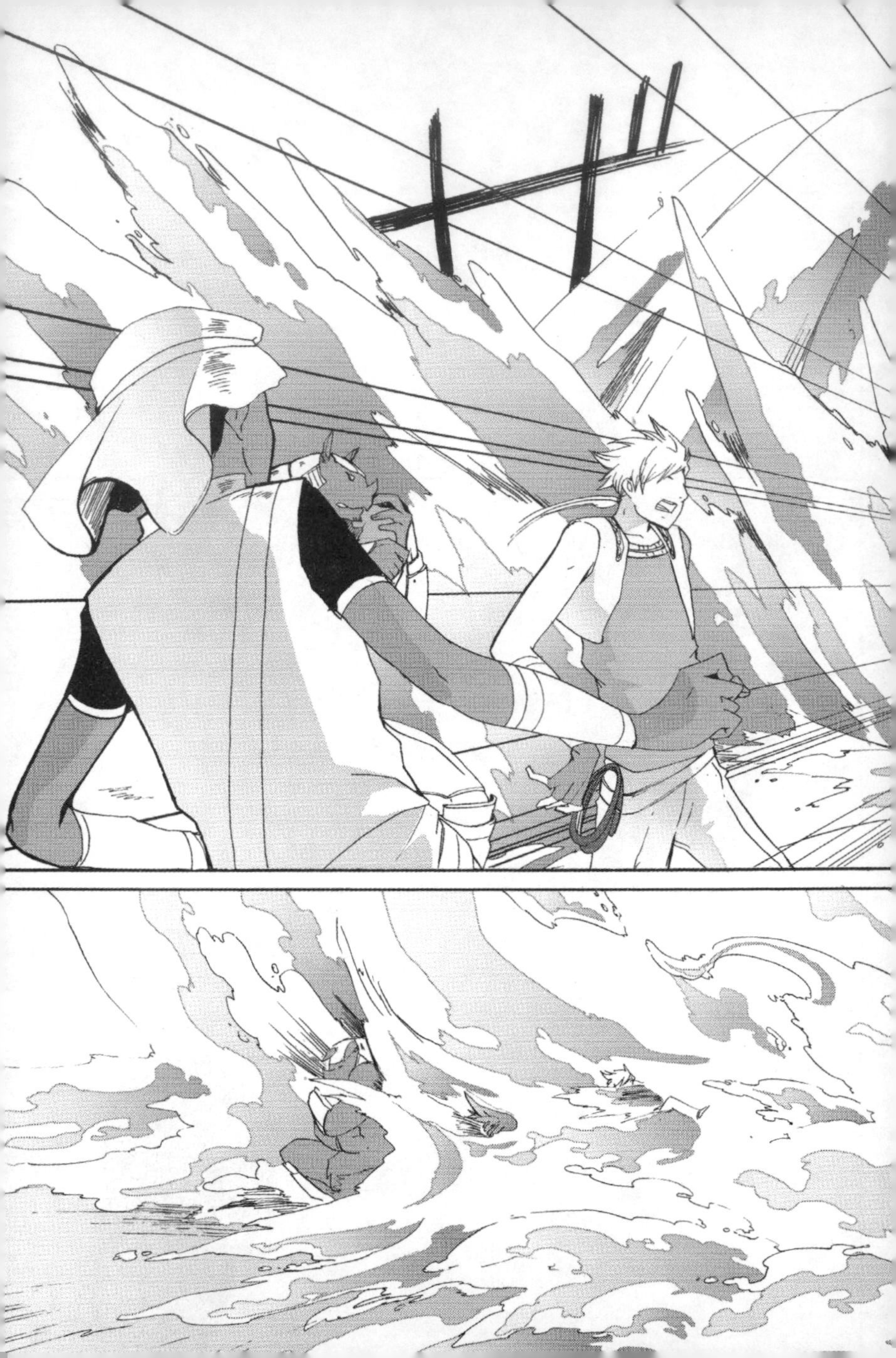

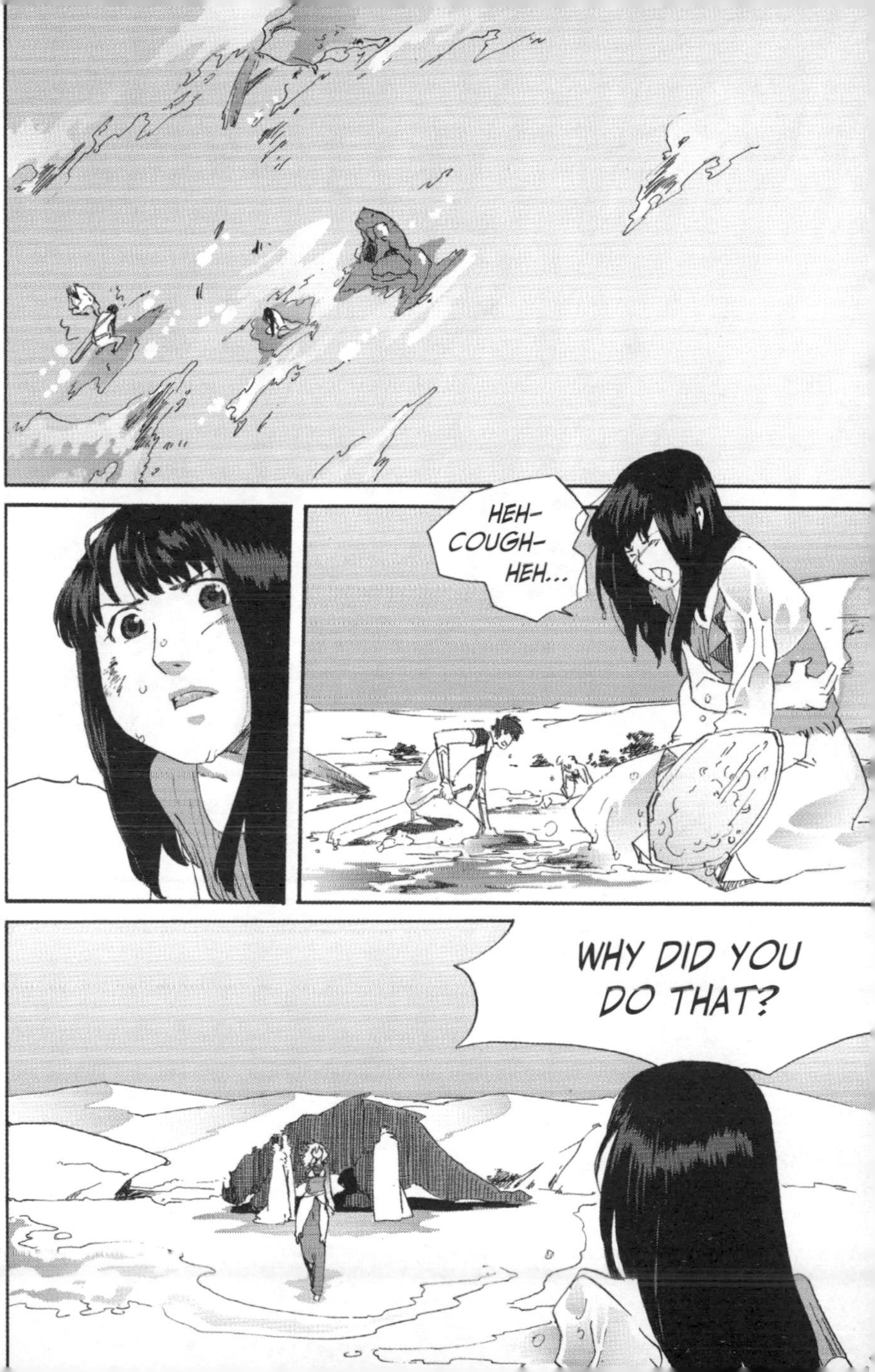
HEH-
COUGH-
HEH...
WHY DID YOU DO THAT?

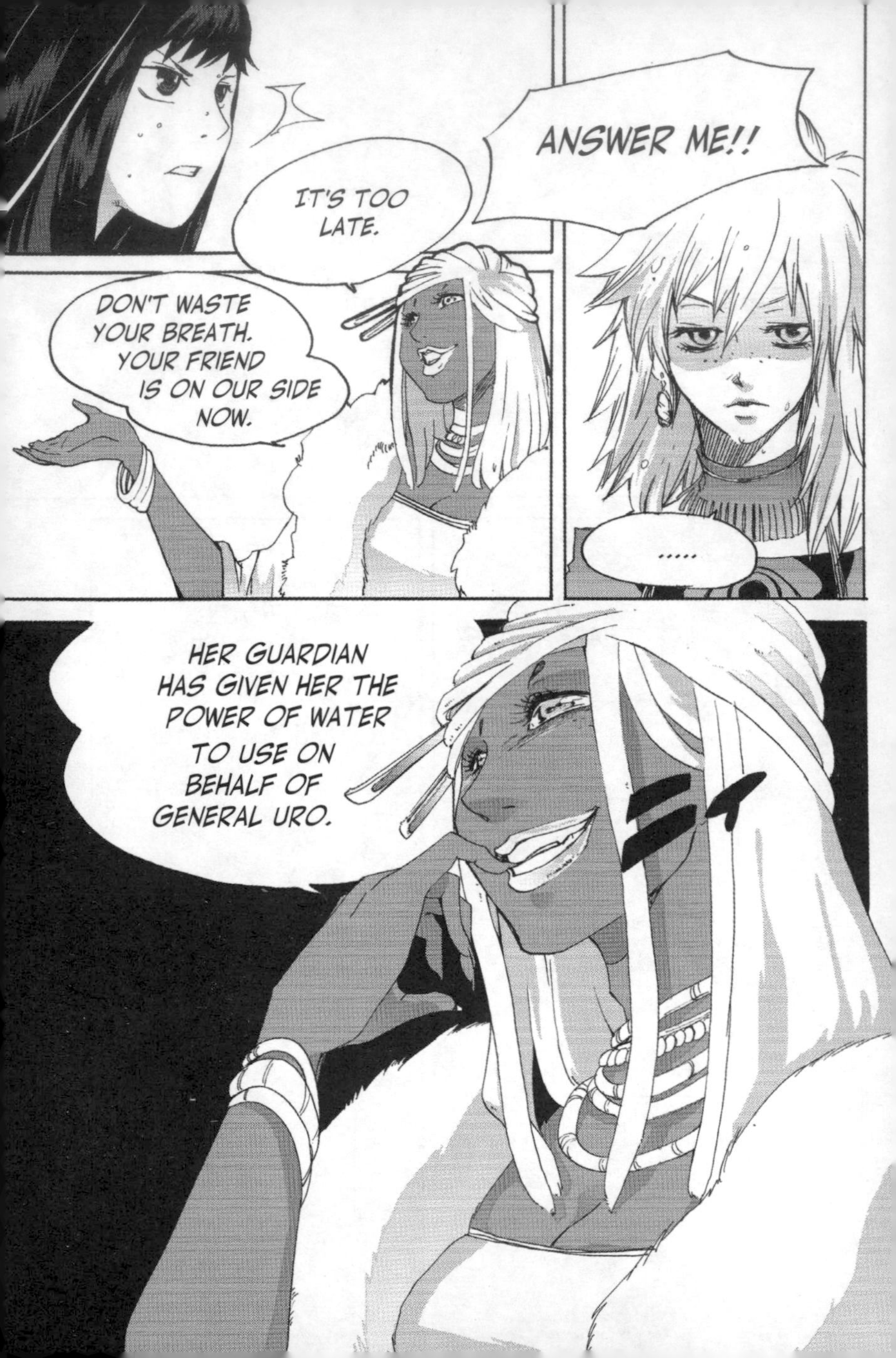
IT'S TOO LATE.
ANSWER ME!!
DON'T WASTE YOUR BREATH. YOUR FRIEND IS ON OUR SIDE NOW.
......
HER GUARDIAN HAS GIVEN HER THE POWER OF WATER TO USE ON BEHALF OF GENERAL URO.

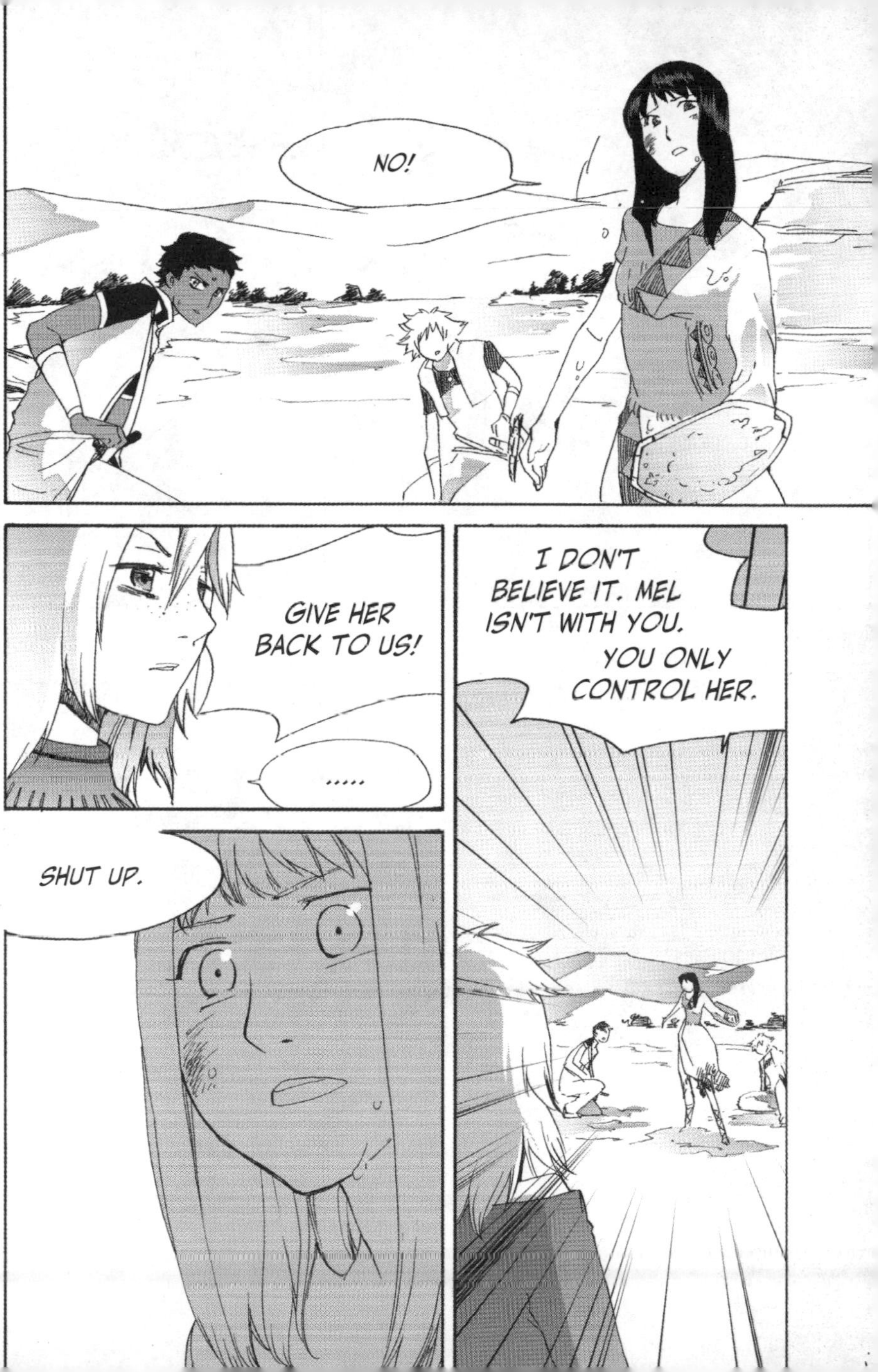
NO!
GIVE HER BACK TO US!
.....
I DON'T BELIEVE IT. MEL ISN'T WITH YOU.
YOU ONLY CONTROL HER.
SHUT UP.

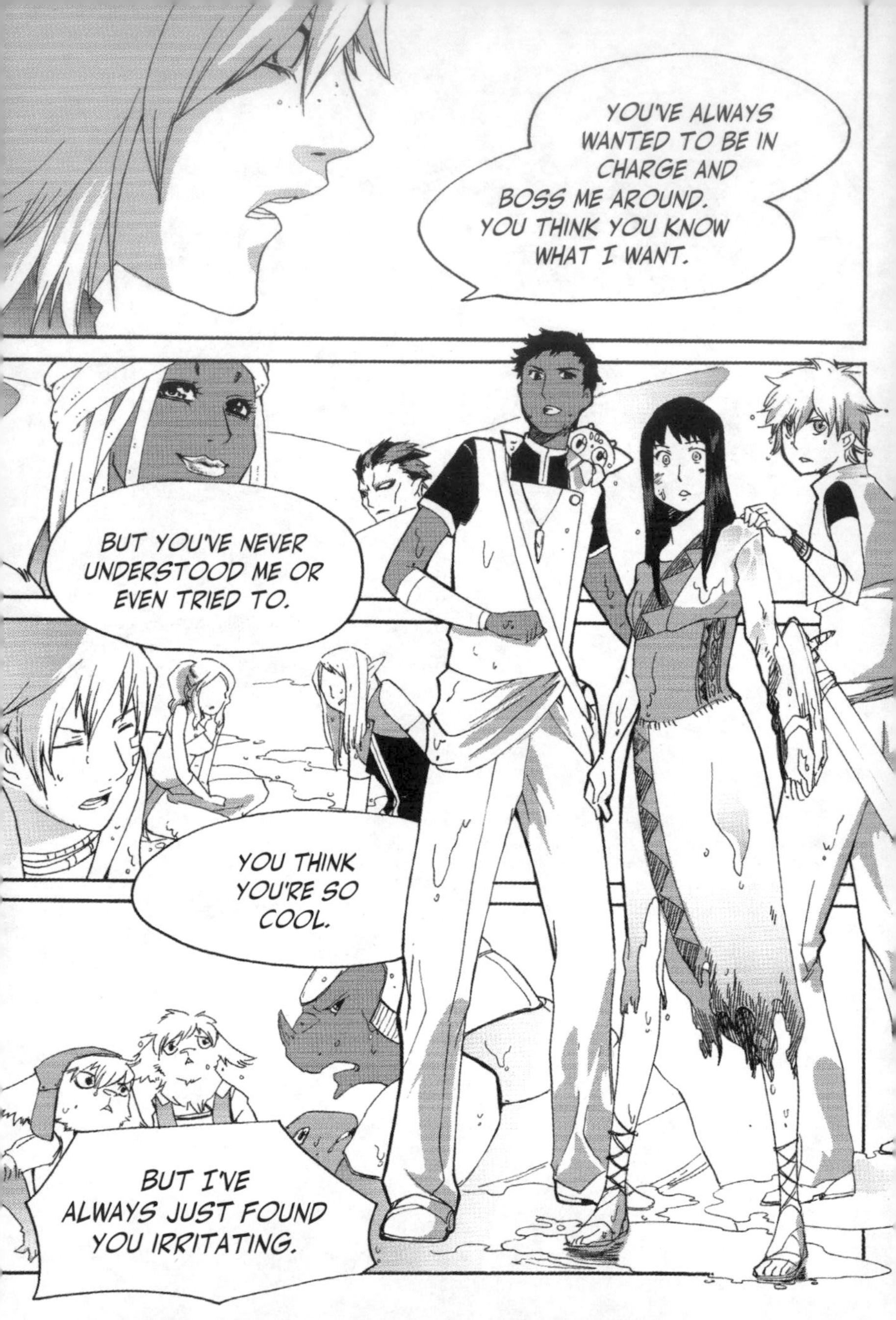
YOU'VE ALWAYS WANTED TO BE IN CHARGE AND BOSS ME AROUND. YOU THINK YOU KNOW WHAT I WANT.
BUT YOU'VE NEVER UNDERSTOOD ME OR EVEN TRIED TO.
YOU THINK YOU'RE SO COOL.
BUT I'VE ALWAYS JUST FOUND YOU IRRITATING.

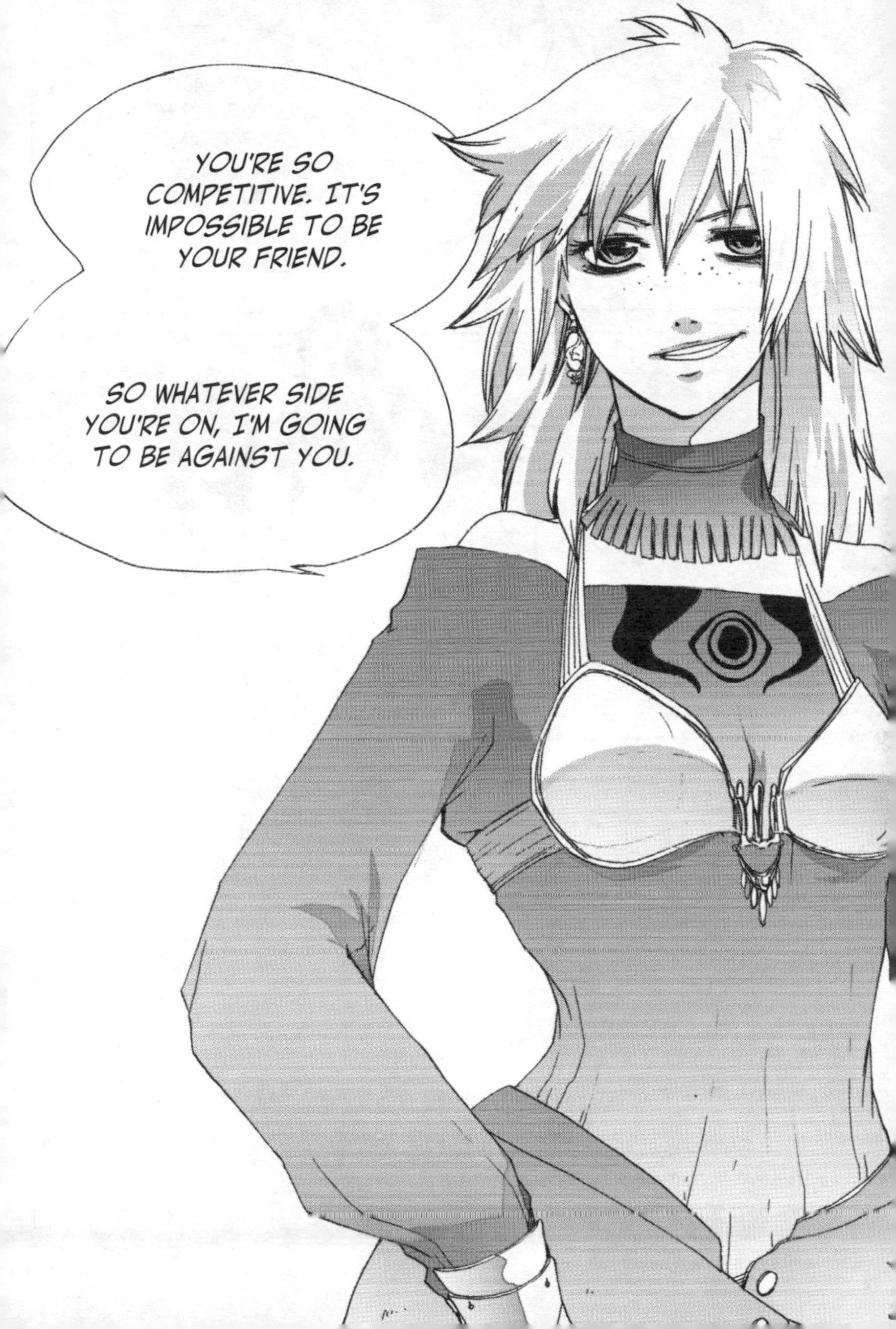
YOU'RE SO COMPETITIVE. IT'S IMPOSSIBLE TO BE YOUR FRIEND.
SO WHATEVER SIDE YOU'RE ON, I'M GOING TO BE AGAINST YOU.

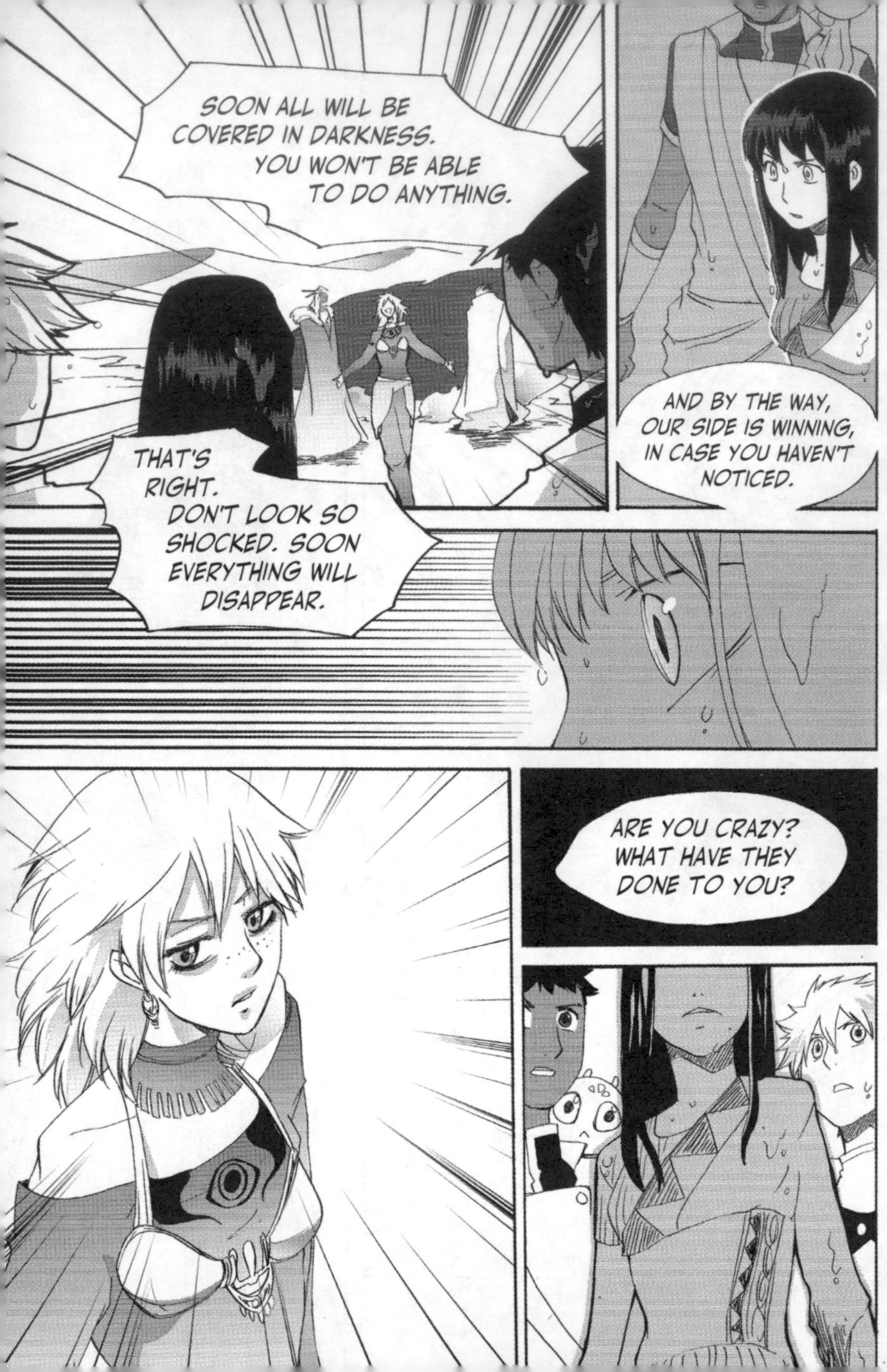
SOON ALL WILL BE COVERED IN DARKNESS. YOU WON'T BE ABLE TO DO ANYTHING.
AND BY THE WAY, OUR SIDE IS WINNING, IN CASE YOU HAVEN'T NOTICED.
THAT'S RIGHT. DON'T LOOK SO SHOCKED. SOON EVERYTHING WILL DISAPPEAR.
ARE YOU CRAZY? WHAT HAVE THEY DONE TO YOU?

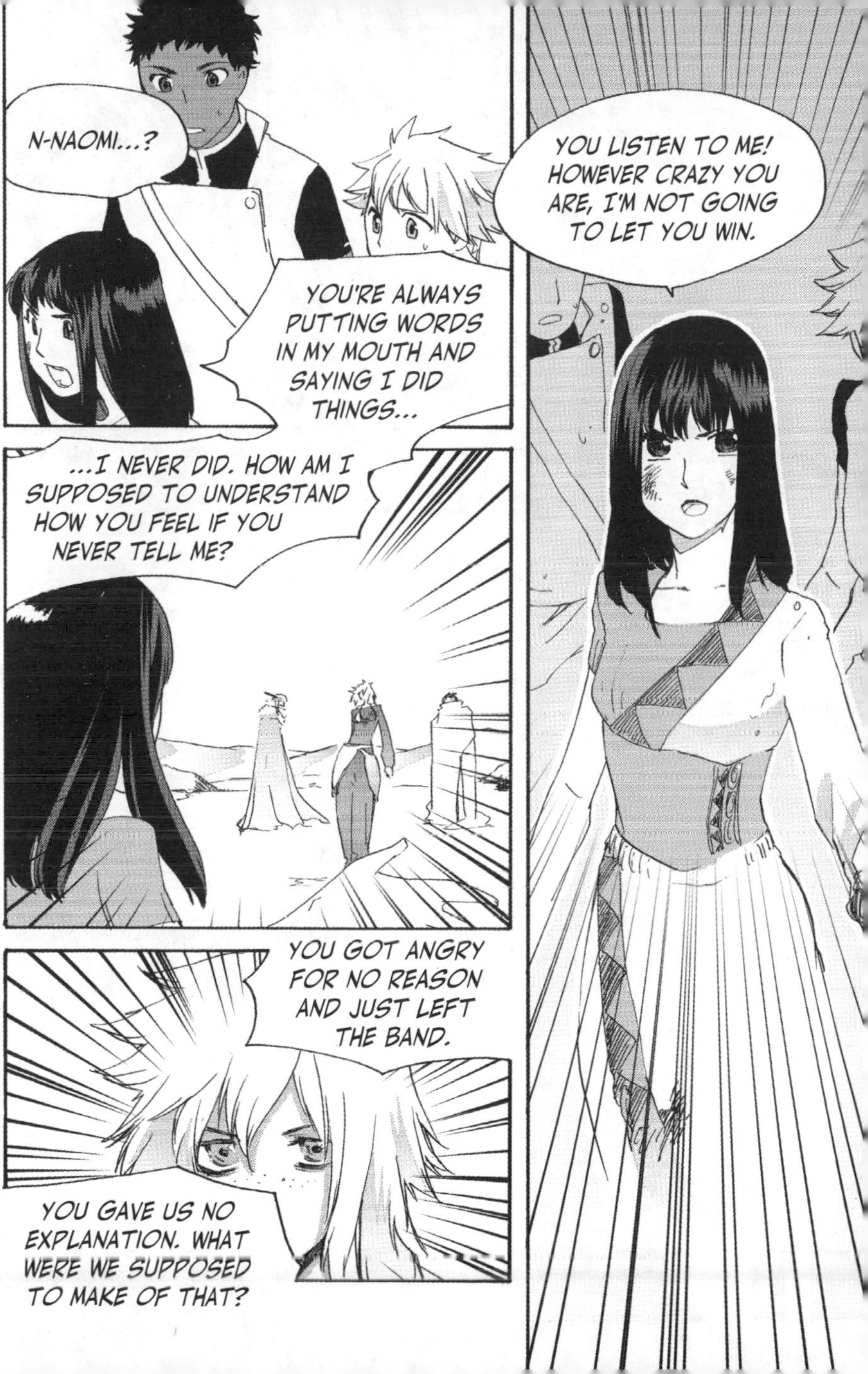
N-NAOMI...?
YOU'RE ALWAYS PUTTING WORDS IN MY MOUTH AND SAYING I DID THINGS...
...I NEVER DID. HOW AM I SUPPOSED TO UNDERSTAND HOW YOU FEEL IF YOU NEVER TELL ME?
YOU GOT ANGRY FOR NO REASON AND JUST LEFT THE BAND.
YOU GAVE US NO EXPLANATION. WHAT WERE WE SUPPOSED TO MAKE OF THAT?
YOU LISTEN TO ME! HOWEVER CRAZY YOU ARE, I'M NOT GOING TO LET YOU WIN.

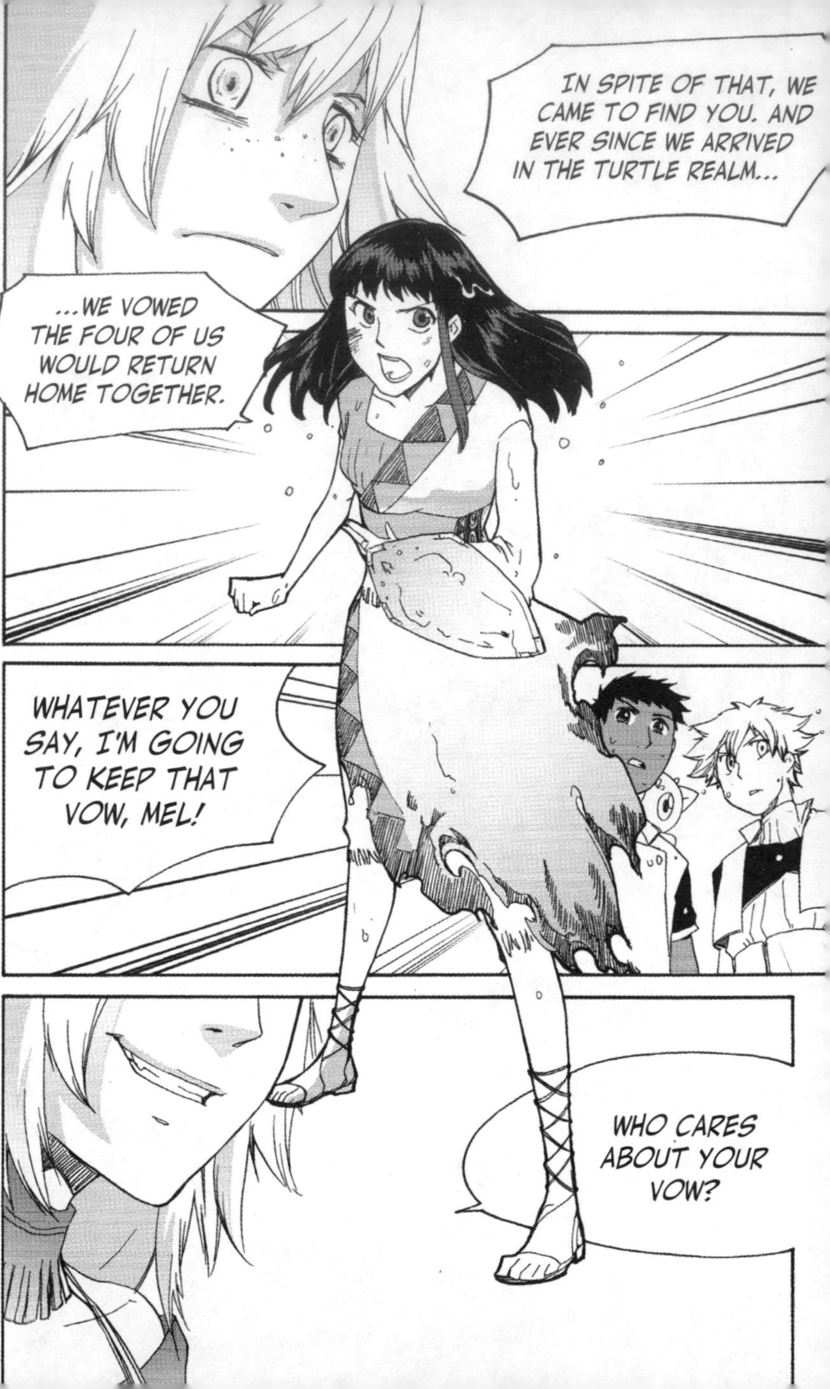
IN SPITE OF THAT, WE CAME TO FIND YOU. AND EVER SINCE WE ARRIVED IN THE TURTLE REALM...
...WE VOWED THE FOUR OF US WOULD RETURN HOME TOGETHER.
WHATEVER YOU SAY, I'M GOING TO KEEP THAT VOW, MEL!
WHO CARES ABOUT YOUR VOW?

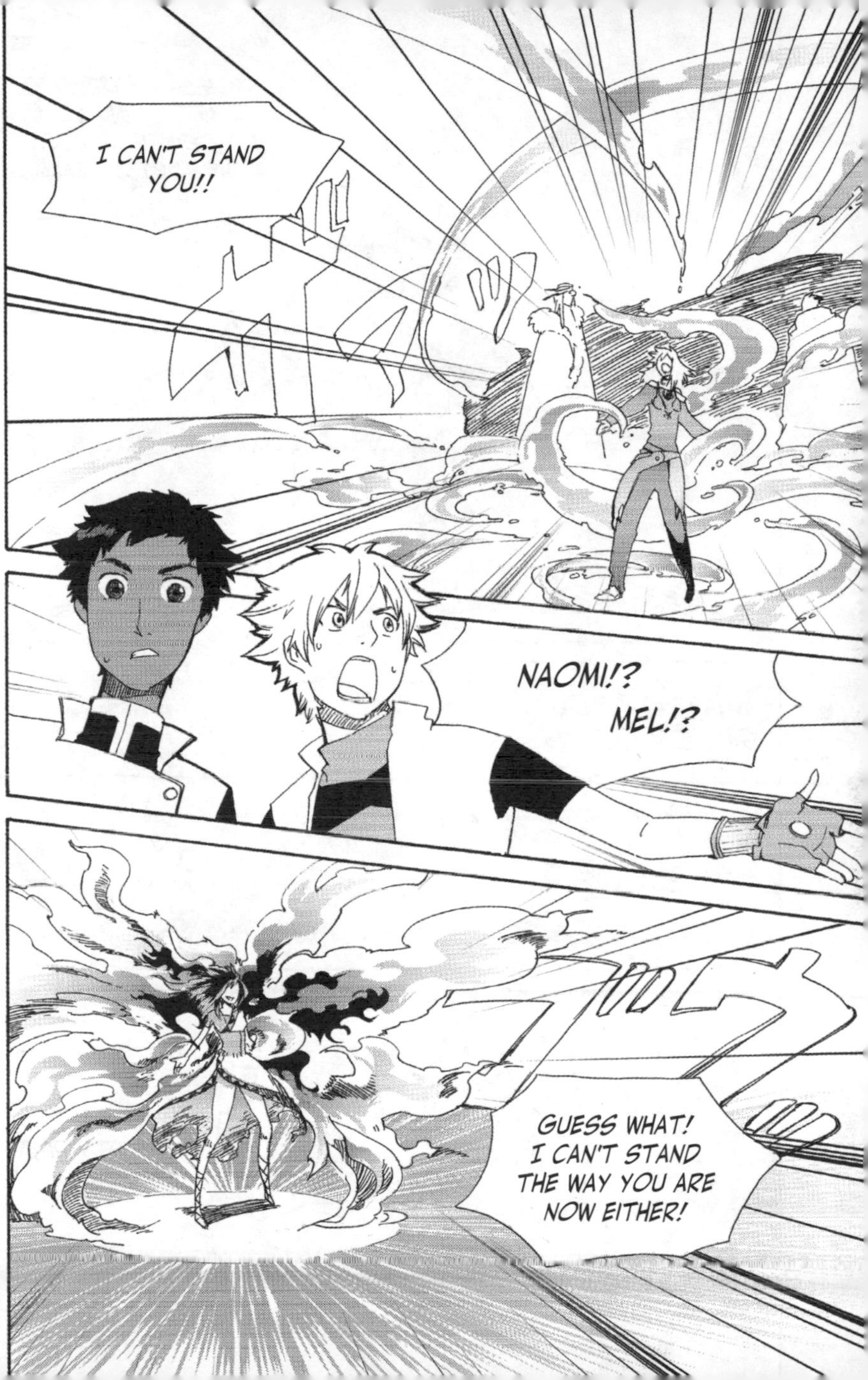
I CAN'T STAND YOU!!
NAOMI!? MEL!?
GUESS WHAT! I CAN'T STAND THE WAY YOU ARE NOW EITHER!

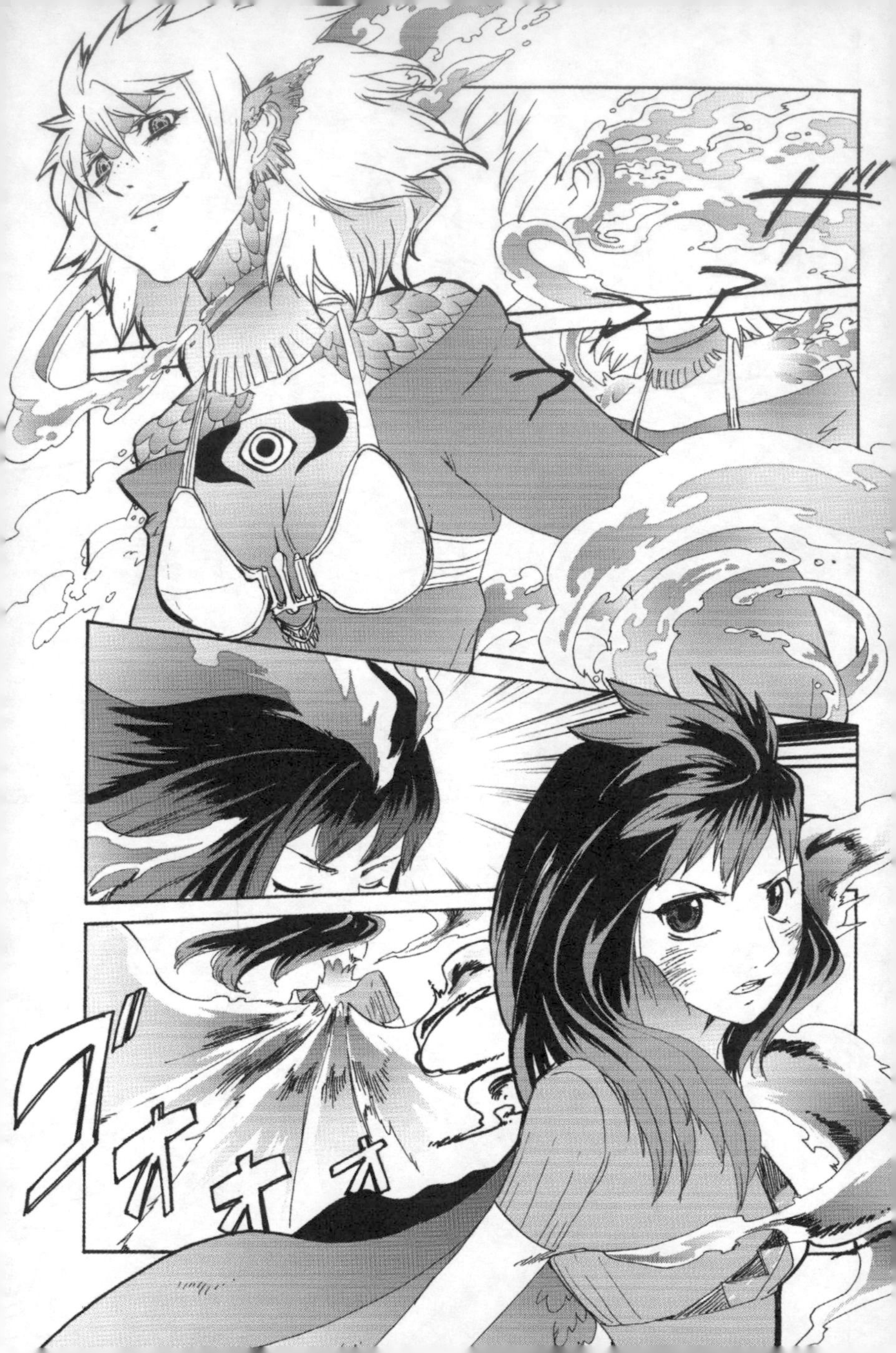
ザ
ゴオオオ

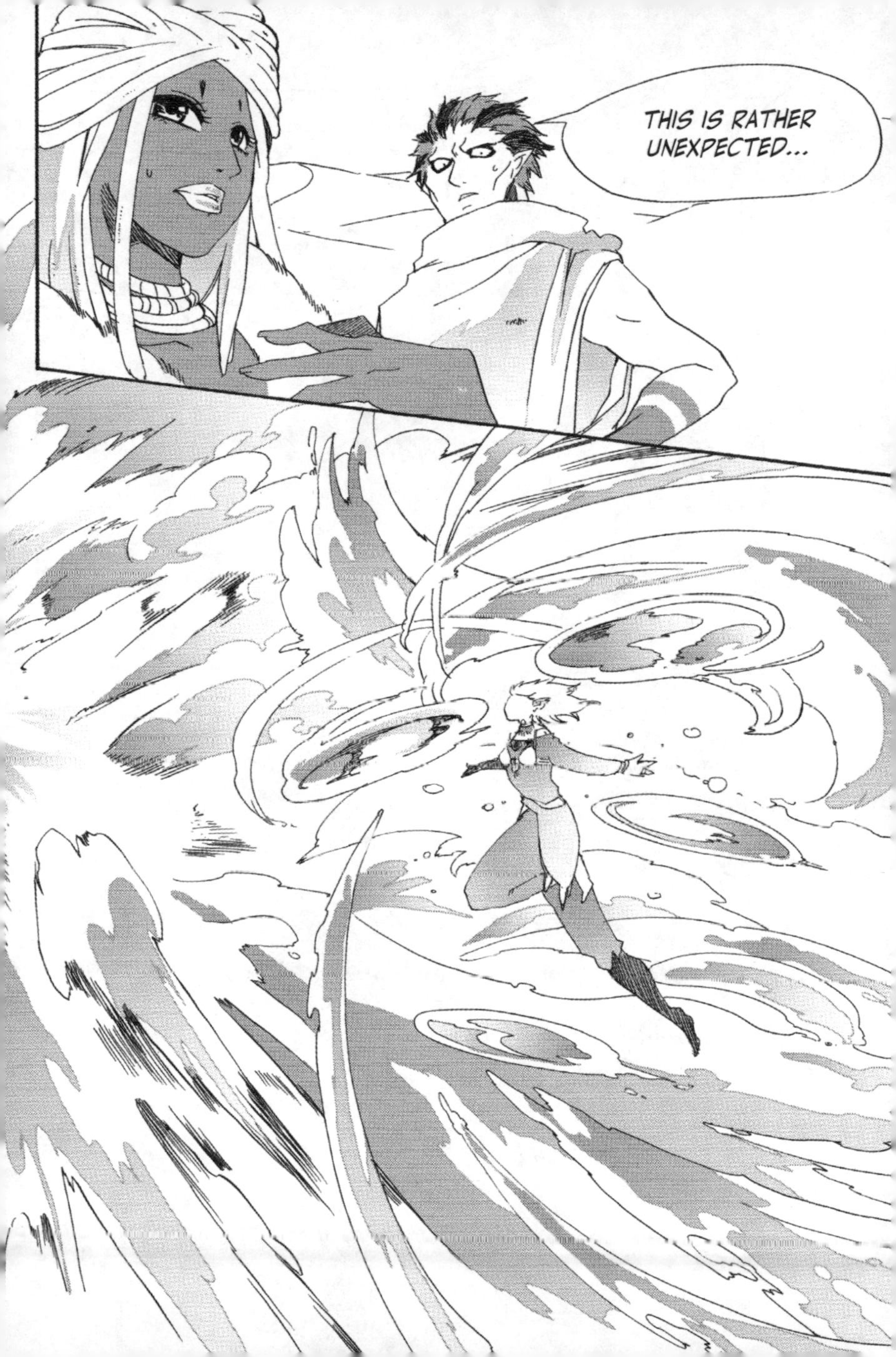
THIS IS RATHER UNEXPECTED...

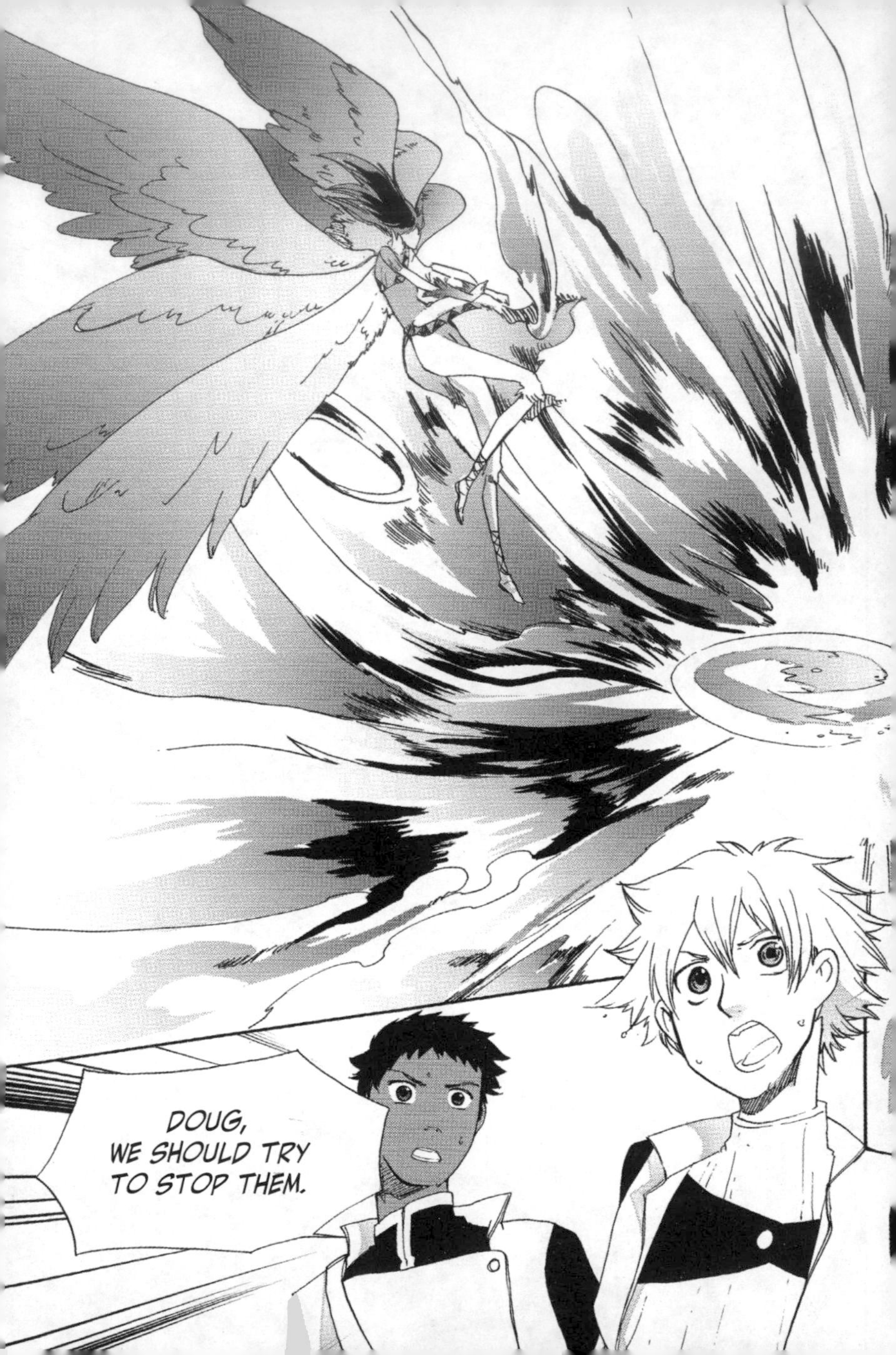
DOUG,
WE SHOULD TRY
TO STOP THEM.

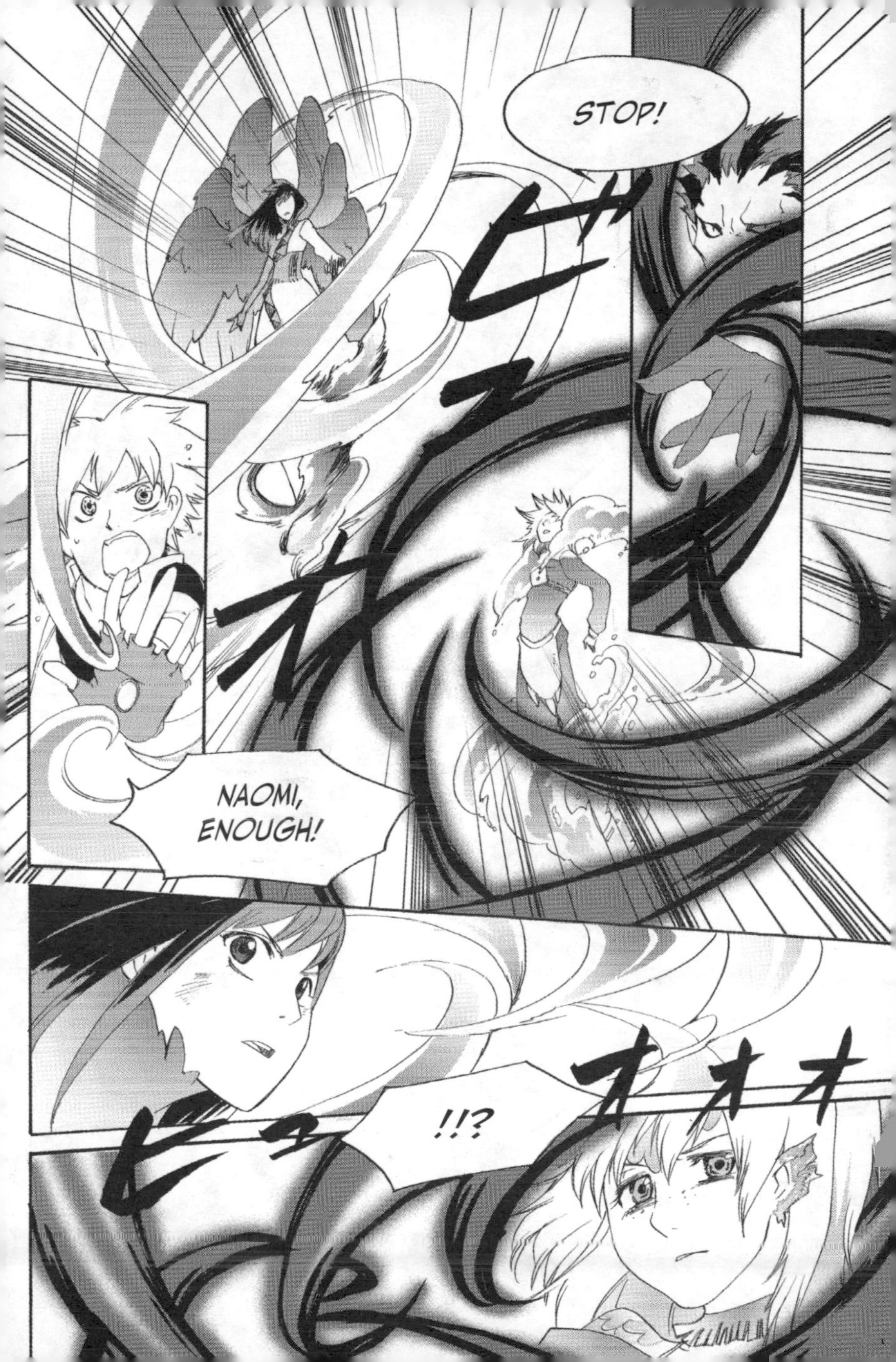
STOP!
NAOMI, ENOUGH!
!!?

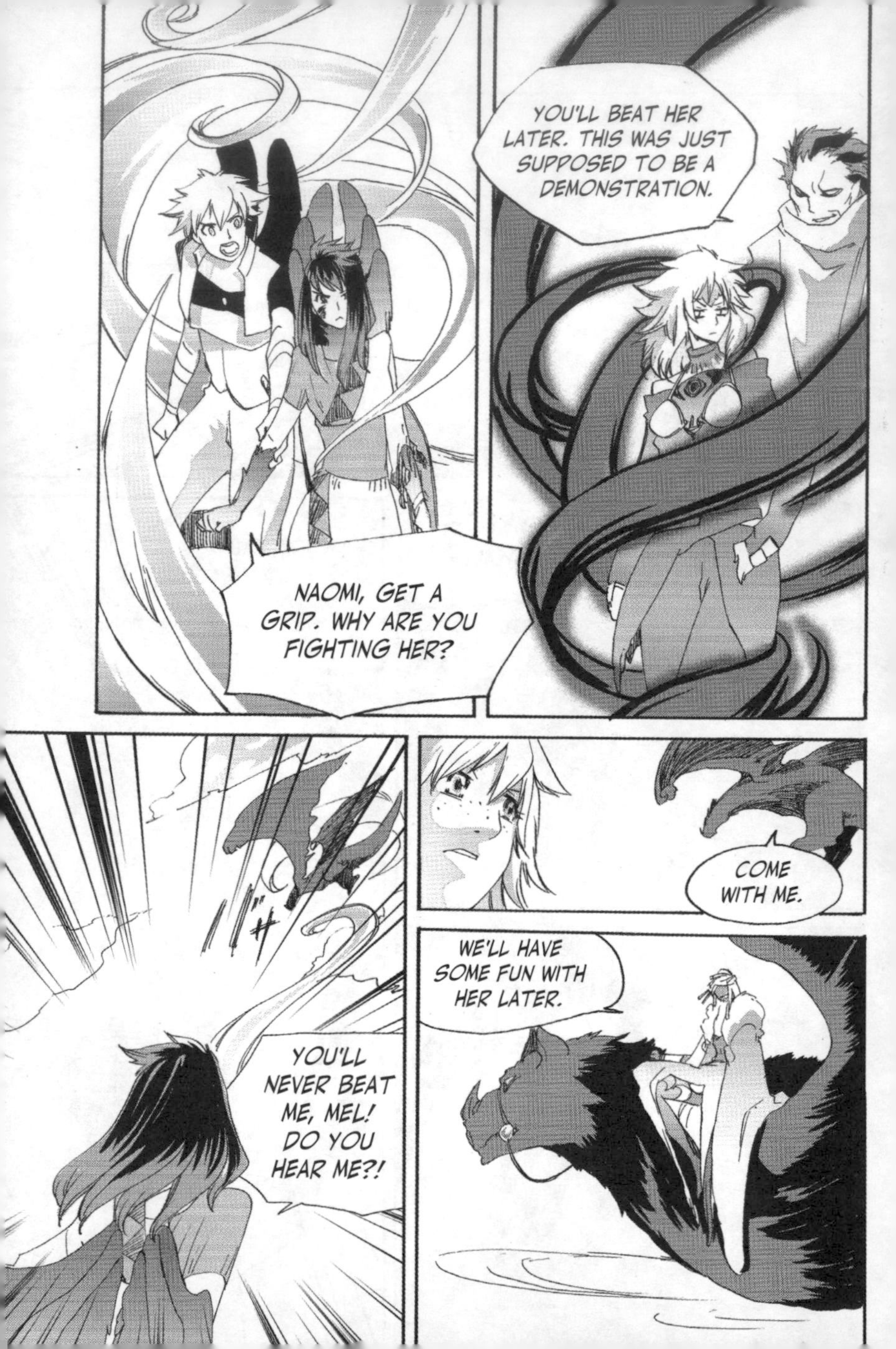
NAOMI, GET A GRIP. WHY ARE YOU FIGHTING HER?
YOU'LL BEAT HER LATER. THIS WAS JUST SUPPOSED TO BE A DEMONSTRATION.
YOU'LL NEVER BEAT ME, MEL! DO YOU HEAR ME?!
COME WITH ME.
WE'LL HAVE SOME FUN WITH HER LATER.

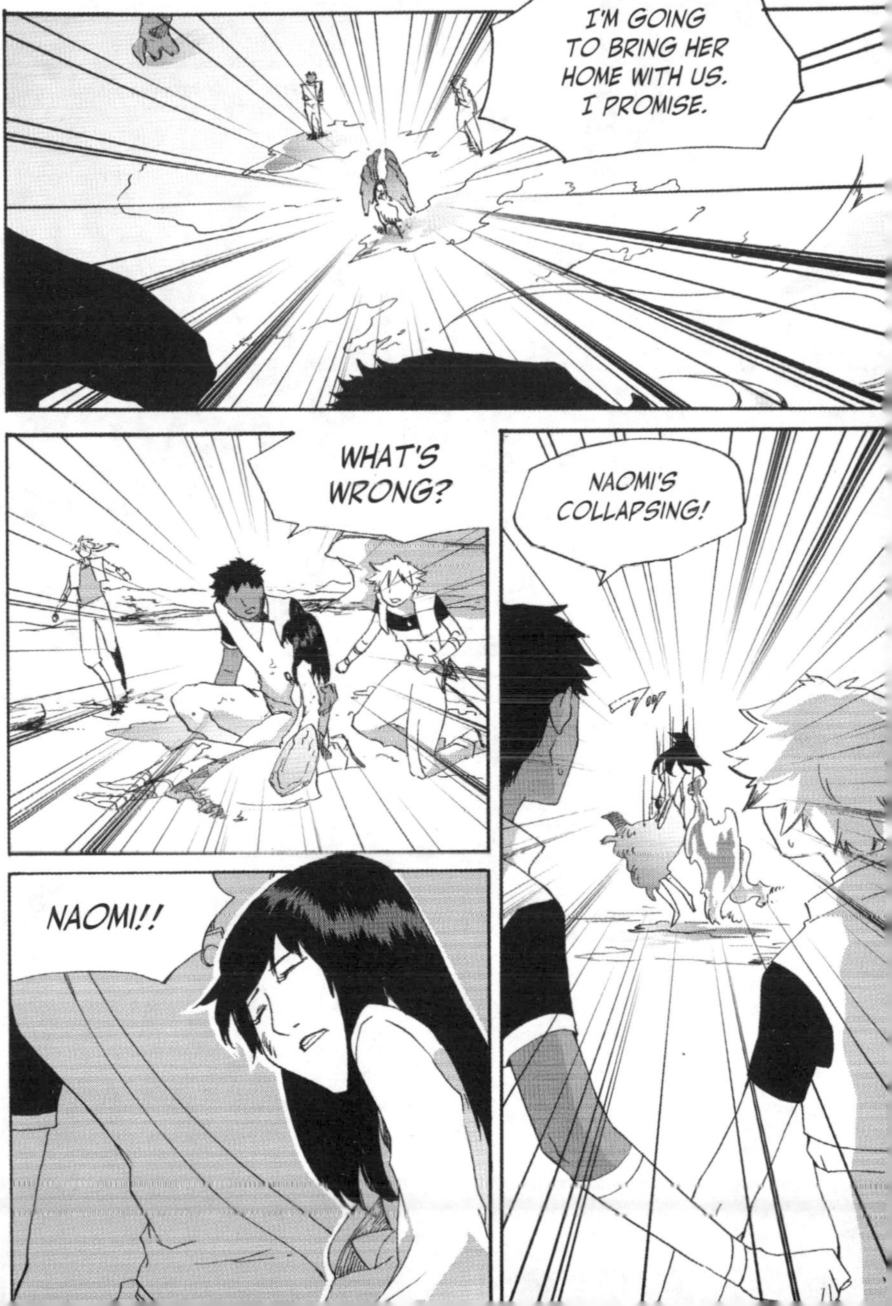
I'M GOING
TO BRING HER
HOME WITH US.
I PROMISE.
WHAT'S
WRONG?
NAOMI'S
COLLAPSING!
NAOMI!!

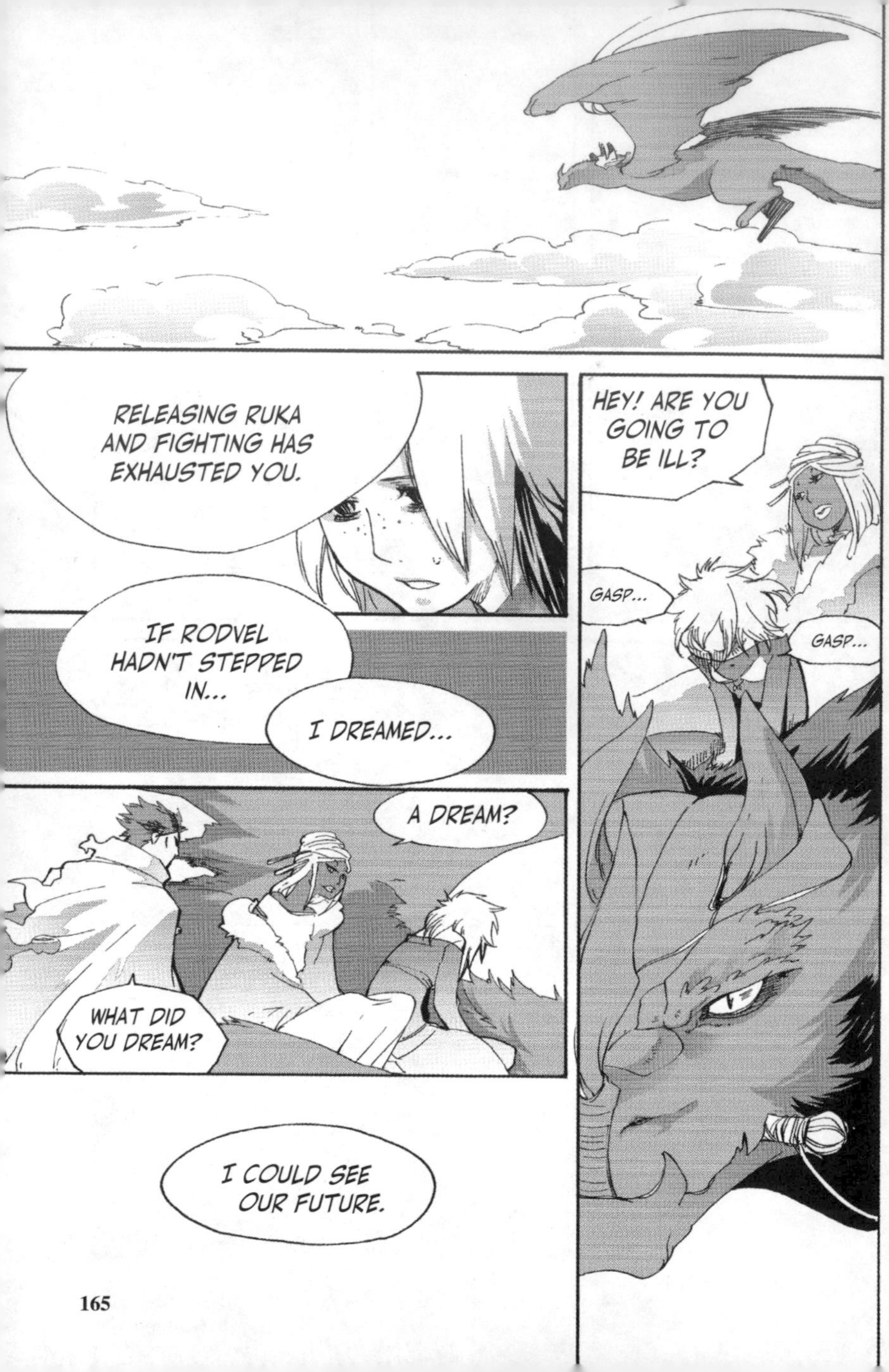
RELEASING RUKA AND FIGHTING HAS EXHAUSTED YOU.
HEY! ARE YOU GOING TO BE ILL?
GASP...
GASP...
IF RODVEL HADN'T STEPPED IN...
I DREAMED...
A DREAM?
WHAT DID YOU DREAM?
I COULD SEE OUR FUTURE.

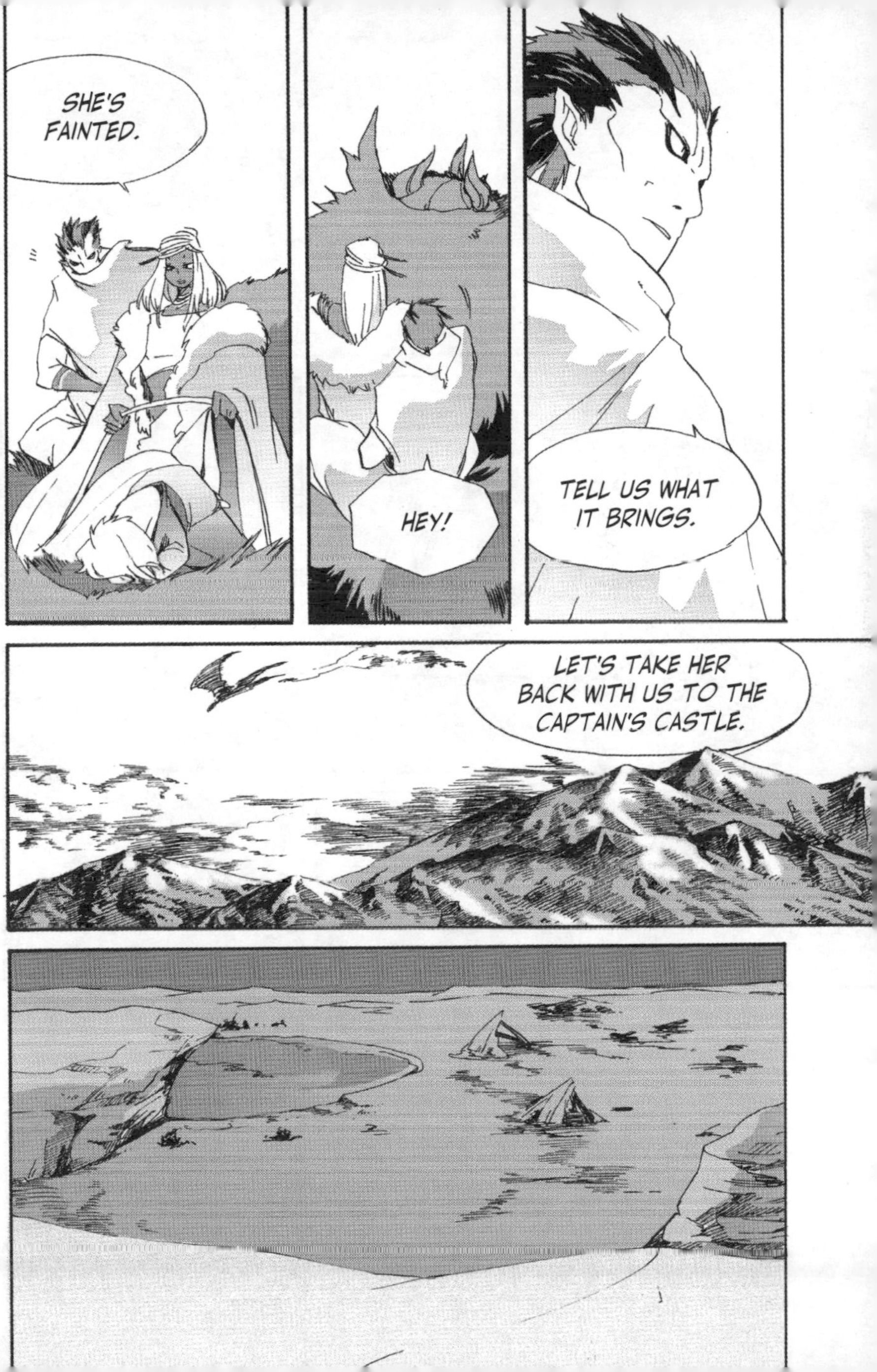
SHE'S FAINTED.
HEY!
TELL US WHAT IT BRINGS.
LET'S TAKE HER BACK WITH US TO THE CAPTAIN'S CASTLE.

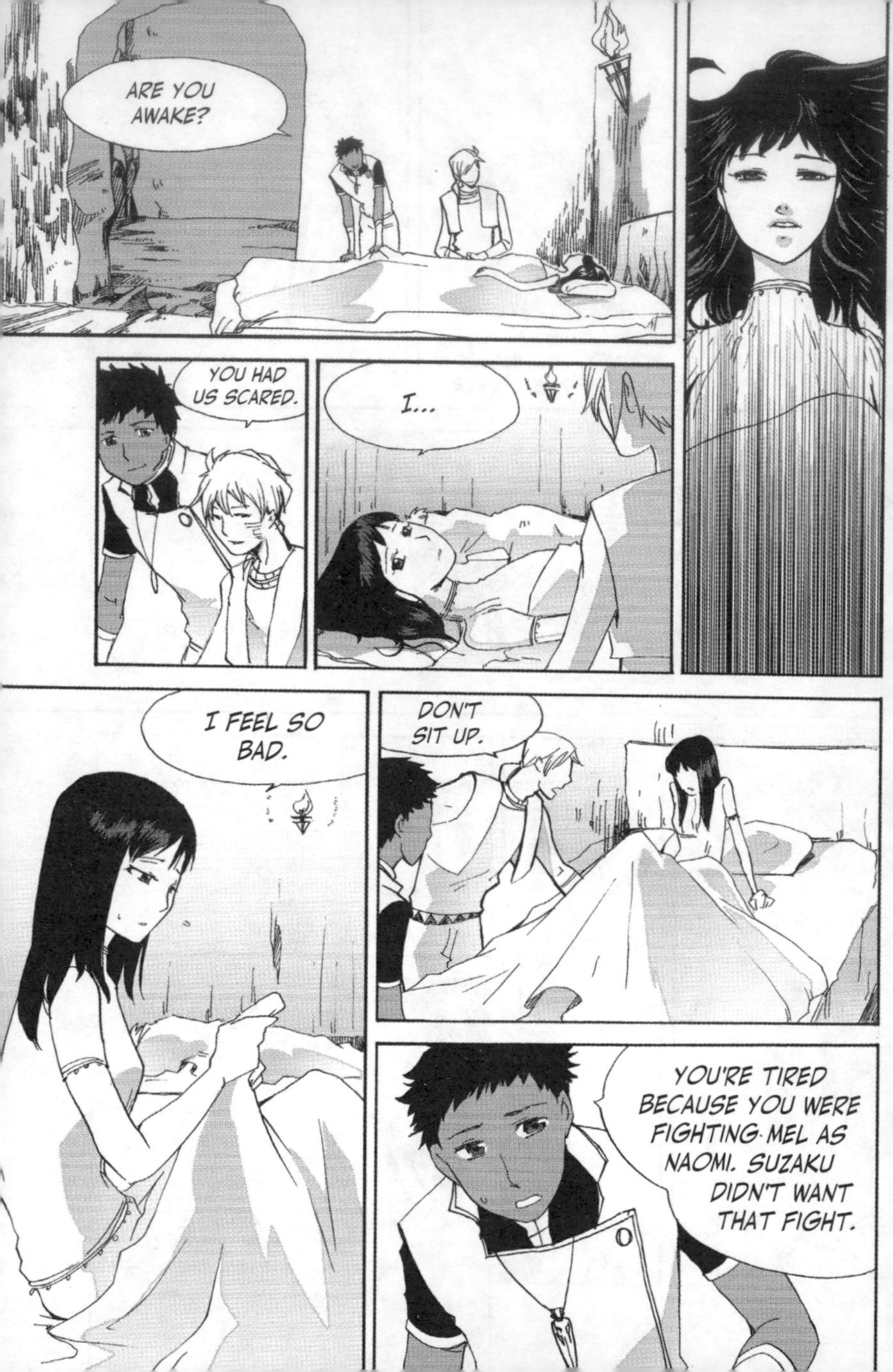
ARE YOU AWAKE?
YOU HAD US SCARED.
I...
I FEEL SO BAD.
DON'T SIT UP.
YOU'RE TIRED BECAUSE YOU WERE FIGHTING MEL AS NAOMI. SUZAKU DIDN'T WANT THAT FIGHT.

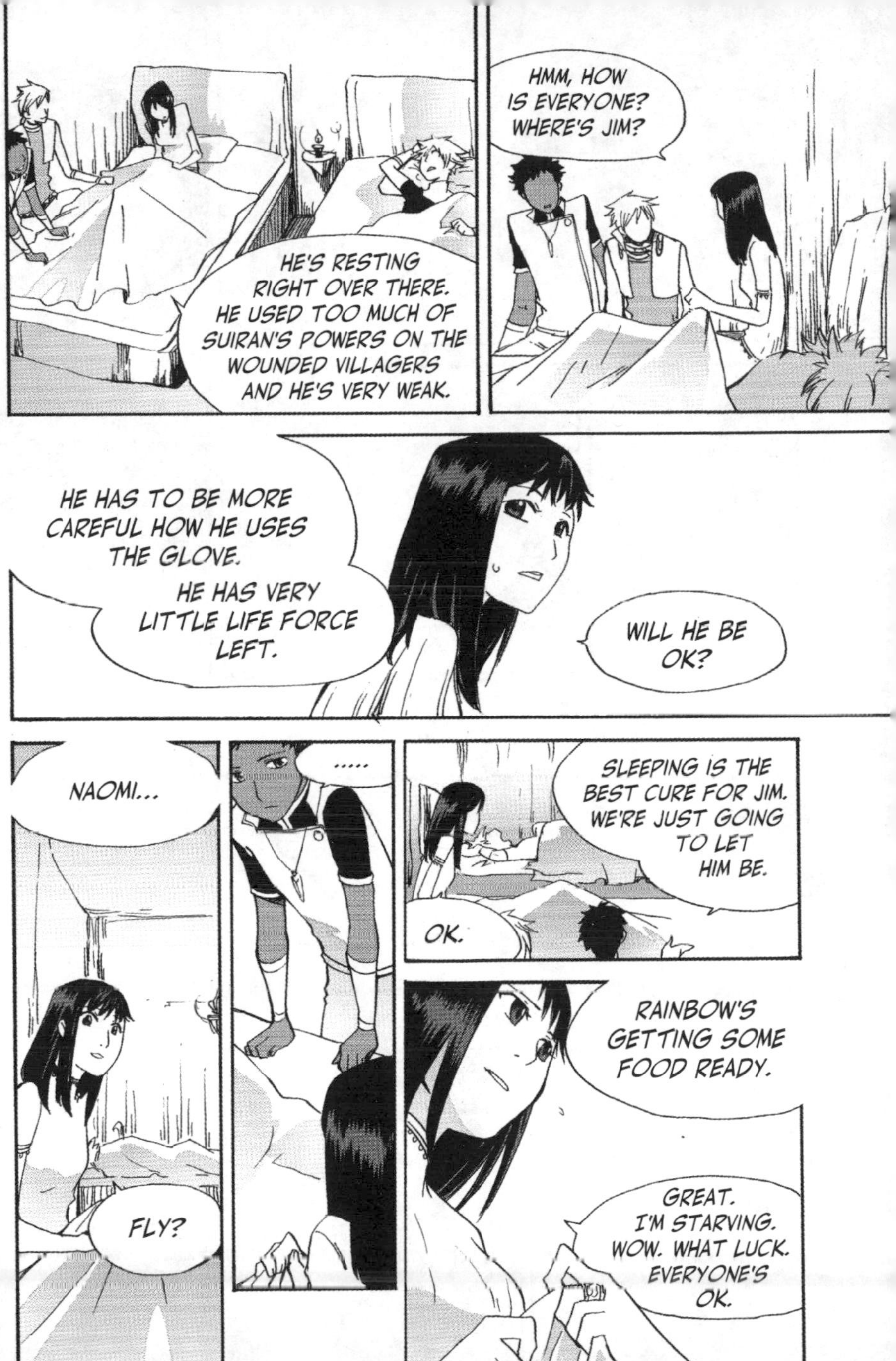
HE'S RESTING RIGHT OVER THERE. HE USED TOO MUCH OF SUIRAN'S POWERS ON THE WOUNDED VILLAGERS AND HE'S VERY WEAK.
HMM, HOW IS EVERYONE? WHERE'S JIM?
HE HAS TO BE MORE CAREFUL HOW HE USES THE GLOVE.
HE HAS VERY LITTLE LIFE FORCE LEFT.
WILL HE BE OK?
NAOMI...
.....
SLEEPING IS THE BEST CURE FOR JIM. WE'RE JUST GOING TO LET HIM BE.
OK.
RAINBOW'S GETTING SOME FOOD READY.
FLY?
GREAT. I'M STARVING. WOW. WHAT LUCK. EVERYONE'S OK.

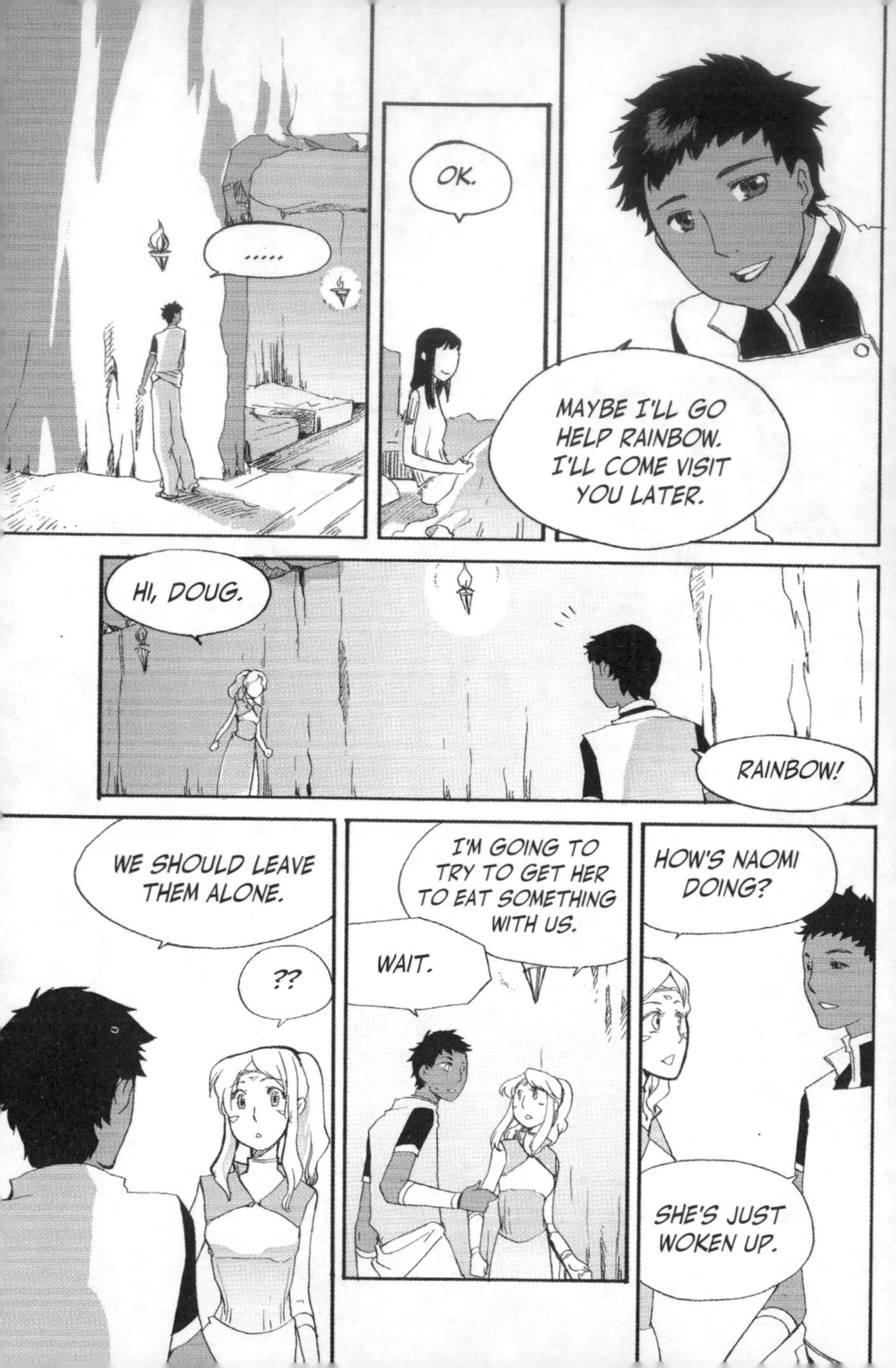
......
OK.
MAYBE I'LL GO HELP RAINBOW. I'LL COME VISIT YOU LATER.
HI, DOUG.
RAINBOW!
WE SHOULD LEAVE THEM ALONE.
??
I'M GOING TO TRY TO GET HER TO EAT SOMETHING WITH US.
WAIT.
HOW'S NAOMI DOING?
SHE'S JUST WOKEN UP.

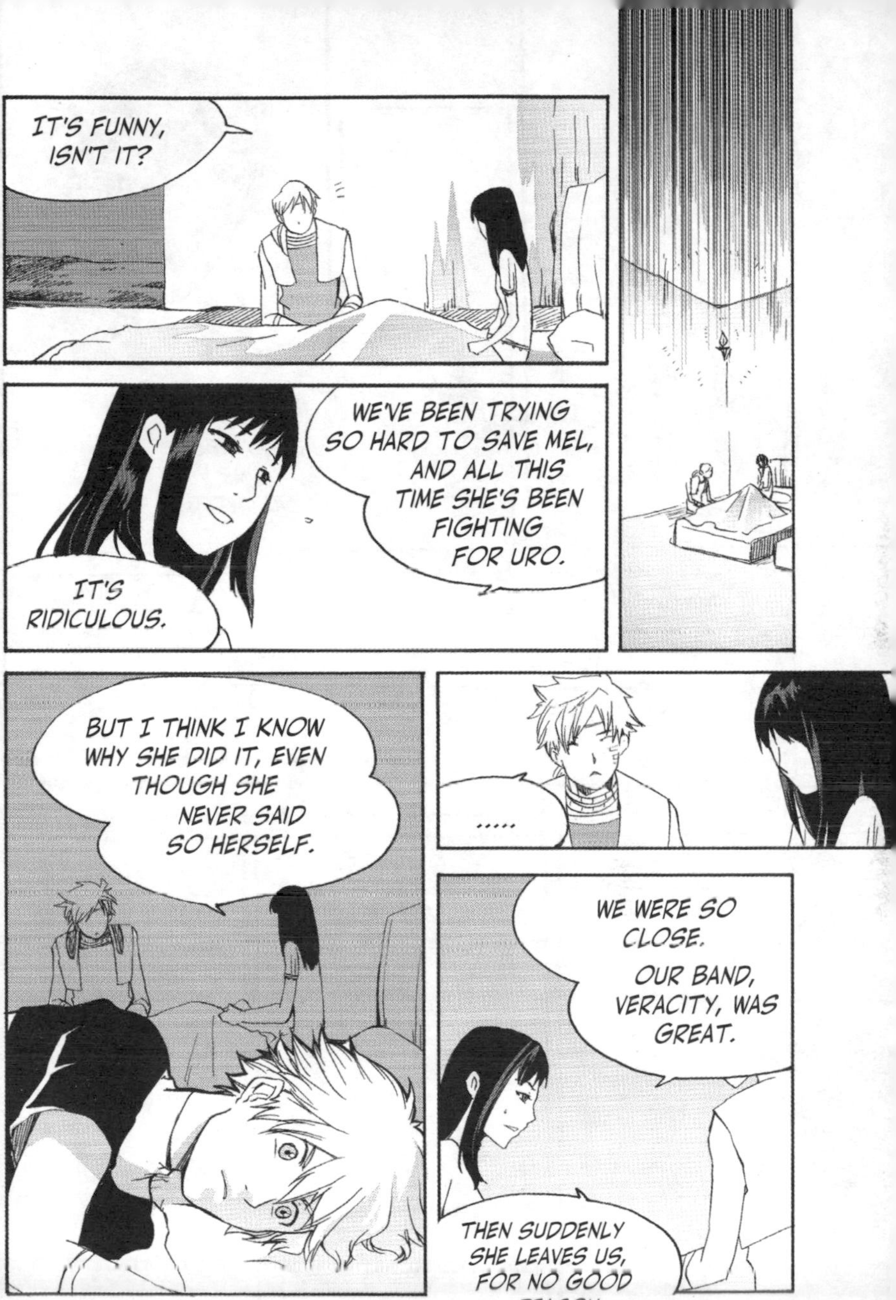
IT'S FUNNY, ISN'T IT?
WE'VE BEEN TRYING SO HARD TO SAVE MEL, AND ALL THIS TIME SHE'S BEEN FIGHTING FOR URO.
IT'S RIDICULOUS.
BUT I THINK I KNOW WHY SHE DID IT, EVEN THOUGH SHE NEVER SAID SO HERSELF.
.....
WE WERE SO CLOSE.
OUR BAND, VERACITY, WAS GREAT.
THEN SUDDENLY SHE LEAVES US, FOR NO GOOD REASON.

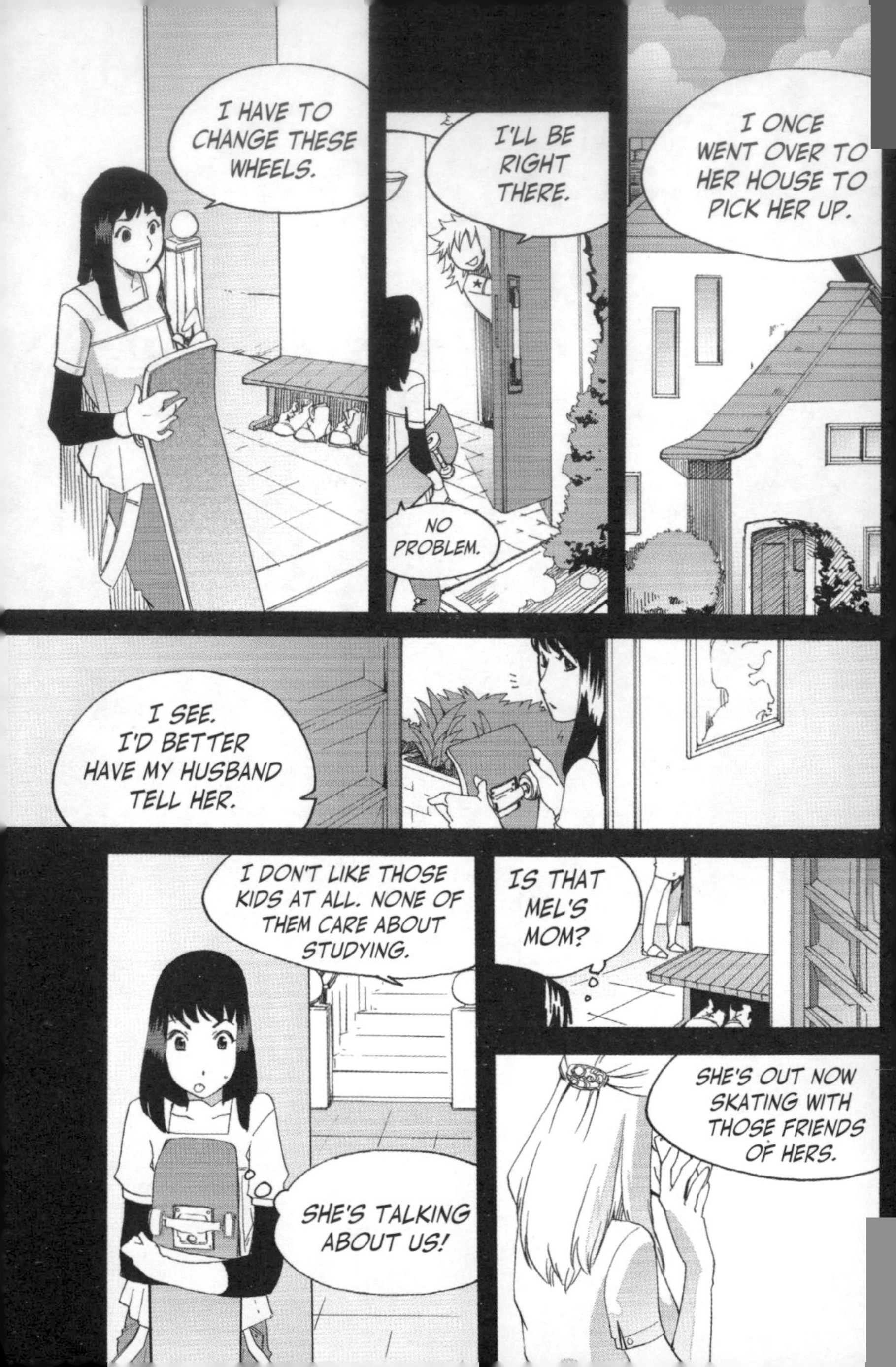
I HAVE TO CHANGE THESE WHEELS.
I'LL BE RIGHT THERE.
NO PROBLEM.
I ONCE WENT OVER TO HER HOUSE TO PICK HER UP.
I SEE. I'D BETTER HAVE MY HUSBAND TELL HER.
I DON'T LIKE THOSE KIDS AT ALL. NONE OF THEM CARE ABOUT STUDYING.
SHE'S TALKING ABOUT US!
IS THAT MEL'S MOM?
SHE'S OUT NOW SKATING WITH THOSE FRIENDS OF HERS.

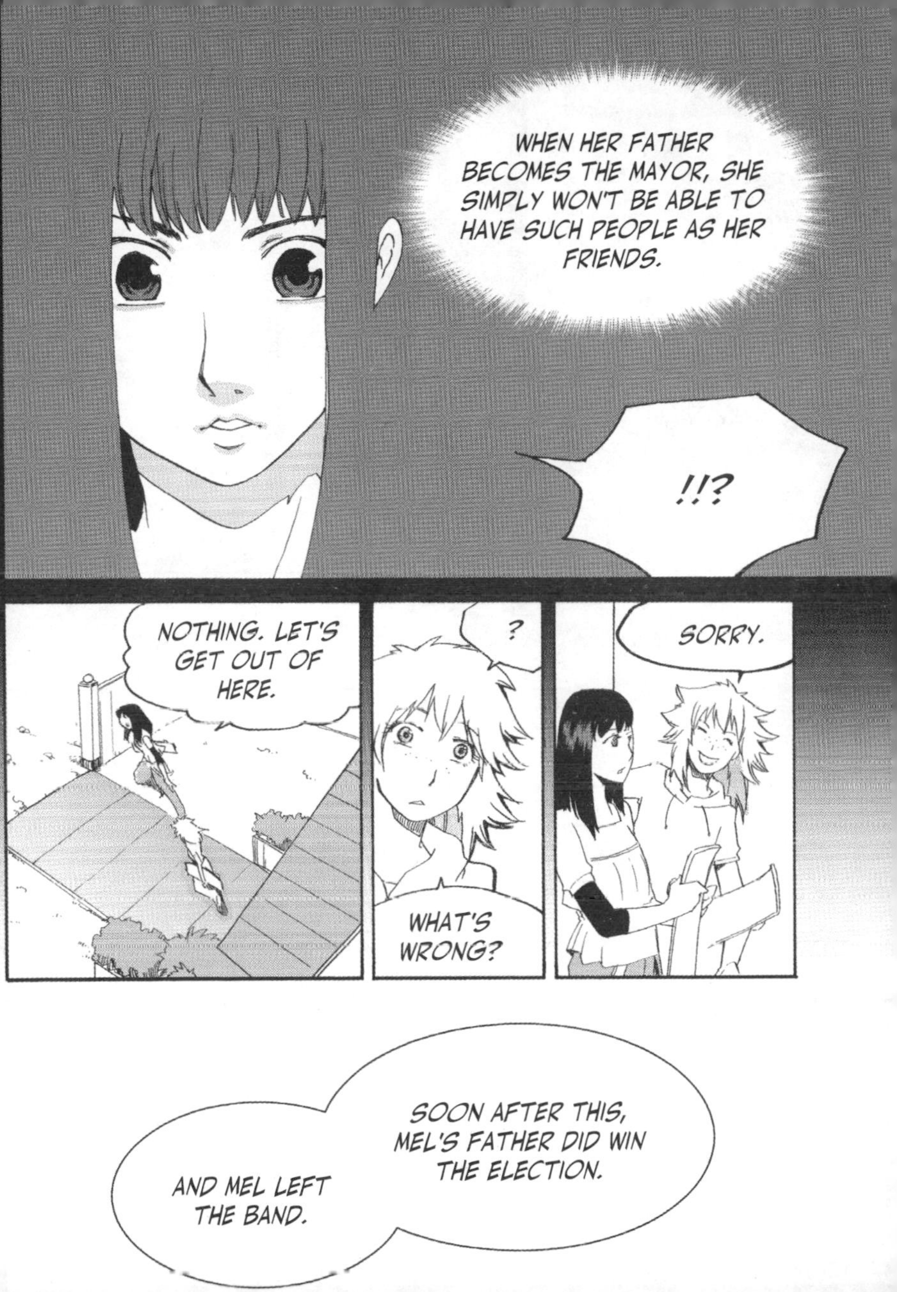
WHEN HER FATHER BECOMES THE MAYOR, SHE SIMPLY WON'T BE ABLE TO HAVE SUCH PEOPLE AS HER FRIENDS.
!!?
NOTHING. LET'S GET OUT OF HERE.
?
WHAT'S WRONG?
SORRY.
SOON AFTER THIS, MEL'S FATHER DID WIN THE ELECTION.
AND MEL LEFT THE BAND.

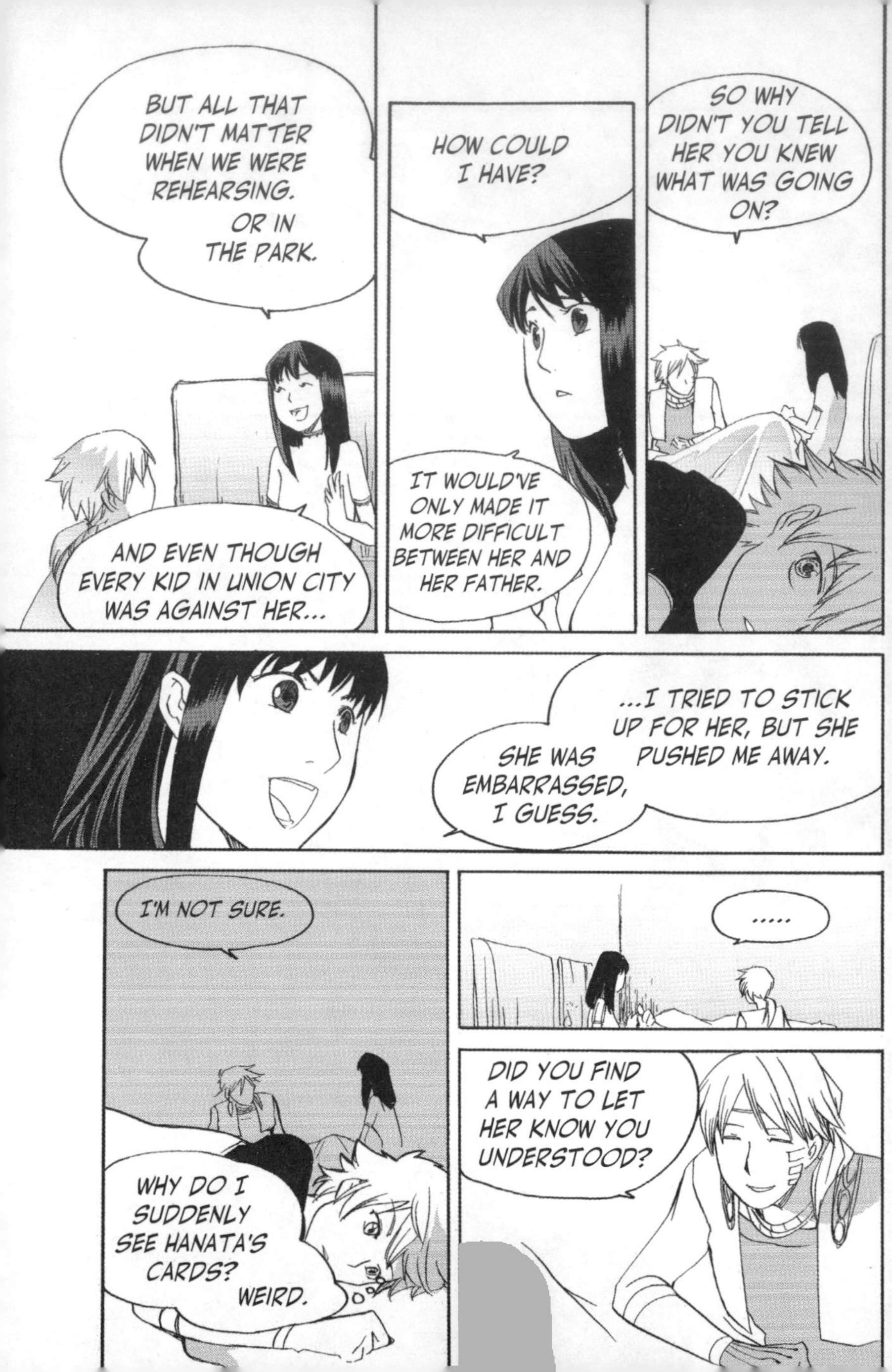
BUT ALL THAT DIDN'T MATTER WHEN WE WERE REHEARSING.
OR IN THE PARK.
AND EVEN THOUGH EVERY KID IN UNION CITY WAS AGAINST HER...
HOW COULD I HAVE?
IT WOULD'VE ONLY MADE IT MORE DIFFICULT BETWEEN HER AND HER FATHER.
SO WHY DIDN'T YOU TELL HER YOU KNEW WHAT WAS GOING ON?
...I TRIED TO STICK UP FOR HER, BUT SHE PUSHED ME AWAY.
SHE WAS EMBARRASSED, I GUESS.
.....
DID YOU FIND A WAY TO LET HER KNOW YOU UNDERSTOOD?
I'M NOT SURE.
WHY DO I SUDDENLY SEE HANATA'S CARDS?
WEIRD.

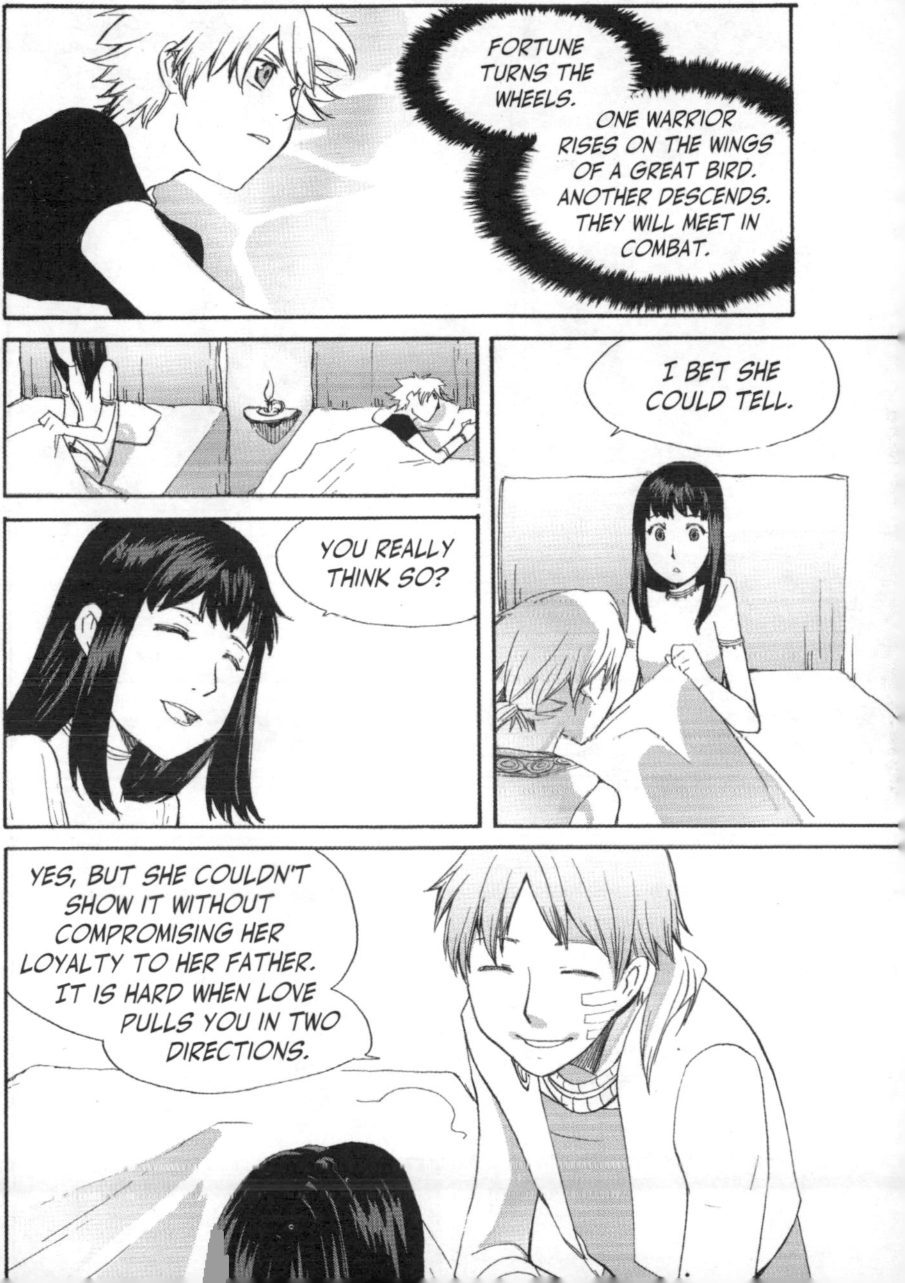
FORTUNE TURNS THE WHEELS.
ONE WARRIOR RISES ON THE WINGS OF A GREAT BIRD. ANOTHER DESCENDS. THEY WILL MEET IN COMBAT.
I BET SHE COULD TELL.
YOU REALLY THINK SO?
YES, BUT SHE COULDN'T SHOW IT WITHOUT COMPROMISING HER LOYALTY TO HER FATHER. IT IS HARD WHEN LOVE PULLS YOU IN TWO DIRECTIONS.

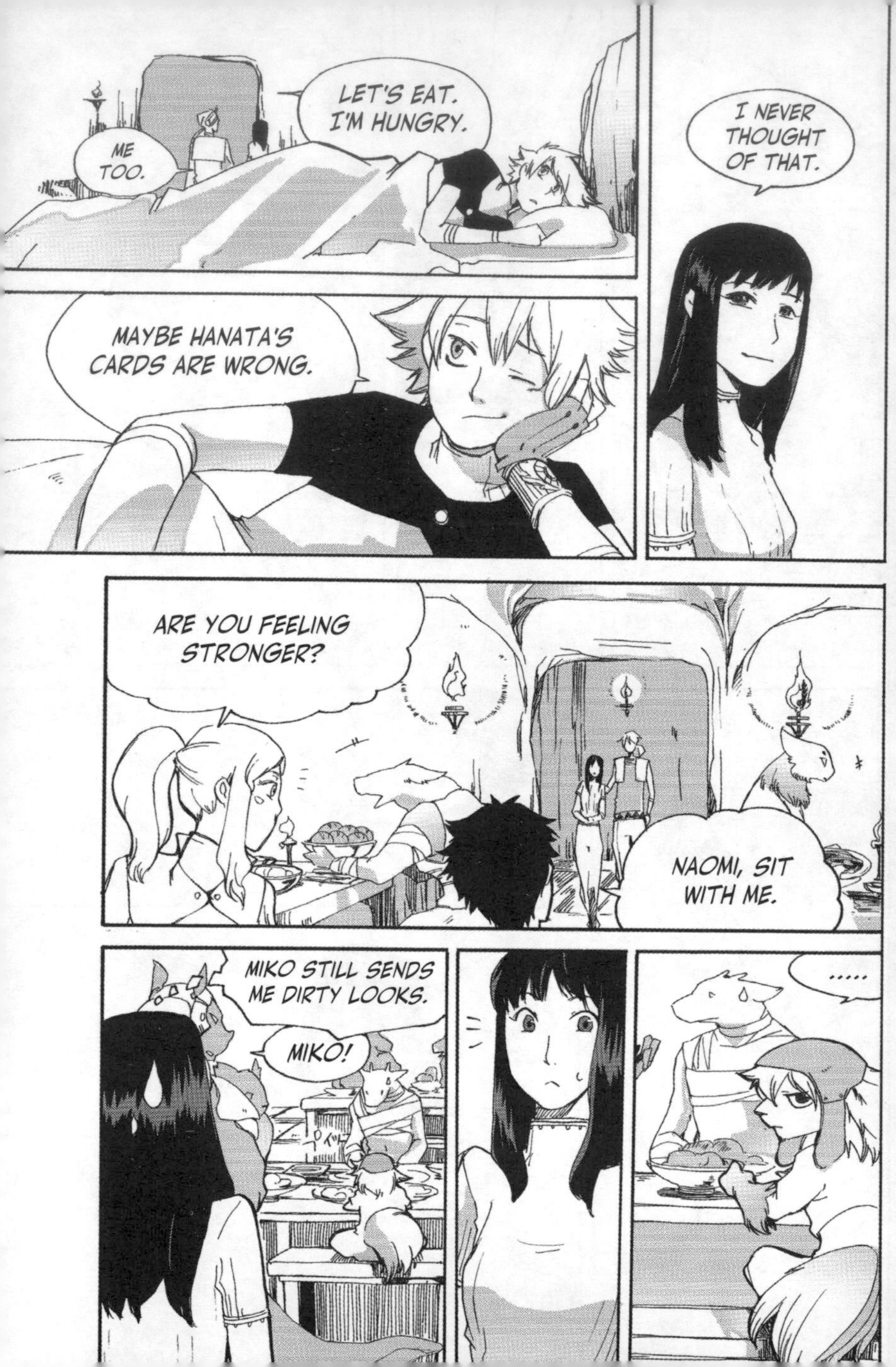
LET'S EAT. I'M HUNGRY.
ME TOO.
I NEVER THOUGHT OF THAT.
MAYBE HANATA'S CARDS ARE WRONG.
ARE YOU FEELING STRONGER?
NAOMI, SIT WITH ME.
MIKO STILL SENDS ME DIRTY LOOKS.
MIKO!
.....

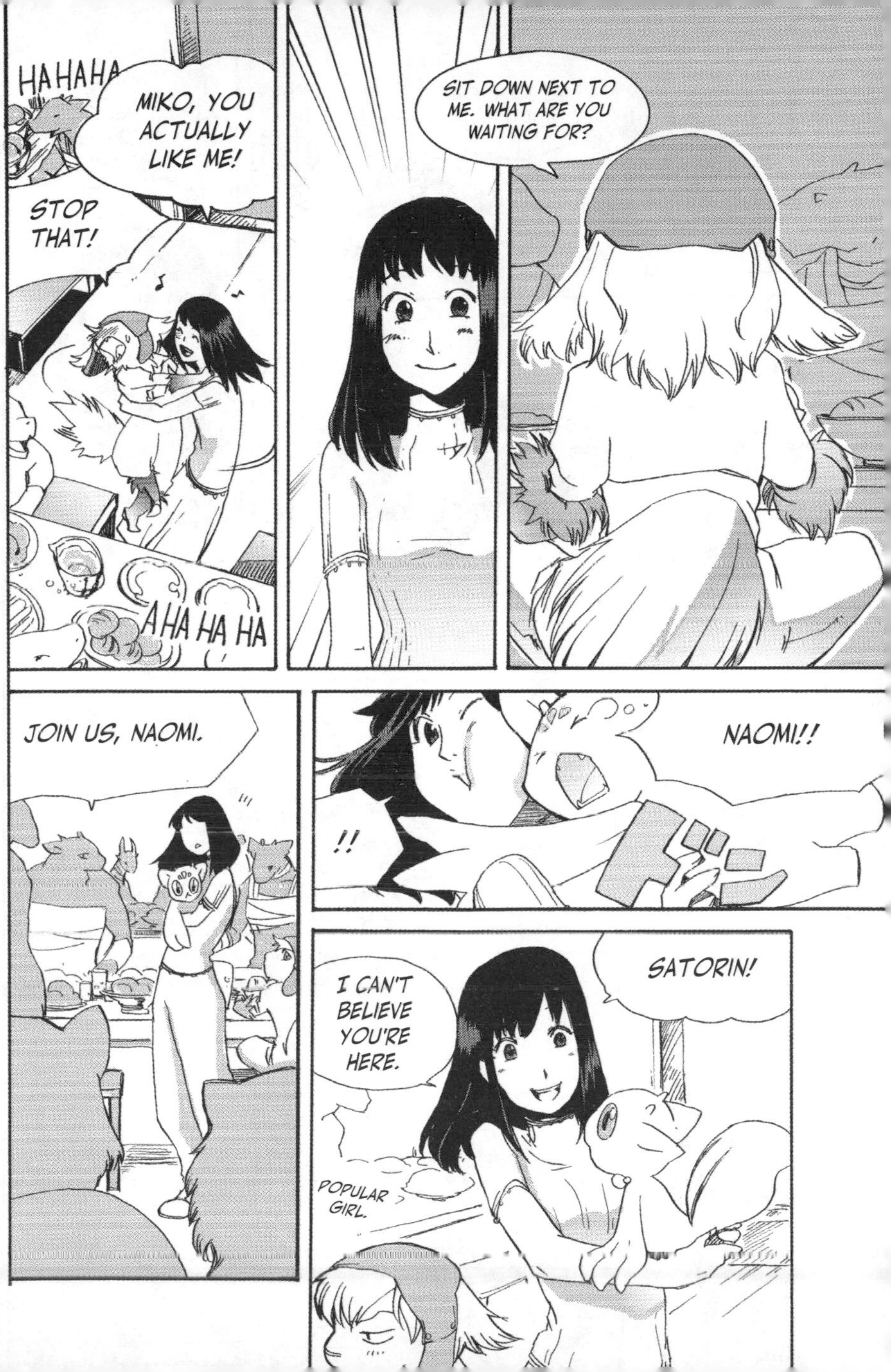
HAHAHA
MIKO, YOU ACTUALLY LIKE ME!
STOP THAT!
AHA HA HA
SIT DOWN NEXT TO ME. WHAT ARE YOU WAITING FOR?
JOIN US, NAOMI.
NAOMI!!
!!
SATORIN!
I CAN'T BELIEVE YOU'RE HERE.
POPULAR GIRL.

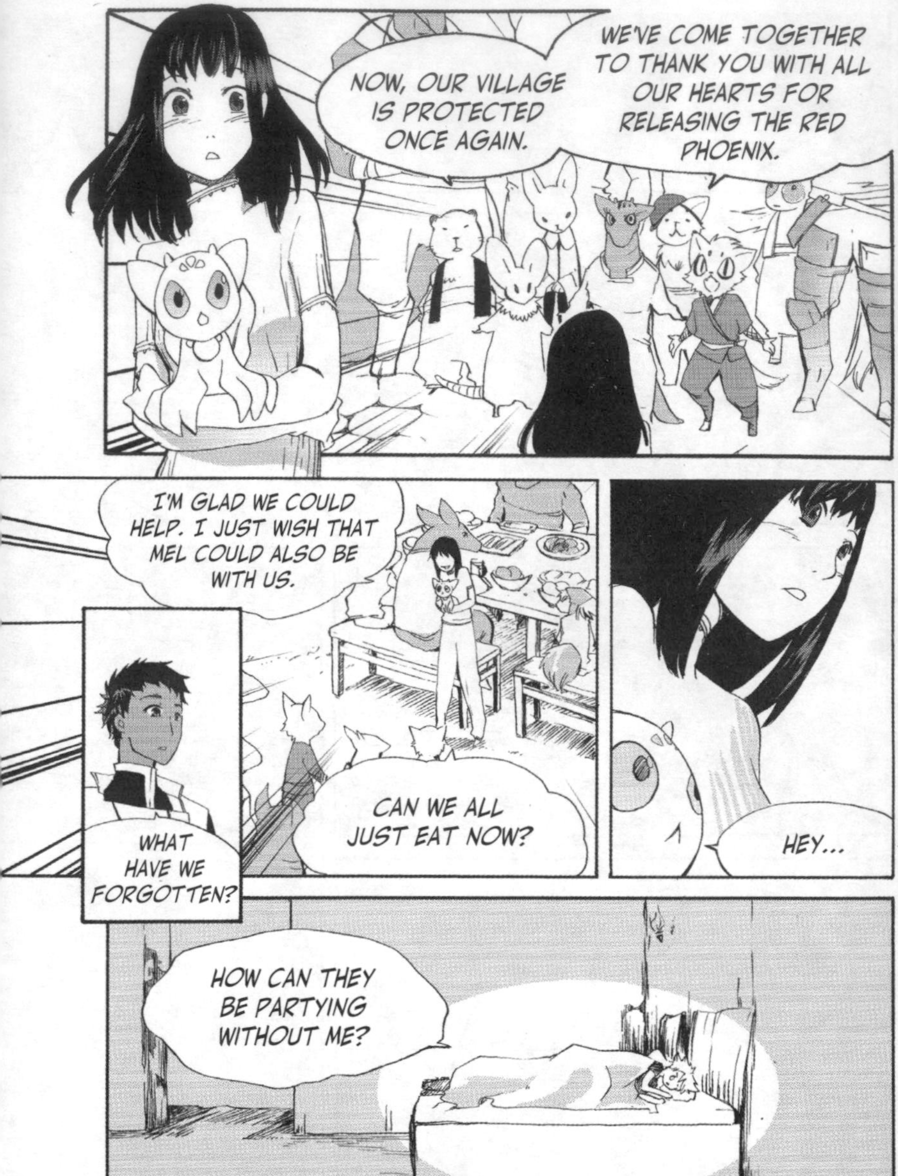
WE'VE COME TOGETHER TO THANK YOU WITH ALL OUR HEARTS FOR RELEASING THE RED PHOENIX.
NOW, OUR VILLAGE IS PROTECTED ONCE AGAIN.
I'M GLAD WE COULD HELP. I JUST WISH THAT MEL COULD ALSO BE WITH US.
HEY...
CAN WE ALL JUST EAT NOW?
WHAT HAVE WE FORGOTTEN?
HOW CAN THEY BE PARTYING WITHOUT ME?

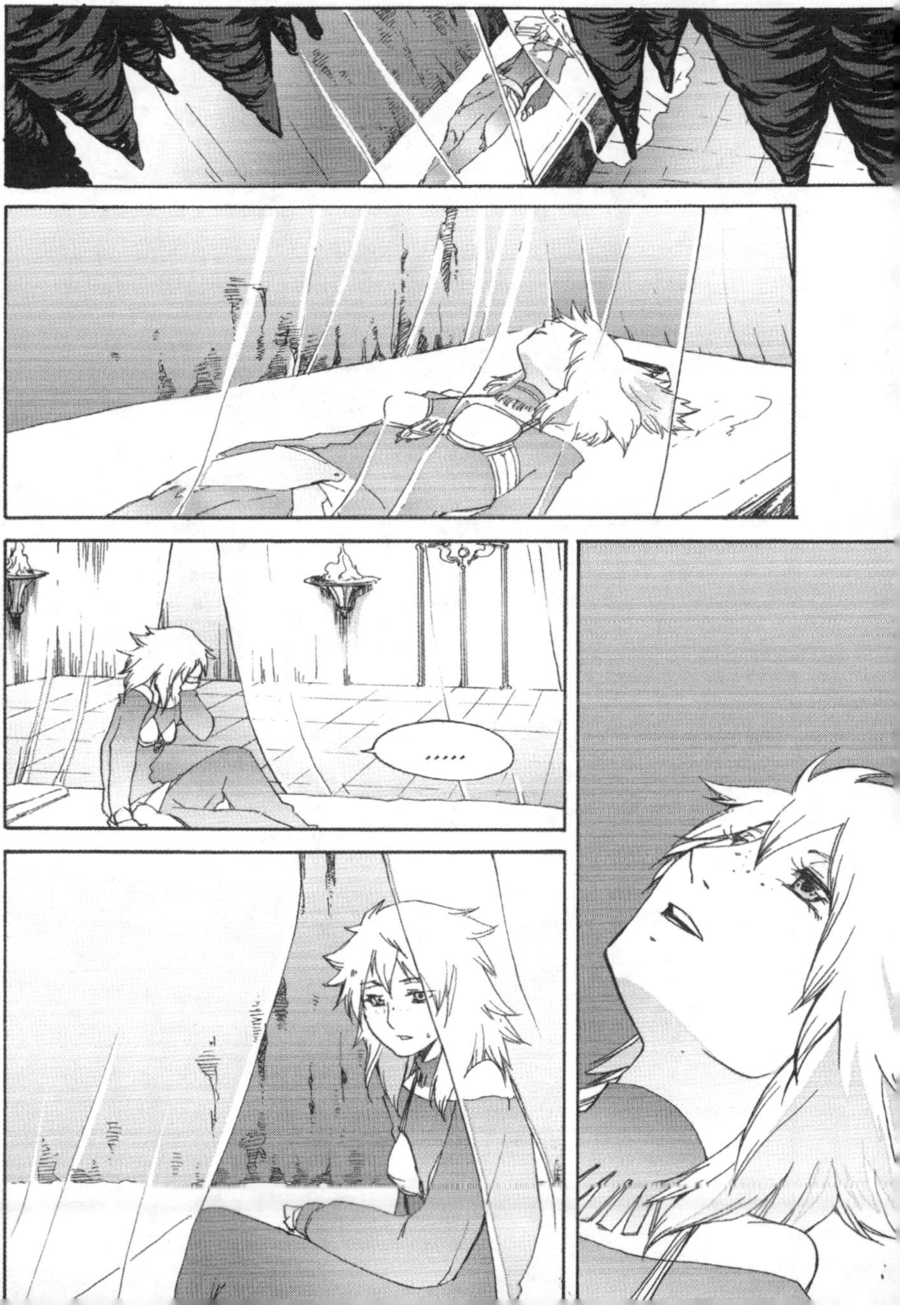
.....

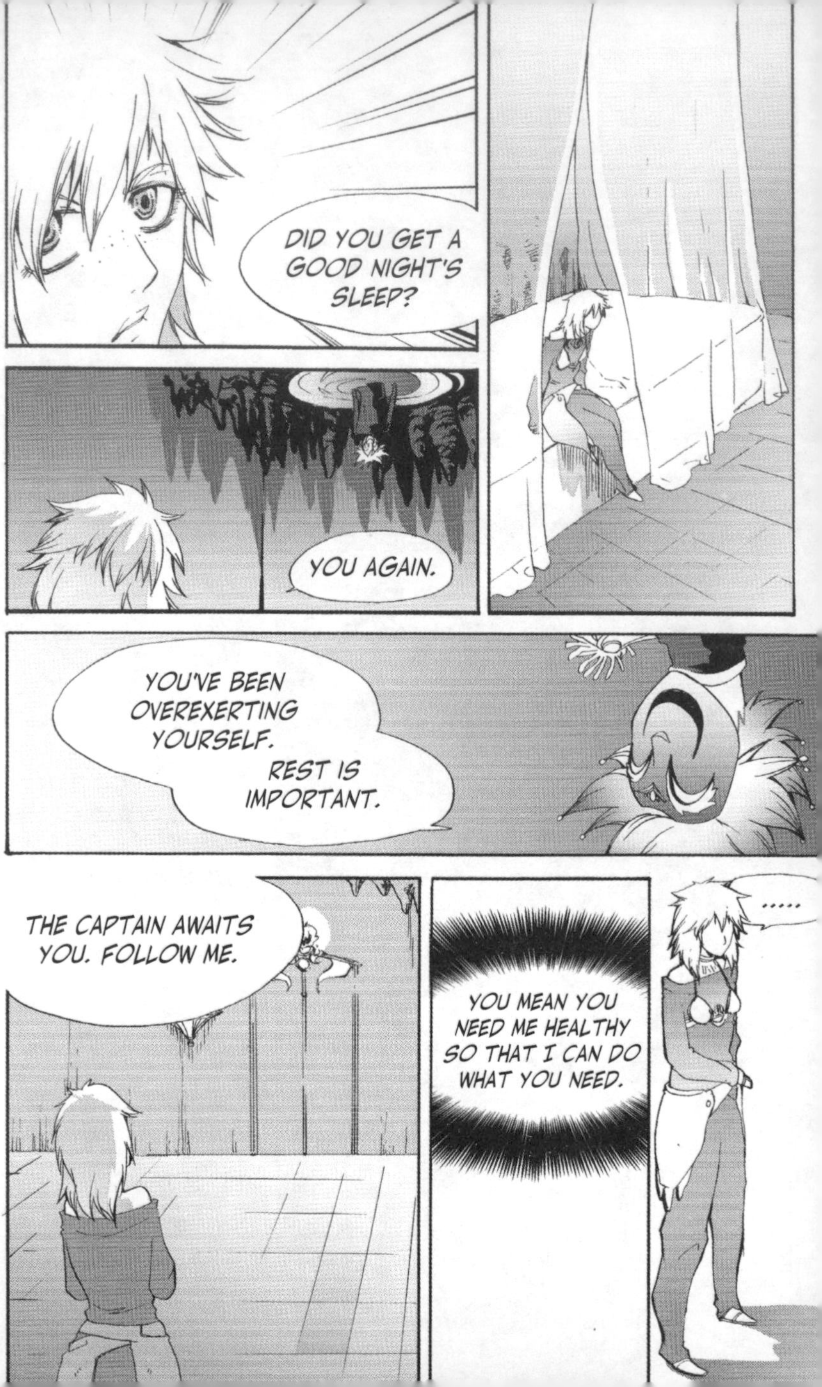

DID YOU GET A GOOD NIGHT'S SLEEP?
YOU AGAIN.
YOU'VE BEEN OVEREXERTING YOURSELF.
REST IS IMPORTANT.
THE CAPTAIN AWAITS YOU. FOLLOW ME.
YOU MEAN YOU NEED ME HEALTHY SO THAT I CAN DO WHAT YOU NEED.
.....

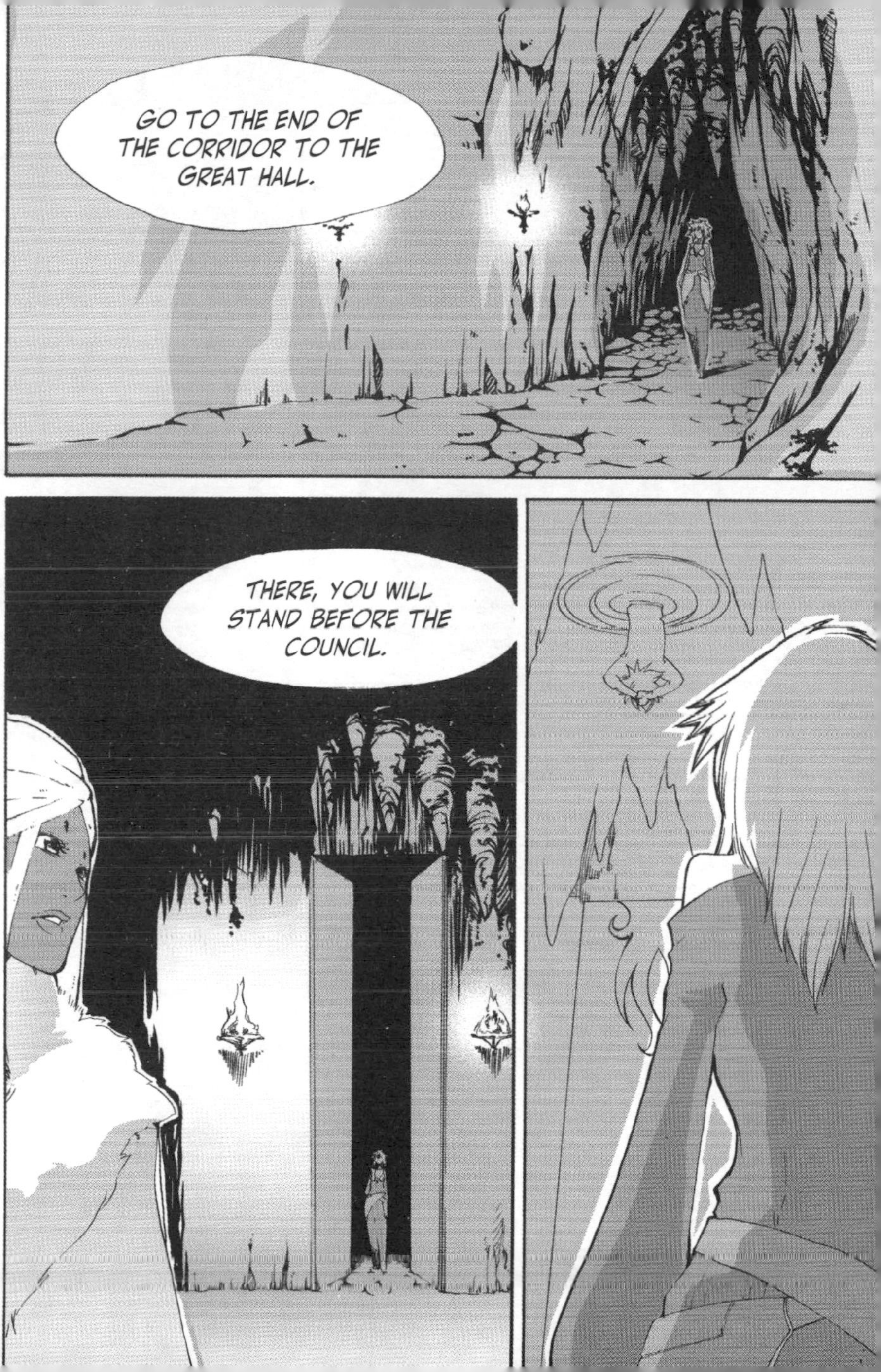
GO TO THE END OF THE CORRIDOR TO THE GREAT HALL.
THERE, YOU WILL STAND BEFORE THE COUNCIL.

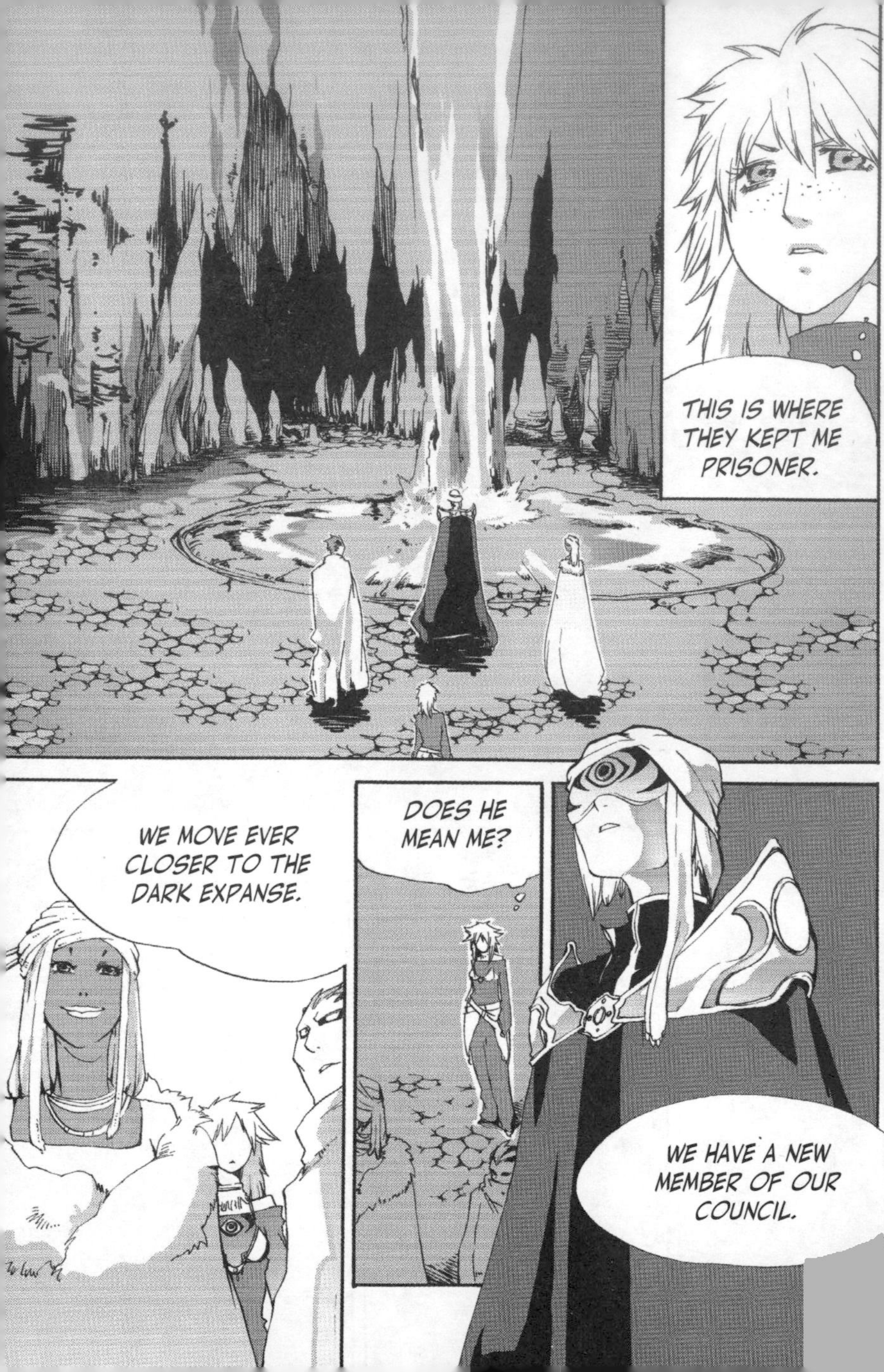
THIS IS WHERE THEY KEPT ME PRISONER.
WE MOVE EVER CLOSER TO THE DARK EXPANSE.
DOES HE MEAN ME?
WE HAVE A NEW MEMBER OF OUR COUNCIL.

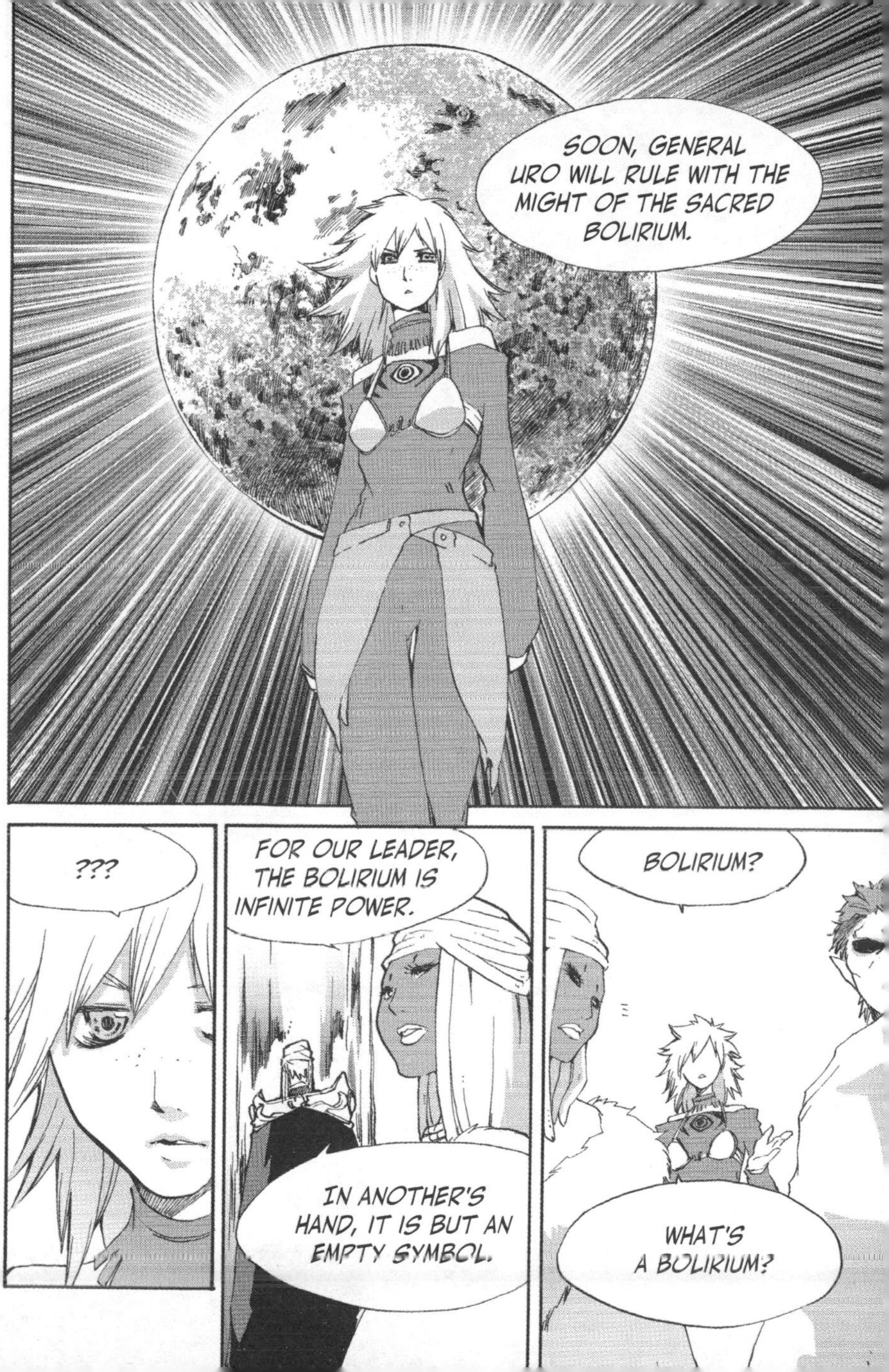
SOON, GENERAL URO WILL RULE WITH THE MIGHT OF THE SACRED BOLIRIUM.
???
FOR OUR LEADER, THE BOLIRIUM IS INFINITE POWER.
IN ANOTHER'S HAND, IT IS BUT AN EMPTY SYMBOL.
BOLIRIUM?
WHAT'S A BOLIRIUM?

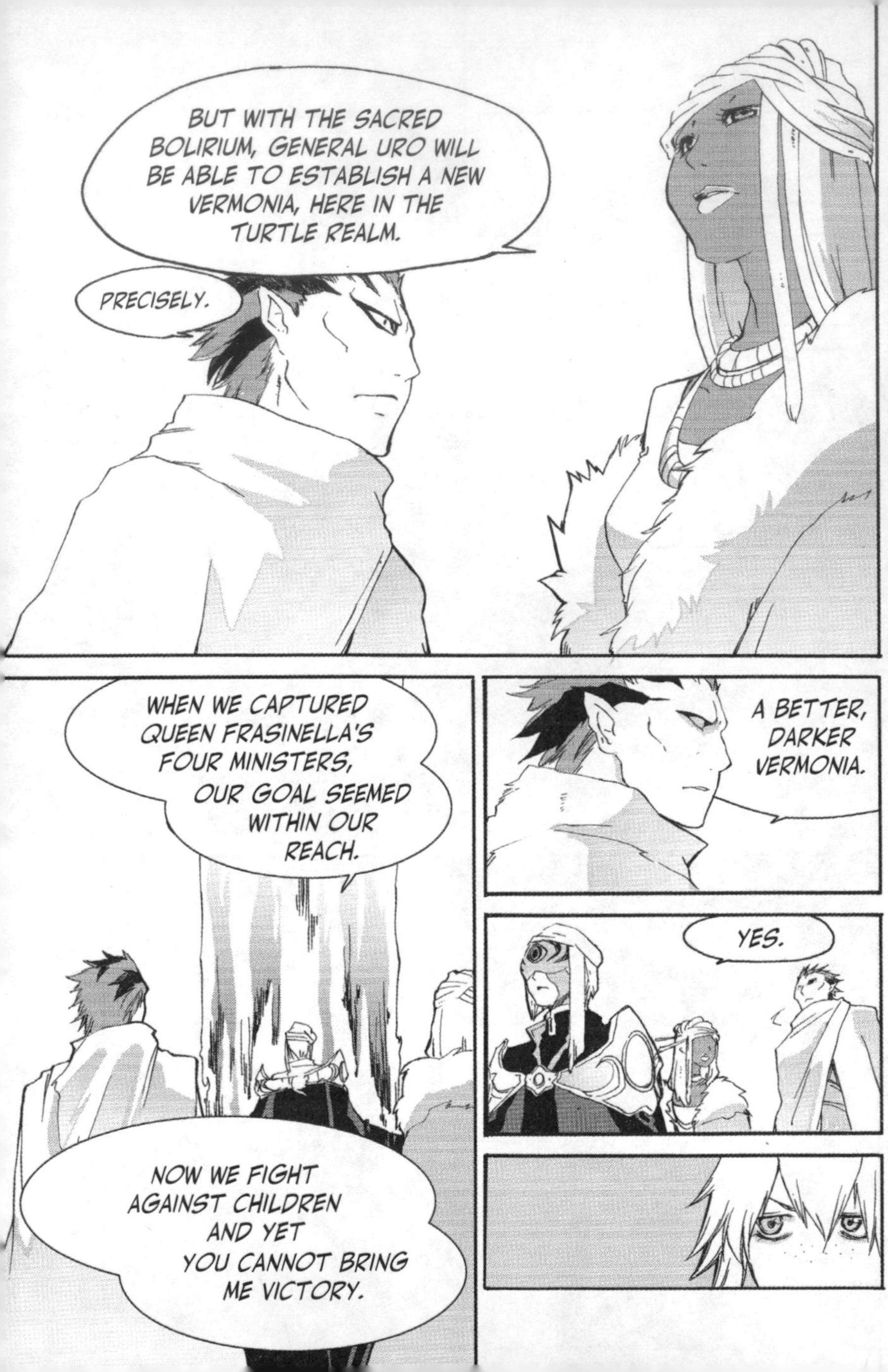
BUT WITH THE SACRED BOLIRIUM, GENERAL URO WILL BE ABLE TO ESTABLISH A NEW VERMONIA, HERE IN THE TURTLE REALM.
PRECISELY.
WHEN WE CAPTURED QUEEN FRASINELLA'S FOUR MINISTERS,
OUR GOAL SEEMED WITHIN OUR REACH.
A BETTER, DARKER VERMONIA.
YES.
NOW WE FIGHT AGAINST CHILDREN AND YET YOU CANNOT BRING ME VICTORY.

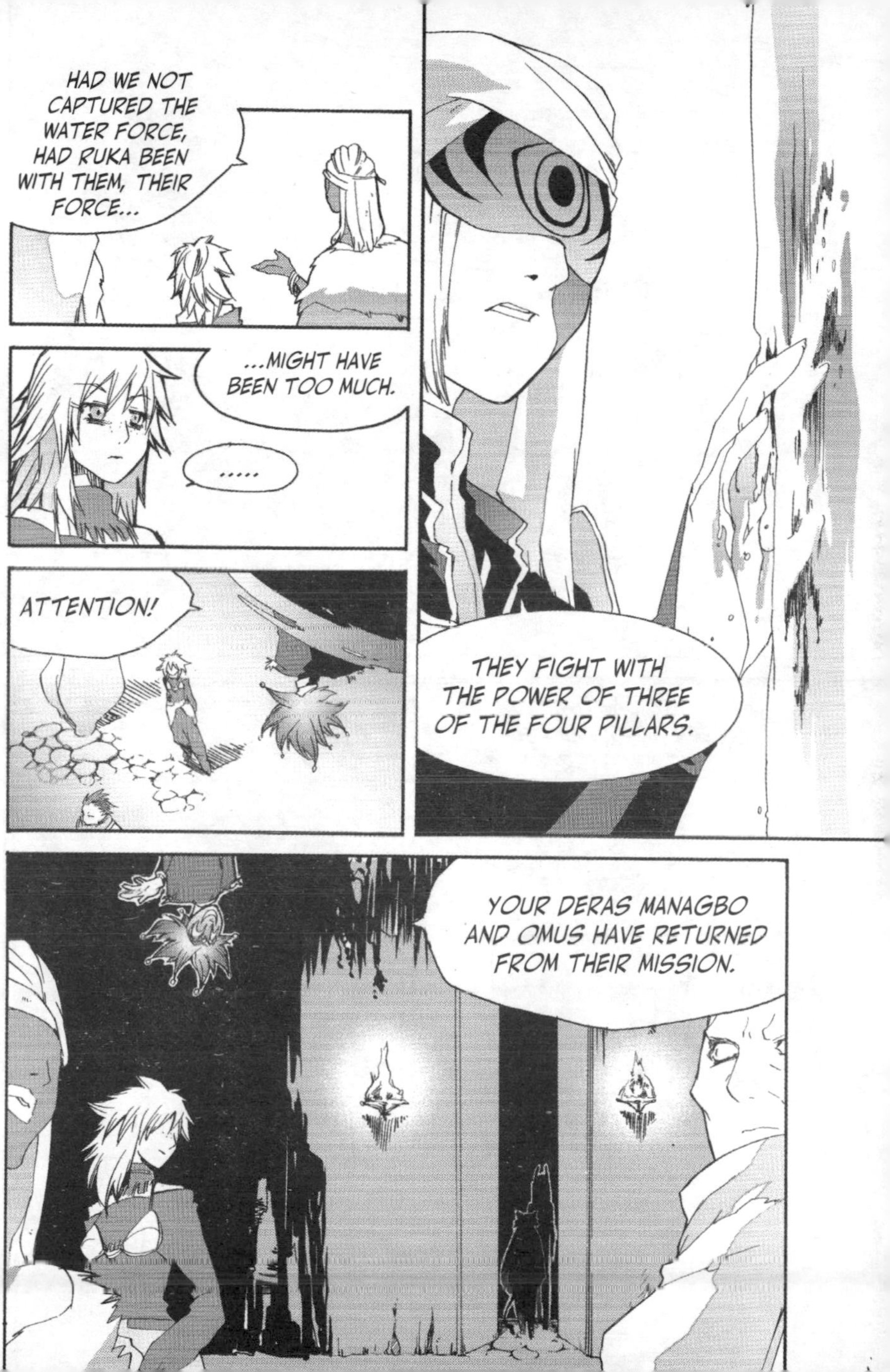
HAD WE NOT CAPTURED THE WATER FORCE, HAD RUKA BEEN WITH THEM, THEIR FORCE...
...MIGHT HAVE BEEN TOO MUCH.
.....
THEY FIGHT WITH THE POWER OF THREE OF THE FOUR PILLARS.
ATTENTION!
YOUR DERAS MANAGBO AND OMUS HAVE RETURNED FROM THEIR MISSION.

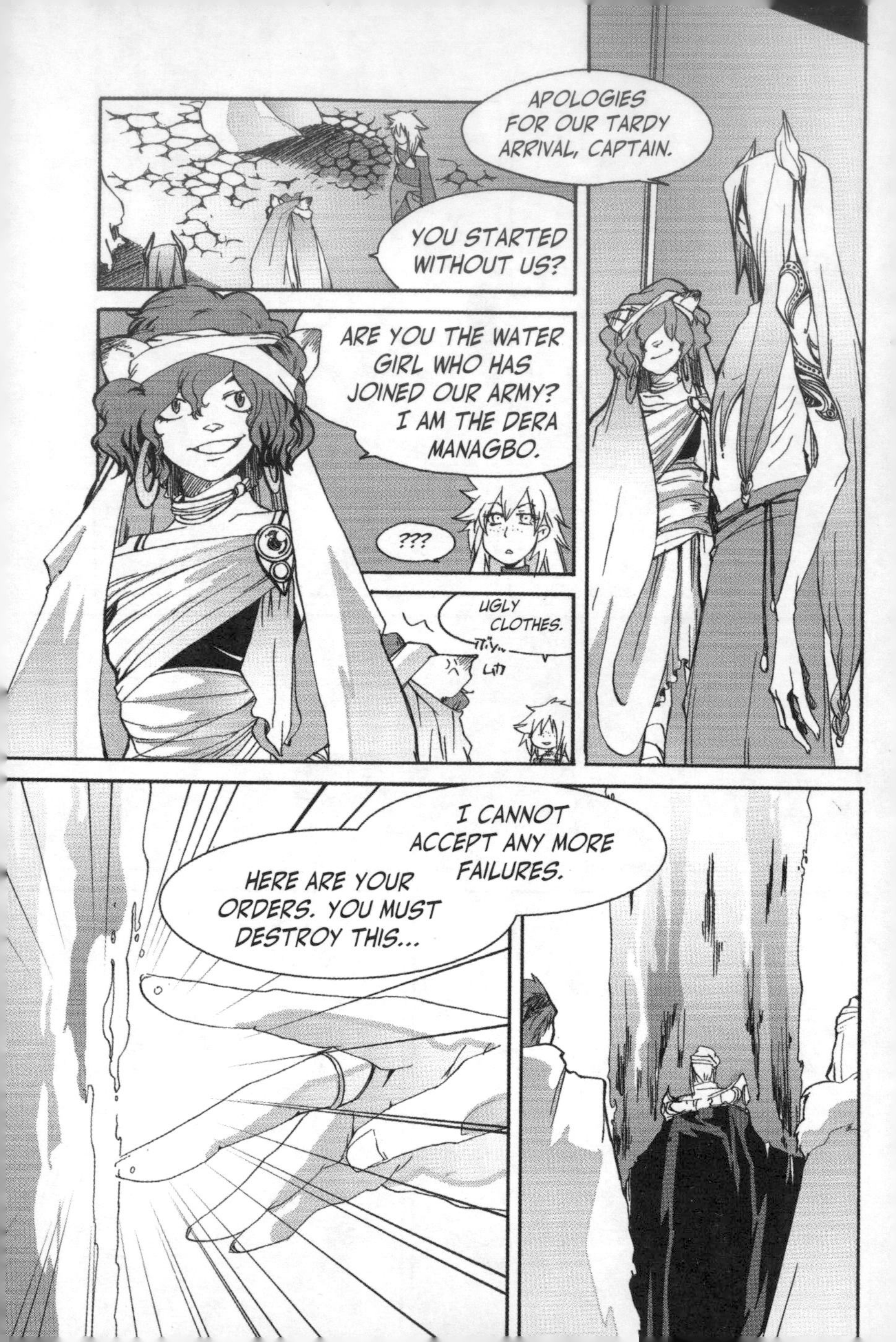
APOLOGIES FOR OUR TARDY ARRIVAL, CAPTAIN.
YOU STARTED WITHOUT US?
ARE YOU THE WATER GIRL WHO HAS JOINED OUR ARMY? I AM THE DERA MANAGBO.
???
UGLY CLOTHES.
I CANNOT ACCEPT ANY MORE FAILURES.
HERE ARE YOUR ORDERS. YOU MUST DESTROY THIS...

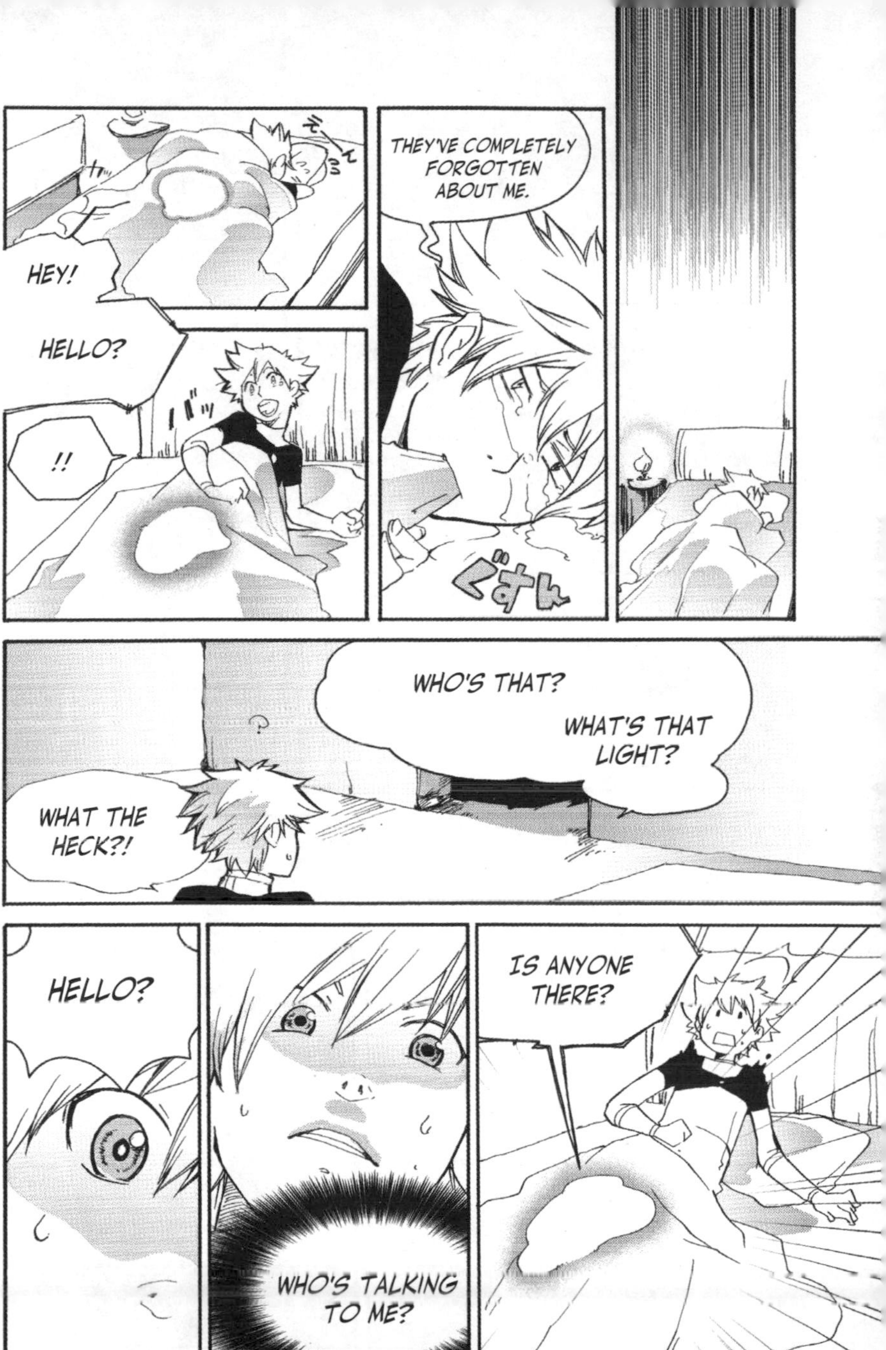
THEY'VE COMPLETELY FORGOTTEN ABOUT ME.
ぐすん
HEY!
HELLO?
!!
WHO'S THAT?
WHAT'S THAT LIGHT?
WHAT THE HECK?!
IS ANYONE THERE?
WHO'S TALKING TO ME?
HELLO?

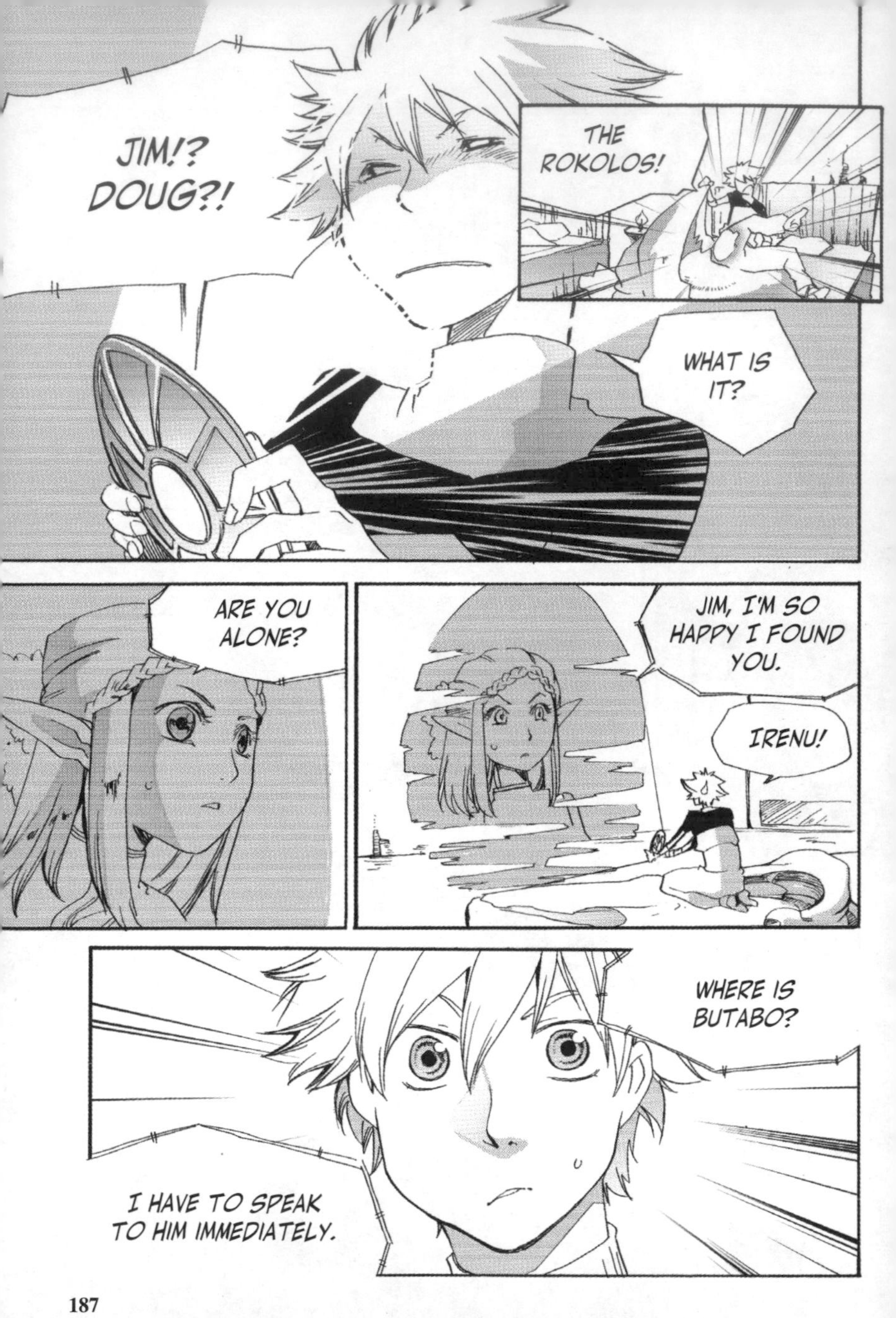
JIM!? DOUG?!
THE ROKOLOS!
WHAT IS IT?
ARE YOU ALONE?
JIM, I'M SO HAPPY I FOUND YOU.
IRENU!
WHERE IS BUTABO?
I HAVE TO SPEAK TO HIM IMMEDIATELY.

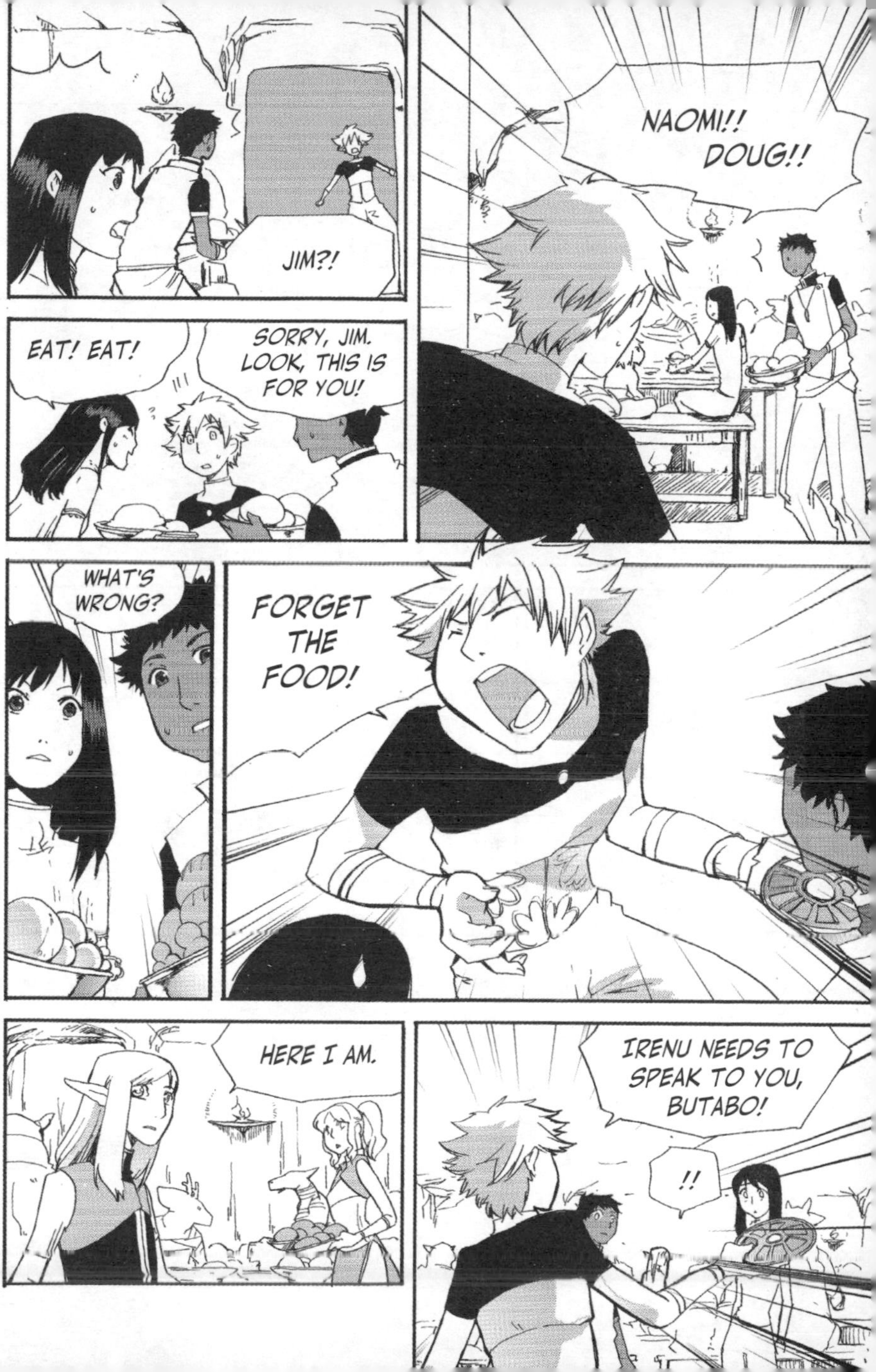
JIM?!
NAOMI!! DOUG!!
EAT! EAT!
SORRY, JIM. LOOK, THIS IS FOR YOU!
WHAT'S WRONG?
FORGET THE FOOD!
HERE I AM.
IRENU NEEDS TO SPEAK TO YOU, BUTABO!
!!

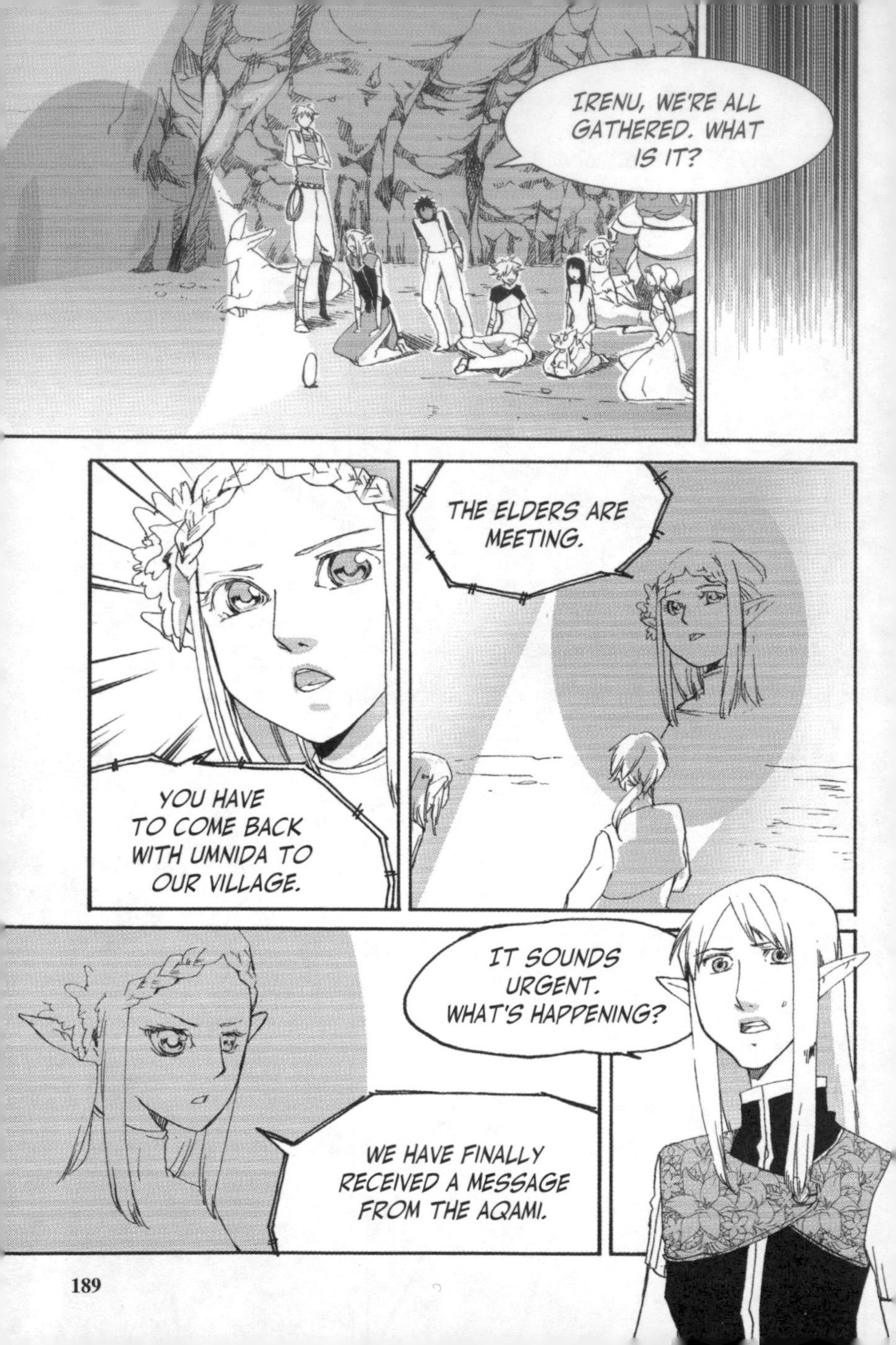
IRENU, WE'RE ALL GATHERED. WHAT IS IT?
THE ELDERS ARE MEETING.
YOU HAVE TO COME BACK WITH UMNIDA TO OUR VILLAGE.
IT SOUNDS URGENT. WHAT'S HAPPENING?
WE HAVE FINALLY RECEIVED A MESSAGE FROM THE AQAMI.

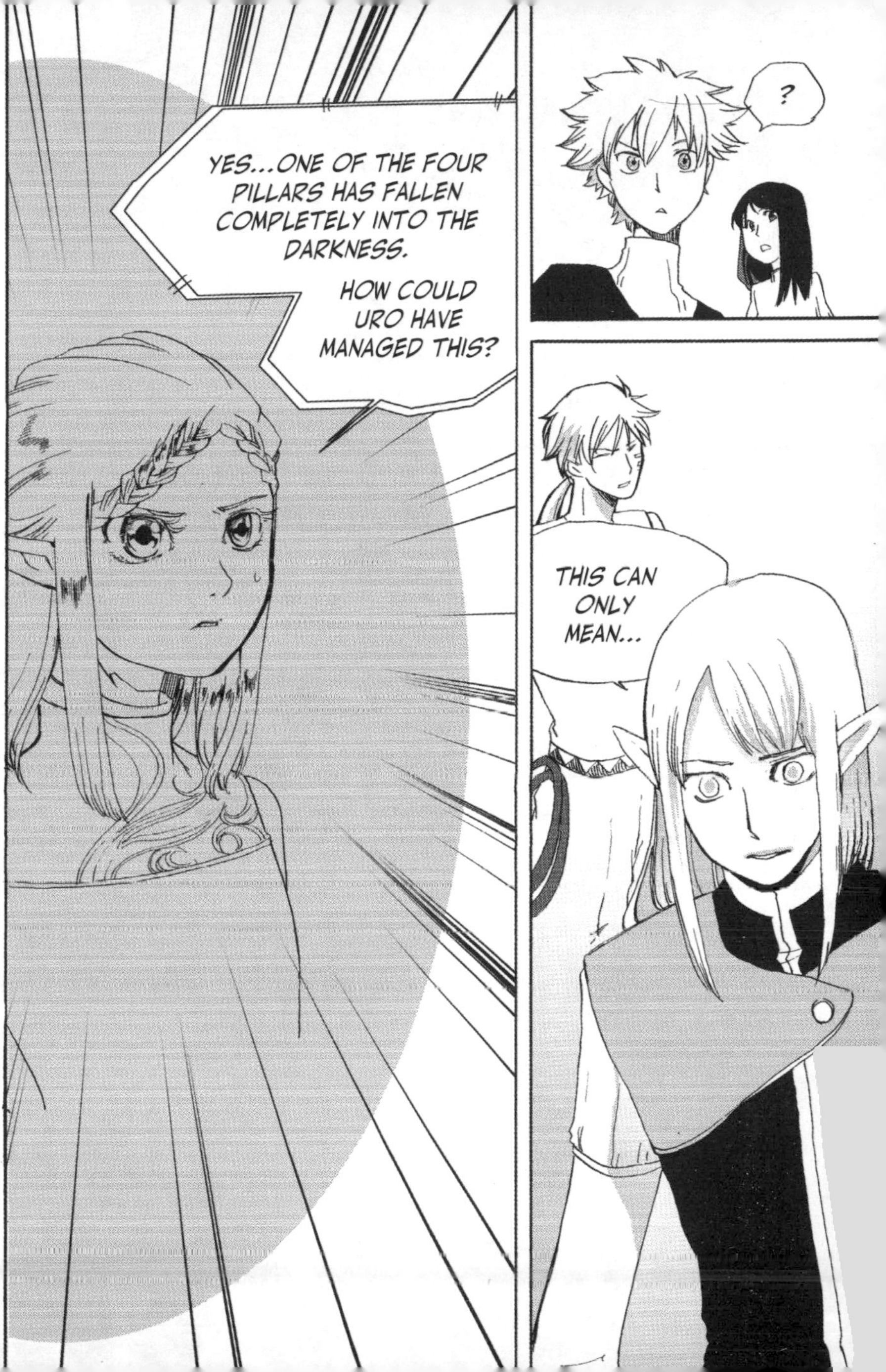

?
YES...ONE OF THE FOUR PILLARS HAS FALLEN COMPLETELY INTO THE DARKNESS.
HOW COULD URO HAVE MANAGED THIS?
THIS CAN ONLY MEAN...

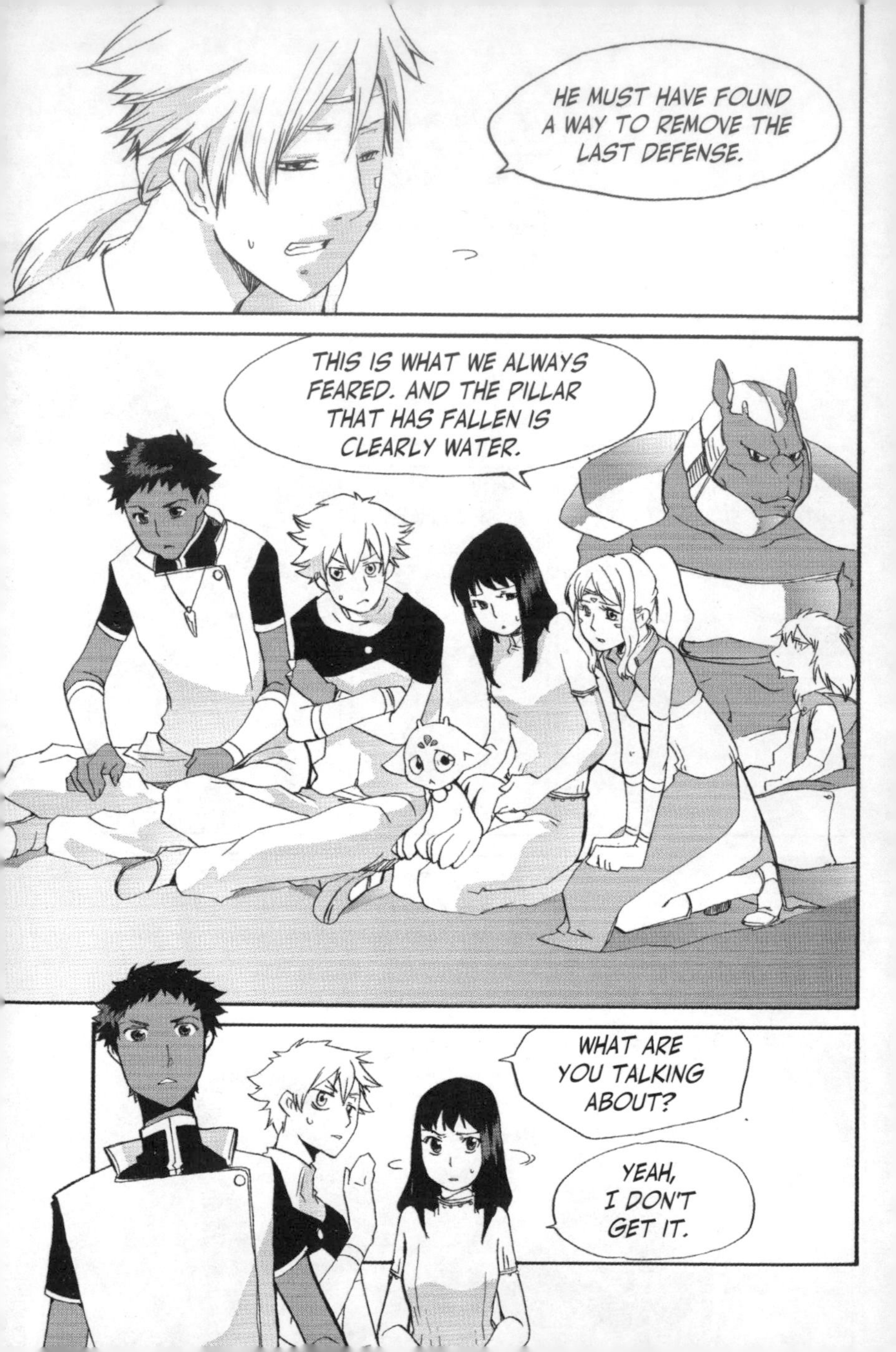
HE MUST HAVE FOUND A WAY TO REMOVE THE LAST DEFENSE.
THIS IS WHAT WE ALWAYS FEARED. AND THE PILLAR THAT HAS FALLEN IS CLEARLY WATER.
WHAT ARE YOU TALKING ABOUT?
YEAH, I DON'T GET IT.

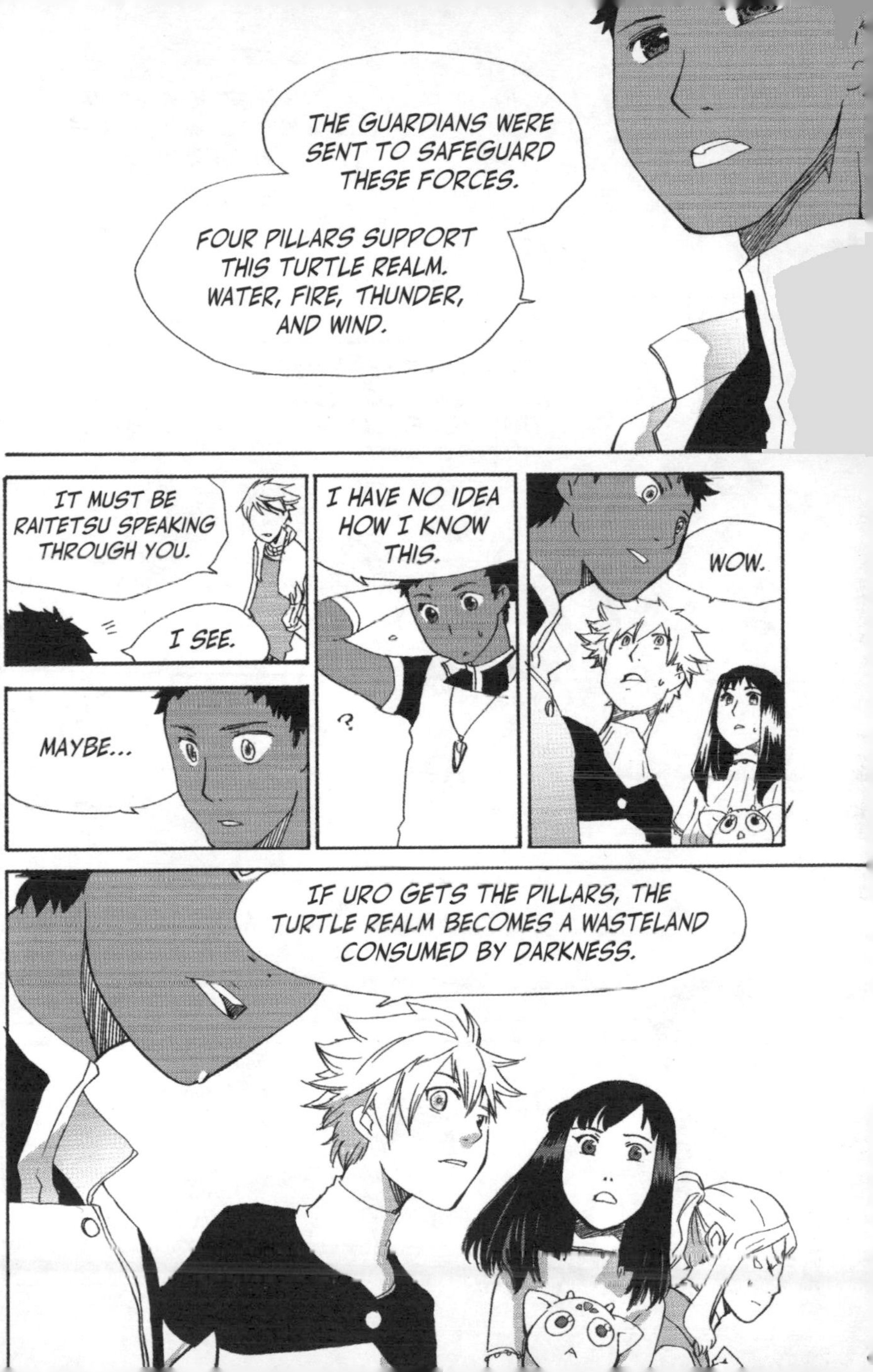
THE GUARDIANS WERE SENT TO SAFEGUARD THESE FORCES.
FOUR PILLARS SUPPORT THIS TURTLE REALM. WATER, FIRE, THUNDER, AND WIND.
IT MUST BE RAITETSU SPEAKING THROUGH YOU.
I SEE.
MAYBE...
I HAVE NO IDEA HOW I KNOW THIS.
?
WOW.
IF URO GETS THE PILLARS, THE TURTLE REALM BECOMES A WASTELAND CONSUMED BY DARKNESS.

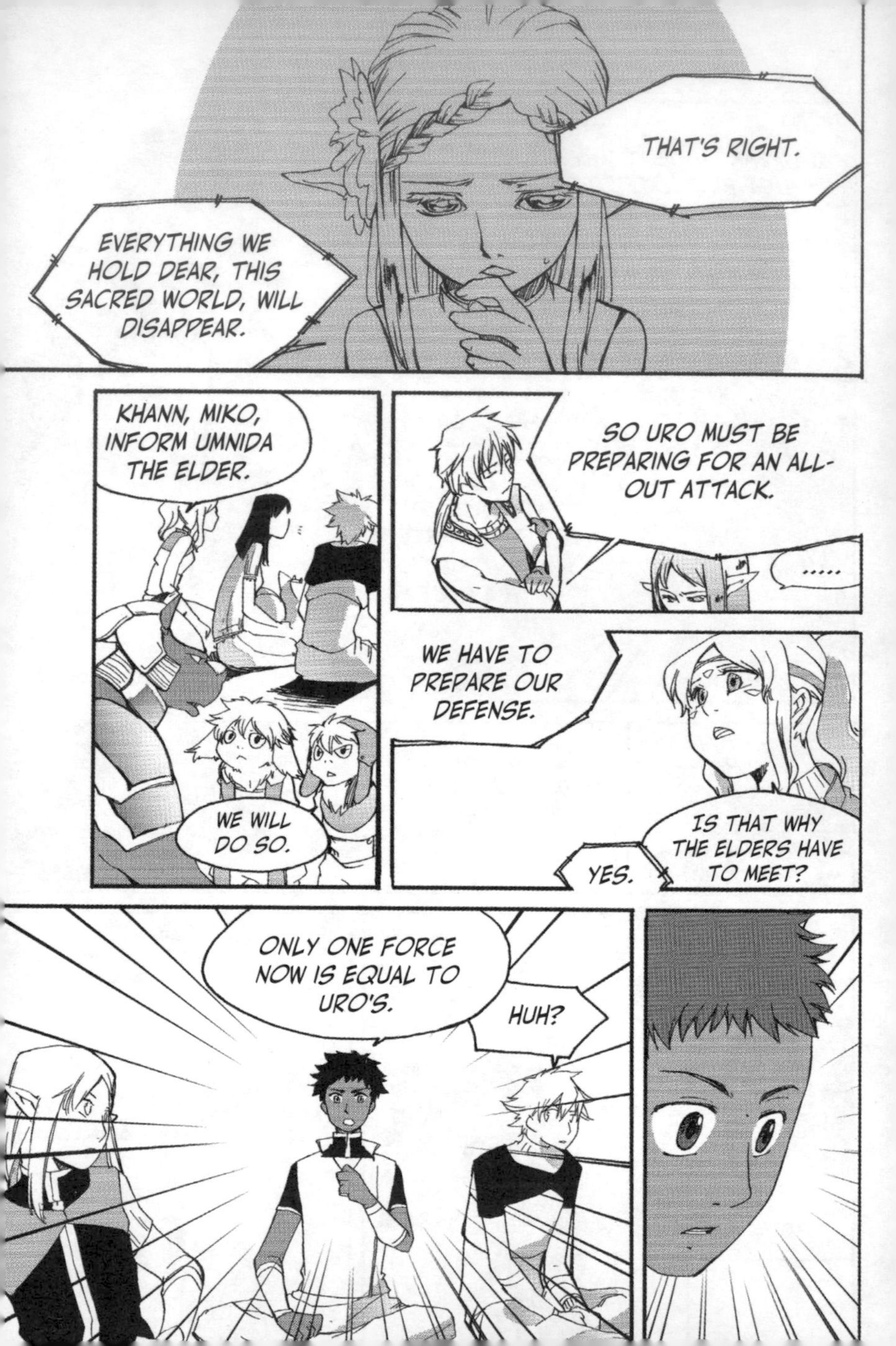
THAT'S RIGHT.
EVERYTHING WE HOLD DEAR, THIS SACRED WORLD, WILL DISAPPEAR.
KHANN, MIKO, INFORM UMNIDA THE ELDER.
WE WILL DO SO.
SO URO MUST BE PREPARING FOR AN ALL-OUT ATTACK.
.....
WE HAVE TO PREPARE OUR DEFENSE.
IS THAT WHY THE ELDERS HAVE TO MEET?
YES.
ONLY ONE FORCE NOW IS EQUAL TO URO'S.
HUH?

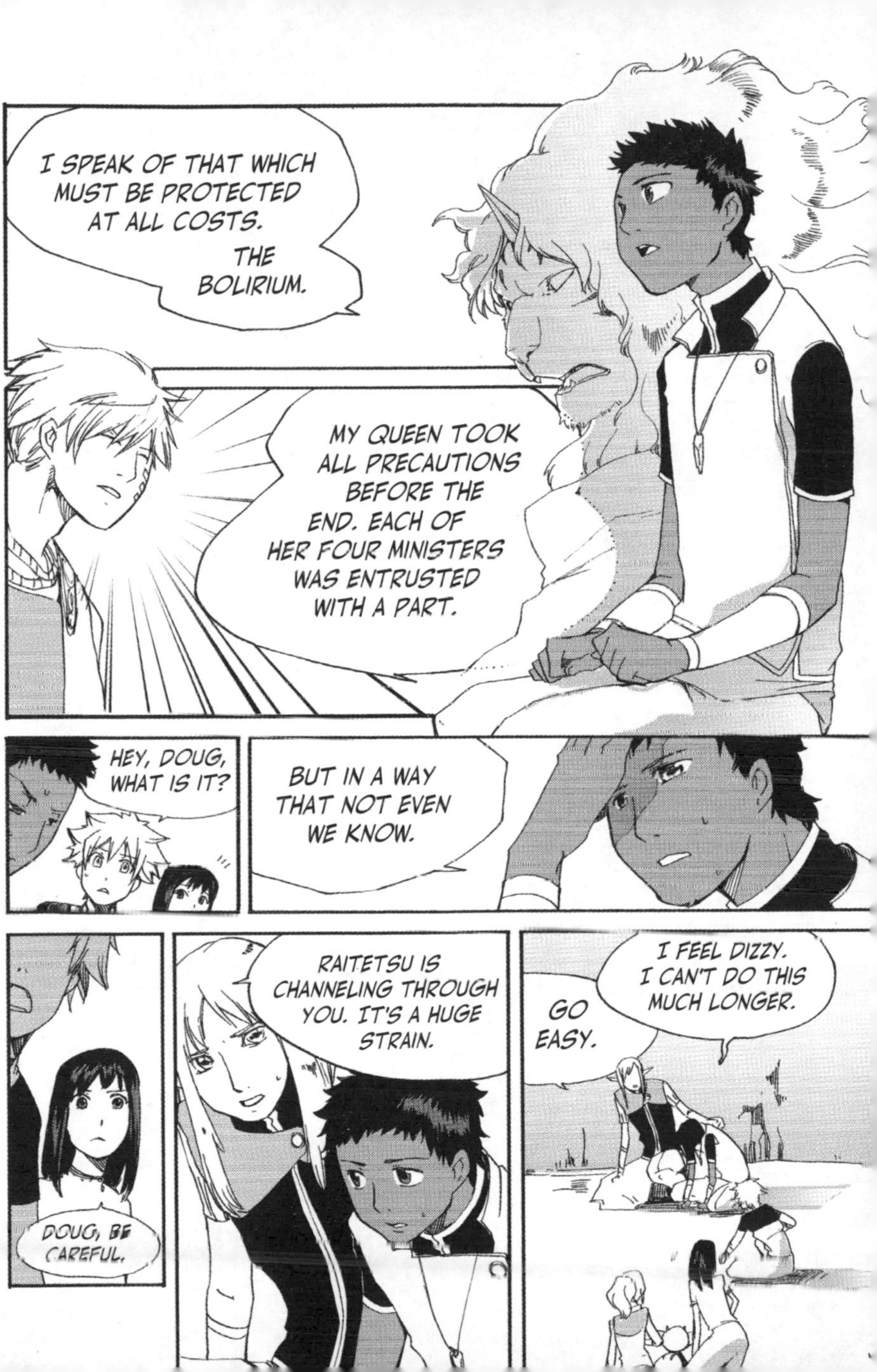
I SPEAK OF THAT WHICH MUST BE PROTECTED AT ALL COSTS.
THE BOLIRIUM.
MY QUEEN TOOK ALL PRECAUTIONS BEFORE THE END. EACH OF HER FOUR MINISTERS WAS ENTRUSTED WITH A PART.
HEY, DOUG, WHAT IS IT?
BUT IN A WAY THAT NOT EVEN WE KNOW.
DOUG, BE CAREFUL.
RAITETSU IS CHANNELING THROUGH YOU. IT'S A HUGE STRAIN.
GO EASY.
I FEEL DIZZY. I CAN'T DO THIS MUCH LONGER.

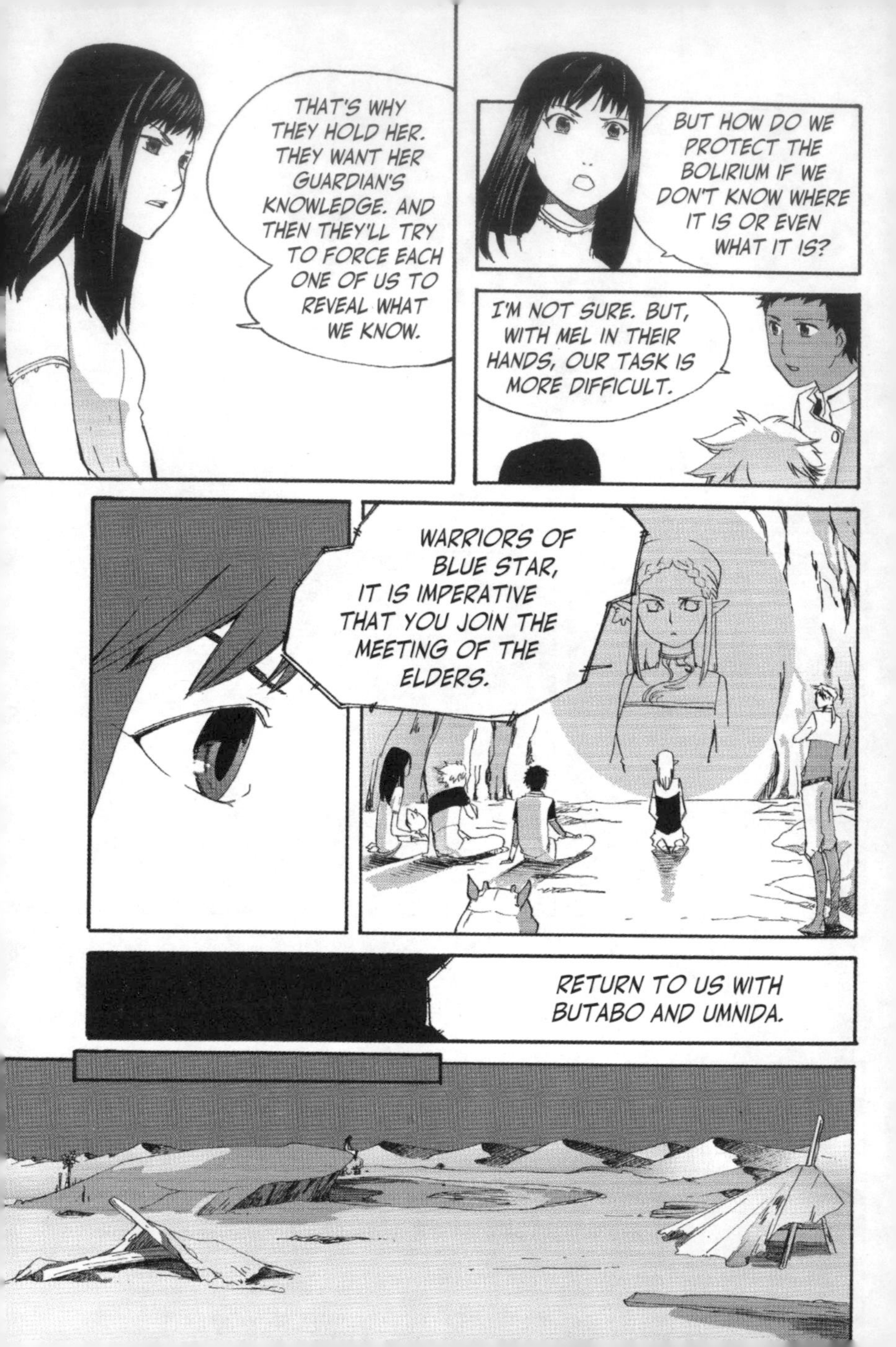
THAT'S WHY THEY HOLD HER. THEY WANT HER GUARDIAN'S KNOWLEDGE. AND THEN THEY'LL TRY TO FORCE EACH ONE OF US TO REVEAL WHAT WE KNOW.
BUT HOW DO WE PROTECT THE BOLIRIUM IF WE DON'T KNOW WHERE IT IS OR EVEN WHAT IT IS?
I'M NOT SURE. BUT, WITH MEL IN THEIR HANDS, OUR TASK IS MORE DIFFICULT.
WARRIORS OF BLUE STAR, IT IS IMPERATIVE THAT YOU JOIN THE MEETING OF THE ELDERS.
RETURN TO US WITH BUTABO AND UMNIDA.

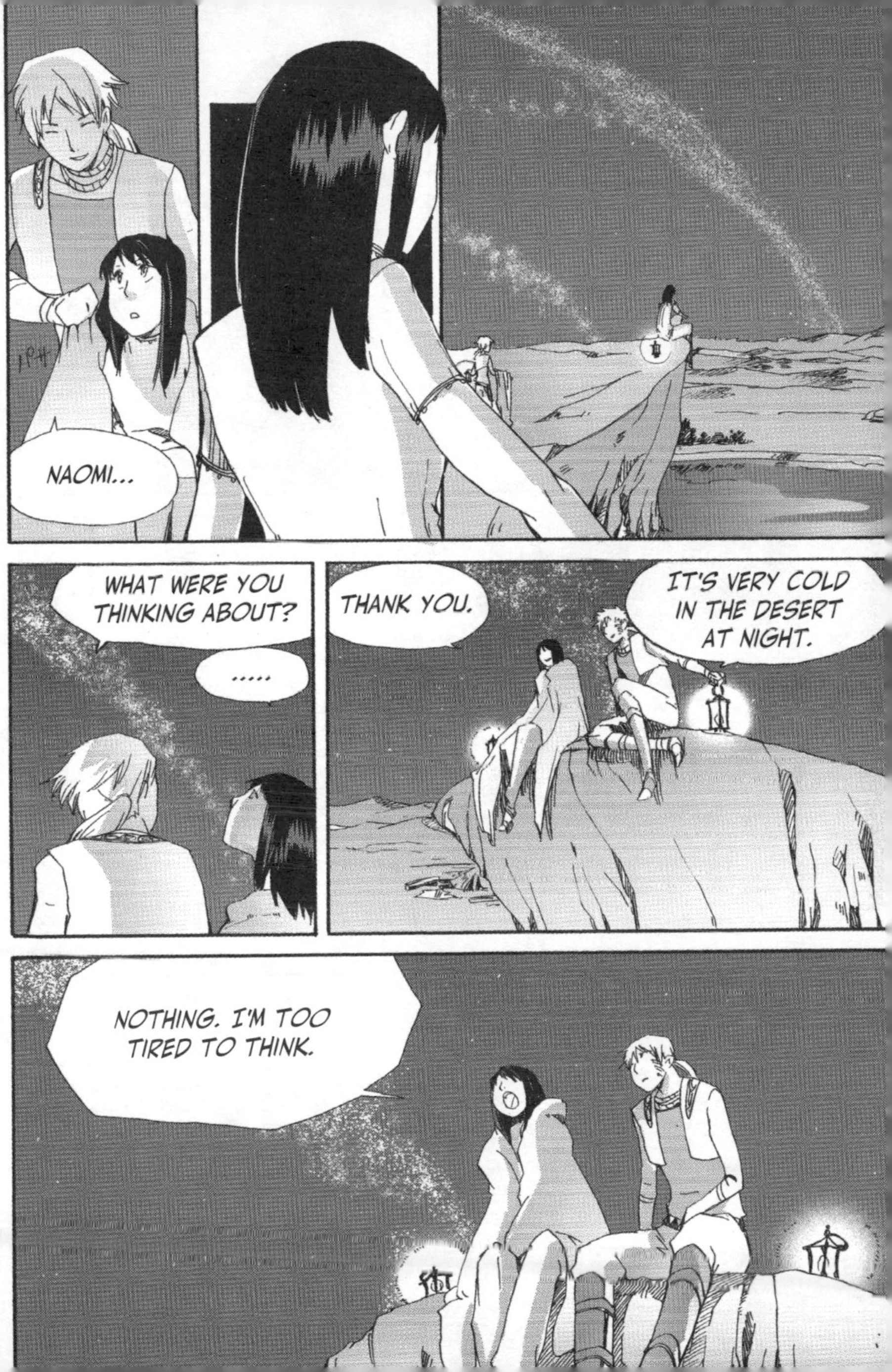
NAOMI...
IT'S VERY COLD IN THE DESERT AT NIGHT.
THANK YOU.
WHAT WERE YOU THINKING ABOUT?
......
NOTHING. I'M TOO TIRED TO THINK.

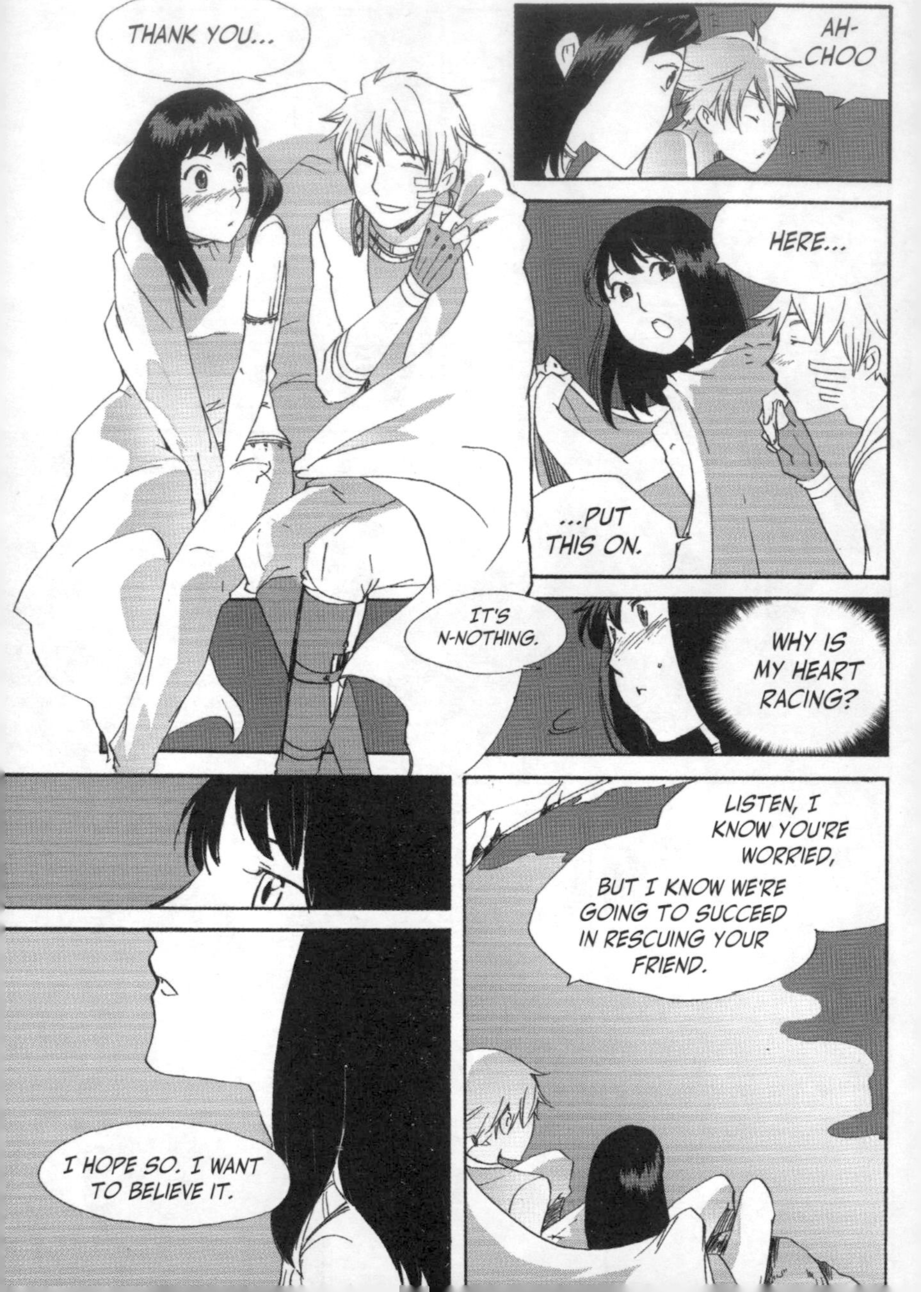
THANK YOU...
AH-CHOO
HERE...
...PUT THIS ON.
IT'S N-NOTHING.
WHY IS MY HEART RACING?
LISTEN, I KNOW YOU'RE WORRIED,
BUT I KNOW WE'RE GOING TO SUCCEED IN RESCUING YOUR FRIEND.
I HOPE SO. I WANT TO BELIEVE IT.

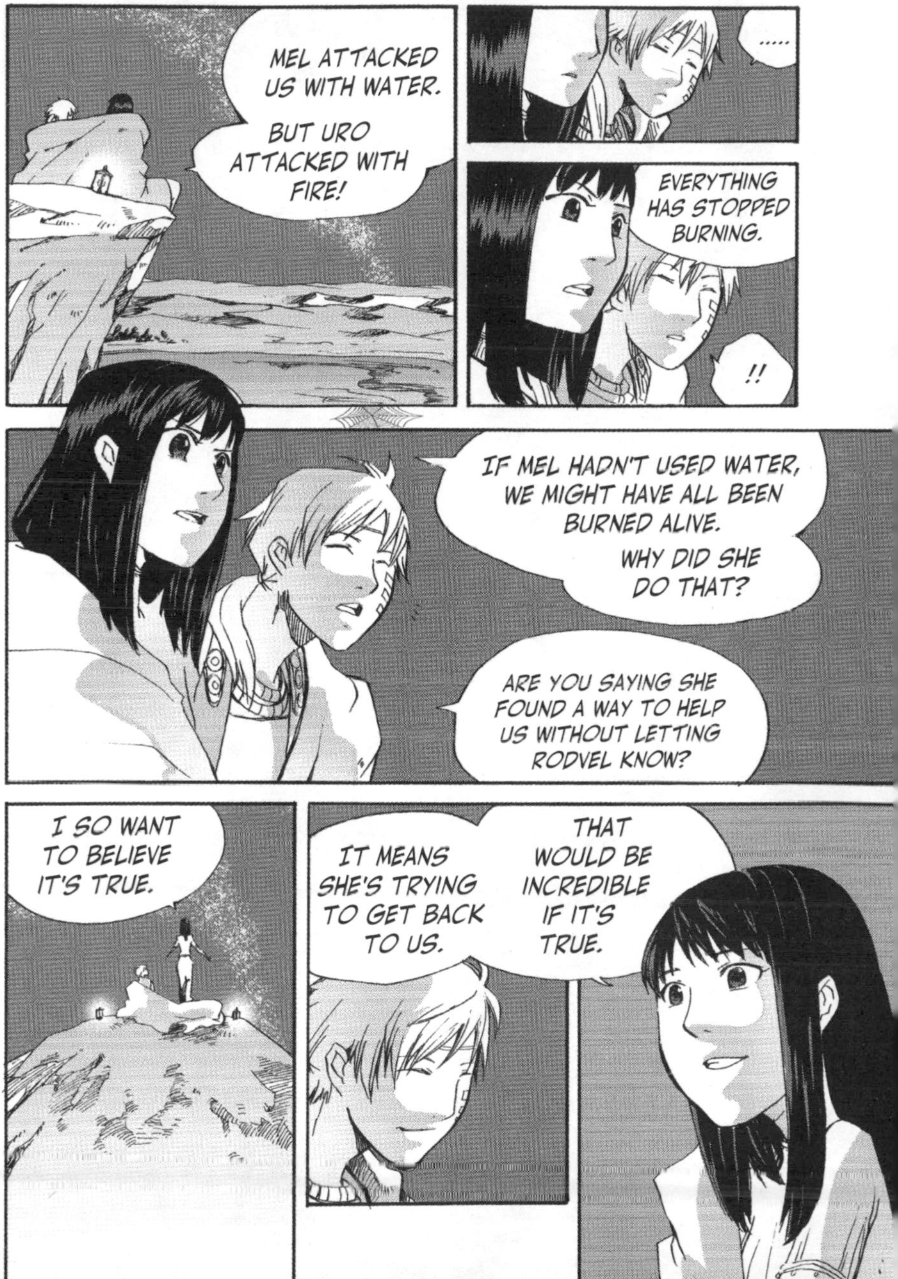
MEL ATTACKED US WITH WATER.
BUT URO ATTACKED WITH FIRE!
.....
EVERYTHING HAS STOPPED BURNING.
!!
IF MEL HADN'T USED WATER, WE MIGHT HAVE ALL BEEN BURNED ALIVE.
WHY DID SHE DO THAT?
ARE YOU SAYING SHE FOUND A WAY TO HELP US WITHOUT LETTING RODVEL KNOW?
I SO WANT TO BELIEVE IT'S TRUE.
THAT WOULD BE INCREDIBLE IF IT'S TRUE.
IT MEANS SHE'S TRYING TO GET BACK TO US.

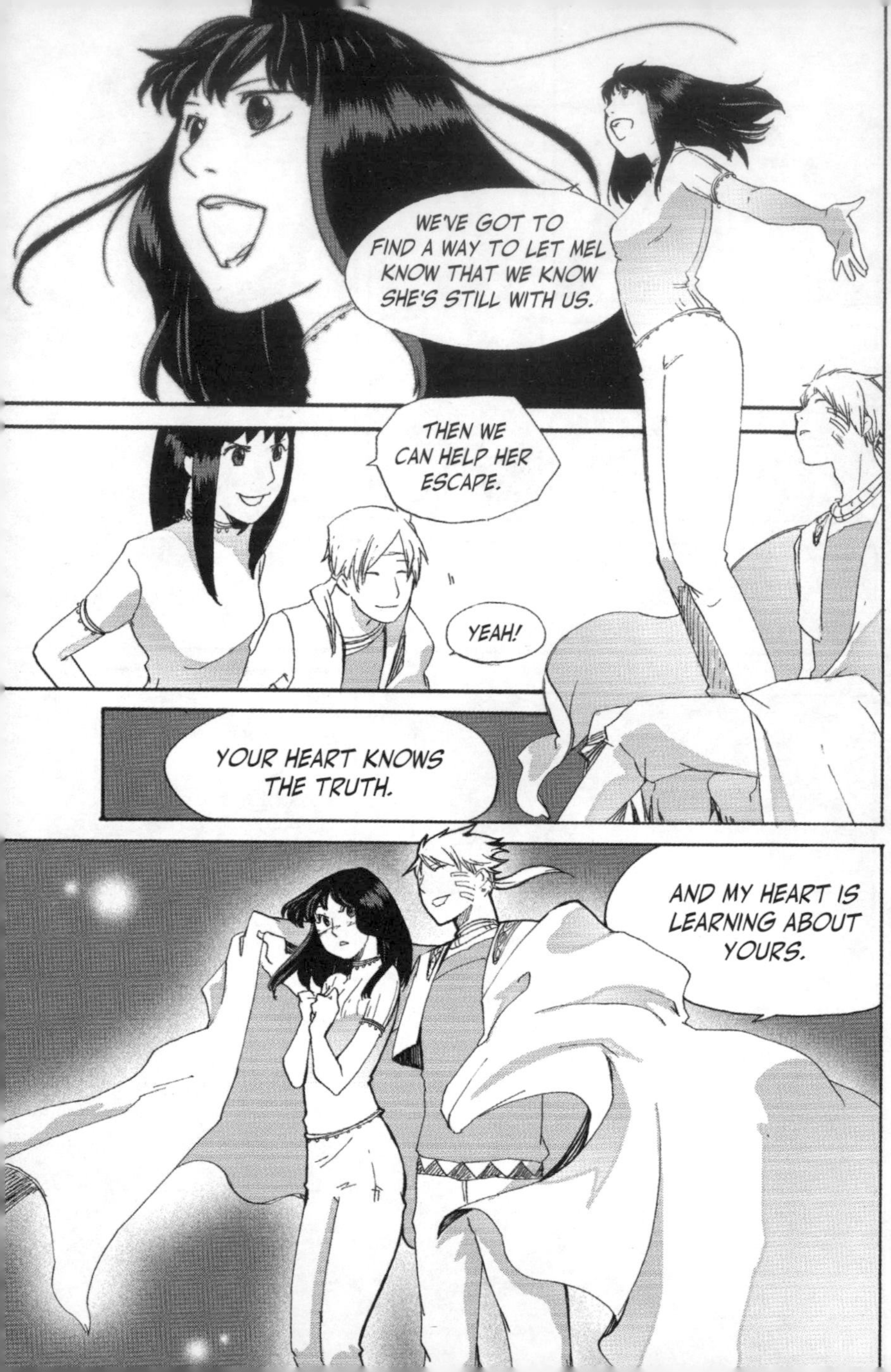
WE'VE GOT TO FIND A WAY TO LET MEL KNOW THAT WE KNOW SHE'S STILL WITH US.
THEN WE CAN HELP HER ESCAPE.
YEAH!
YOUR HEART KNOWS THE TRUTH.
AND MY HEART IS LEARNING ABOUT YOURS.

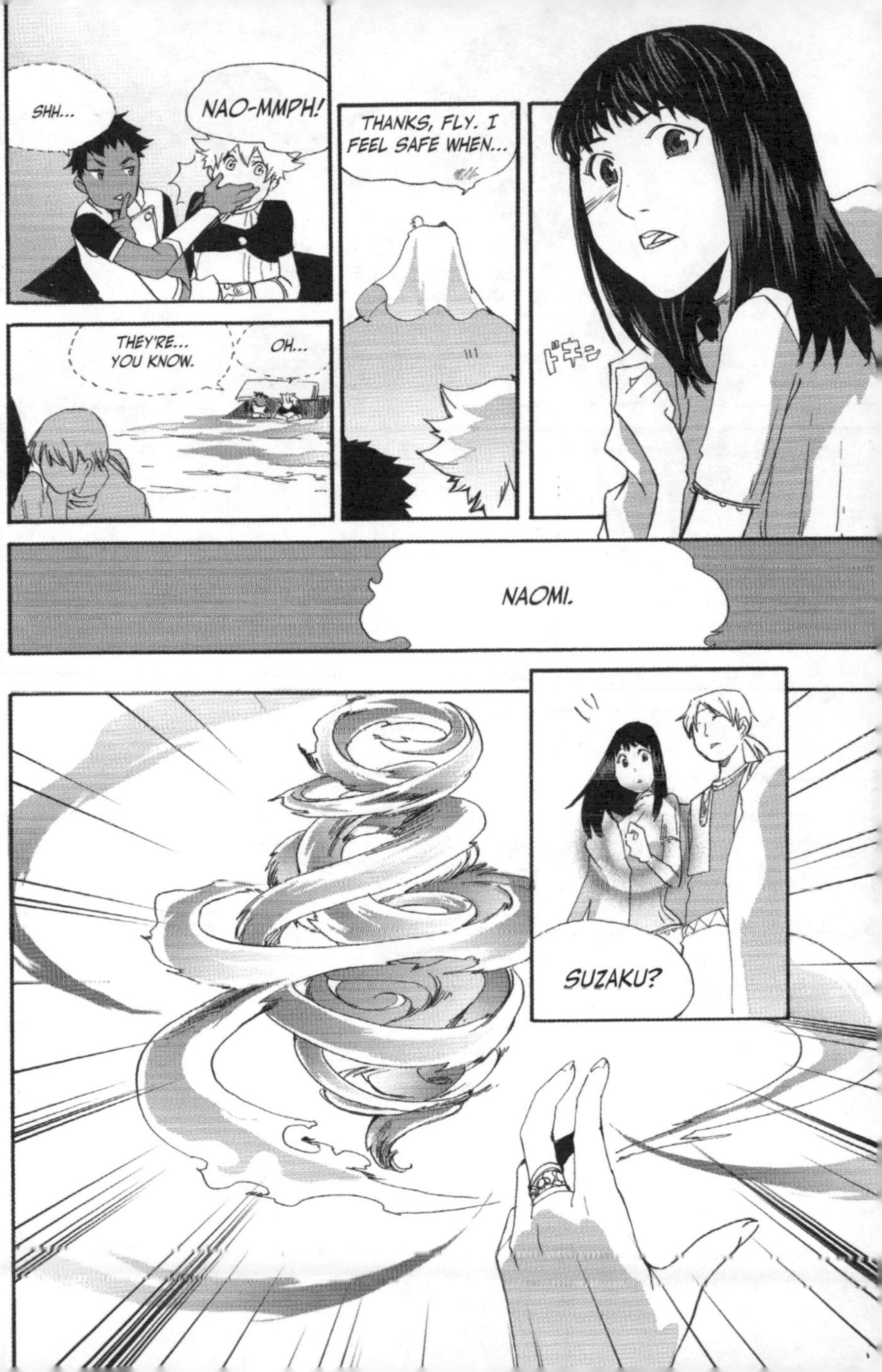
SHH...
NAO-MMPH!
THANKS, FLY. I FEEL SAFE WHEN...
THEY'RE... YOU KNOW.
OH...
ドキン
NAOMI.
SUZAKU?

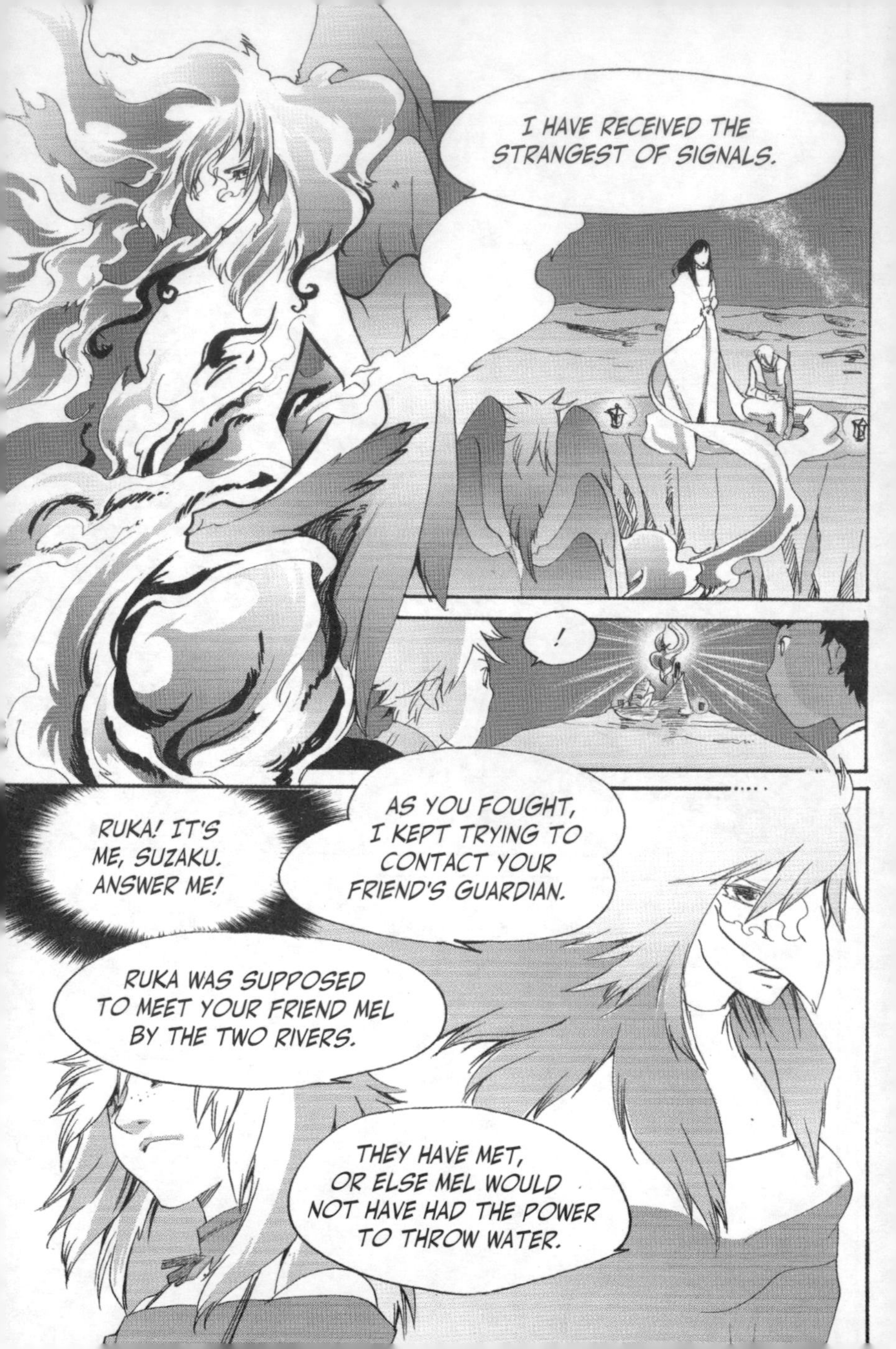
I HAVE RECEIVED THE STRANGEST OF SIGNALS.
!
RUKA! IT'S ME, SUZAKU. ANSWER ME!
AS YOU FOUGHT, I KEPT TRYING TO CONTACT YOUR FRIEND'S GUARDIAN.
.....
RUKA WAS SUPPOSED TO MEET YOUR FRIEND MEL BY THE TWO RIVERS.
THEY HAVE MET, OR ELSE MEL WOULD NOT HAVE HAD THE POWER TO THROW WATER.

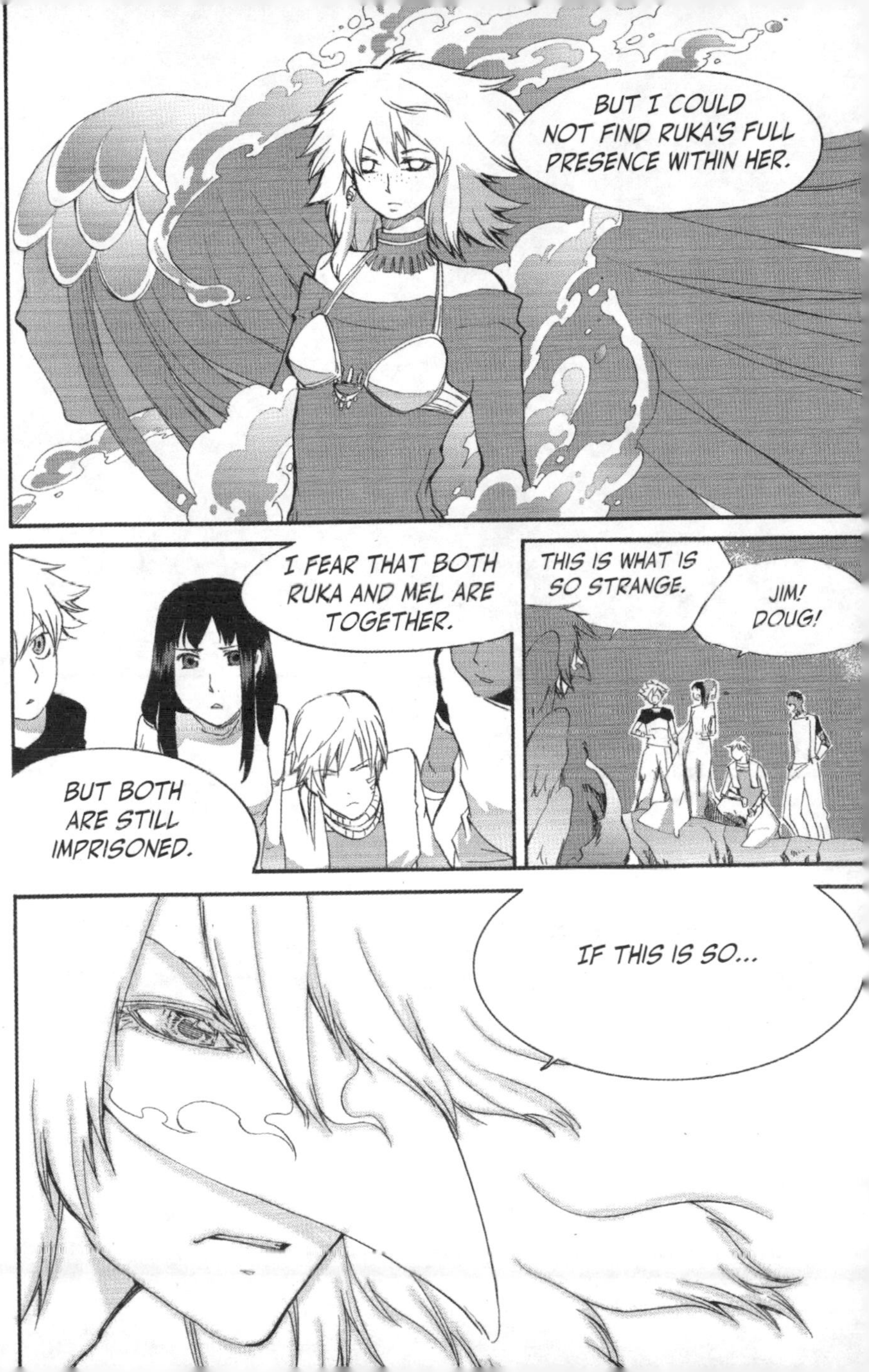
BUT I COULD NOT FIND RUKA'S FULL PRESENCE WITHIN HER.
I FEAR THAT BOTH RUKA AND MEL ARE TOGETHER.
BUT BOTH ARE STILL IMPRISONED.
THIS IS WHAT IS SO STRANGE.
JIM! DOUG!
IF THIS IS SO...

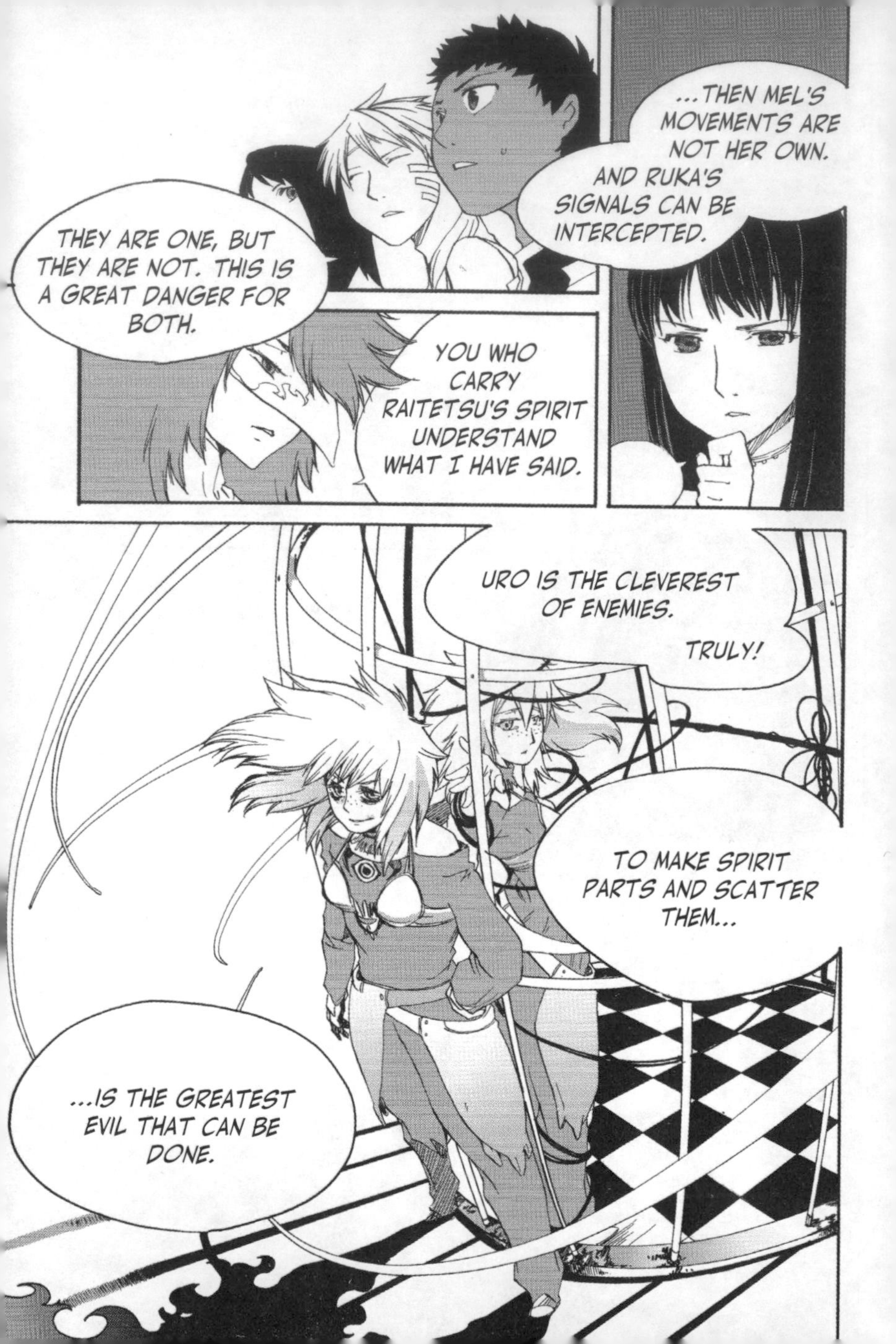
...THEN MEL'S MOVEMENTS ARE NOT HER OWN.
AND RUKA'S SIGNALS CAN BE INTERCEPTED.
THEY ARE ONE, BUT THEY ARE NOT. THIS IS A GREAT DANGER FOR BOTH.
YOU WHO CARRY RAITETSU'S SPIRIT UNDERSTAND WHAT I HAVE SAID.
URO IS THE CLEVEREST OF ENEMIES.
TRULY!
TO MAKE SPIRIT PARTS AND SCATTER THEM...
...IS THE GREATEST EVIL THAT CAN BE DONE.

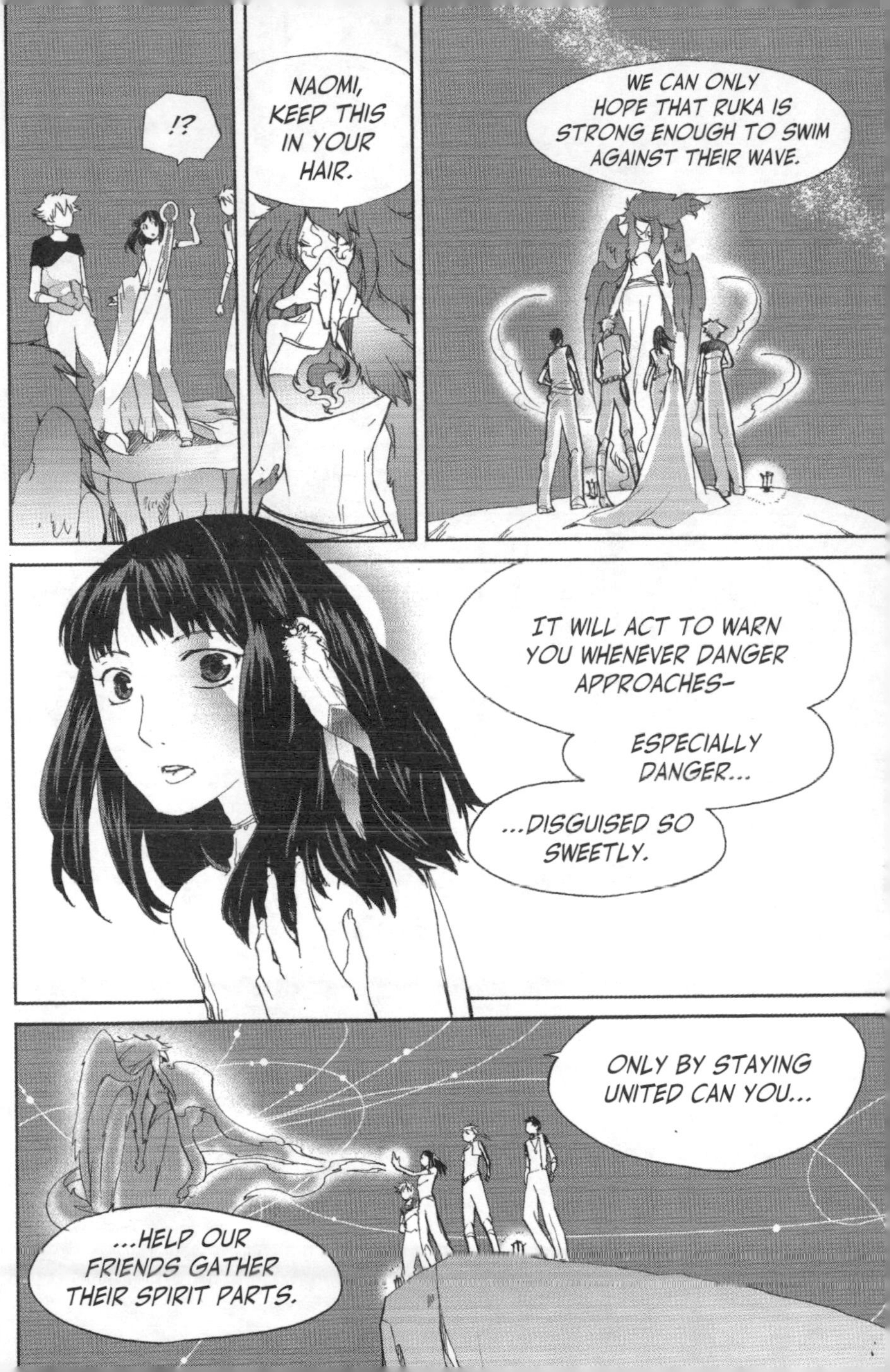
!?
NAOMI, KEEP THIS IN YOUR HAIR.
WE CAN ONLY HOPE THAT RUKA IS STRONG ENOUGH TO SWIM AGAINST THEIR WAVE.
IT WILL ACT TO WARN YOU WHENEVER DANGER APPROACHES-
ESPECIALLY DANGER...
...DISGUISED SO SWEETLY.
ONLY BY STAYING UNITED CAN YOU...
...HELP OUR FRIENDS GATHER THEIR SPIRIT PARTS.

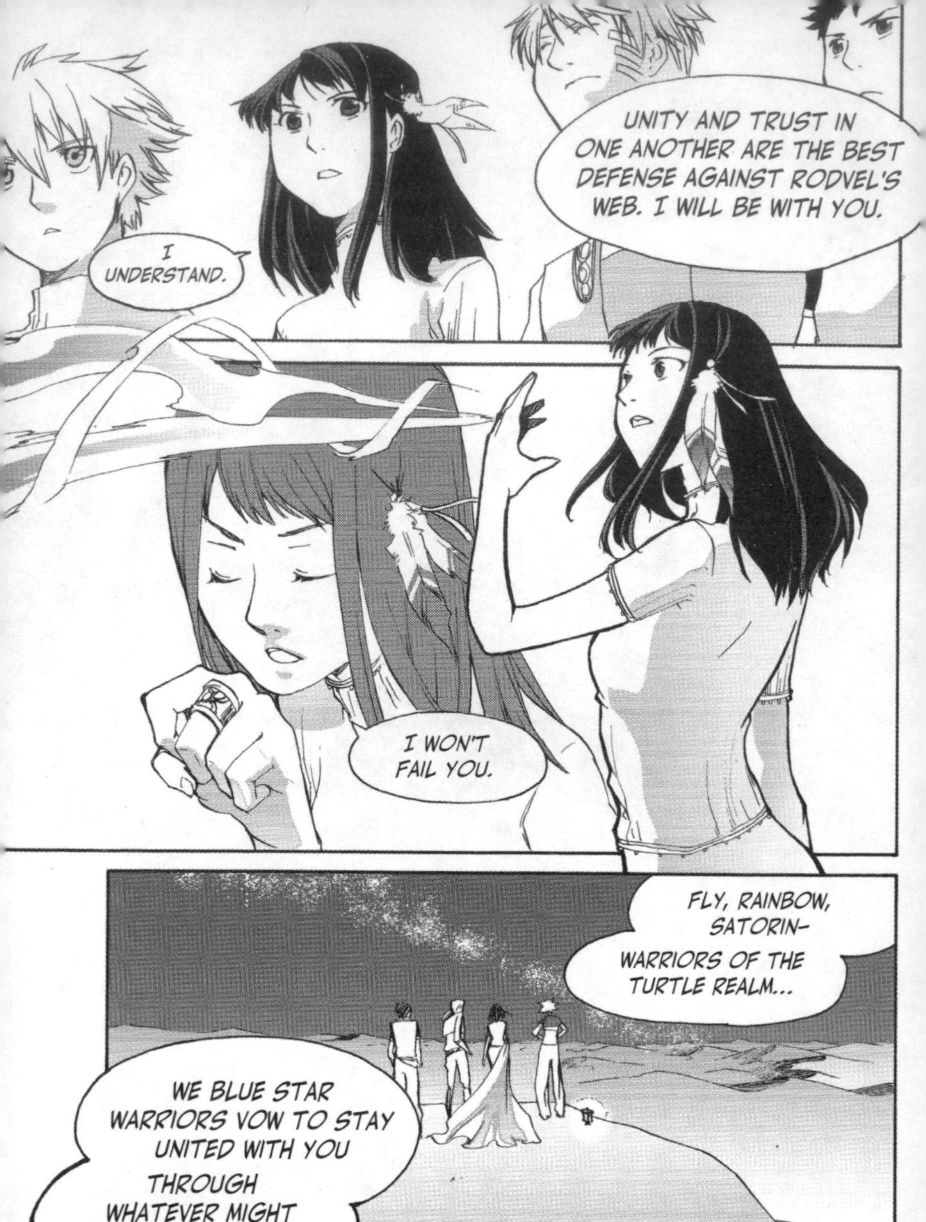

UNITY AND TRUST IN ONE ANOTHER ARE THE BEST DEFENSE AGAINST RODVEL'S WEB. I WILL BE WITH YOU.
I UNDERSTAND.
I WON'T FAIL YOU.
FLY, RAINBOW, SATORIN-
WARRIORS OF THE TURTLE REALM...
WE BLUE STAR WARRIORS VOW TO STAY UNITED WITH YOU
THROUGH WHATEVER MIGHT BE COMING.

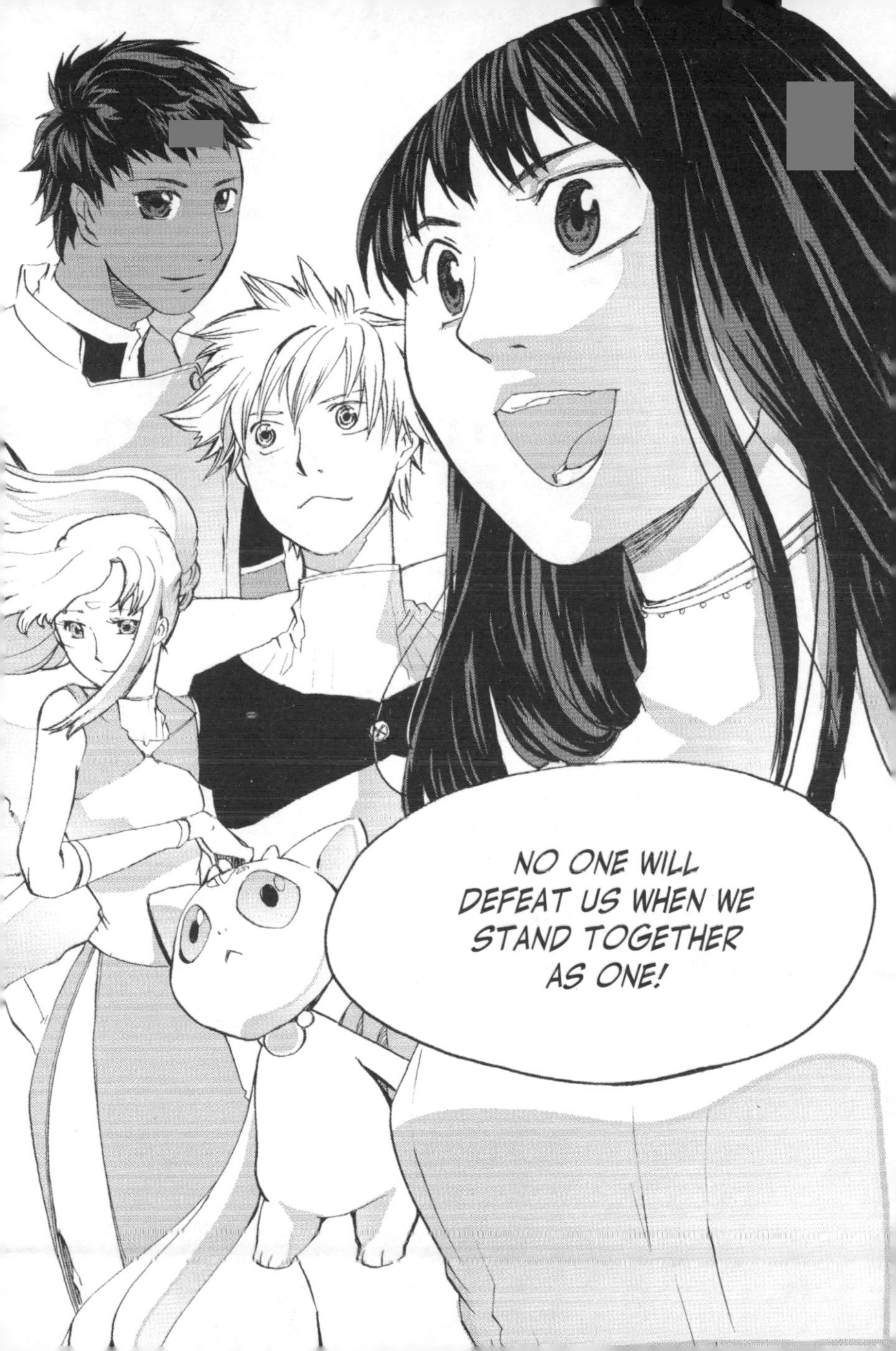
NO ONE WILL DEFEAT US WHEN WE STAND TOGETHER AS ONE!

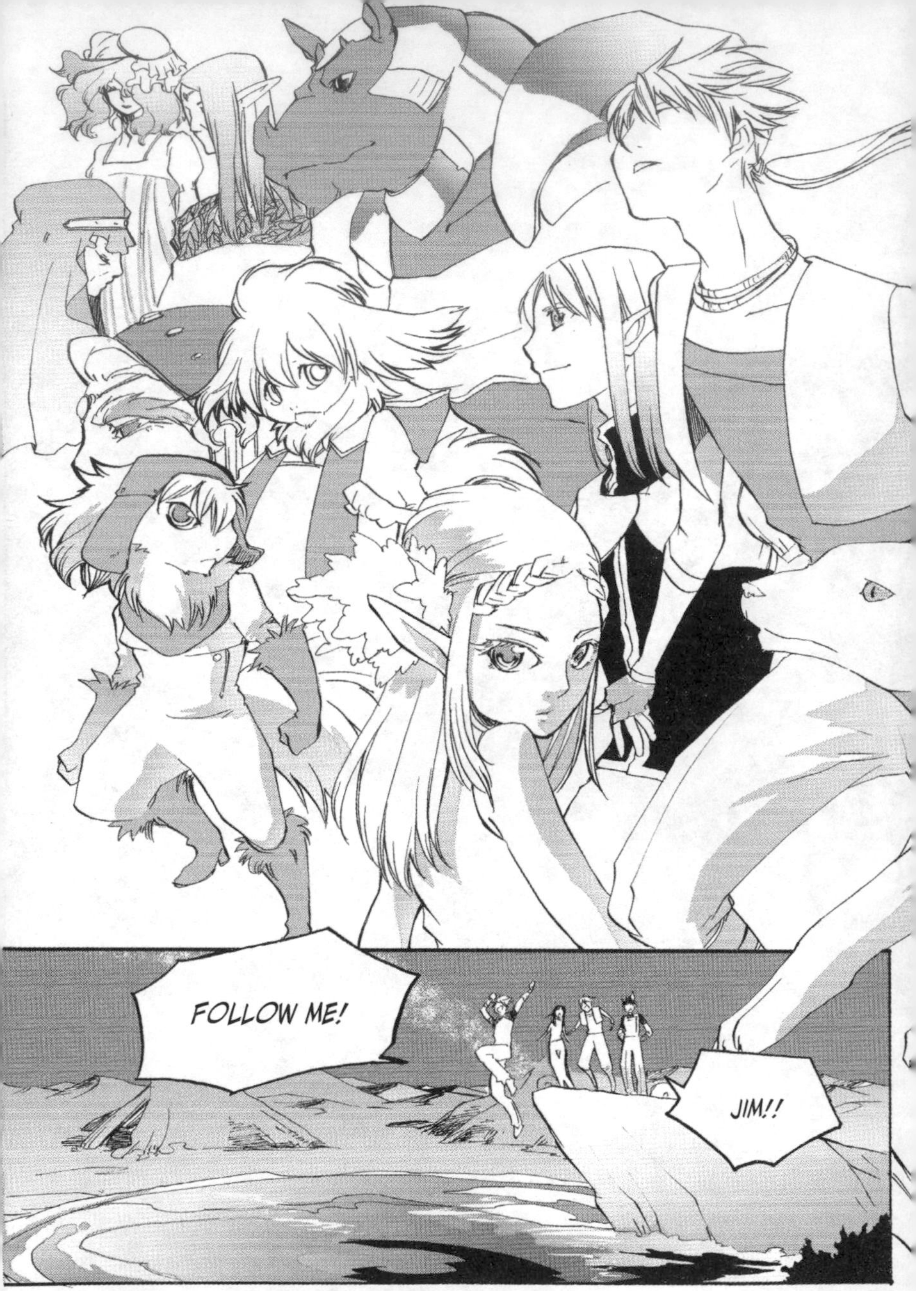
FOLLOW ME!
JIM!!

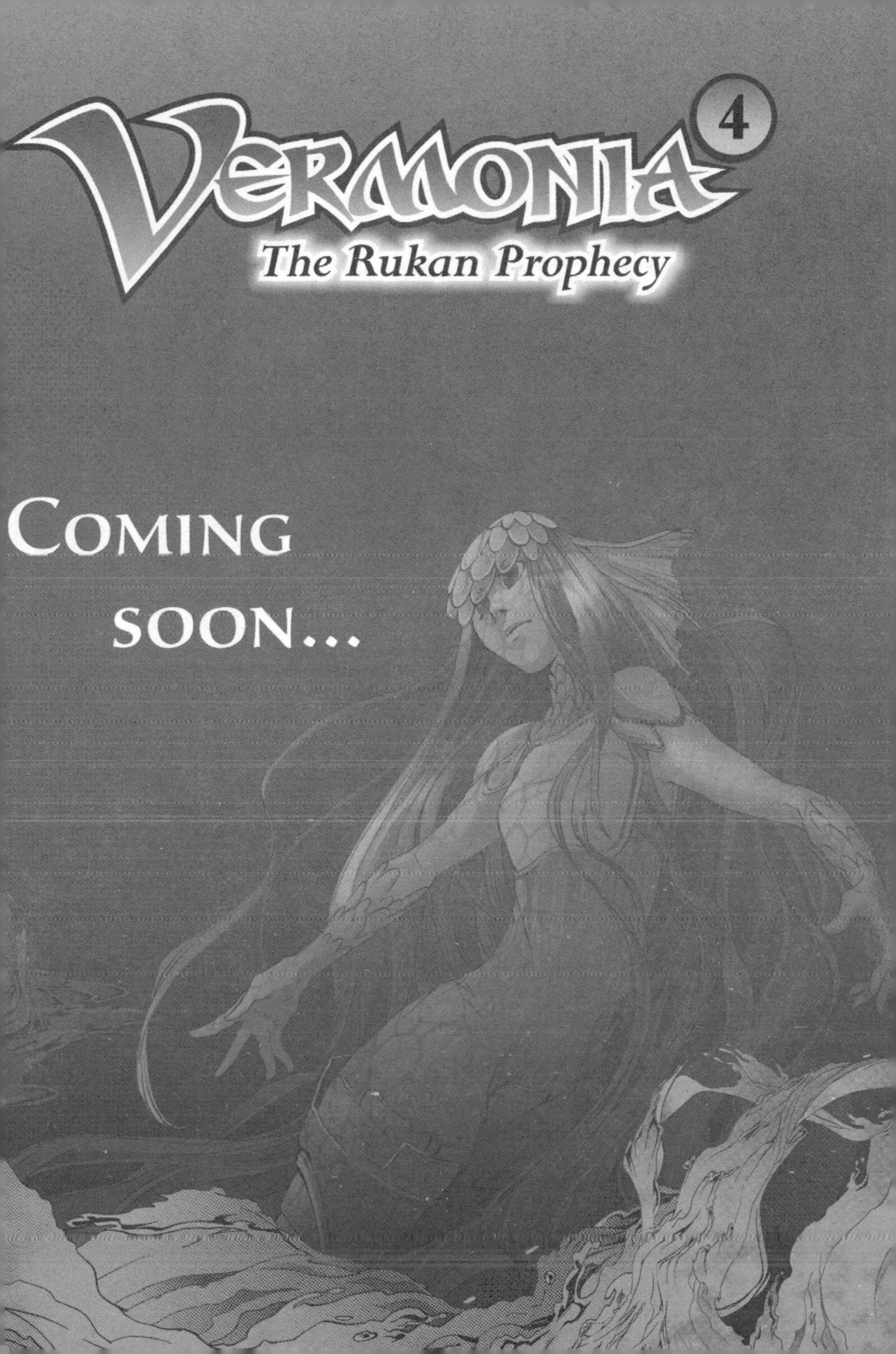
VERMONIA 4
The Rukan Prophecy
COMING
SOON...

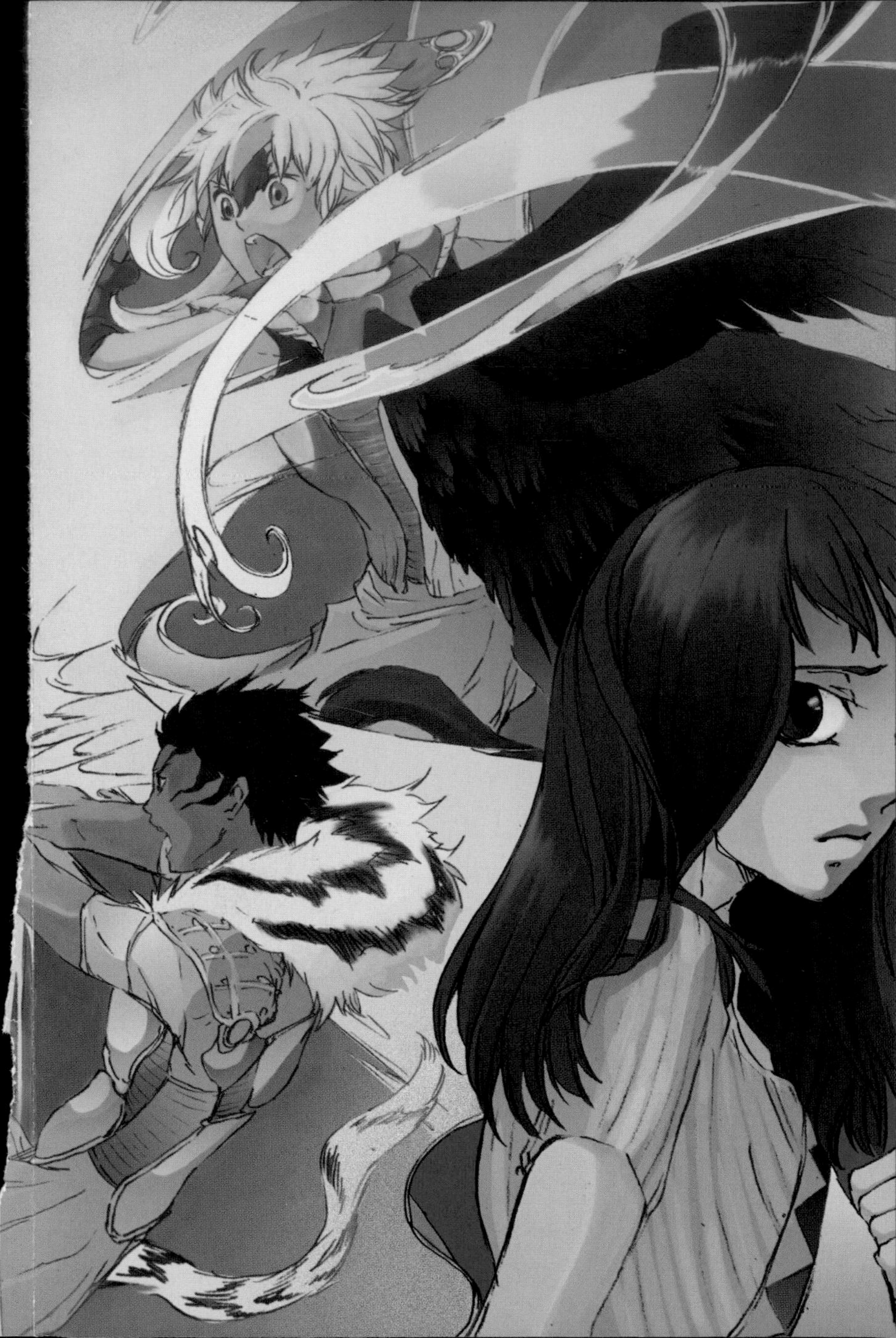

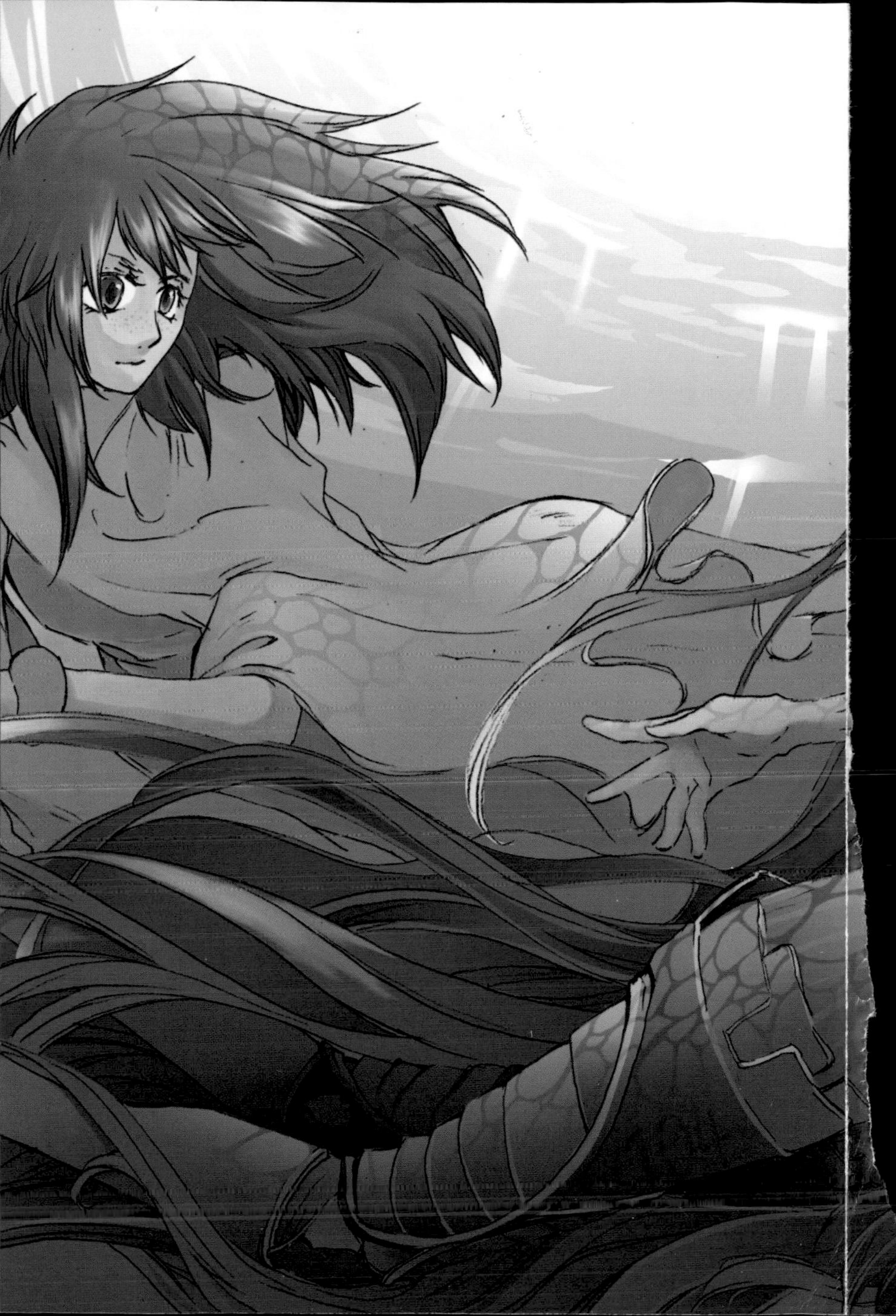

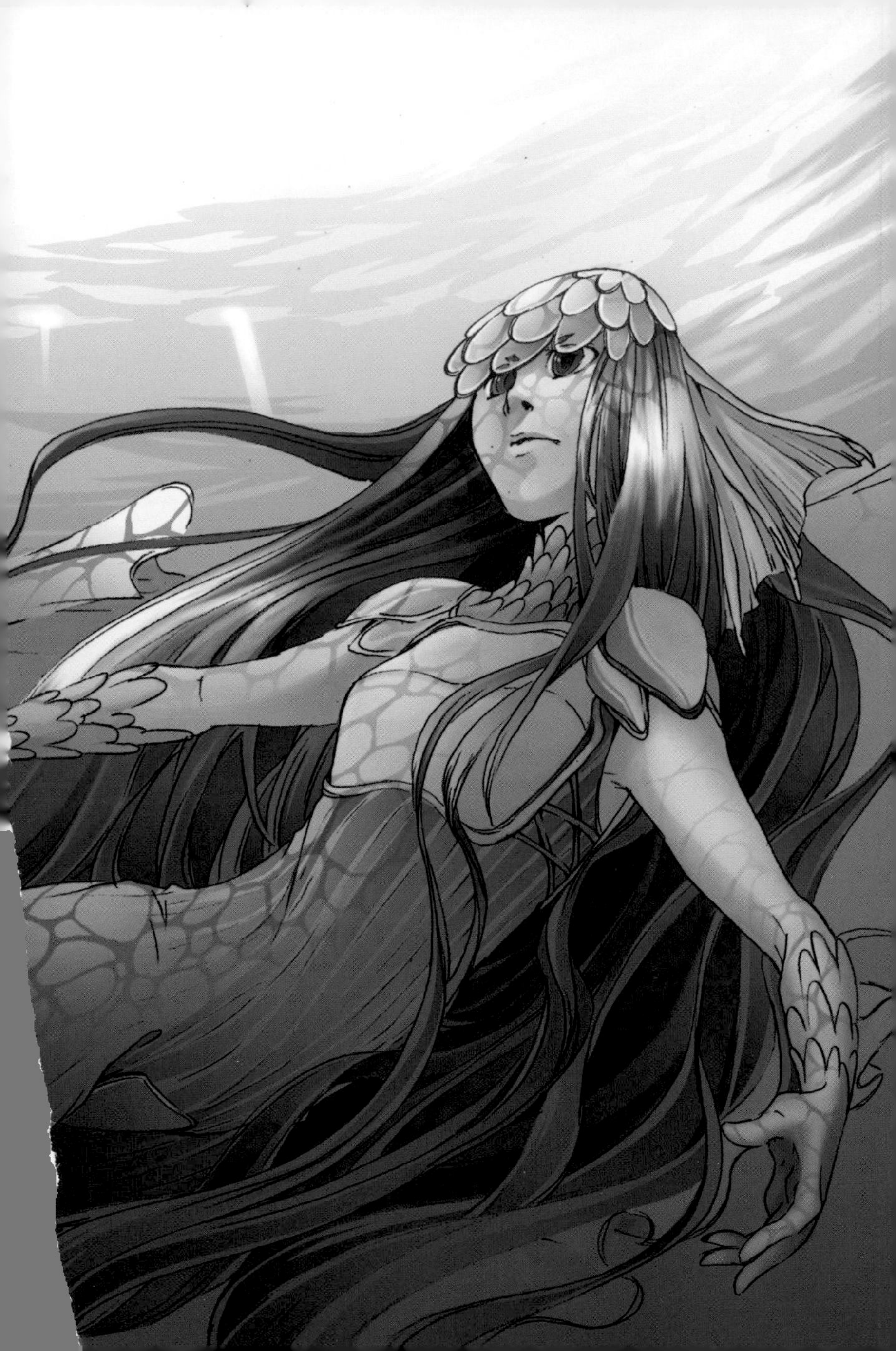

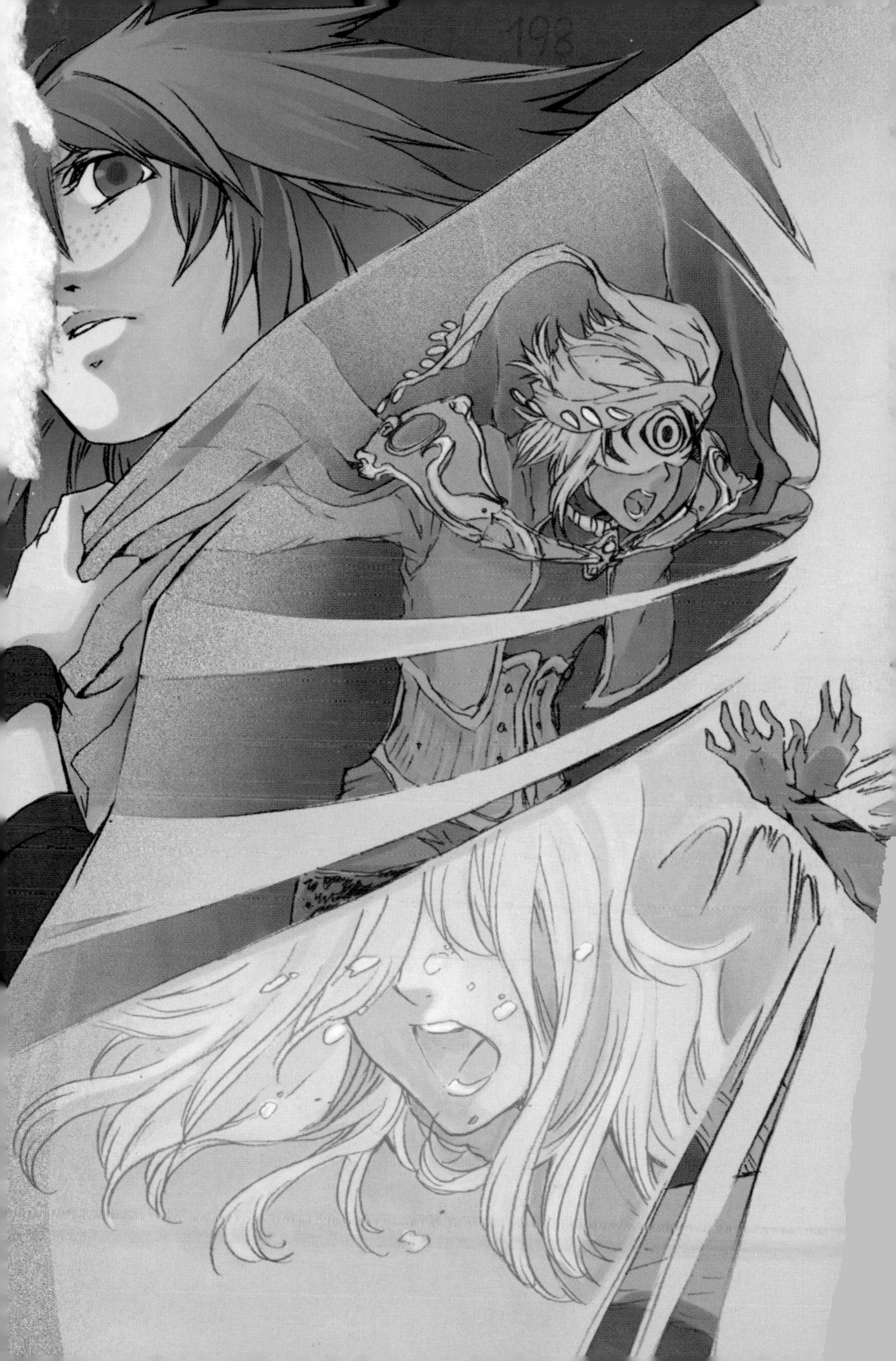

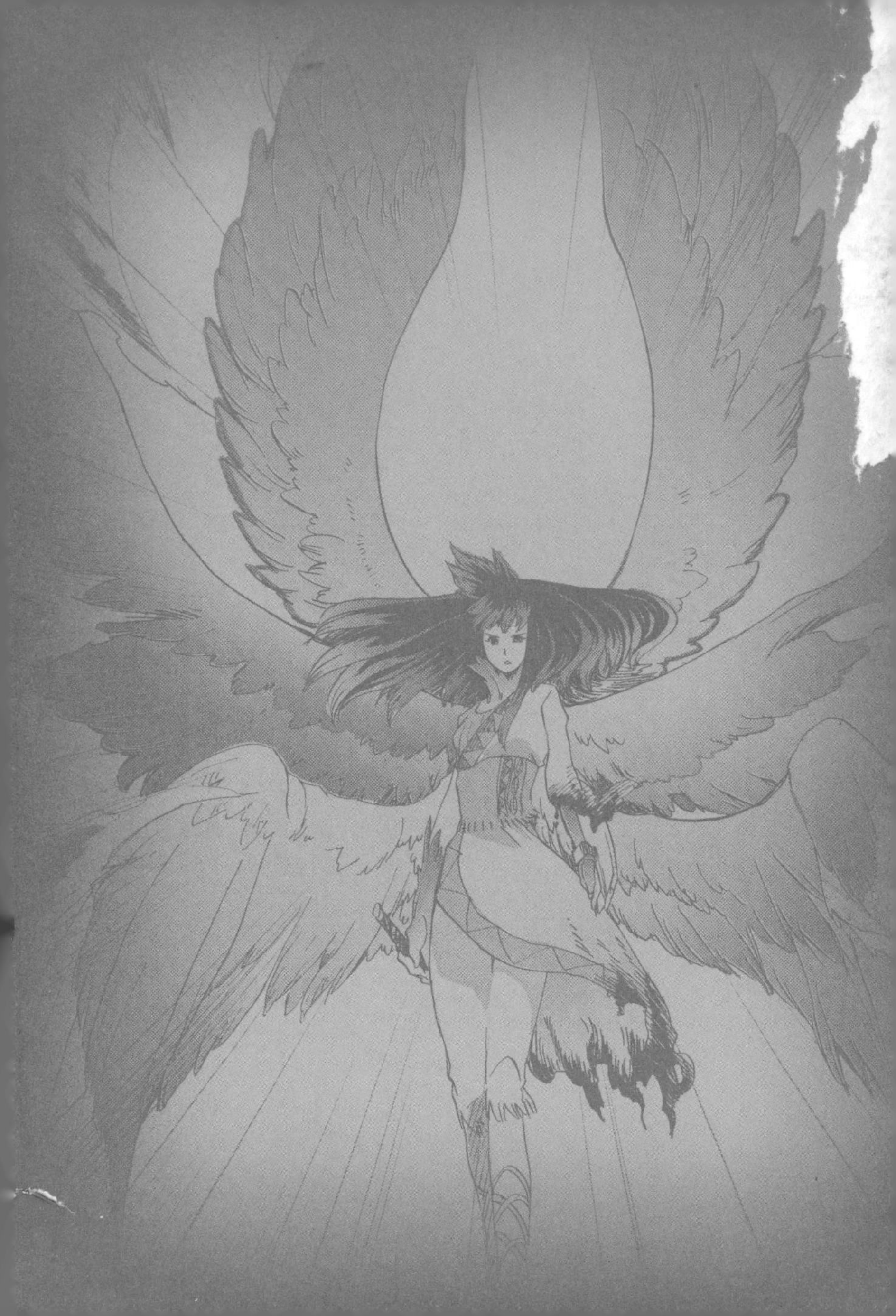

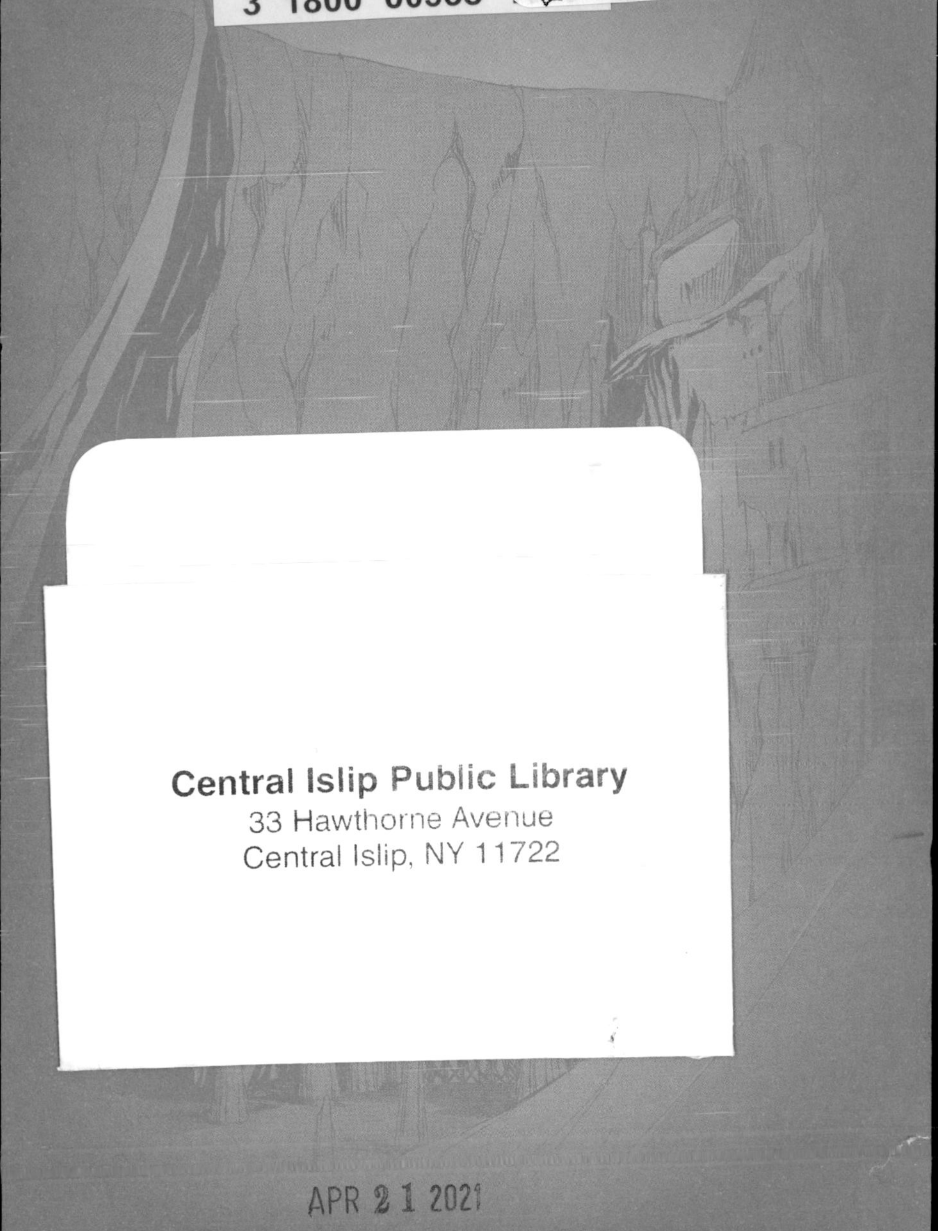